Suddenly Enthroned

THE ROYALS
BOOK ONE

C. R. RILEY

Hermosa Islas

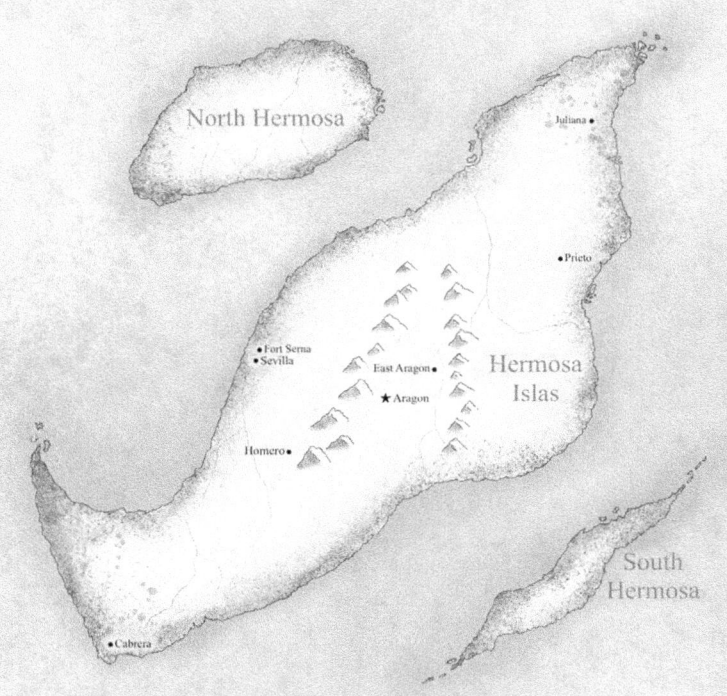

This book is dedicated to my daughter, who, like me, loves reading all about kings, queens, princes, and princesses. Together we have seen all the movies and read several books. And even though she knows she doesn't need a prince to come to her rescue, it doesn't mean she won't find her prince one day to share her amazing life with.

I love you, sweetheart.
You will forever be my little princess.

CHAPTER 1
Antonio

The Royals

A solid knock on my office door while I go over the agenda with my private secretary, Alejandro Sanchez, grabs my attention. Usually, no one disturbs me during this time. Most understand how important it is I get through this quickly so I can start my day.

"Enter." I grant whoever it is permission to interrupt us.

"Excuse me, Your Highness. I apologize for disturbing you, but this is of utmost importance." The head of my father's personal staff bows as he enters.

I should probably introduce myself before I continue. I mean, it's not customary for one person to address another so formally.

I'm Prince Antonio Ramon Reyes of Hermosa Islas, heir to the throne.

You may not have heard of Hermosa Islas, many haven't. We are a small group of islands in the Northern Atlantic. A country that was established when a Spanish prince decided he wanted to explore the world, instead of sitting on his thumbs, wasting away. He wasn't the successor—seventh in line, to be exact—so like many arrogant princes, he did as he pleased. Hired a few former members of the Royal Navy and launched a new adventure.

Long story short, the prince later arranged for his wife and children to be brought to him after a few months. Eventually, he offered a safe refuge to others who weren't satisfied with the current rulers of Spain and its surrounding countries. Over the next fifty years, he erected a port for all to stop and rest from their travels or trade routes. He even extended an offer to settle in a new land if they so desired. A place for those who concluded life at sea wasn't for them, either. It became a new territory to colonize. He named the islands Hermosa, which means beautiful, because that is what the prince thought they were when he first discovered them.

My family—the House of Reyes—has been seated on the throne since the mid-eighteen hundreds. Queen Juliana Teresa Aragon, the first Queen of Hermosa Islas, married Duke Tomas Philip Reyes from Portugal. They had a son, Prince Nicolas Tomas Reyes, who acquired the throne in 1872 after his mother's death. Instead of ruling under the Aragon surname, King Nicolas elected to use his father's surname, Reyes. Moving his people into a completely different era, one that would bring us into the twentieth century and change how this country governed.

Okay, so now that you've had a quick history lesson, and I am certain are bored to death, let's get back to what is happening in the here and now.

I acknowledge the male servant who has been faithful to my father during his reign. "It's fine, Jorge. What seems to have you so on edge?"

"It's just that we haven't been able to locate the King this morning. He retreated to his private chambers last night and hasn't yet emerged," Jorge informs me.

I ask the obvious, even though I know the answer before Jorge gives it to me. "Did you enter the King's chambers? Perhaps he has... overslept."

"I did not enter his chamber, Your Highness. He asked us to give him his space when he retired last night," Jorge answers.

My father is an intolerant man. When he gives an order, he expects all to heed that order, no matter the circumstances. After all, he is King and in this beloved country, the king holds the majority of the power, not all but a great deal of it.

I stand.

When I do, my secretary also stands, because no one remains seated when a royal stands. "Excuse me, Sanchez."

My secretary gathers his items and vacates my office as I am leaving. He is not allowed in the office of a royal unless that person is present. I know where to find Alejandro after I have checked on my father.

While I am walking through the halls to reach the King's chambers, I decide to call him. I am not surprised when he doesn't pick up. As soon as I arrive outside the large wooden door, I press the buzzer and wait. When no one responds, I press it again.

"Have you spoken with the Queen about this?" I hold back the bitter taste uttering those words about my father's second wife.

"Yes, Your Highness. Princess Isabel was not feeling well last night, so the Queen spent the night in her chambers," Jorge informs me.

I push the buzzer a third time. "I hope the young princess is feeling better this morning."

Princess Isabel is my baby sister—technically my half-sister. I fell head-over-heels for the young princess the first day I met her. I swear she was born with a smile on her face. Her innocence captivated my siblings and me immediately. We may not be fond of her mother, although Sofia is a wonderful mother, we all, however, adore the little princess and treat her accordingly.

"Much, Your Highness. Just a bit of a cold that will run its course rather quickly, I'm sure. Dr. Torrez visited last night just to make certain when she sounded wheezy."

"Good." I sigh because I hate I have come to one conclusion now where my father is concerned. "Key, Mr. Gomez."

Jorge produces the key.

"Was he alone last night? Or do we not know for sure?" I ask as I insert the key in the lock and wait for the click.

"He was alone last I knew," Jorge states.

Another detail about my father is that he likes to entertain. That fact ultimately ended my parents' eighteen-year marriage. My mother tolerated it, turned the other cheek for a long time. It was what they advised her a queen does, so it is what she did. Until my sister, Gabriela was born and my father missed it, all because he was not to be disturbed while philandering around with his latest mistress. My mother decided enough was enough, moved her children to the country citadel we frequently retreated to when she desired a break. It became her permanent home, where my brothers and sister resided with her.

I was not allowed to depart with the rest of my family since I was intended to one day become king. At seventeen, I was being groomed in the ways of a future king, and only the current King/Queen seated on the throne is authorized to oversee that process. That meant I could only visit them on holidays and special occasions. *'Tis the price one must pay when expected to one day reign over his people.*

"That will be all, Jorge. If I need you, I'll buzz," I notify the older man as I enter my father's chambers.

Chambers may be a vague description when describing these particular quarters. The king's private chambers are more like a home. There is a large sitting room, a dining area, a kitchen—which is only used when one of our cooks is called to prepare a private dinner—I can't remember the last time that happened. It also has a library that serves as a second sitting room and home office, along with four large bedrooms.

As you might suspect, it is typical for the king to reside in these quarters with his family. It is where my siblings and I spent most of our time when our parents were married. After my mother moved out, and once my father remarried Sofia, that changed. Sofia and Isabel live in a much smaller, but still very large, quarters known as the queen's chambers.

I head to my father's bedroom first. Knock loudly several times before I dare to enter. "King Ramon, are you decent? Sir, it's Prince Antonio. Father?"

After no one answers, I open the door and notice the bed is drawn down—probably from the chambermaids—but hasn't been slept in. That seems rather odd to me.

I continue to the large attached bathroom to make sure he isn't there. Nothing.

Next, I carry on to the library.

Following my parents' fallout, I found my father often passed out in here after a night of overindulging in the Royal scotch. That was always better than discovering him nailing one of his many lady conquests, which I also have had the unfortunate privilege of doing more times than I care to recall.

The door to the library is slightly ajar. I can see a light has been left burning. Meaning, I expect to catch the king with an empty bottle in hand and passed out. And at first sight, that is exactly what I have concluded to be the case.

King Ramon is seated in his favorite chair. A discarded tumbler rests at his side on the floor, where he most likely dropped it. He is slumped over in the chair in the most uncomfortable position. I wonder how he could stand to remain like that. Since I have never been a big drinker, I assume the alcohol in his system makes it so he doesn't care.

"King Ramon," I speak his name, hoping to stir him. "Father."

Nothing. Not even a little flinch from him when I clap my hands loudly.

Shaking my head, I bend to pick up the tumbler, and that is when I notice the coloring of his hands. Grey skin with a blue tinge to his fingers and I realize this will not have a desirable outcome.

I close my eyes and take a deep breath before I lift his hands in mine. They are ice cold—so very cold—and lifeless.

Lowering my head, trying not to let emotions take over, I gather myself before I stand. Staggering over to his desk, I place a call to the security office and wait for someone to pick up the phone.

"Your Majesty."

"Prince Antonio, actually. I require the King's Guards to report to his chambers immediately. Please inform Dr. Flores to join them." I drop into my father's chair.

"What should I mention is the reason for being summoned to his quarters, Your Highness?"

"Tell them that the King has had an... accident."

"They are on their way now, sir."

I hang up and force myself to stand so I can collect them at the main door. It only takes the calvary a few minutes to arrive, and once I have them all secured inside, I explain. "King Ramon Reyes seems to have had one too many scotches last night. I found him when I arrived in the library."

"I'll take care of him promptly, Your Highness. Sober him right up." Dr. Flores starts to head that way.

"That won't be necessary, Dr. Flores. I require you to confirm that the King..." I swallow hard and try to breathe. "That my father has passed."

"Passed?" Dr. Flores' eyes widen. "Are you positive?"

"Cold. Gray. Blue. Yes, I am positive. Although I need you to verify." I motion for him to continue.

Sir Edward Perez, captain of the King's Guard, is right on our tail. As soon as we enter the room, he halts the doctor from proceeding. "Doctor, I order you to step aside. Is this how you found him, Prince Antonio? Exactly how you found him?"

"Yes. I started to pick up the tumbler, but as soon as I noticed his hand, I stopped."

"Very good." Edward takes a slow perusal of the room. "I'm going to ask that you not touch anything until we have conducted a proper investigation. Doctor, you may proceed to confirm, but please do not disturb the King's body any more than necessary."

"Do you suspect foul play?" I ask, disappointed I hadn't thought of that as a possibility.

"I'm uncertain. But one can never be too careful."

Dr. Flores states what we already know. "King Ramon Esteban Reyes, I am regretful to report, is most definitely deceased."

I stare at my father's lifeless body when it hits me. Not just the fact that my father is dead, but what that means. My legs suddenly cannot hold me upright. Sir Edward, along with one of his men, seizes my arms to keep me on my feet.

"Your Majesty." Dr. Flores rushes over as he instructs the men. "Take him into the other room so he can sit down."

Sir Edward barks out a long list of orders. "Send the Queen's team down to her chambers and have them secure her there. We need to call Prince Esteban and Prince Lorenzo to come and sit with King Antonio. Also, make a call to Her Royal Highness Angela; summon her to the palace to join her sons and to bring Princess Gabriela with her. Contact the council for an emergency summit, so they can establish the proper procedures that we'll need to follow.

"We are to keep this quiet until we have done a thorough investigation and confirmed exactly how King Ramon died. No one. No one is to mention we found King Ramon deceased in his quarters until I give the okay."

His men nod in agreement, and Sir Edward turns to me. "Your Majesty, is there anything else you'd like to add?"

"Just that I don't believe you should address me in such a way until we are ready to announce that my father has..." I can't say it again. "I think for now everyone should continue to address me as Your Highness or Prince. That is an order as your King, therefore I expect you to follow it until you hear otherwise from me."

Sir Edward gestures to his men to get moving. "You heard your Prince. Now let's do what needs to be done."

Not exactly how I predicted my day to start, or how I assumed my legacy to the throne would begin. Every Monarch, going back five generations, has willingly passed down the title to the next successor sometime after the heir turned thirty. I am only twenty-five. I expected to have at least five more years before possibly being ordained with that title.

Five years to find a proper queen to rule next to me.

Five years to prepare and learn how to act as I absorbed what to do in certain situations. Being a king isn't just about instructing the people on what to do and how to do it. It is about guiding them while listening to the voices of the nation and elected council. There is so much I still haven't been taught yet.

But like every monarch who has come before me, feeling equally unprepared, this is my time to step up and show everyone that I am qualified. So that is what I plan to do. I will rule my kingdom the best way I can and make Hermosa Islas proud.

I am King Antonio Ramon Reyes, the first unwed king to ever take the throne.

CHAPTER 2
Larkin

The Royals

I stare at the man standing in my kitchen like he has lost his mind. Not once has he even tried to kiss me, and I'm so confused. I've known this guy since I was nineteen. We met during my first year at UIC (University of Illinois Chicago) and became friends shortly afterward. He differed from the people I normally hung around.

Okay, I guess I should explain a few specifics so you understand. I mean, until you know a little of my background, you will never fully appreciate where I am coming from.

I'm Larkin Moon Cross.

Hippie sort of name, isn't it? And if you knew who my parents were, you'd be surprised about that. I have a hard time with it sometimes as well. My parents are not responsible for naming me, so there is that.

I'm adopted. I lived the first three years of my life in the foster care system. My birth parents were messed up. They took me from my mother shortly after I was born, who, at that time, was overdosing on cocaine. Yep, you guessed it, I was a drug-addicted infant.

If you have never been around a baby born in those conditions, then I recommend you do a little research. Basically, it's hell on the baby, the staff at the hospital who is fighting to help the baby, and later the family who accepts the privilege of taking the baby home with them. Both of my foster parents happened to be doctors, so that was beneficial all the way around.

After my birth mother got clean, they returned me to her. I was six months old. My social worker took me away from her again when I was nine months when she was found her high. This pattern repeated itself until I was eighteen months old and my mother successfully OD'd on meth. She landed in the same hospital where my foster father worked. He pronounced my birth mother deceased, then made a very important decision that altered my life and his. At age three, I officially became a member of the Cross family. My new father was also appointed the newest state senator for the Chicago area that same year. Years later, he won a seat as a United States Senator for Illinois. One of his biggest platforms dealt with foster care and how it failed so many children. My new family, Sam and Eleanor Cross, changed the course of my life and loved me like no one else ever could.

Growing up in the home of a senator and pediatric surgeon had its own challenges. It was a privileged life I never was that comfortable with. I was a timid girl who struggled in social settings. Eventually, they diagnosed me with ADHD, and while they couldn't prove it resulted from all the drugs my birth mother did while pregnant with me, everyone knew they didn't help. My parents were great and did their best to teach me ways to cope. They only asked me to attend functions for brief spurts and allowed me to leave when I needed to. Best of all, my parents didn't expose my issues to the world to profit from or benefit my father's career. Instead, they aimed to keep it under wraps until I was old enough to decide it was an important topic to discuss. As I got older, issues were easier for me to control, although I remained reserved and preferred being solitary.

When I left for college, I opted to live on campus. That decision came as a surprise to my parents. It was clear to me I needed to get out from under their wings and learn to survive in uncomfortable situations. That is also when I met this laid-back simple guy, Randal Booker.

Randal was from a blue-collar single-family home. His mother worked in a convenience store in his Fuller Park neighborhood—which, if you aren't familiar with Chicago, is rough. He lived his entire life like mine started. No one came to rescue him from it as they had me. And while his mother wasn't a drug addict, she wasn't living the life of a saint, either. Alcohol was her choice of drug, and when she was drunk, she turned mean, then took it out on Randal and his brother Billy. Foster care was never offered to him because no one was around to notice how it would have benefited both boys. They did have places they could retreat when conditions got rough, but even those homes weren't ideal. Lucky for me, he was a smart guy and knew the only way out for him and his brother was for him to step up and make a change, which he was well on his way to accomplishing.

My parents weren't huge fans of Randal Booker at first. They didn't give him a chance after learning his background until he graduated valedictorian and secured a job at one of the best architectural firms in the city. That's when they decided maybe Randal wasn't hoping to ride the coattails of the wealthy senator's daughter to get out of an unpleasant situation. They came to understand he was doing his best to change his stars by himself and just happened to have my support while he did it.

That being said, the thing I always liked about Randal was the fact he wasn't like everyone else I grew up around. He wasn't politically correct all the time. Didn't care what others thought about him and he always lived life to the fullest. He took each day as it came and strived to make the best of it; I assume it's something he learned growing up.

And no, Randal and I are no more than friends. He has always been a guy I felt extremely comfortable around. I never worried about having to pretend to be someone I wasn't. I could blurt out the gibberish that sometimes slipped into my overly crowded brain and knew he would let it be. Sometimes he laughed because the nonsense I verbalized was laughable, but he never once made me feel like an outcast or was weird about it. We were completely comfortable with each other, and that was something I never really experienced until him.

Okay, so now you have a better understanding of who I am, who we are, even.

Tonight, we are celebrating.

I just got accepted into the master's program at UIC for architecture. I never thought much of the field until I met Randal and he opened my eyes to it. My original plan was to get a degree in something like art and then teach it to young children. Art was always my outlet when I needed to get my head on straight. It was the one thing I could focus on completely, where I could let my mind wander. However, after meeting Randal, I soon fell in love with the art of buildings, really old buildings.

School, until that point, had been a struggle for me. Once I discovered my obsession with architecture and all the wonderful fascinations surrounding it, school became easier. I had Randal to thank for that, which is why when I found out I had been accepted into the program, I called him immediately.

So back to me staring at the man in my kitchen with a shocked expression on my face, mostly because I don't know what to think right now. I told you we were never romantically involved. He has dated a lot of women since he graduated three years ago, and all of those women were gorgeous.

So why did he just kiss me like no one else ever has before?

I'm not completely antisocial. I've had my share of boyfriends in both high school and college. The last guy I dated was probably my most serious relationship. We met during the senior seminar—you know, when the college brings the seniors together to help them transition from college life into the real world. Teaching them interview skills, talking about job fairs, encouraging everyone to use the career center to review resumes, and conduct mock interviews. I met him then, and we started dating. Dated for six months until he took things a little too far one night. After that, I ended our relationship rather quickly, because I just wasn't ready to go there. Not because I am some religious person who believes one should only do that once married. I mean, I guess that may have played into it a little, but not completely. I just wasn't feeling it with him, and afterward, I knew he wasn't for me.

Randal shakes his head and smiles like I have never seen him smile before. "Dang, Larkin. I always knew if I ever got the courage to do that, it would ultimately ruin me."

"Ruin you? What in the world were you thinking, kissing me like that?" I blink a few times. "Why? I mean, we've known each other for three years, and you've never once tried to do... that?" I wave my hand in a circle, knowing I must look ridiculous.

"I've wanted to kiss you, Miss Cross, since the day you ran into me and spilled my hot coffee all over my senior project." A flash of something I don't recognize moves across his face. "I should have done that a long time ago."

Randal drops his head, and I swear he appears sad. Why does he look sad? Does he think I won't let it happen again? Because I can tell you right now, I will most definitely let it happen again. He can kiss me like that as many times as he pleases.

"Why now?" I ask.

When Randal glances up again, I don't like what I detect in his eyes. Pain that warns me something is desperately wrong. So much pain behind his eyes, I am truly afraid of what he will reveal. A quick shake of his head forces that suffering behind a mask he brings in front of it. Then he takes a solid step my way and I can't seem to move. He grabs my shoulders and stares into my eyes for a long time.

"What's wrong?" I ask finally. My voice is so much quieter than it ever has been before.

"I'm so proud of you, Larkin. Never forget that." He repositions his hands to grip my neck and steady my head. "You know I love you, right?"

I laugh lightly. It's not like he's never told me that before. Randal has said that several times over the years. Most of the time, it was done so in a light, friendly way. You know, like when you are laughing hard about something and you look at the other person and say, *'God, I love you. You are seriously disturbed and I just love that about you.'* Or like when you are hanging out and as you're walking out the door you holler, *'Love you. Talk to you later, babe.'*

So, I laugh and nod. "I know."

"No, I don't think you do." He presses his forehead to mine. "I'm an idiot. I should have told you a long time ago how I felt. Too late now though, huh?"

I don't get the impression he is sharing this with me. I get the feeling he is having a private conversation with himself. He's been doing that a lot lately, saying things that make little sense.

"Why?" I grab his face. "Talk to me."

"I wish I could. I wish I had done so many things differently since that first day you showed up in my life, Larkin. Promise me something." He rubs his nose against mine. "Promise me you will never give up on your dream. No matter what happens, you'll finish school and be one of the best dang architects there ever was. Live the dream. Love deeply when you find it. Never lose that person inside of you. Promise me that."

"Why do I get the feeling..." He covers my mouth with his hand.

"Promise me you will live life to its fullest. That no matter what, you won't let it change who you are. I need to know that you will be okay." Randal leans down and kisses my lips gently this time. "I'm sorry, Larkin. Please know that if there were any other way, I'd grab a hold of it with both hands. There's not, so now I just need to know that you and Billy will be okay. Even look after each other for me."

"What are you talking about? Are you going somewhere? What's going on, Randal? You've been weird lately and frankly I don't like it," I tell him.

"You are going to be fine." He smiles and kisses my forehead again. "I have to go. I love you, Larkin. I love you so much that it pains me to think this is going to hurt you." Randal backs away and grabs his jacket.

"What is going to hurt me?" I snatch his arm and the muscles in it tense.

But when he spins to face me there is a smile pasted on his lips. "Nothing babe, just me talking it all out in my head again. You know how I get sometimes. Congrats again. I'm so dang proud of you." He leans in one more time and kisses my cheek. "So proud."

I walk him to the door and watch until he reaches the stairwell. "Why do I get the suspicion you aren't telling me everything?"

A sad smile takes over his face, and I swear I see his eyes fill up with tears. "Because I'm not. I love you."

And like that, he is gone.

I clean up my kitchen and try to piece it all together, but can't. So, after I'm done, I take a shower and get ready for bed. My text tone dings from my phone on my nightstand as I am brushing my teeth. It's from Randal.

> RANDAL: You, Larkin Moon Cross, are one awesome chic.

> ME: Where are you?

> RANDAL: No. No, that is for me to know.

> ME: Are you drunk?

I have only known Randal to get drunk one other time in the three years I've been friends with him. That was when his little brother Billy wrecked his car and ended up in the ICU. Luckily, Billy made a full recovery and has since gotten his life straightened out. He will graduate from North East Illinois University (NEIU) in the spring with a degree in business.

> RANDAL: Most definitely drunk.

> ME: I'm coming to get you. Where are you?

> RANDAL: Nope. Not telling.

I try to call him, but he isn't picking up.

I text several more times, except he isn't responding to them either.

An hour goes by before I hear anything from him, and by then I have worked myself into full panic mode. So, when my phone rings, I answer it frantically. "Tell me where you are."

"Now is that any way to talk to a man on the verge." He slurs out slowly. "I just called to tell you goodbye. It's been nice knowing you, Larkin. Time for me to go meet my maker."

I start to respond, but the loud blast of a horn steals the breath out of me. The line goes dead and I drop to my knees, screaming into my phone, realizing what just happened.

My fears are confirmed a few hours later when I get a call from Billy informing me that Randal stepped off the L-train platform into an oncoming train. They believed he was so drunk he stumbled off of it by accident.

I know differently after having talked to him right before it happened. That is explained a few days later when the coroner released the autopsy report. It reveals Randal had terminal brain cancer. That report, along with the letters his brother and I received several days later, painted a very vivid picture for us.

Randal had been given a death sentence. Instead of suffering, he chose another ending. Made his peace with everyone important to him. Explained he didn't want to force us to watch him suffer while he became an invalid incapable of taking care of himself. Hoped we understood why he did it that way—which we didn't, or maybe we did, but we were selfish and wanted more time with him.

After we picked our broken bodies up off the floor, we did what we knew would make Randal proud. Billy finished school, and I went on to get my master's in architecture. We lived our lives one day at a time. Tried our best to move past the loss of a great man who always encouraged us to do our best.

The one thing I could never do after that was to allow myself to forget what might have been. I compared every relationship I had to the one I had with Randal. I wasn't sure why we never became more than friends, wondered often if we had, if that would have made him want to stay longer. Probably the reason I became afraid of letting anyone in like I had let him in. I wasn't convinced I could live through that kind of pain again, so I kept things casual and kept people at a great distance.

My work became my focus and provided me with the commitments I believed I needed and wanted. At least that is how I made it through each day and night without completely falling apart, knowing my life would never be what it could have been with Randal.

CHAPTER 3
Antonio

The Royals

F ive days after discovering my father's body, I asked the family to assemble at my current residence, Castile Vicente. I've lived here since moving out of the palace. It is located in the heart of Aragon.

While we have now made the world aware King Ramon was found deceased in his quarters a few days ago, we have not announced the circumstance surrounding his death. Sir Edward and his trusted men have not released a cause of death or the details of his investigation.

Three hours ago, Sir Edward summoned me to Aragon Palace so I could meet with him, along with the Prime Minister and Governors. He had new information about King Ramon's death. It was his job to deliver his report to the King's Council alongside the King—which happens to now be me.

Me as King. Something I am trying to wrap my head around. I always knew eventually that would be my burden since I was the firstborn of a family who still faithfully served.

Hermosa Islas is a constitutional monarch where the King/Queen is the head of the government with limited sovereignty. Which means I cannot just create a law and force everyone in the kingdom to follow it. I have to get it approved by the King's Council, who are all elected officials with regulated terms. It makes matters rather interesting.

After I turned twenty-one and graduated from university, I became my father's right-hand man. I did all that while completing my MBA I felt would help me be a better leader one day.

Okay, so now that you understand a little more about how affairs run, you hopefully grasp why the other six members of the King's Council were asked to attend. It is of equal interest they hear why their Sovereign died before his time as much as mine. While the man was also my father, as well as my leader, he was the face of Hermosa Islas. And it is their responsibility to figure out what needs to be done next.

We all sat in one of Aragon Palace's official conference rooms and listened to Sir Edward explain the particulars to us. He was very thorough in his presentation. Producing evidence that supported his findings, suggesting this was no accident, leaving little to no doubt in everyone's mind. His initial investigation painted a very vivid picture.

After he presented his case, the Council and I discussed how to handle this issue. We deliberated over several scenarios that would satisfy what our constitution stated needed to be done in such a situation. None of us wanted to leave until we were convinced, we had all our bases covered and ready to move forward with a solid plan. Then and only then did we disperse with the agenda to reconvene again in a few days. We would then determine if we should take further action.

When I arrive at my home, Sir Edward is with me, as is the Prime Minister, Celia Trevino. There was a rumor floating around that Celia and my father were closer than they should be. This rumor cannot be confirmed, but neither was it able to be proven false. I had to wonder about the truthfulness of the rumor after witnessing her solemn demeanor once we learned how my father died. I would never actually come out and ask her about it. She is a married woman with a family. And since I have rumors flying around about me that hold no truth, I realize she isn't immune to false accusations, either.

"Why is she here?" Queen Sofia, however, doesn't seem to have a problem with it.

"Sit." I point to the chair she just leaped out of.

Sofia must detect the tone in my voice, because after one glance in my direction, I'm sure she comprehends I know what she has done. She drops back down in her seat and just as quickly lifts Isabel off the floor in front of her. Holding her very tightly against her chest as a few tears roll down her cheeks.

I can barely even look at her right now.

"Sir Edward, please ask Isabel's au pair to come retrieve her." I close my eyes and try to maintain my cool.

"Please, Antonio…" Sofia begs me through her tears.

"Say your goodbyes, Sofia. Furthermore, you will address me as Your Majesty or King." I warn her through clenched teeth.

When Beatriz, the young princess's au pair, enters the room, Isabel smiles up in her direction. The young woman makes her way over to the child and waits. After a solid squeeze and kiss from Sofia, she passes her daughter off to the au pair and sobs.

I glance around the room only to discover several confused faces. My sister Gabriela seems to be conflicted about whether she should console Sofia or let her be. Although, my mother halts her after her eyes lock with mine, establishing how that would not be a wise idea. My brothers are also closely watching Sofia, who is sobbing uncontrollably. They seem to have their suspicions. Both peer up at me around the same time.

"Why?" I question the blubbering woman, who I suspect understands her fate has been sealed.

"You cannot be serious," Sofia wails. "I did everything Ramon ever asked me to do. Everything. I gave him a child. Looked the other direction when he brought in his whores. And still, it wasn't enough. It was never enough."

I nod toward Sir Edward, giving him the signal to do what he came here to do.

"Queen Sofia Lopez Reyes, you are being detained for the murder of King Ramon Esteban Reyes. You can confess now and forgo a trial, or you can choose to allow the people to decide your fate." He steps forward with his men flanking him. "What do you say?"

"I beseech for understanding." Sofia falls to her knees. "I beg your forgiveness and ask that you have mercy on me, Your Majesty. Think of Isabel."

"Confess and it will be a swift sentence, carried out in private. Or you can draw this out and let the people condemn you to death. At that time, it will become a public execution, one I will not be able to prevent. I am thinking of Isabel, which is why I am even giving you the first option. The law is clear about how this is to be handled. You are lucky I could convince the King's Council to do the right thing here.

"We found your fingerprints on the tumbler, along with the bottle of scotch. Traces of the drug you slipped into his drink were discovered inside the necklace pendant you used to transport it. A maid saw you slip out of the king's chamber early that morning when you assumed no one was around. The au pair confirmed you called her to sit with Isabel around two so you could shower and take a break, returning around five looking shaken. Security cameras may not have caught you entering the king's chambers, however, they spotted you in the hallways leading to and departing from the area.

"Do yourself a favor, do Isabel a favor, and confess. You should also understand I will not allow you to have any unsupervised contact with her again. From this moment forward, Princess Isabel will be under my protection and mine to nurture as I see fit. And as King, my word in this matter is law."

"Then my life has no meaning any longer. All I ask is that you look after her and do your best to never let her lose her spirit. I, Queen Sofia Lopez Reyes, slipped a lethal dose of sleeping pills into my husband's, King Ramon's, nightcap. I did it after I went to him and tried to talk him out of filing for divorce. What else was I to do? I would have been sent away, Isabel as well, and then all but forgotten. Therefore, I did what had to be done to secure her status in this family, and I accept my fate. Make it swift and please tell my daughter I love her every day." Sofia's body tumbles and the guards have to practically carry her out of the room.

My brother, Esteban, is the first to say anything as soon as the Prime Minister and Sir Edward leave with Sofia. "She killed him?"

"There was even a diary in her suite stating her plan. Seems father was tiring of her and no longer wanted to have her around." I walk over to one of the empty chairs and collapse into it.

"I always told you there was something about her that didn't feel right." My youngest brother, Lorenzo, reminds us. "That there was a screw or two loose inside that pretty head."

"What did the council have to say?" My mother stands and takes the seat next to mine.

She isn't talking about Sofia; there is nothing to discuss anymore where she is concerned. Once the Queen is taken to the authorities and recounts the incident, signs a confession in front of the five Justices, and reads her statement for the record, her fate will be absolute. At that time the Justices will sign off on her death decree and resolve which method seems the most just in this situation. Nothing will be released to the public until after that point, and within a few weeks, they will carry it out in private.

My mother is asking me about my status as King.

"What is there to say, really?" I square my shoulders and try not to appear defeated. "I am King."

"And what about the fact you don't have a Queen?" She is a smart woman to understand that even if they did not bring it up today, it will be soon.

"What of it? As you are very well aware, I was in a lengthy relationship that didn't work out. No matter what others may think about my feelings where any of that is concerned, I will not compromise."

I hate thinking about how it all went down nearly four months ago. The woman I was involved with for nearly two years, whom I deemed might be the one, turned out to not be. We started off slow, friends first. Which as you can imagine, isn't easy when you are the Heir Apparent, for so many reasons. Everyone wants to be your friend. Most women want to date you. There is always a motive behind matters where both are involved.

Lady Dalia Batista didn't come across that way in the beginning. A friendship with her was easy and never seemed forged. After a while, we began dating—my suggestion. She was even hesitant about it. Reported she wasn't convinced she was suited to be royalty if things between us should become serious. Which only made me more fascinated with her and want to prove her wrong. Several months passed and my feelings for her started to grow. I considered telling her I loved her, thought about it seriously.

Until I overheard her talking with her sisters and mother when I showed up early for my lunch date with them. I heard them laughing, and paused so I could grasp what was so funny. That is when I discovered Lady Dalia had played me like a dang fiddle and all along knew exactly what she was doing.

When I stepped out of my hiding place, she realized I had caught her, although she didn't even seem phased by it. She excused her behavior away as acceptable. Even voiced if I believed I would ever encounter a woman who loved me for who I was as a man, rather than as the future king, then I was delusional. Love was a fantasy written for movies and books. Pointed out that my mother and father didn't marry for love, my grandparents and those before them hadn't married for love, her parents hadn't even married for love. Therefore, she also wouldn't be marrying for love. Instead, she would do so for status.

Later, Dalia believed she would learn to love me like her mother loved her father—which was a crock. I told her exactly what I thought about it, then ended things. She didn't take that very well, threw the biggest temper tantrum I have ever witnessed, which only made me that much more relieved I'd eavesdropped on her conversation.

I wasn't a perfect man. I had my flaws and made mistakes along the way. Used my title to get girls to fall at my feet and let me do things with them when I was a teenage boy coming of age. That all changed once I realized I was quickly becoming my father. It happened after I caught him advising a young maid that as King he could do as he pleased. If she liked her job, wanted to continue working in the palace, then she'd keep her mouth shut and please her King.

I swore then I would never be like that; never make anyone feel obligated to do as I said just because I was King. Vowed that I would only marry for love and nothing more. I didn't realize how difficult that would be. I refused to marry only because it was what they expected me to do. A king, after all, is to produce an heir, the next ruler to follow in his footsteps, so there would be those who would try to sway me. Ultimately, I hoped to one day do just that, but I would do it my way and only my way.

A proud smile appears on my mother's face. "You are going to make a great king, Antonio. You will be the leader others can once again look up to. Just be careful to keep your eyes open and your heart under lock and key. They will come out of the woodwork, but only one will stir a fire deep inside of you.

"Let the Lord be your guide. Ask for him to open your eyes when you meet the woman he knows will love you like you so very much deserve. The one who will love you first and foremost and then fall in love with the people you serve second. Lead your people like God has asked of you. You do that and everything else will fall in place as it should."

"I hope you're right, mother. Mostly because I don't know when I'll even have time to take a piss, let alone have the time to court someone while doing this job. I suppose that is why it is ideal to do so before you become king."

Truer words have never been spoken, I'm afraid. Because as soon as we buried my father, King Ramon Esteban Reyes, two days later, I moved into the palace and haven't come up for air yet.

CHAPTER 4
Larkin

Five Years Later

I've worked for Manchester International for three years now. They hired me right before I completed my master's to work in their historical department. That department was quickly growing, and they were looking for someone with my brand of passion.

One of my projects during my studies captured the attention of Zach Greene, a mid-level partner. He came to listen to my presentation and then approached me afterward. Later that day, he invited me to meet senior partner, Timothy Manchester. They offered me a job three days later, and told me it wouldn't take me long to make my way up in the ranks if I had more ideas like the ones they'd seen.

They had been truthful about my advancement. I took their jabber as a way to get me to join the company, and not as seriously as I guess I should have. I accepted the position with them because they had one of the best historical departments around. They took on projects all over the world, and it thrilled me to think where that just might take me.

Chicago has always been my home. The only place I've ever lived.

However, after Randal died, it never felt quite the same again. Working for a company that would send me on assignments far from the city that was a constant reminder of him, was ideal.

It took me two years to get assigned to a project like that. I recently returned from Mexico City, where we restored a crumbling cathedral that had been neglected for way too long. It took us almost a year to complete the project—eleven months and fourteen days, to be exact. It was one of the most challenging projects I've had the privileged of being a part of, and I loved every minute. Mainly because the entire time I was there, my thoughts rarely drifted to Randal. Everywhere I looked didn't trigger some memory that made me sad and lost on the inside. I was able to live my day-to-day life in the moment, while appreciating the beauty of my surroundings.

The one thing that went amiss during that time, was what I allowed to materialize with one of the other architects, Chandler Sloan. The anniversary of Randal's death was always a tough time for me. Chandler and I have worked together since I started. He was the one who urged me to join him on the Mexico City project. So maybe deep down, I felt some kind of obligation to him. We didn't know anyone else in the city, so when he invited me out for drinks that particular evening, and because I was feeling down, I accepted. I mean, it wasn't as if we'd never gone out for drinks before, we had. Except that night I should've known better than to set myself up for disaster.

Now, you should probably understand this about Chandler. He is one of those types. You know, the kind who believes he is all that and a slice of pie. And I'm not going to lie. He is rather pleasing on the eye. His bleached blond hair is cut just long enough to flop around. His eyes possess this light blue tint that is a rarity, so one might tend to stare at them because they are so unusual. And while his smile isn't perfect, it does the job when he flashes it at you in that way. I've watched him use it many times to charm women, so it wasn't as if I didn't recognize what type of guy he was.

However, that night I felt extremely lonely, so I let him kiss me. I mean, like really kiss me. He wanted more; thankfully I was able to fend him off by claiming since we weren't actually dating, it wasn't happening. Not that it would happen even if by chance we were dating, which never happened, so there was that.

The next seven months after that misguided night were filled with me constantly avoiding him, brushing him off, or making plans with anyone but him. Ensuring I had a legitimate excuse not to spend time outside of work with him again. Not that it stopped him from trying his darndest to get me to let him show me what we could have together. Which is why I was relieved when we completed the project and got to return home. I knew he would be different once back in Chicago. For one, he had his friends to distract him here, people he had known a lot longer than me. Plus, we would no longer be required to spend every single working day together. Once work ended, we could go our separate ways.

What I hated about it ending was that I knew as soon as I saw the city, Randal would take over my mind again. After having lived somewhere else for the past year, it was not something I welcomed back into my life at all.

I am positive that explains why I make a beeline to Zach Greene's office two days later. I need to escape this city. I will go anywhere that isn't Chicago, and yes, I do mean anywhere.

Zach acknowledges me as soon as I step into his outer office. "Come on in, Larkin. You look stressed."

I attempt a genuine smile, but I just don't have it in me. "I need to get out of here."

Zach laughs as he leans back in his chair. "You just got back. Ready to blow out again so soon?" He motions for me to take a seat.

"Yes. Don't take this the wrong way, but I hate this city." I admit as I plop down in the chair and sigh.

A sad expression crosses Zach's face as he rocks in his chair and studies me carefully. I know he gets my mindset since he is one of the few people who understands why. Randal and Zach once worked together. His death had been a shock to him and this company.

Oh yeah, did I forget to mention that part? Randal also once worked for Manchester International and his picture hangs in the main hallway as a memorial to a friend they lost too soon. They held high hopes for the kid who worked his way from the bottom to the top.

Randal was an inspiration to those who knew him, but that was too much for me to deal with day in and day out.

"Let me see what I can come up with." Zach seems open to a suggestion, so I give him one.

"I was thinking maybe I could help with the..." I glance at my lap, where I wrote the project's name on a post-it before I walked down here, "... the Hermosa Islas project."

A chuckle escapes him as he straightens and clicks his computer on. "You aren't messing around. That's a five-year proposed project, maybe longer. We are sending a team over in a few days. I'm not sure I have room on that team at the moment."

"I hear Janice isn't excited about being assigned to that particular group. She knows it's career suicide to refuse a project of this magnitude, although I imagine she'd be happier with something closer to home. I'd be glad to take her spot."

I know this because when I was here late last night, trying to figure out what I was going to do, she was around. Janice was sitting at her desk, stressing about the upcoming move she reluctantly agreed to. I'm sure she felt if she informed them she'd rather not accept the assignment, her chances of getting promoted would fade fast. However, if I volunteer to take her place, she can then be reassigned somewhere else, and all is good, right?

"Janice is a Level II architect. You are a Level I, Larkin." Zach peeks up over the glasses he slipped on just a few minutes ago.

"But I should be a Level II after the project I just kicked butt on. Come on, Zach. You and I both know this would be an excellent fit for me. The team you're sending, Cameron, Bradley, and Reginald are all fantastic, but they would be better if I were there with them." I am painting it on thick and I know it.

"Hope is going as well. Timothy thought it would be good experience for her." Zach tries to sound like he agrees.

Hope, by the way, is Timothy Manchester's youngest daughter. She is a few years younger than me and she is good, but not great. Her sister Nicolette is great—spectacular, in fact—which is why she made Junior Partner by the time she was thirty. That woman is who I inspire to be in a few more years, why I work so hard. I mean, I know I will never make

Junior Partner by the time I'm thirty. My daddy isn't the Senior Partner, and I am not the person he plans on handing the company over to when he retires.

And because I am fantastic at selling myself, I see a better reason for me to do it. "Which is an even better reason to send me. Hope and I started around the same time. She just finished her master's and has done very little fieldwork. I can mentor her and she'll be much more comfortable with me than Janice. Janice intimidates her, which, come on, if anyone should be intimidated, it should be Janice just because of who Hope is." Okay, so maybe I shouldn't have said that last part out loud, but I can't retract it now. "Plus, Timothy has always had a soft side for me."

Zach leans back in his chair again and crosses his arms. I realize that means he is thinking about everything I've said. When his desk phone rings, he leans forward and snags it off the receiver. "Zach here." His eyebrows lift almost to his hairline, which you should appreciate is receding. "He's here now? Like in the building and on his way up. Son of a..."

There is a long pause and Zach nearly leaps out of his chair. "She did what? When? Last night? Why am I just now hearing about this? Yes, I'll handle it. I can't believe she would up and leave us like that without a warning this close to an important project. Yes, Bradley, I understand what this means. I know it throws a serious..."

I can hear Bradley Stanton, Project Manager for Hermosa Islas, loudly expressing himself through the phone line. He isn't letting Zach get a word in edgewise. The man is rubbing his face and nodding as if he totally agrees with everything the other man is communicating.

There are footsteps behind me. I can tell by the sound they belong to someone important. Don't ask me how I know these details, I just do. I turn around and nearly fall out of my chair when a large man, flanked by two substantial men, enters Zach's office. One man glares at me like I am doing something wrong by remaining in my chair, gawking at the specimen in front of me. So, I glare back but don't move.

The one who I assume is in charge turns to his companions, and when he opens his mouth, he speaks in this rich, very unusual accent. "You may wait for me outside."

After hearing his rich voice, I slip out of my chair and land on my hip with a loud, "Ugh." I suddenly feel like I did when I was ten after I tripped and landed at the feet of the President. The day he came to my father's office in D.C. to congratulate him.

My cheeks heat as I do my best to save face by rolling over onto my knees so I can stand.

"There is no need to kneel before me, *señorita*." The arrogant male chuckles as he reaches out to give me a hand.

This conceited man no longer impresses me now that he has shown his true colors by making me feel foolish. I slap his hand away and stand on my own, placing a hand on the chair and pushing myself up. It may not have been the most graceful move I've ever done in my life, but at least I didn't require his assistance.

So, what if he is the most stunning male I've ever laid eyes on? He is almost a whole foot taller than me. And I am not short by any means, only two inches shy of six feet in my two-inch heels. His shoulders are broad, giving him a very unyielding posture, dressed in his tailor-made suit and very shiny shoes. Even his square jaw has a deep dimple where it meets his chin, making him appear so much more lethal.

Then there are his brown eyes, which seem to notice everything. They mix well with his skin tone and black wavy hair—not too wavy, but enough to make him look dapper. I mean, who cares what he looks like if he is a complete jerk and doesn't have the decency to ask me if I'm okay.

Did I tell you how I mouth off when I'm frustrated or feeling uneasy? That I blurt out what I'm thinking and don't even care if it offends or makes others equally uncomfortable. It's a defense mechanism my mother desperately tried to break me of but always ended up apologizing for later.

"Kneel? Please! I wouldn't kneel to you if you were the King of freaking England. And since I know you are not the King of England, that can be checked off the list." I make a big check mark in the air and bend to grab my misplaced items off the floor.

"Bowing isn't necessary, either." Again, he chuckles as he clears his throat, visibly amusing himself.

Argh.

I'm pretty sure that is the noise that escapes when I stand and all but stomp my foot at him. "You, sir, are an arrogant, egotistical jerk. One I don't have time to deal with at the moment."

I turn to Zach, who is just now hanging up his phone. He is staring strangely at the man I just chewed out. Whatever. "Let me know what you decide. If that won't work, then I need to figure out what my other options are."

Zach shakes the cobwebs from his head like he just realized I was still there. "Meeting in five minutes. Bring all of Janice's notes. She quit as of this morning, which means if you are serious about taking her place, it's yours."

I do a fist pump in the air and grin widely. "I'll be there."

The large man has relocated and is now blocking my escape, or at least trying to. People don't intimidate me, because frankly, I don't care what they think. When I step right, he steps that way too. I move left, and he does the same. I fake a move and then dart around him, feeling very victorious that I slipped past him without saying anything else to the stunning, annoying stranger.

There are more important matters to take care of right now than to deal with someone like him. I am going to impress the heck out of all those attending this meeting using Janice's notes. And then I am going home to pack. Or maybe I am going home to not unpack.

I need to sublease my place again, or just get rid of it this time, since this project will be a more permanent relocation instead of a temporary move. One I am pleased about.

CHAPTER 5
Antonio

The Royals

I try not to chuckle at the spunky woman who all but stormed past me when I crowded in behind her. Something about her immediately caught my attention the instant I entered Mr. Greene's office. I noticed her seated in the chair facing his desk with her back positioned toward the door. Gifting me with the perfect view of her backside peeking through the wooden contemporary style chair, a design I imagined one might often find in an architect's office. Her slacks were stretched tightly over the only part of her that was exposed, which I thought was a glorious sight.

Don't look at me like that. I rarely make it a habit to focus on that particular area on a woman. However, the bright red slacks she had on begged for my attention.

As I stepped past the door, it was her blonde hair floating through the air as she whipped her head around. Then it was those pale blue eyes, surrounded by the lightest skin I have ever seen, reminding me of the porcelain dolls my sister had growing up. After that, it was those heart-shaped red lips that nearly had me forgetting who I was and why I was here.

It wasn't until she glared at Franco and Isaac, I seemed to come to my senses and quickly dismissed them into the outer office. They wouldn't go far, now that they had secured the room and understood there was no threat to me in here.

Which is when I heard a thump followed by a grunt. By the time I directed my attention back toward the blonde beauty, she was rising to her knees. And for some unknown reason, I commented about her kneeling in my presence not being necessary.

The fire that lit up behind her eyes made me want to say something else, just so I could witness how fiery they could get. When she swatted my hand away, as if I was an annoying fly, it burned me. I have never been treated with such disregard and wasn't sure exactly how to handle her.

I wanted to scold her; except I never got the chance. As soon as she righted herself and had everything back in order, she gave me a piece of her mind. I had to hold back another chuckle, because it was then I knew she had no clue who I was or what I was doing here. There was no way this well put together woman would've spewed all that out if she had.

I just couldn't stop myself when she bent over to pick up her things. And was rewarded with an even fiercer glower that told me she didn't take crap from anyone.

When she turned her back on me to address Mr. Greene, I stepped up right behind her so that when she spun around, we would nearly be touching. I didn't even try to suppress the fact I was toying with her when she wanted to leave. Which is why, when she finally was able to slither past me, she stormed off and never looked back.

"King Reyes." Mr. Greene attempts to address me properly. It's a common error that happens more than one might expect.

Typically, when people are addressed formally, they use last names, but take a minute to think about all the past royalty rulers throughout history. Queen Elizabeth. King George. Prince Henry. We use their first names when we discuss them, don't we? But it never fails that when someone tries to figure out what they should call me, they always go with my last name. Much like they would when addressing other world leaders, President Lincoln, Prime Minister Churchill, President Mandela. Interesting, isn't it?

"King Antonio, if you must address me with my title. Although I am fine with just Antonio since this is personal business, Mr. Greene." I nod politely and then take the seat of the woman who just stormed out, recently occupied. "Who was that?"

A knowing smirk crosses the other man's face, and I'm not sure how I feel about it. "Larkin. She is one of our third years. Just returned to the office after overseeing a major restoration to a cathedral in Mexico City. Spent nearly a year there with a small team and was a critical asset to them, more than proving her worth."

"Larkin." I test her name out on my lips and like how it so easily seems to flow. "She will be joining us; did I hear that correctly?"

Mr. Greene nods. "If that isn't going to be a problem."

"Why would you think that would be a problem? I want the best you have to offer working on restoring my family's estates. They are very important to us, along with those we serve. I'm uncertain when the last time we hired someone to properly appraise the integrity of those particular structures. After the unfortunate fire in the kitchen at De la Peña Citadel, and then the water damage done to Fort Serna when the rainy season hit it hard, it seemed like perfect timing for us to finally get everything up to code."

"Then Larkin is exactly who you want on this team. She has an eye for details that can't necessarily be taught. We were lucky to stumble upon her and then snag her while she was still in grad school."

Mr. Greene stands, and I don't chastise him for rising ahead of me. Royalty in the United States is a régime most of its citizens have no real concept of. I am a firm believer one should not expect those who haven't been trained in the proper etiquette when dealing with royalty to know all the rules. Therefore, I let details like that roll off my shoulders and only concern myself with important matters.

"Shall we join them in the conference room down the hall?" he asks as he moves around his desk.

"That sounds like a brilliant plan. Please introduce me as Antonio and leave the King part out for now. I would prefer to hear their honest evaluations, ideas, and professional opinions before we let them know exactly who they will be working for." I instruct him as we step into his outer office and gesture for my men to follow us. "I hope you understand."

"Too many people focus on the title and forget you are also a client." I catch the twinkle in his eye. "I believe Timothy has explained how we handled this in the past. It's not a problem, Antonio."

There is a playful tone in the way he repeats my name, and it makes me grin. I like this man very much. Know I chose wisely in contracting Manchester International to handle my family and country estates. Their portfolio exhibited all the ways they could maintain the integrity of historic buildings while bringing them into the current century. I knew that the first time I talked with Timothy Manchester and his daughter Nicolette. It was when they made the trip to Hermosa so they could determine what our needs were exactly.

The meeting is already in full swing and I can hear the team chattering amongst themselves, so I stop and listen. Zach seems to understand what I am doing, and he pauses with me. So far, I am very impressed with what I learn and can't wait to let them get started.

There is a break in the conversation, so we start to move again. When I hear her voice, I reach out to halt him. He glances over his shoulder and nods, letting me know he will allow me to enter when I am ready. I just want to hear what she is thinking before I enter and throw her off her game.

Larkin's voice has a crispness to it, like none I have ever heard before. It demands those in the room take notice while letting them understand she knows what she is talking about. There is an authoritative quality to it. informing anyone near, she is in control and not easily intimidated by a room full of men and women more experienced than she. It has me hypnotized and I almost miss my cue when she asks if she can be the one who works on the home my mother was living in until the fire.

I step into the room and don't wait to be introduced before I speak. "I don't see that being a problem. I believe you and the woman who lives there will get along very well. You have the same vision she does for De la Peña Citadel. Perhaps that is where we should start, instead of focusing on Aragon Palace."

"You." Larkin's eyes widen as the realization of who she smarted off to earlier hits her.

I can hear her mumbling to herself, but can't quite make it out. She quickly gathers her belongings, shoving them in a leather satchel in a very agitated way. All I can do is watch, trying to figure out exactly what she is doing.

"I changed my mind, Zach. I think I'd rather take my chances here in Chicago." She stands quickly and heads for the door.

"Larkin," I say her name, stopping her dead in her tracks. "Sit back down... please."

A shiver works its way through her body. She is standing in front of the door opposite mine and slowly twirls to face me. "No."

A smirk overtakes my face when I catch her raised eyebrows, as Larkin dares me to try to make her. Her defiance has me wondering what it would be like to have it out with her. Would she stomp that foot at me again like a petulant child, the way Isabel does when I correct her? I bet she would yell at me like Gabriela has several times these last few years when I refused to allow her some freedom. Perhaps she would even get in my face and tell me exactly what she thinks about my stubborn, unwavering ways, like they both have when I stand my ground. It is something I think I'd like to experience, and the only way I can do that is if I can convince her to join this team.

"Zach told me if I want the best architects this firm has to offer, that means I need you on this team. I won't settle for second best, so that means I need you." And as soon as I say those last three words, something inside of me softens.

"You said that?" The uncertain tone in Larkin's voice as she looks at Zach, has me even more determined to get her to understand her true potential.

"I'm not sure I said those exact words. I believe I also tried to cover the fact that you tend to overreact when feeling overwhelmed." He ducks when a pen flies out of her hand. "See what I mean."

"You killed it in Mexico City." The man next to Zach notifies her.

"Thank you, Cameron." Larkin's head lifts slightly as she gains some confidence back.

"If you had been in the States when this project first came across my desk, your name would have been added to the shortlist," Bradley tells her. I know him because I met with him a few days ago when we were in negotiations.

Now her shoulders square, and I realize we are close to getting her to say yes. So, I turn to the third guy and the young woman seated at the table, hoping they will say something.

The young woman speaks first. "Plus, it will get you away from Chandler before he makes his move again. Not to mention it gives you and me a chance to get to know each other while we make a name for ourselves. I mean, if you are up for that and all." She cups half her mouth as if she is revealing a secret. "I have connections in case you forgot. If you promise not to enlighten my father about what I do on my own time, I promise to lie about how good you are at your job."

That seems to make the room burst into a fit of laughter. Larkin has to take a seat in the empty chair so she doesn't lose her balance and fall on her butt again. I learn right then and there that Larkin's laugh is the sweetest sound to ever invade my ears.

"Okay. One condition." She finally says after the room settles down.

"Whatever it is you want; I can promise you it is yours." I confidently tell her as I breathe a sigh of relief and snag one of the empty chairs.

"You think you are powerful enough to grant me such a wish." Her mocking tone has me holding back a snicker. If only she understood the powers I possess at my fingertips.

"Antonio is a very influential man, Larkin." Zach seems to be enjoying her unawareness way too much. "Perhaps you should..."

I hold up my hand to interrupt him. "Please Zach, let me hear this. I am certain I will be able to accommodate her request."

Larkin crosses her arms and stares at me. Without even blinking, she makes it. "I want an apology for earlier."

I start to give it to her, but she raises her hand to stop me. So, I close my mouth and motion for her to continue.

"I want you to get on your knees and beg for my forgiveness. Perhaps when you stand you can also bow once, to prove you are earnest about it." I understand she is taunting me for how things went down earlier.

I can see her request mortifies the others and they want to put an end to this before it goes too far. However, I don't plan on letting that happen, because right then I realize this woman is going to bring me to my knees so many times before we are ever done.

"If I do these acts you've requested, you will put our earlier mishap aside and join the team?" She nods once and then tries not to laugh as I stand and start to get down on my knees.

"I'm kidding," Larkin shrieks when she realizes I am about to do as she requested.

The funny thing is, I am pretty sure she could've asked for the moon and I would have done everything in my power to give it to her. "You sure?" I begin to lower myself again. "This could be your one chance to get me on my knees, begging you for your forgiveness. You may never get a second chance to make such a request of me."

For the first time since I ran into her this morning, I notice her cheeks growing a little red. "Yes. I am positive. While it has always been a fantasy of mine to have a man falling to his knees before me, I can't ask you to do that. I can, however, ask that you give me a personal tour once we arrive in Hermosa Islas. And let me be clear on why I am asking, so you don't get the wrong idea. This project is passionate to you, so I want to establish what your likes and dislikes are. It will allow me a better understanding of the direction we should go as a team. What do you say, Antonio, do you think you can handle being my personal tour guide?"

I glance around the table and catch Zach shaking his head, truly appreciating now why I requested he not reveal my true identity just yet. There is no way Larkin would so boldly ask me, the King of Hermosa Islas, to escort her around my beautiful kingdom.

"It would be my pleasure, Larkin. I will offer you a tour that only someone with my knowledge and rapport can. It shall be the very first act of business I insist we partake of as soon as everyone is settled."

CHAPTER 6
Antonio

The Royals

We are about to board my plane to head back home, three days after that meeting. I've been gone for nearly three weeks.

The first week was part of my responsibilities as King. I met with a few world leaders, keeping alliances strong.

The second week was more personal, but still a critical part of my job as ruler over a thriving kingdom. It is my duty to ensure our economy flourishes and we can keep our business connections at the forefront worldwide. My youngest brother, Lorenzo, will eventually take over the business dealings our family is involved in. Esteban had been planning to do that, but after my father's passing, his role shifted to becoming the Heir Apparent. A position he will continue to learn until I marry and produce an heir of my own, which right now could be never with the way things are progressing.

I mean, I haven't even had time to deal with all the requests rolling in, asking me to consider them as my future queen. Or maybe it's I just don't want to think about that right now. I have no desire to marry someone to simply fulfill the position of Queen. We all understand how an heir comes about, after all, and the thought of using a woman like that holds no interest to me.

Sure, I guess I can start considering my options amongst the prospects who have been presented to me. One of them could be the woman I am hoping to find. Except when I think about sorting through them one by one, I suddenly feel ill to my stomach.

I should probably get over that quickly, though, now that I've agreed to host several formal balls where a select few of the prospects will attend. After years of hounding, accompanied by the fact I truly don't have the time to do this on my own, I finally consented to do it their way. But if I am being honest, I have my doubts it will lead to more than just a very huge headache on my part.

Week three was for me. I devoted most of my time entertaining my youngest sister, Isabel. We spent our days doing what any eight-year-old girl would want to do. Our first stop was The American Girl store, where we couldn't leave without buying a custom-made doll, along with a few outfits to go with her. We killed an evening on the world-famous Ferris wheel and then watched fireworks from the pier. Visited the Skydeck, where I got to appreciate a little girl lie face down as she took in the scene below her. Those are just a few of the activities Isabel talked me—as well as my security team—into doing that week.

I've done exactly what I told her mother I would do, taken my job as her guardian seriously. She lives with me in the king's quarters along with Helena. I hired Helena a few years ago when I realized I needed a full-time staff member to run my household. She cooks for us, cleans (or oversees the cleaning), keeps Isabel's schedule up to date with her day au pair, Beatriz's, assistance, along with making sure that we have what we need in the evenings.

I've also taken some time to conduct personal business with Manchester International. I made sure it didn't interfere too much with the time I set aside to spend with Isabel. After all, my little sister is topnotch when it comes to laying on the guilt trip. Plus, knowing everything I know about why I am responsible for her, may have me wanting to make up for the mistakes of her parents.

By the time Isabel and I make it to the private airstrip, everyone else is already loaded and ready to go. I should probably apologize since we are an hour late, but it took us longer at Shedd Aquarium than first predicted. We were on a private tour and got held up with the belugas.

What can I say? I'm a sucker and have a hard time making Isabel leave when she is having such a good time.

No one seems to care. It's not as if my staff has ignored them. I instructed them to make my guests as comfortable as necessary while waiting on us. After all, I am the King, and if I can't be late, then what is the purpose of holding such a title?

After we are in the air, I make my way around the cabin, ensuring my companions are happy. I later retired to my small office located on the plane, so I can go over emails and respond to a few executive matters that require my immediate attention.

An hour later, I return to the absolutely most perfect scene. Isabel has somehow convinced Larkin to join her in the sitting area. There are hair bows and jewelry scattered all around.

Isabel's hair is braided in a way I've never seen it done before. It starts at the base of her neck and ends slightly at the side of her crown, where it's gathered into a ponytail. Her long spiral curls are left dangling and two plain white flowers are somehow secured in her dark hair, making her look every bit the princess she is.

And while that is something I notice, it's not what has me leaning against the wall so I can just watch. That would be Larkin seated on the floor in front of Isabel so my little sister can fix her hair. She must have about ten bows strategically placed throughout hers by the young stylist.

Hope joins them and expresses what a lovely job my sister is doing. Then she pulls out her phone and snaps a photo.

"I swear, Hope, if that ends up on social media, you will regret it." Larkin lifts her gaze and then notices me standing there.

"Let's just call it blackmail for another day." Hope puts her phone away and laughs.

"I am going to insist on looking at that photo," I inform the younger woman.

She retrieves her phone and hands it to me without questioning why.

It's a lovely blackmail photo, I must admit, so it is rather unfortunate it will need to be deleted. Isabel's face is glowing behind Larkin, and I cannot allow this to remain on Hope's mobile. There are no pictures of the young princess floating around that have not been approved first by my PR department. I am very protective of her identity being exploited, which is why I pass the phone off to one of my guards.

"Please have Isaac take care of that for me."

"As you wish... sir." I informed my staff to not address me in any way that would give away my royal status.

"Are you serious? I can delete it if you are worried about something getting out with Isabel's face on it." Hope pleads, not understanding how seriously we take this.

"Your phone will be returned to you shortly, Hope. We do not allow photos of Isabel, I'm sorry." I hate how that sounds, but one can never be too careful.

"It's because I'm a princess. Antonio wants to protect me from the world." My ever-chatty sister reveals.

"And what a pretty princess you are." Larkin leans back as she smiles up at the young girl behind her. "You are very lucky to have a brother who looks out for you like that. I wish I had a brother like him."

It seems Isabel has been explaining who I am to her and why she is with me on this trip. I have to wonder if she's said more that she should have. Knowing my little sister, it wouldn't surprise me. It is a complicated relationship we have, but we do well and try our best to keep the lines from blurring.

"Do you want him as your brother?" The little stinker makes a face. "I might be willing to sell him for a price."

"You'd miss him. Who would look out for you if Antonio weren't around?" She stands and drops onto the small sofa next to Isabel.

"I have two other brothers. Esteban and Lorenzo. They will take over for him."

Larkin glances over at me, her hair completely a mess, courtesy of my little sister. And when I tell you she never looked better, I mean it. In that moment, I feel as if I am getting to experience a side of this woman very few people are privy to. I realize we aren't alone on this plane, thousands of miles above the ocean, but I doubt she goes around letting random little girls fix her hair. And since we have a long flight, eight hours to be exact, I get the impression she is letting her hair down, so to speak.

"I get the sense your brother would put up a stink about that. So, tell me something, Princess Isabel. If you are a princess, does that make Antonio a prince?" I realize she thinks this is a game a little girl is playing, but I don't want Isabel to convey too much, so I have to be careful here.

"No, it would make him the king." She blurts out smiling, letting me know she has figured out no one knows the truth about it all being factual. "Would you like to be queen, Larkin?"

"Okay, enough." I push off the wall. "Time for the princess to say goodnight. Hermosa is seven hours ahead of Chicago. By the time we land, it will be morning. We have at least six hours to go, and after our earlier adventures, I have no doubt you will crash shortly after lying your precious head on the pillow."

I wait for her to tell Larkin and Hope goodnight. She even makes a show of it with the three men that joined us, trying to drag it out as long as possible. Finally, we are off and met by her au pair, who shuffles the trouble-making princess off to her private sleeping quarters.

Once I make my way back to the main cabin, I find Larkin cleaning up the mess she and Isabel made playing hairdresser. She is alone once again. Hope has made her way to the front and is struggling to strike up a conversation with Franco.

"You didn't need to do that. My staff would have taken care of it for us." I tell her as I reach down and pick up a hair tie.

"My mother would shame me for hours if I didn't clean up after myself. She always said that it wasn't the job of the house staff to pick up after me when I was too lazy to clean up my toys. I guess you can say old habits are hard to break." Larkin shoves the last bow into the container and then passes it off to one of my flight attendant, who appeared out of nowhere.

"You grew up with house staff?" I ask as I plop down in a chair and accept the glass of bourbon the other flight attendant brings me. I always have a few sips before bed to help bring me down and as a salute to my father.

Larkin stares at the tumbler in my hand as I swirl it around and seems lost in thought. When I stop swirling and take a sip, her eyes follow my movement, and the instant the cool glass hits my lips she bites hers.

"Would you like something?" I ask her as I bring it back down and rest the tumbler on the arm of the chair.

"I don't drink." She shakes her head once and explains a few details on why. "Product of an addict, so I never wanted to take the chance. My parents never kept alcohol in our house growing up so that it was never a temptation. Since they were both physicians, they understood how at risk I was and didn't want to take any chances. Once I got older, I decided it was best to not test the waters and steered clear."

I lift my hand to call over the flight attendant. When she comes to check on me, I hand her the tumbler and order us both a cup of cinnamon sleeping tea. My mother always made us drink a cup before bed when we were children to calm us down and help us sleep. It also has several health benefits, and I guarantee it is way better for me than my usual bourbon.

"You didn't need to do that." Larkin's eyes lock with mine and I notice a swirl of emotion pass through hers. "I had a friend who..." she pauses and closes her eyes as a tear slides down her cheek.

I lean forward and lay my hand over hers. "I'm sorry. He must have meant a lot to you."

"He meant the world to me." Larkin's eyes are open again, but instead of looking up at me, she stares at my hand. "Alcohol I believe gave him the courage to do something he probably wouldn't have been able to do otherwise."

There is a long, drawn-out moment of silence that isn't interrupted until our tea is served. Meaning, I have to remove my hand from hers so I can pour us both a cup.

And in case you were wondering, it is very rare for the king to pour his own cup, let alone pour a cup for someone else. So, when I wave the flight attendant off, it's no wonder why she does a double-take and acts confused about my actions.

"Larkin," I softly whisper her name. "I never thanked you earlier for entertaining Isabel."

A very pleasant smile crosses her lips as she sips her tea. "I can honestly say I enjoyed myself. It has been a very long time since I did anything like that. My girl cousins and I used to take turns doing each other's hair. They were quite a bit older than me, so I suspect I made them look a lot like Isabel made me look. You've done an excellent job with her."

I blush at the compliment. "I cannot take all the credit. Her au pairs, Helena and Beatriz, have been well trained on how to deal with her. When Isabel's mother died mine stepped in to offer advice. She makes sure we don't mess her up terribly and stay within the guidelines set before us."

"Well, whatever it is you are doing, you are making sure it gets done, you should know you are doing it right. I am sure she makes it very challenging."

I slouch down in my chair, which is not something I do when others are around. It causes me to look relaxed and vulnerable; a king is to be neither of those things. "You have no idea."

We say little else while we sip on our tea. Once mine is gone, I glance down at my watch and note an hour has passed. I need to get to bed so I am ready to deal with those who are going to bombard me as soon as I return to the palace.

"We have three sleeping quarters if you'd like to take advantage of one." I roll my neck and watch the woman in front of me do the same. "You should probably get some sleep."

"Are you heading off to bed?" I know she means nothing by her question, but hearing her ask me about going to bed sends warmth to my lower region. "I think I may do the same. I'm still recovering from my earlier trip."

I almost ask if she'd like to join me in my quarters, because the thought of her warm body next to mine sounds like a splendid idea. However, I come to my senses. So instead, I offer to show her to the one I know is empty.

As we walk down the small hallway, I try to figure out what would be the proper way to wish her goodnight. Once we reach the door, I grab the handle and push it open for her.

"Thank you," Larkin tells me as she steps just inside and grabs the door. "Goodnight, Antonio."

I'm not sure why I did what I did next. I've never once

spontaneously leaned in and kissed a woman before. I didn't actually kiss her, I guess. I more like lean in and place a friendly peck on her right cheek and then held it there for a few seconds.

When I pull back, I get the privilege of watching her reach up and touch the spot where my lips brushed her skin. Once again there is a nice red tint to her very light pigmented skin.

"Goodnight, Larkin. I hope you sleep well." And before I turn to walk away, I give her a slight bow, which is not at all appropriate behavior for a king. A king never bows to those beneath him, and since everyone is beneath him, that means he bows to no one except God.

The fact I just showed this woman that I don't see her as beneath me has me smiling all the way to my quarters. I'm not exactly sure what that means, although I believe I have an idea. But before I can even allow my mind to go there, I have to let her know who I am. I know exactly how I will do that, and I hope she will forgive me for not being honest with her from the beginning.

CHAPTER 7
Larkin

The Royals

I t has been five days since we arrived in the beautiful city of Argon. I don't know how to describe the city except to say it is unlike any I've ever been in before. I feel as if I am in an architect's dreamland and often gaze up at the skyline while wandering the streets.

We are staying in a hotel downtown, courtesy of our gracious host. It is only a few blocks from the office Manchester International will use as a home base.

Right now, there are only five members of our team here. We will add to it as the projects develop. Hiring local contractors, as well as employees to man the office. This is the primary reason Cameron York, our Senior Manager, is leading this venture. He will be the liaison between this office and the central one in Chicago. It will be his job to approve all our suggestions while making sure we stay on schedule. His plan is to move his family here after he locates a home for them. Since his kids are young, seven and three, it wasn't as big of a deal relocating them. Instead, he said it gave them a more diverse life and would teach them how to adapt.

Bradley Stanton, our project manager and structural engineer, will also bring his fiancée over soon. They plan on picking out a home together and she will work in our business department. They haven't set a date yet, but if the way Bradley talks is any indication, I suspect they will marry shortly after she arrives.

Reginald Hartford III, Hope Manchester, and I are the architects. It will be our jobs to figure out how to conserve and restore the structures we will be working on while here. Fixing any problems we come across, while doing our best to maintain the original designs and strengthening the integrity of the buildings. We realize a few have some serious issues. Our mission will be to discover ways to save them from further damage, and then ensure they will stand for at least another hundred years.

We most definitely have our work cut out for us. Mainly because my two fellow architects are less experienced than I am. Cameron and Bradley will both be here to help guide us to ensure we do it right. They are excellent at what they do and have made a name for themselves. Janice was expected to be the team leader, the experienced architect they were counting on to teach Reginald and Hope. That role now falls into my barely experienced lap and has landed me a promotion to a Level II Architect. I know I talked big in Zach's office, telling him I could do this. However, now that I am actually here, I am to questioning if I got in over my head.

Our team has done nothing but go over everything we have learned these last five days. I've been doing my best to catch up with the others, getting as familiar with this assignment as they are. Meaning, I have put in twelve-hour days, easily. Once back at the hotel I add in a few more. My plan is to continue to work through the weekend, so come Monday I will be ready to do a thorough inspection of Aragon Palace with Bradley.

Oh, and I've learned a few things since here.

For instance, I learned the king lives in Aragon Palace. I know little about him, although I suspect that will change as we move forward. Maybe I'll ask Antonio about him when he gives me that promised tour. I haven't seen him once after we landed. He was swiftly swept away by his security team, so who knows if that will happen.

According to the adorable Isabel, her brother is an important man and often works long hours. Although she said he never missed one of her school programs or teacher conferences. Made sure to be at her soccer games and piano recitals, no matter what crisis popped up. Since we will work on two of his family's estates, along with those under his care but still belong to Hermosa Islas, I've concluded he must somehow be related to the king.

It's getting close to six, and I am about to call it a night when my desk phone rings. I pick it up as I email Zach, letting him know how things are progressing. "Larkin Cross."

"What are your plans for tomorrow, Miss Cross?" A unique smooth sounding voice asks me.

I swear if I hadn't been sitting down, I might have stumbled over my feet. That would be twice now I have had that sort of reaction to his voice. The first time was when I slid out of the chair in Zach's office. I still can't quite figure out how that happened. Then again, when he spoke my name as I started to leave the conference room, I nearly landed on my rear again when a shudder invaded my body. At least this time he wouldn't be able to see how it affected me, so I took full advantage of that fact.

Leaning back in my chair, I smile fondly to myself and decide to pretend I have no idea who he is. After all, he didn't introduce himself and it has been five days since he last made any contact.

"Who is this?" I try to make my voice sound unsure.

"I don't believe you have been in my country long enough to have men calling you to solicit such a question." He sounds a little upset.

"I've been here for five days. I've met several polite men. A few may have requested to get to know me better." I respectfully declined any such offer, because right now I don't have time to socialize.

I swear I hear a low growl, followed by the solid sound of a slamming door. I can hear him arguing with someone, although I can't make out what it is about exactly. There is a ding, and it sounds a lot like the arrival of an elevator.

"Hello?" I say loudly into the phone.

"Names of the men who..."

"That, I am sad to inform you, is none of your business, Antonio." I snicker, not at all sure why he cares.

I mean, he may have shocked me by placing a peck on my cheek after showing me to the sleeping quarters on the plane. A peck that packed a punch and had me tossing and turning for nearly an hour while my mind tried to dissect what he was up to with that bold move. I met him only a few days before, and yet it seemed like a whole lot longer. His suave move made me wonder if maybe it was a customary way to say goodbye in his country, or if it was a knee-jerk reaction.

"None of my business?" He barks into the phone, letting me know he doesn't agree. "Sorry. I've had an exasperating week, so perhaps I am taking some of my frustration out on you."

I hear the elevator door outside my office chime and watch the doors open. I nearly fall out of my chair when I see him standing there. He is staring back at me through my glass walls.

"You really should be more careful, Miss Cross. Seems you and office furniture don't necessarily get along." He smirks as he steps off the elevator, flanked by four men, who take up position in the hallway, appearing very alert.

"What are you doing here?" I question as I struggle to recover, sitting up straighter.

"I believe I owe you a tour." He hangs up the phone as he steps inside my office. When one man tries to follow, he shakes his head slightly and then closes my door. "Can you frost the glass?"

"Um. Yes. I think?" I try to remember how that feature works.

Antonio steps around my desk and wrenches my chair back, so he has access to my desk. He reaches underneath the front of it and locates the button I forgot was there and presses it. The glass immediately frosts, and I suddenly feel a little uneasy about being alone with him like this.

"What are you doing?" I scoot my chair a little farther back until it bangs against the file cabinet behind me.

He slowly turns, and because of his height, I find myself looking directly at his crotch. I've never been one to inspect that particular region on a man, so I quickly close my eyes tightly and try to forget he is standing there.

When my chair sinks and tilts back, I shriek and reach out, grasping onto the first thing I can. Then I shriek again when I realize where my hands land is the very thing I had been trying to block out. I cannot believe I just groped his private area. I try not to think about it and don't linger there long.

I immediately release my grip and drop my hands. My eyes fly open to discover him perched over me. He is gripping my armrest and has lowered his body enough he is squatting in front of me. A dark, unreadable expression is plastered on his face as he closes the distance between us. A wicked shiver works its way through my body, and I shriek again.

"You really are going to have to keep it down, unless you want my men to use their imagination," Antonio mumbles, a few inches away from my face. "I am going to kiss you, Larkin. If you are not okay with that, you have about two seconds to stop me."

My eyes widen, and because I am not sure how I feel, I do the only thing I can to prevent the act. I turn my head so he misses my lips and instead brushes those soft lips against my cheek. If I thought that would lessen the impact on me, I was completely misguided.

"Oh, good gravy, that feels nice." I swallow and strain to keep the rest of my thoughts locked up. However, when he drops a few more light pecks along my burning cheek until he reaches my ear, they just slip out. "Fudgesicle. W-what are you doing?"

Antonio chuckles and lowers his head. It must land on the headrest of my chair since it seems to have dipped back again. Plus, I can now feel his warm breath against my neck, making me shiver.

With little warning, he stands abruptly, which has me wobbling in the chair. He takes one of my hands in his and gives it a solid tug, forcing me to my feet.

"Do you have a purse?" He looks around the room as if searching for it.

"Yes. I keep it in the bottom drawer." I point to my desk.

Opening the drawer I pointed at, he retrieves it and tucks it under his arm. "Is there anything else you need to do before we leave? Anything you need to take with you?"

I logged out of my computer right before he barged in. While I probably should grab my leather briefcase, I can always retrieve it later. There is nothing in there I need. "No."

Antonio reaches under my desk and presses the button to defrost my glass and then drags me toward to door. "We need to talk."

"Can't we just talk here?" I ask as I allow him to tow me into the hall where four men immediately surround us while we wait for the elevator. "Hello?"

He glances at one of his men when the door opens, and after he notices the car is empty, he states. "We'll ride down alone."

I get the impression none of them agree that is a good idea, if the tightening of their jaws reveals anything.

"Alone." Antonio presses the close button once we step inside as he holds them all back with a stern look.

We are only five floors up, so I know the ride down will be short. "Explain all that, please."

"I will." He squeezes my hand yet refuses to make eye contact.

"Now." I try to yank it free, but he only tightens his grip.

When we arrive in the lobby, Isaac and a man I don't recognize are waiting for us. They both appear angry, although the man I don't know looks like he could commit murder. The flare of his nostrils surely gives away his inner thoughts.

"Don't," Antonio utters one word, and both men seem to gather their disposition. "We will be heading back, so you can stop with all that now."

"We?" The man's eyes land on me as he then does an inspection. "Sir."

"Miss Cross has clearance, so I don't want to hear about it." He gestures for them to move, which they do, only stopping momentarily when a few men step outside and look around. One nod from them and we are moving again.

As soon as we step outside, I notice the three identical black vehicles parked by the curb. Antonio releases my hand as he propels me forward and into the middle vehicle, where he joins me and then grabs it again.

"Antonio, what in the world is going on? Are you some sort of diplomat?"

He doesn't answer me right away. Instead, he waits until the car we are in starts moving. That's when he aims his attention at me. There is a very serious expression on his face. "How much do you know about my country?"

I shrug. "Honestly, until a few days ago, I didn't even know it existed. And after having spent five days here, I find that hard to believe.

Aragon is a very beautiful city; I imagine it displays only a fraction of what Hermosa Islas has to offer."

"It is exactly that in my opinion." He glances out the window just past my head, as he watches the city rush past us. "I'd like to start with something I planned on doing at the end of that tour I promised you. I believe I have misled you long enough, so now it is time for me to correct my mistake."

"Okay." I can't imagine why he looks so torn over something I am sure is not a big deal. "Wait? Are you married?"

The first genuine smile I have seen from him takes over his face. "No, Larkin, I am not married."

"Oh. Good." I can't believe I just said that, so I try to brush it off. "I mean... you know because that would have made all the stuff that happened earlier seem wrong."

He lifts my hand to his lips and places a gentle kiss on it. "I agree, and since it seemed anything but wrong..."

The car slows as we pull through a large gated area. We follow the drive, shut-off by a stonewall, emerging into an open area that looks like some kind of private entry.

"Where are we?" I ask as the cars stop and the men in the other two vehicles get out quickly.

"Home." He tells me as the door on his side opens and he climbs out.

When he reaches in, I offer him my hand so he can assist me. I glance up and try to figure out exactly where home is, except it is nearly impossible to do when you are being ushered inside rather hastily.

Antonio hands my purse to a young woman as she approaches us. We are in a larger-than-life entryway, and I realize at that moment there are several people dressed in uniforms staring in my direction. I suddenly become extremely uncomfortable and attempt to leave. But since my hand is still trapped in his, and he refuses to let go, I am stuck.

"Miss Cross and I will be in the west wing. We are not to be disturbed, no matter the circumstances." He begins to walk and I am forced to follow.

"Where are we, Antonio?" I notice a few of the staff turn when they hear my question. "Did I say something wrong?"

Releasing my hand, he repositions his to the small of my back and leans in. "They just aren't accustomed to seeing me with such a stunning woman."

"I doubt that." I roll my eyes at his obvious lie. "Please tell me the truth."

"Excuse me, Your Majesty." An older woman comes jogging after us. "Princess Isabel has asked if she can join you?"

Antonio shifts his hand to my hip and tightens his hold to halt our retreat. "Tell Isabel I don't need her assistance, and to be a good little princess and mind her own bloody business."

The woman bites her lips together and nods. "Should I say it exactly like that, Your Majesty, or would you like me to summarize it a bit?"

Antonio glances down the hall to where I spot Isabel peeking her head around the corner. He motions for her to step out from her hiding place and then looks at the woman who keeps calling him Your Majesty. "Feed her boiled beets and pigs' feet for supper tonight and make sure she eats it all."

A giggle echoes down the hallway and the little girl twirls around and dashes off in the opposite direction.

"Keep her out of the west wing. If she becomes too much trouble, send her to Gabriela or my mother. I am sure they will have plenty to discuss once they hear what I am up to. But don't allow anyone else to disturb us. When we are ready to make acquaintances, if Miss Cross feels up to doing so, we will meet them in my quarters at that time. Thank you, Helena, you are dismissed." Then he presses on my back again, and once more we are moving at a rather abrupt pace.

"Are we in a hurry? Afraid if you don't get me there fast enough, someone will interpret us again?" I try to move my feet briskly, but since I am wearing rather high heels today—three-inch ones, to be exact—I trip.

The man has quick reflexes. He stops me from making a fool of myself by landing flat on my face. "Maybe we should slow down. We are almost there, and I believe we are in the clear now."

A few moments later, we step through an open door into a room that is museum like. I get the sense the lights have just been turned on when I catch a door in front of me close very gently. I quickly forget about that door when I spot several portraits, mostly of men, surrounding us. Every person has a crown proudly planted on top of his or her head. I move towards one of the few women proudly on display amongst these men and notice the plate under it reads Queen Juliana Teresa Aragon.

I spin and stare at the man behind me. "We are in Aragon Palace?"

"We are." He places his hands behind him as he stares at the portrait in front of me. "Queen Juliana was the very first female ruler of Hermosa Islas. It is said that she is also the one who made it what it is today."

I turn and study her closely. "Why is that?"

"Because unlike most queen's during the era she reigned, when her son was born, she gave him his father's name, Reyes."

"Isn't your last name Reyes?" I ask, starting to put two and two together.

"It is. Queen Juliana is my great many times over grandmother." He motions for me to continue.

I inspect each portrait after hers and notice they all bear the name Reyes and my mouth goes dry. He stops in front of the last portrait and stares at the image that reminds me very much of the man standing next to me.

"This is King Ramon Esteban Reyes, my father."

I reach up and trace the nameplate. "Isabel's father?"

"Yes. My father was the first king to divorce. Eventually, he married Sofia, Isabel's mother. Because Isabel was born to the wife of the King, she became the fifth heir to the throne." He seems to be waiting for me to ask, so I don't disappoint him.

"And who is the first heir?" I can't look at him, knowing exactly what he is going to reveal.

Antonio steps back and motions for me to follow him into a room just to the right of him. When I step in, I know exactly where we are. I have seen photos of this room several times. Studied it meticulously while I was going over all the files handed to me this week.

We are in the Throne Room.

"This room is only used for special occasions now. Tomorrow we will fill it with some very hopeful ladies who would like to seize the attention of their King. There are those who believe it is time for him to marry. Time to stop playing games and select his wife from a collection of women they deem worthy.

"But the king has other plans he hasn't yet revealed to them. No king before him has ever been given the power to freely choose his wife. They all married before taking the throne and were either told who they were to marry, or the sovereign approved of their choice.

"That is not the case here, though. Before the Heir Prince could find a suitable wife, his father was murdered, making him the first unwed king of Hermosa Islas. And while some believe they can influence the king to marry from an elected group they have assembled, he has decided to change history and marry for love rather than position."

I am very aware he has not mentioned this king's name yet, although I'm fairly sure I know who this king is. "Is that allowed? And doesn't it take time to fall in love with someone? I mean, it would take some time to get to know a person, don't you agree?"

"I most definitely agree." Antonio spins and stares at me with his head held high. "If I, the king, say it is allowed, then it is allowed. When it comes to this, I, the king, will stand my ground. Not be persuaded or made to feel obligated to please those who voice their thoughts on the matter.

"I, King Antonio Ramon Reyes, have decided. I know this may not be how one conducts such things where you come from. However, as king, I am required to do things quite differently. Tomorrow night, I'd like to introduce the woman I plan on trying to persuade I am worth her time."

While he is striving to stand tall and strong, like I assume a king is taught, I can see behind the shroud. What I perceive is a man who is unsure of himself as he attempts to impress the woman standing in front of him. He may be king, but that doesn't make him any less secure about his ability as a man.

"What if she refuses such a request?" is the first question that pops into my head, one I ask him.

"Then I'll do what every man has done when he finds himself enthralled by a woman; I'll do my best to change her mind." He takes a step forward until he stands right in front of me. "Are you refusing my request, Larkin?"

"I think I am more like shelving it." I cross my arms to shield myself from him. "I'd like to leave now."

Closing his eyes, he nods once, and I detect disappointment as it takes over his facial features. "As you wish."

He walks me back down the corridors of the palace toward the entry we stepped through almost an hour ago. After he retrieves my purse, he notifies his security team that we are leaving and then rides with me in silence back to the hotel.

When we pull into the underground entrance, and his men have left us to say our goodbyes, he finally speaks. "What are you afraid of exactly?"

"Antonio... Your Majesty." I start to explain.

"To you, I will always be just Antonio." He places his hand over mine.

"That is very sweet of you to offer, but truth be told, you have never just been Antonio, have you? Born with a title securely attached to not only your name but also the person behind the name." I reach up and run my fingers along his jawline, where I discover the roughness left behind after a long day. "I'm not saying no, however, I am also not saying yes. I'm asking for time to consider what you are proposing, although I'm not really sure what that is."

"I propose you allow me to date you. I guess that would be the proper wording." He leans into my hand.

"Do kings, or even princes, actually date?" I snicker, thinking about how that would work.

"As a prince, I had a few dates, girlfriends, even. It can, I suppose, be tricky and complicated. Everything about my life, Larkin, is complicated. Planned out, and often boring. Please give me a chance."

CHAPTER 8
Larkin

I honestly have no idea what I am doing dressed to the nines and getting ready to head to Aragon Palace with the rest of my team. It has to be the absolute dumbest thing I have ever done in my entire life.

Early this morning, the formal invitations came along with the proper attire for the five members of the Manchester team. I guess Antonio decided it was time to let the others also know who he was, since come Monday, we were starting restorations on his palace.

I thought about making up some excuse on why I wouldn't be able to attend. Fake a stomach virus, migraine headache, even a family crisis if necessary. Except that got squashed when Cameron called us down for a meeting. He expressed how privileged we should feel about being invited to such an event, which I learned was actually a celebration for Hermosa Islas.

The Constitutional Ball was an annual event that celebrated the current régime. They were one of the few countries left where the top ruler was born into that position and not elected. A country where that born ruler worked side by side with the elected officials, and together, diligently made Hermosa Islas the thriving nation it is today.

So that meant my thoughts of skipping out on such an important event would not happen. This was not only important to the man who invited us, it was also important to the country where we would work for the next several years. We needed to make friends with those in charge, so they would make our jobs easier and not throw up roadblocks along the way. It is always a good idea to create friends instead of enemies when you do what we do. Otherwise, the process of obtaining permits, setting up building inspections, applying for work visas, and all those other important items we may require could cost us time and money.

I am now dressed in the turquoise chiffon, floor-length gown that hangs off my tall, slim frame perfectly. One that gives the impression I am more endowed upstairs than I truly am. Not that I am lacking, but I am not as full as this dressed makes me appear. That may have been the rhinestones' fault since they outlined the bodice and form a lovely flower shape right between the girls. They even lined the straps of the gown, which cross in the back, stopping just above my shoulder blades.

It pleased me to discover it had a back when I first pulled it out. I wasn't so sure it did, and wasn't clear on what I would have done about that. I rarely wore backless dresses, didn't like how exposed I felt in them. It was intimidating enough knowing I was being put on display in this dress so others would take notice of me. I didn't need anything else to mess with my nerves tonight.

The entire ride to Aragon Palace, Hope chatted about how she was surprised to learn we had been in a royal's presence and didn't even know it. Giggled about how I acted in the conference room when I told Antonio I wanted him to kneel before me and apologize.

I felt my face burning from embarrassment whenever I recalled all those times I made a complete fool of myself. I didn't dare tell her how I mentioned I'd never bow to him, even if he were the freaking king of England. She would never let me forget about it, not that I ever would. I had completely disrespected him and the throne he took pride in being a part of. It's a wonder he didn't have my head for it.

I reach up and rub my bare neck, thinking maybe this was all a ruse, and before the evening, that is exactly what he would have. My head on a platter while he got the last laugh and made a mockery of me and my loud-mouthed, foolish self.

They escort us in like everyone else, which surprises me. I thought we might have to enter through a different entrance since we weren't anyone, really. I'm not sure why I thought that, because it wasn't like this was my first rodeo, or ball for that matter.

Growing up as a United States Senator's daughter, I frequented my share of high-class social events. Even appeared at the Inaugural Ball when I was barely thirteen. My father had just won the election and was personally invited to attend. My mother, unfortunately, couldn't join him, since she was busy in Chicago performing miracle surgeries on children who needed her, so he took me as his date. It terrified me to think I would freak out and embarrass him, but my father had faith in me, and that gave me the courage I needed to get through it.

I haven't thought about that night in a very long time. I believe I may have worn a dress similar in color to the one I have on now. I recall shaking hands with so many people I didn't know and smiling until my face hurt. When I required some fresh air, after having been there for several hours, my father walked me outside to the garden area. I ended up sitting down on a bench while he kept chatting it up with other partygoers.

My mind wanders for a minute as I recall a conversation I had with a young boy while I tried to gather my wits.

"Do you mind if I join you, miss?" The voice had a funny sound to it, an accent I didn't believe I had ever heard before.

"It's a free country," I blurted out and then shook my head, knowing that was rude. "I mean, sure I guess."

He plopped down next to me and the scent of him had my preteen mind swirling. Cinnamon with a tang of something a little more masculine mixed in. I'd smelled nothing like it before; so, I ended up turning my head and taking a deep inhale. That way, I could remember what it smelled like when I thought about this moment later.

"Did you just sniff me?" He chuckled as he leaned in closer.

I scowled, making him retreat quickly. "I am just breathing here, if you don't mind. It helps me calm the nerves." So, I lied, shoot me.

The boy, or more like a teenager, smiled at me, and I suddenly felt like I could pass out. I swayed and felt my body slipping off the bench and nearly landed on my rear. If it weren't for the quick thinking of my bench buddy, I would have.

"Wow. You okay?" His hands wrapped around my arms to keep me steady until I recovered.

"I'm fine." I shook my head and then tried to stand. "Just got a little lightheaded. I'm better now. Thank you."

A heard a man with the same accent call for him. "Es hora de Antonio que entre. Dile adiós a la señorita. Apurarse."

"Vengo, padre. Dame cinco minutos." He rolled his eyes and sighed. "Guess it's time to pretend I actually care about this circus show. It was nice sitting with you and I hope you feel better. I'm Antonio, by the way."

"Nice to meet you." I started to introduce myself, but the older gentleman mumbled something that had his son standing and stalking off.

I haven't thought about that night since it happened. Surprised that it is coming back to my mind now, that we once met even. Seems like even at a young age, Antonio had a strange effect on me.

He is taller now than he was at—I'm guessing—sixteen. Back then, he was a scrawny teenage boy who was just coming into his own. Now he is a man who displays confidence and is so much more of a threat to the clumsy girl who lives inside of me.

We finally step into the Throne Room, which by the way looks completely different now that it is filled with people. Before, the room seemed way too big for the two of us standing inside of it alone. Now that there are a few hundred people gathered in the large space, it appears smaller.

The room is rich in color, with its deep red walls accented in gold trim. The floor has been polished and shines so impeccably, I can see my reflection staring back at me. It's a good thing my heels have a rubber sole, otherwise, there could have been a disaster in my near future. I surely would have slipped on it like it was ice and landed on my backside. I guess that would be fitting, since it seems the host of this event prompts me to stumble and utter words I most likely never would.

We are there almost an hour before an announcement is made that dinner will be served soon and everyone should make their way to the dining area. When large doors open on the opposite end of the room, we head that way. There are palace servants positioned at the doors to help direct everyone to their assigned tables.

Cameron gives our names to the attendant and everyone is instructed to follow one of the men. That is everyone except me. I am asked to step aside and wait until a man named Sir Edward comes to get me. Hope can't help but giggle as she leans in and whispers something about me being separated because I impressed the host with my wittiness.

I skate to the side and wait, and wait, and wait.

The line of guests behind us has now dwindled to about twenty. It has taken a half-hour to seat everyone. I've been left standing here like some castaway and wonder if they forgot about me.

I smell him before I feel a hand land on my back. That hint of the cinnamon I recalled earlier is still present, but there is also a very deep masculine essence that accompanies it now, making me weak in the knees. I turn my head, and if he hadn't slipped an arm around my waist, I know I would have become a puddle on the floor.

I thought the man was a threat dressed in his designer suits those first few times I was blessed to get some time with him. Those suits have nothing on the sight before me now.

Tonight, he is adorned in a black long tail tuxedo tailored to his frame. Underneath his jacket is a gold-threaded vest that stands out against the crisp white shirt and black jacket. Instead of a traditional bow tie, his royal medallion is suspended from a thick red, blue, and gold ribbon, hanging heavy against his chest. Last, but not at all least, inside the left breast pocket of his jacket, is a silk turquoise handkerchief that corresponds with my dress.

I know I am staring at him. But who can blame me? The man paints a very delightful image intended to draw attention.

And then I remember we are in a crowded room, which has become extremely hushed considering the number of people present. I stop staring at the man, who is also staring at me by the way, and direct my attention toward the room that seems to be very interested in what is transpiring behind them.

"Your Majesty, you have guests." I remind him as I twist my head back around, so I can glance over my shoulder at him again.

His eyes scan my body, and he doesn't even bother to stop his inspection when he replies. "And right now, the only one of them who could inspire me to get dressed is standing next to me. It wasn't until the captain of my guards informed me of your arrival that I even bothered."

I gasp, surprised Antonio would disappoint all these people. "You weren't planning on showing up, letting all these supporters of yours down?"

His eyes finally find mine again and the truth behind them lets me know his answer before he says it. "Miss Cross, the only matter half this crowd is interested in where I am concerned, is the one I am only offering you. So, letting them down was going to happen whether I showed up or not.

"Now before my mother breaks protocol and scolds the king in front of his guests," Antonio offers his arm as he smiles down at me with hope, "shall we?"

I study the arm presented before me and know if I take it, that it is a sign to everyone here there is something between us. I still don't know how I feel about all of that, so I hesitate.

"You are making me look bad in front of my loyal subjects. It is never a wise idea to make the king give the impression of being weak. I am not above begging, Larkin. Although, I am sure that would only add fire to the flames already pressuring me." His voice softly rumbles between clenched teeth that have maintained his smile.

Rolling my neck a few times, I take a cleansing breath and then place my hand on the bend of his arm. "This isn't a yes."

"It's a maybe." He pats mine with his free one. "For now, I will accept that."

As Antonio escorts me toward the head table, a middle-aged woman dressed in a beautiful golden gown stands. Once she does, the rest of the room joins her.

As we step into the aisle, it's like the wave at a sporting event has started from the back of the room and moves with us as we progress forward. They don't do a full bow or curtsey, but it is held long enough for us to pass, and done out of respect for the man to my left. I've never been around something so refined before, and I feel unworthy of being a part of it.

61

I hear several, *Your Majesty's,* as we advance slowly. Whispers followed them, questioning who I am and what my status is. Is she a princess from another country? If so, which one? Maybe a Madam or Lady from one of the Scandinavian nations, since her hair is so light and skin so fair? The closer we get to our destination, the louder the murmurs become until they are all I hear inside my head.

"Are you all right, dear?" I hear a voice ask as we approach the main table and make our way to our seats.

I shake my head as I close my eyes, trying my best not to think about the fact I am standing in front of all these people. What was I thinking? I will never be able to handle the undertones are sure to constantly float around us.

There is a reason I never could go on the campaign trail with my father. I couldn't deal with the anxiety that takes over my body when all eyes are focused on me.

The woman standing next to me reaches out and takes my hand in hers as she addresses Antonio. "Move things along before your date passes out on you."

Antonio glances down and takes one look at my freaked-out expression, and then he laughs. Laughs. I kid you not.

I will not be held responsible for what I do next. His laughing ignites a fire deep down inside of me, and I do the only thing I can think of at the moment. I pinch him hard, right there in that tender spot just above his elbow. That's right buddy, don't mess with me. I glare at him as I release his arm and reach for my water.

He snags my hand and holds it while he addresses his guests. "Thank you all for joining me in this celebration of the anniversary when our constitution was established. King Nicolas took a significant leap of faith when he followed his heart and the direction he believed God was leading him. Because of his bravery to give up a portion of his throne, and pass some of his responsibilities over to the people, we are here today stronger for it.

"I am honored to serve my people and offer them the knowledge passed down to me from our previous sovereigns, who were chosen by God and God alone. I will continue to do so until he, decides another should take my place. Let us never forget that our true Supreme Leader is the one who created us. One day we will join him in his kingdom, but until then we will do our best to serve him here. Shall we bow our heads and ask for his blessing?"

I bow my head and wait for Antonio to say more, except he doesn't. It's so quiet you could hear a pin drop. I realize it is like a moment of silence, and we are expected to offer our prayers up to the heavens. Oops.

"Amen. Please be seated and enjoy." Antonio sits down. After he is seated everyone at his table does the same. It isn't until the head table is all settled that the large group in front of us takes their seats.

"Now if you need a drink, you may do so, Miss Cross." He releases my hand. "Are you okay?"

Both my hands are now free. I give them a little jiggle and reach for my glass so I can take a healthy gulp of my water before I answer him. "Like you care," I mutter around the glass as I take another swallow. "I was having a panic attack. I am prone to those when I get overwhelmed. And you laughed at me. Laughed at me while I am literally about to pass out and cause one heck of a scene."

I finish my water and then reach for his. He doesn't stop me, so I think nothing of it until his mother—I assume the woman next to me is his mother—hands me her glass instead. "Here have mine, dear."

Again, I frown at him as I set his back in the exact spot it was so I can accept hers instead. After I drink half her glass and feel somewhat like I am gaining a portion of my control back, I really give it to him. "You were just going to let me drink from your glass, weren't you? Let me make a complete spectacle of myself and really get them chattering about the pale-skinned, extremely blonde nitwit seated next to you, who has absolutely no idea what she should and shouldn't do when in the presence of a king."

I take a breath because I spit that all out in one before I continue. "I bet you even find this amusing, don't you? Me just babbling like the village idiot, unable to stop herself from continuing because she has no control over her mouth when she gets nervous. My mother used to try to stop me when I got like this by encouraging me to eat or drink, but it never worked. I would just keep going until I ran out of things to say, or my father finally stood up and escorted me out of the room so I could say everything I needed to get out of my overflowing, very crowded mind. I think this one time I went on for an entire hour, mumbling throughout dinner under my breath. My friend Randal recorded me once during one of my rants and then made me watch it after I finished so I could appreciate it from a different point of view. All that did was set me off again and had him rolling on the floor while I expressed my thoughts about what he'd done. My mother said it has to do with the fact that the drugs my birth mother took when she was pregnant with me damaged my mind. Said it damaged a section of my brain that tells me to shut up and not just spit out every word I'm thinking. She always thought I'd outgrow it, but I guess she was wrong. Seems it has returned in full force and all because of this really hotter than hot man, who I believe I met once when he was a teenager at an Inauguration Ball, the only one I ever attended. It's all because he has this crazy idea I'm someone he thinks he wants to get to know and has drawn me so far out of my comfort zone, I guess all those crazy defense mechanisms I developed as a young child have kicked back in. You should probably just ask me to leave so you don't have to sit here and listen to me go on and on about absolutely nothing and everything. Because unless you can figure out a way to get me to stop, I don't think I will…"

Antonio grabs my face with both of his hands and plants his lips over my rapidly moving ones.

Oh yeah, that definitely shuts me up almost instantly as it completely turns my mind to mush.

CHAPTER 9
Antonio

The Royals

A soon as we sat down, it was like this switch got stuck inside of Larkin's brain. I have never seen a woman chatter so much in my entire life. She wasn't speaking loudly. So, I wasn't really worried about anyone hearing her gibberish.

I endeavor to follow her line of thought. However, honestly, it is all over the place and makes absolutely no sense. I think she mentions something about being a nitwit, or was it the village idiot? She is neither of those things, by the way. Not even close. I believe I also hear her admit her mother did her best to break her from going off like this when she was younger but unsuccessful at it. Discusses a friend named Randal who filmed her so she could see how adorable she is. Except that only sent her into another rampage. Then she moves on to something about drugs and a birth mother messing her brain up as if that explains all this babbling, which I suppose makes sense.

What catches my attention most is when she mentions something about meeting me when I was a teenager. I attended one Inaugural Ball with my father when I was sixteen and my parents were in the middle of a very long, trying divorce. My father had decided it was time for me to accompany him on one of his public relations trips, so I could be introduced properly to the world.

I hated every second of that weeklong trip, with one exception. Our last stop was the Inaugural Ball in the United States. I was there to meet a few prospective future queens. Several leaders from around the world happened to be present and had their daughters with them. I had to endure giggly girls who thought I was so cute and wanted me to sneak off with them.

It wasn't until I stepped outside to escape a very persistent princess, and spotted this blonde girl pacing the garden, that I started thinking things were looking up. I watched her from a distance for a while. Listened to her talk softly to herself, using her hands and face to express those thoughts escaping her mouth. After about fifteen minutes of non-stop chatter, she took a deep breath and plopped her weary body down onto a bench. Which is when I saw the perfect opportunity to determine if I could get her to talk to me.

She was younger than me, probably closer to Esteban's age, thirteen, maybe fourteen. It wasn't like I was there to do anything more than just talk, so that didn't matter to me. The closer I got, I realized I was in way over my head if I believed she would look twice at me. Even at thirteen, Larkin was a sight to take in.

So, I did what any young man would do and asked if I could sit next to her. When she spat out, it's a free country and then attempted to correct her outburst, it captivated me. No one talked to me so bluntly, and I liked she didn't seem to care I might be someone of importance. And when I caught her sniffing me, I found I wanted her to remember my scent, in case we ever ran into each other when she was older. Then when she nearly slid off the bench after getting a good look at me—my ego may have burst, I can't be sure—and I had to reach out and touch her. It was then I thought this girl just might do.

Unfortunately, our time was cut short when my father came looking for me because some lame highborn was asking about me again. For that reason, I had to leave before I even caught her name. As we were walking away, my father strictly forbade me from associating with the American girl.

I didn't think all that by the way while Larkin was letting her mind dump. Speaking all those thoughts overloading her brain. There is no way I had time to think about it, but I thought maybe you'd like to know I caught what she said and later recalled the moment. Which I guess could be why I finally seize her face when she says something about sending her away because she doesn't think she can stop. That is unless I can come up with some way to stop her.

There is only one action I can think of that might work.

I have been thinking about kissing those soft lips since the plane. Nearly got my chance in her office yesterday, except she stopped me before I reached my destination. This time, however, I know I will be successful when I go for it.

I didn't warn her, I just grabbed that stunning face of hers with both hands and kissed those moving lips once and for all. She stops talking immediately. Thank God, which allows me to kiss her properly. Making it so I could give her a lingering appropriate embrace, which only makes me want more. Larkin is definitely a sweet piece of candy I want to spend more time sampling.

A throat clears behind me. I know it is my brother, Esteban, attempting to let me know we are drawing attention now. I pull back, bringing her forehead to my lips, holding it there while I catch my breath. Once I am sure I can speak without sounding like someone on the verge, I decide to see if she has recovered yet.

"So, how was that, Miss Cross? Did I come up with a way to calm the nerves?" A slight shake of her head has me withdrawing so I can gaze down at her. "Do we need to step outside for a minute so you can get some air?"

"No," Larkin whispers and blinks slowly. "You kissed me. You kissed me in front of all these people and you want to know if I feel calm. Have you lost your mind, Antonio?"

I smile at the sound of my proper name being used so openly amongst a crowd who wouldn't dare. To them, I have always been a member of the royal family, the Heir Apparent, who would one day accept his place on the throne. So, they have consistently addressed me as Your Highness, Prince, Sir, Your Majesty, or King. I was only Antonio when the members of my family used my name without adding a title. Even the women I dated never felt comfortable enough to get that personal with me.

My brother leans around me to answer her question. "You are

suggesting he has a mind to lose, love. Antonio, as the precious heir, was taught to take first and ask permission to do so later. I'm Esteban, and you must be Larkin. Isabel has chattered about you non-stop. It's nice to finally appreciate what all the fuss was about."

Larkin gets a little color in her face as she extends her hand. "Pleased to meet you, Prince Esteban. I hope I addressed you properly."

I want to correct her when she lifts her hand as if to shake his. It is an unwritten rule that states unless a hand is offered to you then one should keep his/her hand where it is. Offering a royal your hand is expressing you believe you are equal or above them, it just shouldn't be done.

My brother doesn't even hesitate. He seizes Larkin's hand and brings it to his lips. "The pleasure is all mine, Miss Cross. You did just fine and have my permission to call me Esteban, lets drop the formalities. After all, you are seated at the family table, are you not?"

"Oh, no. I couldn't possibly disrespect your family like that." She informs my brother while shaking her head frantically.

"Are you refusing my request? *Dime con quién andas, y te diré quién eres.* Tell me who you hang out with and I will tell you who you are." My brother releases her hand and gestures to all those seated at the curved table where we are gathered. "*Cuando entre lobos debes aprender a aullar.*"

Our food was delivered sometime during Larkin's outburst, so I motion for her to eat. I am pleased to discover my guests broke protocol and didn't wait for me to get started. I assume that was my mother's doing. She most likely began eating when she realized the woman seated next to me entranced me, and showed my guests it was fine to go ahead and enjoy this great food.

Larkin glances down, as if to just realizing what I did. She picks up her spoon and takes a sip of her soup. After she has finishes about half of it, she wipes her mouth off with her napkin and glances over at my brother.

"I have no idea what those words you said means. I hate to admit this, but I failed Spanish in high school. I was an awful student. Unless it had something to do with art or music, I couldn't focus long enough to follow. My mother and father gave up expecting me to be on the honor roll or even follow in their footsteps. Both of them, by the way, are doctors, or at least they were at one time. My mother is a pediatric surgeon, so she works long hard hours. My father started as an ER doctor and spent twelve years there before changing career paths after my birth mother overdosed in his ER. That's when he decided our foster care system was failing so many children like me. I spent the first eighteen months of my life in and out of their home. What happened to me wasn't uncommon. That day, he called my social worker to report what had happened and then made it very clear he was taking custody of me, permanently. Rang my mother to let her know he was quitting his job for two reasons. One, because he knew I would require one parent to oversee my care until they caught me up with my peers. The other, because he decided it was time for him to take a stand and find out what he could do about changing things. By the time I was three he had successfully caught me up to kids my own age, or at least had me hitting the milestones, and won a seat in the State Senate. Seven years later, he won his seat as a United States Senator and has been one ever since. So, as you can imagine, they had to learn to accept that not every child was a prodigy, and sometimes getting a C in Math was something to celebrate. It wasn't until college when I met someone who introduced me to architecture, that I discovered when something inspired me, I could actually pull off A's and B's in subjects other than art and music. Which means you are going to have to explain to me what you said because I have been sitting here wracking my brain. Struggling to decide if I should admit my flaws or just pretend, I am equally as smart as the rest of you. I asked, because my mother always said if you don't understand something never be afraid to ask, otherwise you will learn nothing." She finally stops speaking so she can take a drink of her water.

I was beginning to wonder if I was going to have to kiss her again to get her to stop. Honestly, I was looking forward to it, although I'm not sure she would have appreciated the action again right now. So instead, I let her continue.

This time I could follow her easily because she wasn't rambling like before. It was done at a nice leisurely pace. While I get the impression she is still very nervous, I also can see she is relaxing some now and I like that.

I would love to reach over and hold her hand, except I am right-handed, so that isn't possible at the moment. Instead, I shift my foot toward her and stop once my leg is firmly pressed against hers.

Larkin twists her head to look at me and smiles, then drops her left hand into her lap and slowly allows it to slide across it until it settles on my knee.

"Okay?" She questions me as she gives it a little pat.

"More than okay," I notify her as I bump her leg slightly. "*Cuando entre lobos debes aprender a aullar.* I believe that is what Esteban said at the end of his decree. It means when among wolves we must howl."

I can see her mind turning that over in her head while she finishes her soup. "I still don't get it. I'm sorry. You all must think I am the reason they created dumb blonde jokes."

My youngest brother finally joins in on the conversation. He is seated next to Esteban and, until now, has been a silent observer. "You are referring to the fact that blondes are nice to look at but unable to understand the simplest of things."

Larkin nods once, so he has a little fun. "Three blondes walk into a building. You'd think at least one of them would've seen it."

Larkin laughs, as do the rest of us.

A wicked smile takes over Lorenzo's face. "Why did the blonde get fired from the M&M Company? Because she kept throwing out all the W's. What did the blonde say when she saw a box of Cheerios? OMG! Donut seeds. Why do blondes love boob jobs? Because it's really the only job they are qualified for."

"Okay, that is enough, Lorenzo. You've made your point." I glare at my brother, who is so very proud of himself "You will have to excuse the young prince; he sometimes takes things a little too far."

"And you will have to forgive the king, because he doesn't have a funny bone in his body. Father had it removed when he was just a wee little lad. Replaced it with a boring stick that he shoved up his bum. That way when everyone called him the snobby king with a stick up his backside, they wouldn't be arrested for being mendacious."

"Boys." My mother's stern voice has all three of us glancing her way. "I apologize, Miss Cross. You can add the most prestigious titles in front of their names. Make them take all the proper etiquette classes required to teach them how a prince should act. Even scold them more times than one could even count. One would expect that would do the job. One would think men who look as honorable as they do would have some manners around a woman who isn't accustomed to their form of banter. Please understand I did my best, but boys will always be boys, even when they are a king or prince."

Larkin rotates to face my mother. "No apology necessary, Madam. It is Madam correct? Or should I call you something else? I have no idea what I'm doing here."

"Madam is fine, dear." My mother takes her hand and rests it on top of Larkin's. "I am no longer a woman with a title. I lost it when I divorced. However, I am the mother of the king and the rest of these royal brats."

"Hey." The four of us loudly object.

My mother only grins as she continues her explanation. "Therefore, I may be addressed as Her Royal Highness Angela, but there is no reason for you to address me in such a way. Madam or even just Angela is fine by me."

We continue to eat our meals and talk freely amongst ourselves. My family takes the time to ask Larkin a few questions about herself. I am pleased to find them welcoming her so freely while doing their best to make her feel comfortable.

Gabriela even joins in after having sat there so quietly most of the evening. She has always been self-conscious around people she doesn't know. So, I am pleased when she questions Larkin about her job. Even seems very interested as she listens to her passionately explain why she loves it so much.

The women talk about the De la Peña Citadel. Larkin is sharing with them her thoughts on what she'd like to do to it. My mother and sister are ready to get back to the place that has been their home for years and seem very excited about her enthusiasm.

"Time to howl, Larkin," Lorenzo warns before we are graced with the presence of someone I know I didn't invite.

Looking as lovely as always, the woman curtseys when she stops in front of our table. Most of the women in this room would never make such a bold move as to approach the king while he is obviously having such a grand time. However, this woman's familiarity with my family and me seems to have made her bolder than most.

"Your Majesty. Your Highnesses. Your Royal Highness." She takes the time to acknowledge everyone except Larkin. "I am honored to have been invited to attend such a celebration. May I speak freely, Your Majesty?"

"Lady Dalia, I believe you forgot someone." I lift my chin and wait.

"My apologies, sir. Please introduce me so I can address her properly."

I notice the overconfidence in her right away. I will not have this woman making Larkin feel as if she is less than the one standing before me.

"I'd love to. Titles are not as common in the United States like they are here, so allow me to improvise." I know she will not object because no one questions or corrects the king. "Her father is a member of the Senate, so that would make her proper addressing title to be Lady. Then again, her mother is a pediatric surgeon. We all know how highly we hold those so gifted and often make them Dukes and Duchesses. Therefore, as king, I have granted her equal status, and encourage you to address her appropriately. This lovely lady seated next to me shall be known as Countess Larkin..."

I hold up a hand and turn to face the woman next to me. She is staring at me like I have lost my mind again, but I don't care. I know exactly what I am doing. "Larkin, what is your middle name?"

She shakes her head slightly at me. "You do not need to do this. Just introduce me like you would anyone else, Antonio, please."

I hear Dalia softly gasp as she utters. "The audacity of such a woman. She has no respect for him at all."

I tilt my head to let her know I heard her loud and clear. With just my eyes focused on her I then speak. "Did you say something, Lady Dalia? Something perhaps you'd like to say about how I allow the countess to freely address me when we are having a private conversation?"

"No, Your Majesty." She lowers her head the way they have taught her to do. "Please, forgive me."

I roll my eyes and turn back to the only person I am interested in right now. "Middle name Larkin, or I will be forced to make one up and you will be forever stuck with it. Shall we go with Luna, perhaps?"

"Moon."

"Luna means moon, yes. See, you learned something in that Spanish class after all. Maybe we should go back and get your grade adjusted," I tease her.

"Ha, ha. I believe Lorenzo was correct about your funny bone being removed." She sighs before she continues. "My middle name is Moon, Larkin Moon Cross. I'm pretty sure my birth mother was high when she filled out my birth certificate."

"Or perhaps when she looked at you, it reminded her of how we all need a light to lead our way through the darkness, so she gave you the name of the brightest light available once the sun disappears, hoping you could be her light."

"But I wasn't," she whispers as a tear slides down her cheek.

"Maybe not, however, you are mine. You shall guide me out of the dark by always being the brightest light amongst a sky full of stars that will never compare." I lean forward and kiss her lips quickly, letting her know I mean every word I just said. "You okay?"

"You have got to stop asking me such a stupid question right after you kiss me like that. I'm as fine as a woman would be after such an act, I suppose." She brushes her hand against her cheek. "Thank you."

I wink at her before I turn back to a very apathetic woman, who is doing a poor job of withholding her thoughts right now. "Countess Larkin Moon Cross, and in case you haven't figured it out already, let me paint a very clear picture for you and anyone else out there interested. I, King Antonio, have my sights set on the beautiful woman seated to the right of me and only her. She captivates me like no one else ever has. I plan on doing my best to get her to agree to date me. She hasn't accepted my invitation yet, because she has this crazy idea that kings don't date. This king however plans on showing her how very mistaken she is about that. Now, I believe you had something you wanted to say?"

"Madam Larkin, please forgive me for not addressing you earlier." Dalia clears her throat. "I was going to suggest we move this celebration along since everyone seems to have finished dinner. Perhaps we could start with dancing in the Throne Room to allow everyone to socialize and get to know the countess."

I know how hard that was for her to suggest. What she really wanted to suggest was that I forget about Larkin and let all these eligible women who were invited so they could impress their king, be given the chance to do so.

I turn to glance at my family and decide it would probably be a good idea to let them mingle. After all, my brothers are also present and single. Maybe they would like to socialize with some of the single ladies here tonight.

Plus, I believe I might enjoy dancing with Larkin, showing her I do not have a stick up my butt as Lorenzo suggested. I can let loose and have fun if I so choose; and tonight I plan on letting her see just how much fun this king can have.

CHAPTER 10

Antonio

The next two hours are like they have always been at these types of events. There is your traditional dancing, where an orchestra plays lovely waltzes, mixed with a few upbeat, big band tunes.

I do what I have done every year these past five years. I mingle and talk to a few people I haven't seen since last year. Mainly because that is what the king does, he makes himself available to his citizens.

Every member of the King's Council is present, as are all other elected and appointed officials. Which was why I didn't care if I offended any of them by not showing up. Most of the guests present are from that crowd, and the ones who invited the eligible women they envisioned would make a suitable queen.

I wouldn't have been the first king to skip an event, protesting what these officials proposed. It was a silent practice performed by a monarch to let them know he disagreed when no one seemed to be listening.

I also knew my mother would have made a formal announcement about me getting caught up in royal business and then apologizing once. Afterward, she would suggest they continue without me, and that perhaps when I was finished, I'd join them. Everyone would receive the message and they would either back down or they wouldn't, but at least I wasn't taking all of this sitting down.

However, I was given the privilege of doing something better. I got to attend one of my favorite events while publicly declaring I would be in charge of my love life. All while declining offers to socialize with the women they invited, since it would be rude of me to ignore my date, leaving her with strangers. I wore a genuine smile and then suggested that perhaps one of my brothers would appreciate some company. After all, both are currently single.

Eventually, that backfired on me, though. Lorenzo came walking up to me with one very enthusiastic looking Lady Maribel Allegro on his arm. She was one of the approved that none of us had any interest in. Her family has been trying to marry her off since she was sixteen. They were apparently in negotiations with my father before he died, although he had not brought it to my attention.

Please don't take this the wrong way, and know that I wish there was another way of stating this, but there is not. Lady Maribel is very sweet. She is a year younger than Lorenzo, so in her early twenties. I have tried to be nice by implying she was too young for me in the past. Although that wasn't the real issue at all. To put things as kindly as possible, she is very stout, with unique features and tastes.

"OMG." I hear Hope whisper to Larkin. "Who is the mutt attached to the young prince's arm? He deserves a Golden Globe for his acting skills. I honestly have to say he appears interested and has her eating it up. Okay shhh, they are coming this way."

Larkin swats her friend/coworker. "Me, shhh? You are the one calling... oh wow... yeah, that is something else. Save him, Antonio."

"What am I supposed to do about it?" I smile as they approach us.

"Your Majesty." A high screechy voice pierces our ears. "You are looking very well put together this evening as always."

"Is she meant to look like a pumpkin?" Hope mutters.

"I was just talking to Prince Lorenzo, saying how I was so looking forward to sharing at least one dance with you." She makes a pouty face that does nothing to help her cause.

"Make it stop, please. Maybe when the clock strikes midnight, her dress will go away." Hope quickly decides that may not be a good idea.

"Oh wait, if that happens, then can you imagine what is buried underneath. Perhaps the pumpkin dress is just fine."

"Stop." Larkin scolds through clenched teeth, struggling not to laugh.

"I'm sorry to disappoint you, Lady Maribel. It would be very rude of me to leave Madam Larkin alone after I personally invited her and all." I smile and then start to give her the same little spiel I have offered all night long.

However, I cannot get it out, because my little brother cuts me off. "It would delight me to keep Madam Larkin company while you two dance a little jig. Lady Maribel and I have already completed a few spins around the floor, so now it's your turn, brother."

Maribel claps her hands several times and squeaks. "Oh, what a lovely gesture, Your Highness. I do believe you have earned a favor."

I hear Hope again as she speaks softly in Larkin's ear. "Oh boy, a favor. I do so hope she kisses him."

I cough, hoping to cover my laugh, and then almost completely lose it when Maribel reaches down the front of her dress and pulls out an orange hankie. She holds it out for Lorenzo to take, and I can't say that I blame him for not wanting to accept it.

"I'm afraid..."

I reach out and snatch it out of her hand, then tuck it neatly inside his left breast pocket. Making sure it is displayed just enough for all to see.

"When a lady offers you a favor, you should accept it, brother." I pat his chest hard. "Now everyone here will know she has laid claim on you this evening. As you can see, Larkin gave me one earlier as well."

I hear her clear her throat to cover up her words. "Liar."

"Are you ready, Your Majesty?" The poor woman is practically bouncing now.

I turn to Larkin, not wanting to do this. "If this will be a problem, I can decline. I don't want you to misunderstand."

The little nymph turns her lovely smile towards Maribel. "I am placing the king in your care. I believe I need to use the ladies' room as it is, and this way I know he won't be bored while I am gone."

I lean down and kiss her cheek right before I warn her. "You will pay for that later. Mark my word."

A visible shiver travels down her body, but even that doesn't keep her silent. "I look forward to it, Your Majesty."

That little move from my brother ended up keeping me on the dance floor and away from Larkin way longer than I planned. I danced one very long ballad with Maribel, while listening to her shriek at me the entire time. About what, I am not sure. My attention was on Larkin and Hope as they watched my brothers gathering all the women I turned down earlier. Once I finished dancing with the orange blob, I quickly realized there was no way I would get out of dancing with a few others. They all noticed me out there and now knew to use my brothers as she had.

So, it began, and I end up dancing with seven eager ladies.

Esteban escorted his current leech to the edge of the dance floor, ready to get her turn as soon as Maribel and I were done. Then Lorenzo was there with another after that. It went back and forth like that until I noticed Dalia standing there as if she planned on making her move next.

As soon as the song ends, I bid Lady Bella farewell and thank her for coming, which is also when I feel a hand land on my back. I don't need to turn around to know who it belongs to. Only one woman would be brave enough to touch me so freely without permission. I can see Larkin still standing a few feet from me, talking to my brother, not at all aware of what is about to happen.

"Your Majesty, if I may." Dalia steps in front of me and curtseys. "It would be my honor, sir, if I could have the next dance. Perhaps we could discuss a few issues and clear the air between us. I miss you, and..."

Thankfully, right then my mother steps up to the microphone to make an announcement. "I believe it is time to let the younger crowd have their fun, as is tradition. I'd like to thank all of you for coming. As the orchestra packs up and clears out, I invite King Antonio, Princess Gabriela, Prince Esteban, and Prince Lorenzo to wish all those who will be departing, farewell. The rest of you can make your way into the dining hall again. I believe that is where the after party will take place."

I don't even bother to acknowledge Dalia; I make a beeline for

Larkin and invite her to join us. There is no way I am letting her leave, so I explain to her exactly what will happen next.

Typically, the king and queen, along with those who are over a certain age, leave all celebrations around midnight. It all started when I turned eighteen and requested to be allowed an after party. Surprisingly, my father thought it a noble idea and so the tradition began.

This will be the first year Gabriela is old enough to join, so it is her coming of age party, so to speak. She has invited several guests to join in on the festivities, and I know she is looking forward to seeing what all the fuss is about.

Since I am a young unwed King, I have been known to stay and have some fun as well. I may not have stayed the entire time, because I wasn't really into that kind of thing any longer. However, it made me feel more my age and gave me a chance to spend some time with my brothers. It was a more relaxed environment, where we got to pretend we weren't royalty while we partied with our peers.

As soon as the last of the older crowd leaves, my mother reminds us to remember that everyone is watching us. We need to keep in mind that even though we are young and allowed to have our fun as much as anyone else, we are not just anyone. There are those who are taking notes, and there are those who are hoping to get their claws in us. She wants us to have fun, of course, but not so much fun that come morning we end up with a few regrets.

Last, she reminds us to look out for Gabriela. Since this is her first party, it is likely she may get caught up in the celebrations. It is our job as her brothers to make sure no one takes advantage to use this against her one day. It's basically the same speech I have gotten since this all started.

The heavy doors close behind her as I reach up and remove the medallion around my neck as well as my jacket. I pass them off to the footman. My brothers do the same. Then I loosen a few buttons on my shirt so I can breathe again before removing my cufflinks, allowing me to roll up my sleeves.

Once I am as comfortable as I can get, I take Larkin's hand in mine and wait for my brothers to signal they are ready. Esteban links arms with Gabriela so he can escort her properly. I see him offering her some encouraging words and probably some subtle reminders as well. They are close and she will take all that better from him than me.

When he is finished, he looks up, "Well, what are we waiting for? *A beber y a tragar, que el mundo se va a acabar.*"

Larkin lets out a very nervous laugh. "Sorry. What was that?"

"Eat, drink, and be merry, for tomorrow we die." We all say in unison with great expression.

The doors open in front of us and we pause momentarily as we line up like we have done so many times before. I glance down at my brothers and nod.

Lorenzo does a visible count down for us and right before we enter the room we yell. "*Santiago*!!"

CHAPTER 11

Larkin

The Royals

I am on the verge of freaking out all over again. Everything about tonight has put me on edge and one little push will send me tumbling.

Anxiety is a real thing in case you have your doubts. It can make people do all sorts of unusual things. My standard reaction is to babble uncontrollably until I simply run out of words. It can take hours for me to run out. I may eventually stop verbalizing to those around me, but I continue blabbing softy to myself long afterward.

It hasn't been any different tonight, really. I have just gotten good at talking to myself without actually moving my mouth or using my voice. Sort of like a ventriloquist, except I don't let my voice make any noise while doing it.

It was easy to screen during dinner. Sipping on my soup, which I learned was called *caldo galego*, made it fairly easy. I could pretend I was blowing on the hot spoon when, in reality, I was mumbling.

When the appetizers—that reminded me of crawdads—*gambas al ajillo* arrived, I simply stared at it for a moment. These black beady eyes peered up at me from amongst the steamy spices and lemons. I sat there, not sure how to tackle it. That is when Angela tenderly encouraged me to try them while she displayed the proper way of eating it. I discovered, after my first taste, it was shrimp with the heads still attached. Why they left them on, I had no idea. Personally, I preferred my shrimp headless.

The main course came after a traditional salad with a sweet vinaigrette dressing on the side. It was duck glazed in honey, served with figs—probably my favorite course. I had never tasted duck or figs and after my first bite, I decided I needed to eat this more often.

Then came dessert, which was flan, otherwise known as custard with caramel sauce poured over it. I am not a fan of custard. But I didn't want to be rude, so I took a few bites, commented on how delicious it was, and then dropped my fork like I just couldn't possibly eat another bite. That was probably because I couldn't unless I wanted to make an even bigger scene by gagging.

All the chatting during the meal helped keep me from melting down again.

I still can't believe I did that.

It has been years since I had a public reaction like that one. I could usually hold myself together until I was alone, in a safe environment, before letting go. The only other person who had seen one of my disturbing, rambling messy freak-outs, besides my parents, was Randal. He'd laughed so hard that first time I started, he ended up as a human ball rolling around on my floor. It hadn't stopped my rant, but it had eased the embarrassment and even had me snickering while I continued.

I really miss him.

I nearly had a second one when Lady Dalia approached, just so she could poke Antonio with her words. The tension that radiated between them was thick and could probably be cut with a knife. His desire to protect me by granting me a title, was both flattering and disturbing.

Flattering because he wanted everyone to see me the way he saw me, as his equal—or at least worthy of being seated next to him, since no one here was equal to the king. No one had ever done that for me before. My status wasn't an issue in the U.S., really. I dated who I wanted to date based on attraction, not because of their net worth, social status, or how high they sat on the food chain. Some of my best dates had been with construction workers I met while on the job. They were always exactly who they were, never trying to sell themselves as something better.

I guess that is what was disturbing about it. I didn't like the fact

Antonio felt I needed a title to compete with Lady Dalia. Who I have learned since is the daughter of Justice Ivan Batista, one of the five main justices in this country appointed by the king and the King's Council. It was as if he was trying to sell me as being worthy, instead of considering me worthy just the way I was.

So maybe that had me wondering if that was really the case. Was I good enough as Larkin Moon Cross, an architect from Chicago, Illinois, daughter of a drug addict who overdosed when I was a baby? Adopted into a family that gave me what he considered worthy status, because of the jobs they did and not who they actually were? If you stripped them down to the people they were, would I still be worthy, or would I just be another woman lost at sea?

The last couple of hours had been exasperating all the way around. Being dragged around by the most powerful man in this country was fascinating and educational. I learned a lot about how things worked here; not all that different from back home.

I also began to understand how important it was that Antonio marry and produce an heir. If he never married, then his brother, Esteban, and his offspring became next in line. That practice had never been put into action in Hermosa Islas' history. Each one of their leaders had married and passed the torch on to their firstborn child. The sovereigns wed spouses who were chosen for them by their fathers and held some kind of noble heritage, be it firsthand or distant. None dared to marry outside of the approved class, meaning none of them had married a commoner. While it wasn't officially penned that a king/queen was not permitted to marry below a particular social class, it was an unspoken decree.

Antonio had rolled his eyes several times whenever someone brought that up. Mentioned how it was time for that to change. Went on to remind them he did not need their permission when it came to selecting the woman he married. He clarified that he was retaining control over his love life and would not be goaded into feeling guilty about not doing things the way they had always been executed. Last, he pointed out that until him, no king had ever maintained his bachelor status when he inherited the throne, either. That seemed to shut them up quickly, and he always walked away afterward with his head held high.

By the time we are ready to join the after party in the dining hall—that is after the four of them howled at the top of their lungs to something that sounded like a battle cry—it had been transformed to look like a classy nightclub. Most of the guests have already made their way inside and are standing around socializing while they wait for their hosts to arrive.

The door seals behind us, and the music pounds almost instantly. Antonio grabs hold of my hand and tows me across the room. I am not much of a dancer, never really dared to attempt a place like this. Thankfully, it's mostly dark in here, so no one will see us or me. They won't be able to watch me when I most likely have another panic attack, and this time pass out right here in the middle of the dance floor.

I am, however, relieved to see he doesn't pull me onto the very crowded dance floor. Instead, we make our way to a roped off area. Fewer people are waiting inside of it. None of them I recognize.

Gabriela seems to know about half of them. They immediately flock to her and drag her over to join them. For the first time all night, I notice her relax, as if the people she is with right now make her feel safe.

I've never had that before. Okay, not true entirely, I guess. I had one person who I felt like I could let my hair down around. That person has been gone for five years now, so seeing her shed her protective layer and let loose makes me start to miss him. And I hate I am even thinking about him right now when I am here to have a good time.

"Hey." Antonio places his hands on my hips and I catch myself tense even more, but for different reasons. "What's wrong?"

I jiggle my head, dropping my chin, not wanting to let him see the stress on my face. What is wrong? Where should I start with my explanation?

One large finger lifts my chin, forcing me to gaze up at him.

May I just say that I have never in my life seen a man as handsome as this one? He is so much taller than me, too. I am no shrimp, five feet eight inches to be exact, and this man towers over me, as well as everyone around us. I have no doubt he can easily gaze over the crowded room, which means he can also easily be seen.

His broad shoulders are stretching his bright white shirt, not hiding the fact that he works out. The sleeves he rolled up earlier display the dark hair that covering his forearms. There isn't an overly obscene amount, but there is enough to take note of. It makes me ponder what he would look like without his shirt on. Would he have hair on his chest? Would his muscles be hard and defined? Would I ever get the chance to determine if I liked the way they felt against my hands, my body...?

Hold on, where did that thought come from?

Why does my face suddenly feel like it is on fire?

"Have I ever told you how much I adore it when you blush?" Antonio dips his head and angles it slightly. "Why are you blushing, sweet Larkin?"

"No reason," I lie and try to step back.

Antonio slides his large hand around the backside of my waist, situating it just above the curve of my butt. My breathing quickens, and I am pretty sure I am going to hyperventilate soon if I don't gain some control. So, I lift my hands to I can rub my forehead and conceal my eyes, hoping to block it all out.

"Am I going to need to kiss you again to get you to relax?" I feel his hot breath tickle my ear. "Drop your arms and wrap them around me?"

I drop them, but I don't dare wrap them around his waist. Instead, I let them fall freely to my side. My eyes meet his and they lock, making my breath catch in my throat.

Now you need to remember we are supposed to be dancing. Everyone around us certainly is. He most definitely seems to be rocking his hips and shuffling mine with his hands. Apparently, even my feet have been moving, since they stop when his lips collide with mine. They are extremely soft and moist. Full masculine lips that know how to move over mine perfectly.

Earlier, when he kissed me to shut me up, I don't think I took the time to appreciate any of that. So, this time I decide to soak it all in and memorize how they feel against mine.

Antonio tugs me closer, forcing me to reach out and grab the first thing I can locate to steady myself. Which, by the way, is his butt. The lower part of his butt, to be more accurate, so I can paint you a better picture. Compelling him to bring that part of his anatomy forward, pressing his groin against my stomach.

A whimper escapes my mouth when I sense something expand down there. All that does is seem to encourage him to kiss me harder while tightening his grip on me. Coercing another whimper from me. It's like every time I notice him getting harder, I whimper, which only makes him get harder. A vicious cycle we have found ourselves in.

Antonio stops kissing me for a second so he can say something. "Open up so I can get in?"

I have no idea what he is trying to tell me—mush, remember? That is what he turns my mind to when he kisses me. As a result, I start to say *what* but can only get the *wh...* out before he delves his tongue inside my mouth.

Oookkkaaaayyyyyy.

He moans as his tongue freely roams around inside my very happy mouth. And here I thought his closed mouth caresses were mind-mushing. This style of kiss is the kind that erases all other kisses before this one, ordering your brain to only remember how this man kisses. Forges a memory inside your mind that will remain forever, no matter what happens later between the two of you.

The kiss ends slowly, and I find my head being pressed securely to his chest. I can hear the pounding of his heart in my ear. When I come to my senses, I decide to remove my hands from his very tight butt, placing them on the small of his back instead.

"Larkin." He whispers my name into the top of my head.

I breathe in his cinnamon scent before I tilt my head back so I can glance up at him. His eyes are now glazed over as if he is high on something. High on me, perhaps, and I wonder if I look the same way.

When we spin, I spot Hope and Reginald in the main crowd. I invited them to join us because I need a distraction right now. This is all getting too serious, too fast, and if I think too hard about what I just let him do in front of his guests, I just might run out of this place screaming.

After a few songs, Antonio motions for us to follow him to the couches that have been strategically situated in our area.

Hope drops in one and swipes at her forehead. "Wow. Who knew royalty could be so cool? This is actually the most fun I have had in a really long time. So, do you do this often, King Antonio?"

He shakes his head and reaches for my hand. "No. My brothers are still into the party scene. Lorenzo more than Esteban. Now that I keep him busy with, *I could be the next king,* type of business. But these last five years, since I inherited the throne, most of my free time has been spent with Isabel. I was getting a little bored with my all this anyway, so there is that. If you three hadn't come tonight, I probably would have made an appearance for a half-hour and then retreated to my quarters."

I quickly see my chance to voice my opinion on the matter. "We don't have to stick around. I don't mind, really."

Hope rolls her eyes. "Seriously, Larkin. Live it up a little. Come on Reggie the III, let's get back out there and see if we can get one of those eager ladies to notice a wealthy American."

"You are welcome to party here with us." Antonio extends a heartfelt invitation to Hope when she stands and moves toward the main floor.

"Thank you, Your Majesty. But seriously, when will I ever get the chance to party with a room full of lords who have no idea what kind of trouble I can get them into?" She winks as she drags poor Reginald into the larger crowd again.

"She is a handful, isn't she?" He turns and looks at me as if I am the only person in the room.

"Hope definitely gets around from what I've been able to figure out. So, this is crazy." I scan the room and inspect all the action going on around us.

Both of his brothers have selected a few females that caught their attention earlier and seem to be having a good time. They aren't hanging all over them, but they are giving them some attention. The women are eating it up, although I get the impression the guys are just having fun and nothing will ever come from any of it.

Gabriela is dancing with a young man. She notices her brother watching, so she sticks her tongue out at him. That is totally a little sister move she seems to have perfected over the years. I am sure she has had to listen to him lecture her several times about being careful and not letting guys take advantage of what she represents.

"Do you want to get out of here?" Antonio asks, sounding hopeful that my answer will be yes.

"If you do."

He stands and pulls me up with him, then leads us to a door on the other side of the main dance floor. I'm guessing he has an idea where he wants to take me. This palace is his home, after all.

Palace his home. Tell me that statement makes absolutely no sense.

Isaac, one of his guards, notices us moving, so he clears a path to make things easier for us to get through the crowd. Antonio arranges me in front of him, preventing me from getting swallowed up in the sea of people. The door opens the moment we reach it, and he shoves me through quickly. I hear it close behind us just as fast. I realize then where we are, in a beautiful garden area that is only lit by the light of the moon.

The moon.

That thought has me recalling what Antonio said about why my birth mother gave me such an unusual middle name. I'd never taken the time to consider it may have any meaning, other than she was probably high when she named me.

I didn't mind my first name, really. It wasn't common, but I was always told it was a pretty name and fit me. Moon on the other hand was odd. People who are considered eccentric, or under the influence of a substance, they are the only ones that end up naming their children after objects found in nature. You know, like Star, Cosmo, Ocean, or Indigo are all names you know were thought up by someone who was a few sheets to the wind.

Antonio's explanation blew my mind into a thousand curious pieces. Had my birth mother actually given some thought to my full name when she picked it out? I knew from a little research that Larkin means fierce or rough. I had always just thought she was thinking of the bird, Lark, and added -i-n. It made the most sense to me at the time. I'm still not completely convinced it was more than that. And my middle name, Moon, I had accused her of being stoned while gazing up and catching the bright light shining, before absentmindedly writing it down.

Had she maybe held out hope I could be the light to her darkness?

Something that could pull her out of whatever it was that had her using drugs so intensely they eventually took her life?

I have no idea, although I kind of enjoy thinking that perhaps I had been wrong all these years. That my birth mother loved me enough to give me a name with some real meaning behind it.

So, I glance up at the sky and stare at the bright moon, letting my mind ponder that for a few moments longer.

CHAPTER 12
Antonio

The Royals

I needed to get out from under the eyes of those who thought my personal life was any of their business. Living inside a glasshouse can be very exhausting. Even when you have been raised inside of one and have learned how to ignore most of it, there is only so much one can take. Privacy can be an advantage people born into this life never get to experience all that often without fighting for it.

I maneuver us through the nosey vipers, and as I do, I move Larkin in front of me. I don't want to lose her amid the crowd and have to fight my way back to her. I just want to get us out of here as fast and as quietly as I can.

I head for the doors that lead to my private garden. A place no one will be allowed to enter without my permission. As soon as we approach the large exterior doors, my guards open them so we can slip through and then secure them just as promptly. Now that they know I am out here, security in this area will be tightened, meaning Larkin and I will not be disturbed.

Because I am behind her, I get the pleasure of watching her body completely relax the moment we step outside. I continue to watch as she saunters toward the concrete railing and takes in a deep breath of fresh air. It is as if she has been holding herself together by a few weak strings, and now that she is away from it all, she can let everything go. Her head tilts back, and she seems to stares at the sky above us where the moon is shining brightly.

I wander up behind her, trapping her by placing my hands on the railing next to hers. A shiver travels through her body, and I notice her grip tighten around the edges.

I bury my nose into the crown of her head, where her hair is gathered into a messy but stylish bun. Instantly, I am hit with the fragrance of something sweet that causes my mouth to water.

Another shiver travels through her, so I move my hands to her arms and begin running them up and down hers slowly. Her skin is soft and warm under my caress.

When was the last time I touched a woman like this?

I have to think hard about that. I ended things with Dalia a few months before my father's death. I had touched her in lots of ways, ways I probably shouldn't have since she wasn't my wife.

Don't judge me, please. I'm not making excuses for myself. I'm admitting I have faults where I allowed a woman to manipulate me. I am, after all, only a man, king or not. I can fall just as easily as the next guy when things are offered freely and willingly by a woman.

I trusted her at the time, so I allowed her to take some advantages to help me relax when I was stressing over matters concerning my father. Touched her body when she blatantly displayed it to me, and then encouraged me to touch her while she pleasured me.

I know it was wrong. I knew it was risky and wrong. Everything I had worked so hard for, all my plans could have gone up in smoke if I allowed matters to go much farther. I hadn't, though. Right before I was about to make a huge mistake and give in to temptation, my brothers made an unexpected visit to my home, bringing everything to an abrupt end. I had given God the credit later for sending them to make sure I didn't get trapped in a loveless marriage because I did something so stupid.

After our breakup, I have only kissed a few women, striving to get her betrayal off my mind. Shortly after that, I became king, and my days, nights, and weekends have been filled with balancing my responsibilities as king and raising the child left in my care. Isabel has become my haven after long, hard days. I didn't have time to think about dating or entertaining a woman. That little girl has kept me on my toes and given me more than I could have ever hoped for.

It wasn't until I saw Larkin in that office that I even seriously thought about how much I missed that part of my life. She awakened something inside of me that had gone dormant over the years.

Which probably explained why I agreed to let my advisors suggest I start looking for a queen. Allowed them to invite potential prospects that would satisfy the criteria they felt necessary to uphold the integrity of the position as queen. That is all it really is to them, a station of the highest honor. And they want to fill it with someone who looks suitable on paper and will make their jobs easier. It benefits them if my future queen is someone they can use to influence me during my reign. Everything about it is political and follows those unwritten guidelines that suggest a king/queen marry for power rather than love.

I can see where that was probably important back in the Middle Ages, when power and the size of one's kingdom displayed their strength. But in today's world, things are completely different. We no longer conquer other nations; take them over simply because we can. It does me no good to marry a princess from one of the other monarch families who holds no power whatsoever. It isn't as if by doing so it will suddenly give us a portion of their land, pay a dowry to settle debts, or gain political status in the eyes of the world because the sanctity of marriage now joined our nations. It would mean more to them than it does to us. It would allow them to experience how it could have been if they hadn't been forced to give up the power to their thrones.

Then there is the other option of marrying someone of status that lives here in this great country. The consortium of women who are considered elite, those I have known most of my life, and none of them has ever done a thing for me. I can't fully trust any of them to not have their own agenda, nor believe they will always look out for my best interest. I have no desire to marry one of them just so they can finally fulfill their fantasy of being granted the highest title in the land.

I want what most men out there want; someone to love them for the man they are underneath the facade. Someone they can come home to at night and know it is the one place they can relax and let go. I want a woman who loves me more than she loves the country she serves. Actually, I want a woman who couldn't care less about all this and only see me, love me, even if it all one day went away. Finding a woman like that, when you are in my position, feels like a fairytale fantasy, because they just don't exist. Or at least I didn't believe they existed until perhaps now.

I kiss the top of Larkin's head before I back away from her. "Come with me. I don't want to chance someone overhearing us, spying on us. There is a vine-covered structure in the center that will keep us hidden from the nosey vipers."

Larkin lets a pleasant giggle slip past her lips. "Nosey vipers? They sound dangerous."

I tuck her arm under mine and begin leading her down the stairs toward the path. "They can be dangerous if you allow them to be. Give them power over you and they will use it to get whatever they want. That is why it is important to always keep them underfoot. Do you understand?"

I can hear her letting out a deep exhale. "I think so. It's why you gave me that made up title earlier. I'm not comfortable with that, by the way. If I am not worthy enough as simply Larkin Cross, then perhaps we should put a stop to this before it gets even more complicated."

My feet stop dead in their tracks as I glance down at her. The light of the moon is bright, making her hair glisten. I have never seen hair reflect the moon the way hers is right now. Then she tilts her face up to look at mine, letting the moon light it. The glow off her porcelain skin is nearly blinding, and I become hypnotized momentarily.

"Is that what you think? That you are not worthy to be standing next to me, Miss Cross?" I ask when my mind returns. "Because I can assure you my reasons for anointing you with a title had nothing to do with my thoughts on that matter. You are here right now because I want you to be here. None of that matters to me, but unfortunately, it matters to them."

"Which means it also matters to you." Larkin slips her arm out of mine and then walks again.

Does it? Do I really care what they think?

"No, it doesn't."

Larkin is now about ten steps away from me, so when I respond, she spins to glare at me. Her pale blue eyes sparkle in the light and a defiant roll shows me she disagrees. Then she spins around, moving even faster. I can hear her mumbling, although I can't make out exactly what she is saying.

When she is a good fifty steps from me, she spins quickly. Lifting her hand, she points her finger at me as she loudly voices her views on the matter. "That, Your Majesty, is a bald-faced lie. If I may speak freely, sir, as not to offend, if you truly believe what you are saying, then you're a fool. A fool who was provoked by that venomous woman earlier and ended up giving her exactly what she wanted."

Larkin huffs and then twirls around just as quickly. This time when she retreats, she is practically stomping off in those heels I know are hiding under that lovely dress. I momentarily get distracted by the way it fits her form, showing off her backside the way I imagined it would when I picked it out.

Yes, I picked it out for her. I had my mother's stylist bring several different styles to the palace early this morning. One look at that dress and I knew it would look exceptional on her, and I was right. The color against her skin tone is the perfect combination. Bright, vibrant colors are definitely kind to her, and she should wear them often.

When I can no longer see her as well as I'd like, my feet move again. She is heading to the place I suggested, and I hope I catch up with her before she veers off in another direction. At first, I thought maybe she did, because I don't spot her when I step through the archway.

"For a man who has lived his entire life under a microscope, one would think you smarter than you act. I guess it just goes to prove that there is a sucker born every minute." Larkin's voice emerges from behind me. "That woman knew exactly what she was doing. She dangled that carrot in front of you and you took a bite, like she knew you would. Well played, sir, well played."

"Stop it, Larkin," I warn her.

"Or what? You seemed to like it when that woman poked her stick at you, am I wrong, Your Majesty? Do you not like being nudged? Maybe you are more like a paper tiger, something that appears dangerous but is nothing more than a piece of harmless paper."

Larkin's comments do exactly what she intended. They're getting under my skin and stirring up something deep inside of me, reaching a place that up to this very day has never been disturbed.

"Does it bother you, King Antonio, to realize how easy it is for them to know what buttons to push? Showing that woman, who obviously knows you intimately, who clearly hurt you once, letting her prove to them just how vulnerable you are? That while you claim to not care about their approval, the reality of it all is you need it, whether or not you want to. I think I should go."

While she blurted out her thoughts, I stalked toward her slowly. Each word she speaks chips away at my ability to remain calm. As soon as she is finishes, I pounce.

She wants to call me a tiger; I'll show her exactly how dangerous of one I really am. Would a helpless tiger be able to attack her so fiercely? I don't think so.

I back Larkin up against the concrete pillar behind her, my hands clenching her hips. When her back hits the hard, cool stone pillar, my lips take hers. This time I don't ask for permission when I want to enter her mouth. I demand my way inside as I plunge my tongue through her whimpering lips. Talk about someone who displays her weakness. This woman is like putty in my hands whenever I get close to her.

Larkin gets her hands between us trying to shove me away, but I am having none of that. So, I grip them and press them into the pillar next to her head, not letting up at all on my attack.

I have never in my life taken a woman like this before. I have always asked permission before kissing them, or at least warned them what was coming. But even then, I never went after them like I just can't get enough. It is as if Larkin is feeding the tiger that has been trapped in his cage, teaching him just how good it feels to be free to roam.

Her body sliding down the pillar has me stepping back to give us both a chance to catch our breath. I release her arms and end up watching her slither her weak form into a crouched position. She drops her head into her hands and I notice her trembling.

I immediately crash to my knees. "Larkin. *Mi lunita*. Are you okay?"

She drops her hands, revealing a smile that tells me what I need to know. "You really have to stop asking me such a ridiculous question after you kiss me like that, Antonio."

"I will always ask." I reach up and cup her cheek. "Especially when you have such a reaction to me kissing you. You are okay, then?"

"I'm fine." She reaches up and pats my cheek. "Your Majesty definitely knows how to knock a woman off her feet."

I growl at the formal way she addresses me. "No more, *mi lunita*. You will stop that right now. Call me Your Majesty one more time and I will show you what a king does to those who blatantly disobey his orders. I am Antonio to you, always and forever. I will never correct you, not even in public, for addressing me so informally. I am not your king, nor do I want to be. What I want from you, Larkin, is to earn your respect. I want you to see me like no one else ever has. I am looking for a woman who isn't afraid to tell me what you did tonight. Call me out when I am acting like a fool. I want a woman who will look out for my best interests, our best interests. I need a woman who will stand by my side always and not care should any of this ever go away. One who I can love, and one who will love me back with everything she possesses. That is what I want and need, and I am hoping I can find that in you."

"Well, then." She offers me her hand so I can help her stand. "That gives me a lot to think about now, doesn't it? I can assure you I couldn't care less about all of this, but that doesn't mean I don't know how significant it all is. That it's a part of you and should I decide to date you, it would mean accepting one day it could possibly be a part of me as well. Which means I need to think about how I feel; if I am even capable of being a part of this world. Can I handle the pressure? Am I willing to take a risk on my sanity? Are you enough for me to willingly put myself in the public eye and have them all up in my business? I'm not sure of that right now.

"I also think you need to take time to think about it as well. Are you willing to fight for me no matter what it may end up costing you? Is love really that important to you? I mean if we should date and this turns into more." She blushes and I laugh. "Because if you have any doubt about that at all, then I ask that you let tonight be a lesson to us both. Some things sound really good, even feel good, but the reality of what it may take to obtain them sometimes just isn't worth the risk, and so we have to let it go."

"You are worth the risk, Larkin." I don't even hesitate with my response. "Never doubt that."

"You say that now, Antonio. But this is just the beginning, and as I have learned so many times during my life, things always get harder, not easier."

CHAPTER 13
Larkin

The Royals

T wenty-four days.

That's how long I've lived in Hermosa Islas after practically begging my boss to get me out of Chicago. It's also three days shy of the number of days I have known Antonio.

Eighteen days.

That would be the number of days I last heard from Antonio. The last time I saw him was when he escorted me back inside the party to join the others. Shortly after that, he got called away on matters that required his immediate attention. Left me in the care of his brother, Esteban, who did his best to entertain me while my colleagues partied it up. Once the party started dying down and I was more than ready to get out of there, he escorted us back to our hotel and wished us farewell.

Farewell.

That is a word I am wondering if meant more than I first predicted. It sounds so final, doesn't it? Maybe Antonio instructed his brother to do his dirty work and send me on my way so he didn't have to.

Five days.

That's how many days it has been since I got called into Cameron's office and informed Chandler Sloan would join us. They then instructed me to hand over all my designs for Aragon Palace to him once he arrived later today. I didn't argue about it because I hated working in the palace. It was a constant reminder that the man whose home was inside of it was ignoring me.

I was being reassigned to work on Maximiliano Chateau in Homero. Homero is a town located an hour South of Aragon with rich rolling hills. Maximiliano was once the home of an English noble who fled to Hermosa Islas in the mid-1700s. It is a beautiful chateau that has been neglected for far too long and eventually sold to the Reyes family around a decade ago. They bought it as an investment and a way to preserve a piece of history that otherwise would have been torn down. The chateau in Homero was more up my alley. I looked forward to moving on from here and getting started on it. Cameron told me there was a habitable cottage on the land where I could live while overseeing the renovations. It would serve as my home and office, courtesy of the Reyes family, since housing in Homero was limited. I wasn't sure how I felt about that.

Whatever.

I was just happy to be leaving Aragon, where I wasn't expected to visit the palace every few days and wonder if he knew I was there. I hated I even cared. Working on the chateau would get me out of this city and away from my newest obsession.

I guess my speech about him reconsidering what he was risking had been a fantastic one. Good enough to scare him off and then conclude I just wasn't worth risking all of this. (This being the palace plans I am currently reviewing so I can answer any questions Chandler has for me.)

The knock on my glass wall has me glancing up. Once my eyes refocus, I spot Hope standing there, making some sort of gesture with her hands. She is mouthing something, although I can't quite make it out. My eyes are tired from staring at blueprints and tiny little words for the last two hours. Then I catch her straighten quickly when she notices someone coming her way. She glances back in my direction and mouths, *'Oh my Gawd.'*

"Ma'am, I am going to need you to clear the hallway." I overhear the man in a black suit and a visible mechanism in his ear order her as he passes my door.

"Sure thing. Just leaving." Hope turns so she is looking at me full-on and makes this crazy face that has me laughing.

Or had me laughing. That is until the elevator dings. When it opens, a man I have decided I don't really like very much is standing inside of it. He stares at me in a way no man ever has, with this expression that reveals what he is thinking. Well, the joke's on him if he thinks I will be that easy.

He struts the short distance to my office door. "Please leave us. Miss Cross and I would like some privacy."

"No, we wouldn't." I roll up the plans on my desk and gather them in my arms. Before I speak, I secure them tightly against my chest. "Miss Cross has a meeting she is going to be late for if she doesn't get moving. You are dismissed."

Yeah, I did. I dismissed him in that way I've heard him do to those below him. Not all that long ago, he told me he wasn't my king, meaning he didn't want me to treat him like one. Fine, I won't. I will treat him like the stupidest man alive, one who obviously thinks he can ignore me and get away with it because, after all, he is king.

"Excuse me." I glare up at him as I make my way to the door. "I need to get going and you are blocking my path."

"I came here, Larkin, so we could talk." He stubbornly holds his ground.

"Talk? Now you want to talk? The time to talk, Antonio, was fifteen days ago. Sixteen days would've probably been better, but fifteen would have been acceptable. Ten would have likely gotten you into my office had you shown up like this. Five may have had me chewing you out first, with a real good tongue-lashing to go with it. After I notified you how your silence has affected my overactive mind, how if you were any other man, I'd have dumped you out with the trash. I may have let you explain had you shown up then. However, it has been eighteen days, and yesterday was the day I decided I was over it. You made your decision, obviously, so I am forced to live with that decision. Put my big girl panties on and move forward." I believe I said all that in one very long agitated breath. "So, now move or I will not be held responsible for my actions."

His stupid smirk does nothing to make me any less angry. It only lights the wick that will send me into a raging woman who once allowed herself to think she might actually have a chance with this man.

"Step aside, sir." I know he hates it when I use anything other than his name.

"Don't call me sir again, Larkin," he warns as he leans forward.

"Then move that royal butt of yours before I move it for you." I detect my anger building up deep inside of me. "I mean it, Antonio. I am not playing around here. I'm completely serious."

The arrogant prick laughs before he leans forward and kisses me. Kisses me like he has the right to put his lips on mine after all that has transpired between us.

Well, he doesn't.

Even though it feels nice and right and I can smell that cinnamon mingled with him, and it is clouding my brain, it does not cloud it enough to stop me from reacting.

The loud slap echoes off my walls and makes his men jump into action. I watch them yank him backward and soon realize they are not removing him to get him out of my way, but coming for me.

I am sure my wide-eyed expression alerts him I wasn't thinking about the fact I just slapped the king, because in my mind I had only slapped the man who pissed me off.

"Stand down!" Antonio shouts when he also realizes what they are about to do. "Do not touch her."

"Your Majesty..." The closest man to me questions him with his eyes. "My job..."

"Is to protect me from danger, not a woman who has every right to do what she just did. Stand down now or you will find yourself jobless." He shakes the other men off of him. "All of you back to your post."

Antonio directs his gaze on me and nods once. "All right. I deserved that. You do seem to suffer interesting responses when I kiss you, Larkin, although I think I like the other ones much better."

I lift my chin and start advancing out my door now that it has been cleared. "You will never kiss me like that again without my permission. Next time I won't think twice about giving those family jewels a good kneeing."

His hands instantly cup himself, but his stupid grin expresses I don't really scare him. "I'll remember to look for my athletic support before our next meeting, then. Because kissing you is sure to happen once you start throwing orders around as you do."

I spin to scold him and catch the red mark of my handprint across his cheek. I've never slapped anyone before; no one has ever given me a reason to. However, I sure presented him with a nice one that still has to be stinging.

"You should instruct your men to grab you some ice before your precious face gets any worse. Farewell, Antonio."

I sense him following me, not to mention the fact his men are mumbling as they try to clear a path for us. I am pretty certain they hate me right now.

"It would save me a lecture later from Sir Edward on how being spontaneous makes it challenging for my team to do their jobs if you would just tell them where we are heading." He nods at the men doing their best to check offices and corridors. "Or we could just go back to your office and..."

I concentrate on the man standing next to me in a black suit. "I'm heading to Cameron York's office, it's at the end of the hall to the left. Then I have a meeting in the opposite direction in one of the bigger conference rooms. Chandler Sloan should be there by now, ready to take these from me."

"What are those?" Antonio reaches over and yanks the plans out of my arms.

Okay. Whatever. "My designs for Aragon Palace."

Antonio passes them off to a man standing behind him. "Make sure those get to Mr. Sloan. Tell him we will join him shortly."

I stop walking and lean against one of the cubical walls. We are now in the open office area where our ten new employees sit. They do odd jobs, anywhere from accounting to making sure we hold the proper permits. A few are interns who are just getting their hands wet in this field. They are all doing their best to act like they don't know exactly who Antonio is, or that he is standing five feet from them.

"No. You're not coming to my meeting with Chandler. In fact, why are you still here?" Again, I realize we are quickly drawing a crowd. I don't care. I'm not the one who just showed up at his work and started acting like an idiot. There is work to do, and I don't have time to deal with this right now.

"I am here..." he glances around the open space. "Can we please find someplace more private?"

I roll my eyes and start walking again, shoving open the first door I come to. I check inside and then motion for him to enter.

"Larkin, that is the ladies' lavatory." Antonio shakes his head when he realizes he has no other option. "Gino, please do what you need to do."

Gino takes a step into the bathroom and has a thorough look around. Pushes open the doors to both stalls, studies the ceiling, and checks behind the door. It's a small bathroom, for Pete's sake. Did he expect someone to be hiding in the visible space under the sink or maybe inside the trashcan? And yes, Gino checked those spaces as well. "All clear, Your Majesty."

Antonio motions for me to step inside and then follows. I lean my backside against the small sink, leaving him in the area in front of the stalls.

"We are really doing this here?" He seems completely unsure of how he should feel about that.

"You have five minutes. Five minutes before I walk out that door and never think about you again," I lie, but it sounds good, right?

He stands there and just stares at me for a full minute.

"Four minutes now," I inform him as I glance down at my Apple Watch.

"Shut it." His tone is firm. "I've never done this before, okay?"

"Done what? Stand in a women's restroom and tried to explain why you are a jerk?" Yeah, I am so done being nice. "What? You wanted to explain it all, right? So, start talking, you're down to three minutes and thirty seconds."

A growl rises out of him, reminding me of how he attacked me in the garden after I called him a harmless paper tiger. His hands grab his hair and begin rubbing it, making a mess out of his put together mane.

"Three minutes and counting." I am agitating my head now.

"You are really going to make me say it, aren't you?" Antonio looks like he has swallowed a piece of glass that is stuck in his throat.

"Two and a half." I am not kidding. I will walk out that doorway madder than I was when I walked in here.

Sweat forms on his forehead and his eyes dart around rapidly, looking everywhere but at me. He is making this way harder than it needs to be. However, only he can decide for himself if he is man enough to fess up.

"Two minutes, Antonio. In less than two minutes I am walking out of here and if I do, then..."

"I'm sorry!" he shouts and his voice vibrates off the walls of this small space. "I am freaking sorry that I had you worrying about what was going on. I should have called you so you understood I was working on some specifics to clear the path. I messed up, okay? I'm sorry and I messed up because I don't even know how to do this."

"Apologize?" I squint my eyes at him. "You've never apologized before?"

One arm drops to his side, while the other lands firmly on the back of his neck. "No. I mean, of course, I've apologized before. To my family mostly, a few friends, probably when I was little. But never to a woman, never to someone who means the world to me as you do."

"Don't! Don't you dare go on about all that when I haven't heard hide nor hair from you in eighteen days, Antonio. Don't start in on all that while we are standing in a women's bathroom."

A stupid smirk crosses his face. "You are the one who made me do this in here, remember? I wanted to have this conversation inside your office."

"Oh, no. No, you never wanted to have this conversation at all. You were hoping as soon as you stepped off that elevator, I'd see you and all would be forgiven. Well, guess what? That is not how it works out here in the real world. Prince Charming can't just show up with all his hotness and powerful façade and expect the little lady to just go all goo-goo eyed over him. It's going to take more than that to get me to buy into the fantasy. You are going to need to do a whole lot more groveling and offer a detailed explanation about why you were such a jerkwad. However, all that will need to wait because I have a meeting to get to." I push off the counter and head for the door. "I believe you know your way out."

"Larkin." He says my name as a plea. "When will you allow me to grovel? I'm free this evening if you are."

I yank the door open and spin to face him again. "Leave your number with my secretary. I'll ask her to check my schedule and get back to you when I find the time to do so. Right now, I am a little busy getting organized so I can work on this irritating king's chateau. I'm thinking I may charge him double the cost just because he has been a real pain in my butt."

A loud, very sincere laugh echoes from behind me as I leave him standing in the bathroom. "I'm sure he'd pay triple if you'd promise to always be honest with him."

Jerk.

Three seconds.

That's how long it took for me to realize I was going to give him the chance to explain. But this time, there will be no messy, mind-boggling kisses to distract me from what needs to be done or said.

CHAPTER 14
Antonio

The Royals

Larkin made me wait three days before clearing a spot. Apparently, she wasn't lying about being busy.

I stopped by her secretary's desk on my way out of the office. Of course, I had to ask one of the ten speechless employees, who I knew overheard part of our conversation, where I could find her. The young woman got the giggles when I approached and then nearly fell out of her chair when I spoke.

That act reminded me of the first time Larkin actually tumbled to the floor, the first time we ever met. Had I known then how much my life would change after that incident, I might have been nicer to her. Although, I do believe our little bantering experience showed me she wasn't afraid of anyone, or at least as long as she didn't know who that person was.

Her secretary wasn't quite as giggly, though she seemed to smile a lot. Apologized when she knocked over her container that held all her pens and pencils, scattering them all over the floor. I helped her pick them up, which only had her apologizing more for making me do something so simple.

Finally, she pulled up Larkin's calendar like I asked so she could look at it. When I requested her to put me down for seven that evening, she frowned up at me. Apologized again as she informed me Larkin had a meeting for the rest of the day. One that was in red and extended into the evening. Red, I learned, meant under no circumstance could it be missed or rescheduled. Therefore, I tried for the next night but was once again told it was blocked off in red. She explained they were currently under a deadline and staff change, so without permission from Larkin, she couldn't just pencil me in.

Which meant I had to wait for her to get back to me. I started to wonder if maybe this was payback. Perhaps she was making me wait like I made her wait. I guess I can't say I blame her, really.

This morning when I walked into my office, my personal cellphone finally rings and her name appears on my screen. I was just about to sit down with Alejandro to go over my agenda for the day and discuss all the issues that *need* my urgent attention. Suddenly, all of that will have to wait, and I can see he gets the message when I signal to the door. He immediately jumps up and vacates my office.

"Hello, *mi lunita*," I answer as I lock the door behind him. "Are you paying me back?"

"Did you just call me a loony?"

I chuckle. "No, Larkin. I called you my moon."

"Oh. Whatever. Look, I'm sorry it's taken me this long to finally call. However, I've been extremely busy. Your people are not making it easy for us right now, and it is causing all sorts of headaches and long, arduous hours. Think you could head down to the Historical Preservation Offices and have a word with them? I'm sure that would help speed things up and allow us to get started on restoration to the lovely palace you live in." I hear her ruffling some papers around as she pauses from her little rant.

"I'll add it to my diary. Anyone, in particular, I should speak with? Someone who is giving you a hard time?" I grab my pen, ready to write down a name and make it known that I want this matter resolved ASAP.

"What?" I can hear the surprise in her voice. "No. I was kidding. Okay, so I'm calling because I told you I would and I haven't yet. See how that works? Shocking, isn't it."

She is still obviously angry with me, but at least she took the time to call. "Did you get the flowers I sent you yesterday?"

A creaking noise sounds across the silent line. I assume it is her chair as she leans back in it. "They were very nice, thank you."

I've never sent a woman flowers before. After everything went down with us at her office, I wanted to make sure not to totally screw things up again. So yesterday during breakfast I asked Helena about how I could go about doing that. The older woman's surprised expression to my question did not go unnoticed. She recovered quickly, though, and then wrote down the name of the florist the palace staff used. Recommended roses because she said that is what men typically sent. Suggested I personally compose a note to go with it, then send a footman to take it over to be attached to the arrangement.

I'd taken most of her advice. Wrote a personal note, which, by the way, took me an hour to do. I wanted it to be perfect and express how I planned on doing better from here on out. I finally went with this.

Larkin,

I know I am a jerk and a fool. Please understand, however, that I am your jerk and fool and hope you understand I am new to this. I'm a quick learner, though, and promise to not repeat the same mistake twice. Please accept these flowers as my first attempt at groveling and appreciate there will be so much more of that once we get together. I have cleared my evenings for the rest of the week and am also available this weekend. Just tell me when and where and I'll be there to commence groveling like a desperate man.

Antonio

The flowers I finally decided on, after I delivered the note myself, were tulips, yellow tulips. The older woman helping me, who, by the way, wasn't at all surprised to see me there, said it was an excellent choice. She even suggested yellow because yellow was the color that bestowed a thoughtful apology. And before I left, she winked and said, "Well done, Your Majesty. I hope this works and she forgives you. You deserve to be as happy as the rest of us."

I hoped they worked, too, because I was pretty certain my happiness depended on this woman. It has been three days since I've seen her, and with each passing day, I could feel my good mood fading.

"You are most welcome, *mi lunita*. So, you called so we could finally sit down and hold that way too late conversation?" I try to get us back on track.

"I'm sorry, Antonio, but that isn't going to happen," she informs me and I interrupt her.

"Don't make me show up to your office again, Larkin. I'll do it and get lectured again by my head of security about how they need advance notice before I wander aimlessly around the city, *correndo atras de uma bela mulher*. The man is going to call my mother and encourage her to have a very stern talk with me. Unless you want me to go through all of that, you will provide me a time." I grunt my frustration into the phone. "Please."

"I don't know what all that mumbo-jumbo in the middle means. However, if you would let me finish, before rudely interrupting me and going berserk, I would let you know my week is fully booked.

"Timothy and Nicolette are flying in to check on the progress of each of our current projects. Which means Hope is freaking out on top of everything else. So, between that and Chandler requiring my assistance with all this palace business, along with the new project that is starting next week in Homero, and the fact I still need to pack, rent a car or buy one—that probably would be best—I'm lucky if I find a minute in there to pee, eat, or sleep.

"So, setting aside time for a conversation that should have been done days ago, is going to just need to wait. I'm sorry, but unlike you, I can't just drop everything and do as I please. People just don't bow down and do as I say, when I say. And I can't keep the lights on if I don't have a job that gives me the resources to do so. Not all of us are privileged enough to be born into such a prestigious life."

I try to say something but she just keeps going. I don't want to be rude and interrupt her, so I listen and smile thinking about how adorable she must look.

"Oh, and let us not forget that five minutes before I called you, my father rang and told me he was coming for a visit. He is even bringing mother with him. Don't know how he pulled that one off, but good for him. They deserve some time away from their lives for a few days.

"So, that just added one more unexpected matter to my already overflowing load. Okay, so now I am even further behind because I've spent the last several minutes talking to you when I should be working."

Finally, she stops and I hear her taking a deep breath. Pretty sure that if I don't speak now, I won't get a word in for another five minutes.

"First, the mumbo-jumbo means chasing after a beautiful woman. And I believe I learned to release my thoughts from you."

"Hardy har har," Larkin says, unimpressed. "There's a comedian in every bunch."

"Second, I get you are busy with work. But you need to eat, right? Pee, even, and most definitely get some sleep."

"Pee?" she repeats, sounding horrified. "Please tell me I did not say that."

"It was very refreshing to hear, actually. My point is that surely there is an hour scheduled in there for lunch, perhaps. Dinner, maybe. Coffee, even. I need to see you, Larkin. I am having withdrawals. And trust me when I tell you that when that happens, my staff hides and begins sending in all those people they hate so I can put them in their places.

"Last week I made the Minister of Treasury cry after I shoved her overly exaggerated budget back at her and ordered her to start over. The Minister of Education left my office with a stack of papers so high he could barely carry them. My proof that we are not using our resources properly and relying too much on printed materials rather than these great tablets that save trees and keep our trash to a minimum. Don't even make me tell you what the Heads of the Church and I discussed. I basically warned them to fix the problem or I would fix it, and then they'd both be replaced, effective immediately.

"I believe I have a meeting with the Minister of Defense in the morning. He will most definitely benefit if I am in a better mood. Otherwise, I might bring up the fact that our recruiting classes are not up to the standards I'd like them to be. Make a few suggestions on how I think he can rectify that for me. He has been mad at me ever since I stole Isaac from him to oversee my personal detail. It could get ugly very fast. All because a woman can't find one hour in her day to have dinner with me." Desperate times call for desperate measures.

"Wow. You've gotten pretty good at the whole letting it all out. One hour, Antonio." I can picture her holding up one finger in my mind to make her point. "I'll meet you outside my office building at seven. That's an hour after my meeting with Cameron, Bradley, and Chandler is due to end. That should account for it going over. I need to be back by eight, eight-thirty, at the latest. Nicolette and I have a conference call at nine, and I cannot be late or unprepared for it."

"I can work with that. Are you always this busy?" I relax back in my chair now that I know we have a date tonight.

"Yes, and no. I bet I've put in forty hours already this week and it's only Wednesday. Typically, a normal week for me consists of ten-hour days, five days a week. Occasionally, I'll end up working on a Saturday if a project is running behind. Towards the end of the project, my hours usually jump to twelve-hour days to make sure we don't fall behind and to keep our contractors on schedule. So, if you are asking me if my job is a nine-to-five one, the answer is no. I'm a workaholic who loves her job and strives to do the best she can do. I've never really had a reason before to not put in the long hours." Larkin drops something and I hear her mumbling to herself. "I need to go, Antonio."

"One more question and then I will let you go. You said you never really had a reason before not to put in those long hours. Are you saying you have one now?" I close my eyes as I wait for her response.

"Well, I am rearranging my very hectic schedule for you, tonight, aren't I? Goodbye. I'll see you at seven."

"Goodbye, *mi lunita*. Tonight, I shall make sure to make the most of our hour together." I hang up and smile at no one.

I have a date.

I have a date!

Oh crap, a date.

I need a plan and I don't even know where to start. Helena will help. I pick up the phone and call and ask her to come down to my office

ASAP. When I'm done, I send a text to Alejandro letting him know I'm ready.

"Sir." Alejandro is standing at my door. "Your agenda?"

"Yes, of course. You're married, right?" I believe he is. Why do I not know this for sure?

"I am, Your Majesty. Four years now. Why do you ask, sir?" He takes a seat in his usual spot.

"Your wife, how did you meet her?" I relax back in my chair and play with the pen now in my hand.

He chuckles as he places everything on the side table. "Well, I met her working here, sir. She greets you every morning."

"Helena is your wife? Isn't she a little old for you?" I stop toying with my pen. "How does that work with her living in my quarters?"

"No, sir. Not Helena. Triana. Triana is my wife." He blushes as if embarrassed to admit that.

"How did I not know this?"

"We didn't make a big deal about it. Keep things professional and all while we are here at work, Sir. We both put in the same long hours as you, for you, so it all works out, as it should. It wasn't a secret, sir, but we felt it best not to go public with it. I mean, of course, people around here know we are married, but we also know it could be frowned upon and all. We spoke with HR before ever dating. I believe I even discussed it with you at that time, but you were likely distracted by all that was transpiring around you."

Light bulb moment, they probably started dating and got married during my first year as king. That first year is one big blur, so yes, I am sure I don't recall such a conversation.

"First, congratulations. She is a great woman, and you are very lucky to have snagged her. Second, there is no need to be discreet about it. She is *tu esposa* and you should never hide that fact. Celebrate it every day. Tell her you love her as often as you wish, kiss her for goodness' sake when you greet her every time you walk into this office. You are lucky enough to have a wife and therefore you should take advantage of the fact you work together. Drag her off to your office after an extremely stressful meeting. Let her help you relax, and vice versa. There are plenty of others having sex in this palace and doing it with those they should not be doing it with. So, you might as well be doing it with the one who will one day make you a papa. If I had a wife, that is exactly what I would do, especially if she worked within twenty feet of my office."

I've known Alejandro for several years now. Not once has he blushed like he is right now.

There is a knock on my door before it opens again. "Your Majesty, Helena is here to see you. Said you were expecting her."

I gesture toward the door as soon as Triana steps through it. "Send her in. Why don't you stick around as well? I believe the four of us may be more successful at conquering this issue. Alejandro, don't just sit there. Grab your wife a chair so she can sit down."

My personal secretary jumps to his feet as he clears his throat. His gorgeous wife is now blushing as well. However, she isn't blushing as much as she is a minute later when Alejandro takes her into his arms and kisses her like I am certain he does every night when they get home.

"Well done, Alejandro. Well done." I laugh loudly for the first time since I left Larkin a few days ago. "Now tell me, I have a date tonight and I need to knock the socks right off of her. This is a do or die situation, and as we all know, I refuse to die without a fight, so we need to make this really, really good."

CHAPTER 15
Larkin

The Royals

I press the down elevator button several times while I wait for it to arrive. I gave myself an extra hour and still, I am running late. How is that even possible? This was supposed to be a simple meeting that finalized all the work I've done so far while clearing up a few questions hanging in the air.

Oh yes, I know why it happened, because Chandler freaking Sloan is being a prick. As soon as it hit six forty-five, and an alert on my phone went off, he decided he had twenty more questions about my proposals. He noticed the message as it flashed across my screen the moment it buzzed on the table. Even dared to read the text that quickly followed, because his eyebrows disappeared under his floppy hair.

My phone then started going off every five minutes after that until I finally responded. Which I did only because nosey Chandler made it a point to act irritated after the fifth one came through.

"Are we keeping you, Miss Cross?" He'd asked with an unmistakable tone to his voice.

"Actually, you are." I grabbed my phone to respond before Antonio stormed the castle. See what I did there?

I reread his texts quickly to make sure I provided him with all the correct responses.

ANTONIO: I'm here so if by chance you are ready early, you can join me.

ANTONIO: Did you forget you only have one hour, Miss Cross?

ANTONIO: Are you ignoring me?

ANTONIO: Standing me up?

ANTONIO: Did you fall asleep at your desk?

ANTONIO: Maybe you are in the lavatory emptying that very full bladder? I'm giving you five minutes before I see if I can track you down.

ME: Sorry, no to all the above questions. I'm stuck in a room with a man who knows exactly what he is doing. Note to self, never ever make out with a man you work with, and then later blow him off. Men are very prickly creatures who get their panties in a twist when they don't get their way.

I put my phone away and began explaining my changes again to a particular portion of the palace supports. I've been over this with him a dozen times already. While it isn't something we would typically do, with some of the alterations they are suggesting, it is a necessity if we don't want to run into future complications.

Cameron's phone started vibrating on the table. He glanced down at it and smiled. I'm sure it's his wife expressing something sweet and wondering why he was still here as well.

It goes off again ten minutes later and his eyes finds mine. He waits for me to stop before letting me know what that one was about.

"Next time you have an engagement with the king, please do not keep him waiting." Cameron closed his folder and began to stands. "Sloan, I think we've taken enough of Cross's time. As her very eager companion just pointed out to me, we expected this meeting to end an hour and twenty minutes ago. Stanton, we good?"

"I can't possibly think of what else there is to know about this project. Larkin did a superb job on this, as usual. Honestly, I'm kind of worried that maybe we should have kept her on this project and sent him to Homero." Bradley glared at Chandler, not pleased with his little stunt.

"Thank you." I shoved everything into my briefcase and didn't bother asking if there was anything else.

Chandler steps up next to me while I wait on the slowest elevator known to man. He is staring at the numbers, watching them rise. "Date?"

"What?" I hit the button again.

"Do you have a date?" He asks as it finally reaches our floor and opens.

We both start to step inside as soon as the doors release, but a large hand jets out to stop him. "Sorry, sir, but you are going to need to catch the next bus."

"Are you serious?" Chandler sounds annoyed.

The sea of black suits part, and I am blessed with the sight of the man who has been on my mind since our conversation this morning. He is casually leaning against the wall.

"Ma'am." The same man says to me. "I believe we are running late as it is."

Antonio doesn't look at me when I step onto the crowded elevator. Instead, he glares at Chandler, giving him a once over. His arm wraps around my waist the second I step close enough to him. He draws me into his side and addresses me in his own unique way. "*Mi lunita*. I was beginning to think I would have to make a scene."

As soon as the doors close, I step out of his embrace and lean against the corner of the elevator. I am so exhausted, the last thing I honestly want to do right now is talk about topics that are going to wear me down even more. So, I close my eyes as I prop my head against the wall, trying to relax.

When I open them again, I am in a car, tucked securely in the nook of Antonio's arm. He is on the phone with someone and does not seem all that pleased right now.

"She fell asleep standing up after closing her eyes for a brief second. She is exhausted and obviously requires sleep. I had to carry her from the elevator to my vehicle because I was afraid to lead her out like that. She looks like a zombie and has been mumbling incoherently." He now seems to be listening to whoever it is he is talking to.

I strain to open my eyes, but they are so heavy. "I'm fine. Just a quick five minutes and I'll be good to go."

"Shhh." He hushes me as he pats my hip. "No mumbling allowed. Yes, she said something, although I don't know what it is. I'm all about working long hours when necessary, but there is a limit when enough is enough. Larkin's body is stating she has had enough, and since she has no one to speak for her besides me, I am saying it."

I swat at him, or I think I do. I feel my hand land against something hard, thick, and solid. "I'm fine."

His hand grips mine and transfers it away from the area I patted, placing it gently somewhere lower.

"Thank you. Yes, that makes me feel better. I'm sure if you have any questions you can let Mr. Sloan take the conference call. He should be well informed on all subjects dealing with the palace since he just kept her an hour and a half longer than first planned. I'll make sure she gets the message when she is coherent. And thank you again, Miss Manchester."

I feel his lips land on top of my head and hold it there. He mumbles something in Spanish, I believe. I am going to need to take a crash course in the language so I can understand him when he does that. Portuguese too, I believe is mixed in at times. I remember reading something about that while I was doing research on their culture.

The creaking of a car door opening, followed by a male voice, is what I hear next. "Why are you... what did you do to her, brother?"

"Nothing, Lorenzo. Are you going to just stand there staring, or help me?" Antonio seems irritated.

"Help you? Oh, no. No, I am not taking care of your drunk friend." His voice is getting farther away as if he is backing up.

"I don't drink. Not drunk." I struggle to tell him.

"What did she say? Hey, is that Larkin?" Lorenzo's voice gets closer, and then he rambles very fast in some other language I cannot understand at all. I hate I don't know what they are discussing.

"*Escutar. As paredes do palácio têm ouvidos.*" Antonio scolds his brother, from the sound of his voice. "I cannot risk taking her there. Your place doesn't have a constant flow of nosey vipers coming and going like mine. If I take her there, come morning, it will be in the papers and give them fuel to fan the fire. I just got them off my back about all of this. And for the record, I'm not leaving her here for you to take care of. I'm just searching for sanctuary for an evening."

"You'll owe me." It's not a question. "And when I come to you for something, it will be a no questions asked kind of help. Come on. I sent my staff away hours ago. It's just Valentina and me. Hope she doesn't have allergies."

I'd like to be able to tell you what happens next, except I can't. The two brothers carry on for a while and sometime during that time, I must have passed out again.

When I wake up the next time, I can hear ice clacking against a glass as a deep voice declares, "Check."

"Nope. Not happening. You may be king, but that doesn't mean I am letting you win." Lorenzo's voice sounds confident. "So how long do you suppose she'll sleep?"

"What time is it?" I ask as I stretch and then feel something wiggle up my body. When I open my eyes, a wet tongue licks me, as a fuzzy face stares down at me.

"Valentina, no." Lorenzo sternly corrects the little ball of fur.

I sit up and gather the cute little wiggle worm in my arms. I've never really been around dogs before. My parents didn't feel it fair to own a pet when they were always on the go.

"Well, aren't you an adorable little bundle of fur? What kind of dog is she?" I snuggle right in and get lots of kisses from her.

"She won't be so cute in a few months when she is twice that size and is chewing on everything she can get her mouth on. She's a Saint Bernard." Antonio answers without looking up from the board. "Checkmate."

"I hate you." Lorenzo slides his chair back and strides over to me. "You sure you want to get involved with a man who thinks all dogs are evil?"

I lift my eyebrows as I hand the puppy off to him. "Who said we are involved?"

"That a girl. Make him work for it, love. Although falling asleep on a man when he comes to take you out on a date could possibly suggest that. Groping him while he is trying to..."

Antonio growls. "Shut it."

"What? Come on, man, that was priceless. If you didn't want me harassing her about it, then you shouldn't have told me." Lorenzo grins. "Don't worry, Larkin, your secret is safe with me. Okay, Valentina, time to do our business outside and then off to bed. Brother King wants some private time with the woman who grasps his future in her hands." The grin on his face informs me he knows exactly what he is suggesting.

I watch Lorenzo make his way out of a door and disappear. When I turn around, I can barely look at Antonio. "I'm sorry I fell asleep on you. I've never had that happen before. Nor have I ever groped a man in my sleep." Or awake for the record.

"You didn't... never mind, it's not important. It's a little after two. You asked what time it was earlier." He stands and motions to the spot next to me on the couch. "Feeling better?"

I yawn as soon as he asks. "Still tired, I guess, but better. Sorry I ruined your evening."

"Not at all. Sometimes sleep is more important. We will try it again when you are fully recovered and completely alert. I'm not so sure it would have been such a great idea to hold the conversation we need to have while you were a walking zombie." He reaches down and takes my hand in his.

"That sounds serious." I lean my head against his shoulder. "Why did you wait so long, Antonio? Tell me that at least, would you?"

He takes his other hand and encases mine between his. It takes him some time to start, but when he does, I realize he was very busy those two weeks and they certainly weren't fun. "I've learned a lot since that night. There are those who don't like how I acted at the party. Said that I made them all look like shmucks and liars. They made some assurances with a few very important people who have gotten them to where they are today. So, they requested I help them recover some of their reputations and spend time with those they invited."

I yank my hand out from his and leap up off the couch. "Wait. You were going out on dates with all those women while I was..." My voice shrieks louder with each word.

Antonio reaches out to grab my hand, but I step away from him. All that anger that has been building inside of me since that night comes to a head. I feel like I've been deceived in the worst of ways.

Is he revealing that him showing up the other day was to inform me we could never happen? The flowers. The note. Was that all just his way to...

"Would you stop and let me finish before drawing any conclusions? Of course, I didn't go out on dates with those women." He throws his head back against the couch and talks to the ceiling. "Before I met you, I agreed to let them introduce me to a few prospects. As you can imagine, finding my own dates is extremely difficult. It's not like I can just walk up to someone and start a conversation out of the blue. Everything is planned out, and we make arrangements to ensure things don't take a turn for the unexpected. It's all so rather boring, honestly, and not at all how a man pictures meeting the love of his life. Probably because a man like me isn't intended to marry for love at all, I guess."

"That's so sad." I drop into a chair and let my anger slowly subside. I never really thought about how true that is. Even in the United States, many times those who are involved in politics marry for reasons other than true love.

"I agree. It is completely disgusting and something that should have been done away with years ago. Perhaps that is why God decided I needed to become king. To change some of these ridiculous traditions that have created a bunch of adulterous men, all because they felt trapped and married to someone they never even liked."

"But they all produced heirs; surely they at least liked them at one time or another." I can't even imagine letting a man do that if I didn't love him. "Those women allowed all that to happen just so that the next rightful heir could take the throne? That is so not something I understand at all. I could never do that."

"I believe that is exactly why they did it, actually. What those women loved was the advantages being queen provided them. The men as well, I suppose, since it also brought them several. And because of that, it was very common for the king to keep a lover in the palace, sometimes more than one.

"I grew up watching how that hurt my mother. Saw my grandmother ignore her husband's philandering ways and pretended she was clueless, even though we all knew she was not. Watched her lose it when my grandfather's long-term mistress dared to show up to his funeral, wearing the royal colors he claimed as his. My mother was at least brave enough to finally say enough was enough when my father decided to openly embarrass her the day my sister was born. It wasn't easy to get those in charge to grant her a divorce since it had never been done before. But she never gave up until she was free from the lies and out from under the thumb of my father." He pauses before he says more.

"I don't want that, Larkin. I would rather be the first unwed king than live a life of lies. At thirty I know my chances of finding love dwindles rapidly, so I guess that's why I agreed to do things their way. Reasoning that perhaps I could learn to love the woman I determined would fit best as my queen and wife. A strong aspiration for intimacy can make a man begin to doubt his own beliefs and force him to consider options he swore he never would.

"Life has a funny way, sometimes, of rewarding you when you least expect it. God really, I guess should get the credit, not life or fate. Tell me you understand, as I am doing my best to explain it all to you."

I stare at him, not sure I'm ready to acknowledge what is happening between us completely. The last time a man expressed his feeling to me, it all went so very wrong hours later.

Do I believe Antonio is unstable and planning to do something drastic? No, at least not in the same way Randal did. I do suspect he has a plan he is not sharing with me right now.

"Larkin." He rolls his head and lets his eyes find mine.

"Yeah, I get it. So, what's the plan exactly?" I dare to ask, even though I'm not sure I want or am ready to hear it.

His lip raises on one side as he shifts his weight so he is now sitting a little awkwardly. "Last week I sat down with two different groups of women. Invited them to have dinner with me, along with my mother and brothers. They were there for moral support really, but I guess they were also there so I could make a few things clear to everyone we invited as well. I wanted them to see us as a united front, a family that is supportive and wants the best for each member, whatever that may look like. During our time together, two things were made perfectly clear to them.

"First and most important, as far as they were concerned, I had chosen none of them to go any farther in my pursuit for a wife. While I believe they were all very lovely ladies, and one day would make a wonderful wife if the right man came along, they would not be mine. After that, I lost about half of them, and the other half, as I suspected, turned their attention to my brothers. Therefore, I had to break it to them that what I said also went for Esteban and Lorenzo. None of us planned on entertaining any of them in the future with hopes of anything more than a possible friendship.

"The other thing I made clear was that I deceived them all and wanted to clear a few matters up. I told them I was ashamed to have misled them the night of the celebration when I introduced you. In reality, you were just an everyday woman who caught my attention without even trying. Knocked me right off my feet before I even knew what was happening. Then I mentioned that if I were lucky, you'd give me a chance to do the same thing to you."

Tell me how you really feel Antonio, my brain screams as my heart races. Funny thing about it all is I'm not completely freaking out about it, maybe it's because I'm too tired to let my brain process the reality of what he is saying.

I'm not sure how long we sit there in complete silence regarding the other person closely. I know one thing, though; I've only ever felt this comfortable with one other man.

When I yawn, Antonio stands and stops right in front of me. He offers me his hand, and when I take it, he tugs me to my feet. "Time for bed *mi lunita*. My brother has laid out one of his t-shirts in one of the guest rooms."

"I'm staying here tonight? Where will you sleep?" I yawn again.

He leads me to the stairs and guides me up them from behind. "A few rooms down the hall."

"Okay. Why not just go home? Take me home?" I glance over my shoulder.

"Because if we leave now, everyone will wonder where I've been all night. If I take you back to the hotel, they will all question why I'm dropping you off so late, it's nearly three, Larkin. *As paredes têm ouvidos.*" He stops in front of a large door and opens it for me.

I am suddenly reminded of the first time he walked me to a room so I could get some sleep. He kissed me for the very first time then, catching me completely off guard.

"What does that mean?" I know he said that earlier tonight.

"The walls have ears. Something I learned very well growing up in this world. One has to be careful, so those who have it out for you, don't carry ammunition to use against you later." He gently directs me inside.

I grab the door and turn to look at him. "Am I ammunition against you?"

"No. That is not what I meant. But I've done my best to keep matters between the women they have seen me with respectable. It is even more important to me they don't make assumptions where you are concerned. I don't want you to be known as the woman who trapped the king." He winks at me, and I roll my eyes.

"No, we definitely wouldn't want that now, would we? Goodnight, Antonio." I wait for him to lean in and kiss me.

Instead, he takes a step back. "Goodnight, Larkin."

He takes another step back, and I laugh. "What, no kiss?"

"My family jewels kind of don't like it when they get kneed. They are protecting the future heir in there and have advised me to not risk it." He shrugs as he takes another step backward. "Plus, I couldn't find my athletic supporter."

I laugh like I haven't in years. "What if I promise to keep my knees to myself?"

That's all it takes to get him moving in the other direction. He wraps his arms around me and drags me forward to meet his lips.

"I thought you'd never ask," he whispers right before his lips crash against mine.

CHAPTER 16
Larkin

The Royals

I slept better than I have in a very long time. I'd like to blame it on the fact I was just so dang tired, so I had no other choice. And while that probably contributed to my restful night's sleep, it wasn't the only reason.

If you've never slept on really good sheets, I'm guessing the best money can buy, then you've never really slept. Holy crap is all I can say. My parents always bought high thread count sheets for us. When I got my own place I went with jersey, mainly because I liked how soft they were. My jersey sheets will never feel the same again.

I stretch and kick the covers off.

I am wearing the t-shirt that was neatly folded on the bed last night. Again, I'm guessing it is better than the store-bought ones other men wear. This one is gray and soft—so very soft against my skin—with a little embroidered bird just to the left. I've never seen it before, but I feel I should probably know what the GA inside the bird stands for. So, I start naming all the famous fashion designers in my head, three in, and the name Armani flashes across my brain. I then assume that this undershirt costs as much as my entire outfit I had on yesterday.

Placing my feet on the soft plush rug, I wiggle my toes and then bend down to scratch an itch on my ankle.

"Nice knickers." I hear a male voice behind me declare.

I rise so fast I end up knocking the back of my head against the side table and tumbling back onto the bed. My throbbing head has me forgetting the reason I reacted so quickly.

I reach back and rub it, and notice Antonio seated on the cushioned bench attached to the window. He is sitting there sipping on a steaming mug of coffee, dressed in jeans and a dark t-shirt. Looking like a dream more than a king.

"What are you doing in here?" I whisper at the upside-down vision of him.

He points to the steaming mug on the silver tray next to him. "Thought you might like some coffee."

I sit up and yank the covers over my bare legs. "Give it to me."

He sets his down and stands, before he moseys my way. "I tried to call you, but it went straight to voicemail. Guessing your phone ran out of battery sometime during the night. Sugar? Cream?"

"No. Black is fine." I want to retrieve my phone. It is next to the window inside my leather satchel, but I don't dare move. "Could you also grab my phone? It's in the outside pocket."

Antonio bends down and grabs it for me. He brings both with him as he advances the few feet toward the bed. Then he sets both on the side table and sits down on the edge of the bed. "Good morning. So, if I kiss you..."

"Oh, no. No, you are not kissing me." I squeal when he pounces like a predatory tiger on the hunt. "Stop!"

He catches me and I find myself on my back with him hovering over me. "I am. I've been watching you sleep for the last fifteen minutes."

Breathless at the sight of him above me, I quickly respond. "Why didn't you just wake me?"

Staring directly into my eyes, he doesn't give me a chance to deny him. His lips drop to mine, where he kisses me hard. Although there is no breaching of his tongue, it is still a very telling kiss. After a bit, he rolls off of me and lays flat on his back, gawking up at the ceiling as if seeking to recover.

I get it. That is pretty much how I feel every time his lips connect with mine. And if I didn't need to pee so badly, I'd have stayed there with him.

As soon as I start to sneak out of the bed, he snags my arm. "Stay."

"I need to use the bathroom," I tell him as I tug on my arm so he will release it.

"Pee and then hurry back." He orders with a playfulness to his voice.

I do my business and hurry back after I snag the terry-cloth robe that was hanging in the bathroom. One look at my reflection in the mirror told me why he commented on my panties, or knickers, as he put it. I was relieved to see I at least had on a pair that covered me mostly, although they are lace, so I'm sure he enjoyed that.

Antonio is completely stretched out on the bed when I return. His bare feet are crossed and his arms are tucked firmly behind his neck, making his t-shirt tight against his torso. Which is when I notice it is lifted just enough on one side to reveal his skin and the dark hair that lightly covers his stomach.

Not that I am staring or anything. But if I were, I'd regard the dips in his abs, along with the way his hipbone forms half a vee. Maybe even the three moles circling his navel, right above the thick dark line of hair that disappears behind his Balenciaga labeled waistband. I've never even heard of that brand of underwear, so that probably means they are very high end.

"Larkin, are you even listening to me?" Antonio's voice finally breaks past the fog clouding my brain. "What are you staring at?"

I know I blush. I can feel my face heat instantly, but that doesn't mean I am going to just admit I was checking out the five inches of exposed flesh he was displaying. I go for option number two and lie while I blink back the image burned in my mind.

"I was just thinking I have so much to do that I should be going. Do you think someone could run me by my hotel so I can shower and change? What time is it, anyway?" I notice there are no clocks around and my phone is on the other side of the bed. My guess is it is around seven, maybe eight.

"Ten-thirty, last time I checked." He says it so casually I almost miss the fact that I have never in my life slept past eight. "Probably close to eleven now, is my guess, though."

I jump straight up off the bed and start frantically searching for the pantsuit I had on yesterday. Who cares if anyone realizes I wore it yesterday? Which I doubt they will, since I own several black ones that are only slightly different.

"Where the heck are my clothes?" I thought I folded them and put them on the chair in the corner, except they weren't there.

"I sent them with Lorenzo so they could be dry cleaned. He called his staff this morning and directed them to not bother coming in. Since that is nothing new for him, they are all enjoying a day off on his dime. Sit back down so we can talk." He hasn't moved and I cannot help but drink in how lovely he looks.

There is nothing I'd rather do than... never mind. I will not allow my brain to veer that far off track.

"I need clothes, Antonio. I have to get to work. Timothy and Natalie are coming in later today. Scratch that, they will be here at one. Since I missed my conference call with her last night, I need to make sure I'm prepared to discuss it all when she gets here."

I open drawers frantically, searching for anything I can slip on. "Do you people not believe in keeping extra clothes in the house?"

That has Antonio chuckling and I can't help whirling around so I can glare at him. Which you may have figured out was a huge mistake, because dang it, now his shirt is even higher than before and he has risen to his elbows. Those abs that I was studying before are scrunched up and making my mouth water. I may or may not lick my lips and swallow hard.

"We rarely invite women to sleep over, so no, we don't keep extra clothing suitable for your type around. Which I would think would make you happy?" He sits all the way up, making my obsession disappear.

"This isn't your home, so why would I care?" I mean that sincerely.

If I were at his place and he had women's clothing stashed away, I'd probably not like it. This is his youngest brother's home, and while I find that refreshing, right now it would sure be handy if he were a planner and all. Kept an extra pair of women's stretchy pants and a t-shirt around just in case some chick passed out on him while they were on a date.

Hey, it can happen.

"So, could you tell him he needs to rectify that? I mean, because you just never know when an extra pair of yoga pants and a t-shirt might come in handy. Just saying." I drop into the chair and pout. "So, now what?"

Antonio leaps to his feet. I don't miss the pep in his step as he passes me and heads for the closet. When he returns, he has a black bag in his hand and hands it to me.

I take one look at it and immediately know where it is from. I've shopped at Sax a few times in Chicago. Mostly hit the clearance section to save a few bucks. Although I don't suppose whatever is inside was on clearance or sale.

Inside is a set of tan underwear and a white camisole. Both look expensive, but not nearly as expensive as the pantsuit he returns with that is dark gray with faint pinstripes. Or the shoes dangling from his fingers that I know are Armani, because I can read the name scribbled in gold across the inside heel.

"You bought this? When?" I stare at the extremely well-made suit. "Why?"

He laughs as he lays it across the bed. "Well, most importantly because I didn't think letting you leave my brother's house in only that would be acceptable. And the other reason is because I wanted to. I had Helena pick it out for me and bring it by. She was about to let me have it when she thought I'd done something that was out of character for me. That is until she walked in here and realized I was actually just doing my gentlemanly duty and rescuing sleepy beauty."

I want to scold him for letting someone witness me like this. I'm not sure I like anyone knowing we spent the night together. I mean, I know nothing happened. He knows, as does his brother, that it was all a very innocent affair. But if someone else were to hear I spent the night at Prince Lorenzo's place with his brother, the king, we know what others will think. If I heard that story, I'd think it too. So, the fewer people who know, the better, right?

"I'll let you get ready. She also picked up some toiletries for you and put them in the bathroom. I had no idea what to even ask her to bring, so I just left that up to her. I'll meet you downstairs when you are done." He heads for the door. "Oh, and I'll keep in mind next time to tell her you like lacy knickers."

If I had anything in my hand to throw at him, I would, but I don't. "You should not know what my knickers look like for a very long time. Now get out of here before I hurl something at that royal head of yours."

"At least we are in agreement that there will be a day that I should." He shouts over his shoulder. "Not sure we agree on the timeline, but we will discuss that another time."

The door closes and I drop to the bed. What just happened?

The first thing I do while I am trying to figure that out, is retrieve my phone. Sure enough, it is dead to the world, so I grab my charger and plug it in. While it is charging, I decide to take a quick shower. Lucky for me, I have all kinds of hair trinkets in my leather satchel. I tend to mess with my hair a lot during the day, depending on what I am doing. So, I secure it high on my head and opt not to wash it this morning.

After my shower—that was absolutely perfect, I didn't even have to wait for the water to heat—I find the makeup bag Helen left me. I am surprised to find exactly what I need, all the way down to my signature red lipstick. Once my face has been covered the way I prefer, I try hard not to think about how Antonio saw it bare. I wear more on the days I dress for the office than I do when I head out to the field. It's not like I care about being completely put together all the time. But only a few people have seen me barefaced. My complexion is very pale, so I like adding some color. With no makeup on, I look way different. I have no pigment to my cheeks, lips, or eyelashes. So even on the days when I'm not going anywhere, I add mascara, a light dusting of blush to my cheeks, along with some color to my lips. I'm no Gwyneth Paltrow, who is just naturally beautiful, but I also don't think I'd scare little children and make them go screaming because they saw a ghost. It sure didn't seem to frighten Antonio off, so I guess that means something, right?

Once my hair is brushed, braided at the base, and tied off, I decide I don't look like I just spent the night with some hot guy. I've never performed the walk of shame and I didn't expect the first time I'd be doing it would be with a man who put the title King before his actual name.

It hits me as I descend the stairs he led me up last night and I spot him standing in the kitchen. He is buttering a piece of toast, whistling of all things. As soon as he notices me, the reality of everything seems to slam to the forefront of my mind. I have to grab the railing so I don't tumble down the last few steps.

Suddenly it's like I realize two things at once.

First would be, the man looking so normal right now, is not normal at all. He is a very powerful man and will continue to be a powerful man for years to come. He runs a freaking country, and the good of that country rests on his shoulders. Unlike other leaders around the world, his reign only ends when he says it ends, and then passes the torch down to his successor, preferably his firstborn. Until that time comes, he is a leader first and foremost, a king. He is King Antonio of Hermosa Islas, and it is one of the most sacred and ordained jobs one can hold.

This is when the other reality of this situation has me wanting to throw up. Not because I am sick to my stomach about it, like it is the most awful thing anyone could bestow on me. That isn't it at all. It's that he wants me. The girl from America who only speaks one language and freaks out at the thought of being put on display. The one who suffers from anxiety and rambles when the stress of it all gets to her, making her say all kinds of crazy things. The girl who prefers the background rather than the spotlight.

Yeah, reality sometimes sucks. I know deep down inside of me that this is by far the dumbest thing I have ever done before. That I am going to end up in the nuthouse before it's all said and done. But one look at him standing there—and while I am scared completely out of my mind —I know there is no way I can walk away now. I'm going to have to suck it up and pray God knows what he is doing. Because if all goes as well as we both hope it will go, then that means I could actually become queen.

Mind about to explode in five... four... three... two... one.

CHAPTER 17
Antonio

The Royals

W hen I glance up, I find Larkin frozen on the stairs, staring at me. I know something is going on with her because she has that deer in the headlights expression on her face. So, I put down my knife and head her way.

To say I am surprised at what happens next would be an understatement. When I approach her, she drops her leather satchel and leaps at me. I have to be quick so I can catch her before she ends up knocking us both on our butts. Her arms wrap around my neck as her mouth attacks mine. It's the first time since this thing between us started she has made the first move. Can't say I hate it, because I don't. I like it very much, in fact. Therefore, I hold her dangling body against mine and kiss her however she decides she wants me to kiss her.

When she pulls back, she laughs. "Oh. I guess I should have thought about that before I attacked you."

I lean in and rub my nose against hers. "No thinking required whenever you want to do that. Are you hungry? I made toast."

"Toast?" She squints her eyes. "Tell me something, Antonio. Is toast the only food you can make?"

"No!" I protest as I set her back down on her feet and lead her to the kitchen. "I can also make peanut butter and jelly, any type of meat sandwich you may crave, box macaroni and cheese with hotdogs, and frozen pizza. There are probably a few more items in there. Like frozen waffles. I make a very mean frozen waffle; ask Isabel if you don't believe me. We've had frozen waffles for dinner before with a side of that pre-cooked sausage you throw in the microwave."

She settles in one of my brother's stools and grabs the fresh mug of coffee I made for her. "So, what you are saying is that if I want a proper meal, then I am the one who is going to have to cook. Otherwise, it will be frozen dinners or prepackaged meals."

I slide the plate of toast and jam in front of her. "Not at all. If you require a proper meal, there are plenty of chefs at the palace who would be more than happy to cook one for you."

She takes a bite of her toast and makes this crazy face. "Best toast I have ever tasted. Thank you."

I roll my eyes and try to ignore her. "So, you know how to cook?"

Larkin waits for me to take the spot next to her and then picks up the napkin to wipe off my lips. "Red lipstick doesn't look as good on you. Yes, I can cook. How good I can cook, I guess you will have to wait and see. I've never poisoned anyone yet."

"That's good to know. Poisoning a king is no joking matter. It's a crime that comes with a very severe sentence." I know she is teasing, but after what happened to my father, that one isn't as funny to me. "Isabel's mother poisoned my father, and had she not taken her own life, it would have been taken for her."

She chokes on her coffee and coughs several times. "I was kidding, by the way. That being said, I realize after something like that happens, the joke gets lost in the reality of the situation. I promise to not poison you ever, so maybe to be safe we should let your trained staff cook."

A smile creeps across my face as I shake my head nonchalantly. "Oh, no. You are not getting out of that so easily. You'll just have to make sure to be careful and taste all the food first. Plus, I've never had a woman cook for me before. I think I might enjoy watching you."

She shoves the last of her toast in her mouth. "There will be no watching. If you are in my kitchen, then you are required to help. Otherwise, you are not allowed in it."

I can't help but be a smart aleck about her suggestion. "But it will most likely be my kitchen you cook in. Therefore, I can watch."

"We shall see." She finishes her coffee and looks at the clock on the stove. "I need to get going. I don't even want to think about the all comments I am going to get when I show up this late."

"I guess it's a good thing I called this morning, then, and told them we had a meeting. That I wanted to discuss your ideas for Maximiliano Chateau." I offer her more coffee, but she declines.

"But we don't have a meeting. And Cameron, Bradley, and Chandler were there last night when you came to collect me. You don't think they're going to be suspicious and assume a few things?" Larkin rests her head on her hand propped against the counter. "I thought that was the whole reason we came here instead of going to your place."

I reach behind me and grab my laptop. Since I am playing hooky this morning, I thought I'd look over a few matters while she rested up. I pop it open and click on a new document, then begin typing.

"So, Miss Cross, tell me what are some of the ideas you have for my personal property in Homero. It has forever been a favorite of mine. I always envisioned it as a nice place to raise a family. Lots of land for little ones to roam and run off all that extra energy they seem to possess."

"A family home? I thought the king's home was here in Aragon." She stands and retrieves her bag. "I assumed it was strictly a restoration."

"I'm open to suggestions. Lately, I've had this wild thought probing my brain that it might make a nice wedding present." I see her pause and swallow hard. "Do you agree?"

"I don't have an opinion on the subject." She pulls a folder out and opens it.

"Is it something maybe you'd like?" I stop typing and turn to look at her.

Larkin has started frenziedly flipping through her detailed drawings. I'm pretty sure she's not searching for something she wants to show me. I get the impression she's not comfortable with where this conversation is heading.

"Larkin." I reach over to stop her. "Talk to me."

"I can't talk about this. I'm not even close to being ready to discuss something that huge." Her eyes slowly lift to meet mine, and I can perceive how unnerved she is right now. "I need time to wrap my mind around all this. I already had one epiphany today about how my life was about to change. I don't think I could handle another one at the moment. I need my wits to get me through later today. If you start bringing up," she blinks, "wedding gifts... I'm going to lose my handle on my sanity."

"And what epiphany did you have earlier?" I scoot my stool closer to hers.

"I thought we were going to discuss Maximiliano Chateau?" Her eyes don't leave mine, and I don't dare shift mine off hers.

"Sure. If you don't want to tell me, we can definitely do that." I hook my foot around one leg of her stool and tug it toward me. "My home is wherever I decide it will be. Each property is prepared to accommodate the needs the monarch on the throne requires.

"Aragon Palace is the capital because my father named it the capital. Before then, it was Juliana Castile, the property my grandfather, King Esteban, believed was the most beautiful of the three. Queen Victoria ruled from Fort Serna. Her husband was a commander in the Royal Navy, so she wanted him to be able to be close to his post. King Francisco built his own, De la Peña Citadel. He loved the Prieto countryside, hence the reason he constructed a home there, where he remained long past his reign as king.

"I have only remained in Aragon Palace for a few reasons. One being that it was where my father ruled and I had no desire to pack it all up and move when I first took over. I also had Isabel to consider. It was hard enough for the two of us those first few years. I didn't want to simply move her out of the only home she ever knew. She loves Maximiliano Chateau as much as I do. Talks about acquiring some horses she can train and ride. We talked about it a lot that week she spent with me in Chicago."

"I believe the chateau has a lot of potential. The property has been neglected for way too long, so we will definitely need to get an engineer out there first thing to determine if the foundation is stable. Once we have that taken care of, then we can discuss exactly what you want. Isabel, even, if you are all right with that. Knowing her, she has quite a few ideas I am sure we can incorporate into my designs. Any questions?" Larkin's professional response does not go unnoted.

"I have several actually." I glance down at the drawings she hasn't shown me yet. "Are those yours? Your vision?"

She peeks down at the first one visible to me. It's the front view of the chateau.

What I have always admired about the structure of the chateau is its artful design. An English noble built it, so it definitely has the appearance of a castle, yet it doesn't scream that it is a castle. The entry is tall and rectangular with two-cylinder-shaped towers. The rest of the structure looks more like a traditional manor, with its rectangular shape and steep roof. On the west end is a tower that stands taller than all the rest, with windows circling it all the way up. She has sketched a very accurate three-dimensional perspective of it, and I can't wait to see all the others.

"They're nothing." Larkin starts to pack them. "I was just doodling out some ideas."

I snatch the folder from her hand and open it before she can prevent me. Each one has been freehanded with very specific details. There is one on each side and the back. One that opens the home up so you can picture the inside, each floor, including the cellar.

My favorite though is the last one. It's only of the tower and her obvious proposal on what we should do with this large open space. She has turned it into a three-story library, with a spiral staircase erected in the center so a person can access each floor easily. A large desk is positioned on the bottom floor, a desk fit for a king, I imagine, by the design of the room. It is an office area much like the one I have at the palace, except way better. The second floor is lined with bookshelves that go from floor to ceiling, with two large window seats that are very inviting. The third floor is what catches my attention, though. There is an architect's desk placed against one wall between two windows where the light is good—two desk, to be exact, on opposite ends. Amid the two is a sitting area that has a couch and chaise, smaller bookshelves, and a child-size desk. Across the way is an easel that allows the artist to look out over the property for inspiration. A workable office for my *dama*, an area all her own, where she can work on her designs or art whenever she desires. I don't miss how it is as detailed as all the rest, leaving nothing out, not even the children's area.

I must stare at it for too long, because Larkin seems to misunderstand what I am thinking. She gathers them all up in one big swish and shoves them back inside the folder. Shifting her weight, she tries to escape off the opposite side of her stool.

"Hold up there. Give those back so I can study them again." I seize her by the elbow. "Those are not doodling. That is hours of work, outstanding work."

"They are doodles. I only started them once I got assigned the property a little over a week ago." She won't turn to look at me. "I just drew whatever popped into my mind. You weren't meant to see them at all. I doodle like that when I need a release. You shouldn't read anything into it."

No way am I letting her get away with that. I realize she may not be ready to discuss in detail what is transpiring between us yet. That she needs some time while we do this dating stuff first, really get to know each other. I accept it, I do. However, that doesn't mean I will not discuss details that are difficult for her right now, because this tells me exactly where her mind has been.

"Did you *doodle* the library before or after I stopped by your office?" I reach for the folder and tug it gently from her hand.

"Does it matter?" Larkin's irritation with me right now only makes me push harder.

"Answer me. Before or after?" I leave no room for her to think I will accept anything but the truth.

Shaking my hold off of her, she twists her body back around so she can stare at the sketch I have pulled out again. This time I watch her as she studies it. I can distinctly grasp her going over all the little details in her mind, picturing the space in that beautiful brain of hers.

"I started with the first-floor office first. Worked my way up. Left the third floor empty." Okay, so I don't get a straightforward answer from her.

"When did you add all that to the third floor? I love it, by the way. I never could figure out what to do with the tower. This is perfect and I want you to build it exactly like you have it drawn out."

I move closer and wrap my arm around her waist so I can lean in and whisper in her ear. "I want it all, Larkin, including the studio you have designed for yourself. Visions of you sitting at one of those desks, doodling while I watch secretly from behind, are very vivid. I imagine sneaking up behind you because you are so focused you don't hear me. Startling you when I kiss the crook of your neck. Hoping to coerce you back into bed with me, because it's gotten late and you seem to have forgotten all about me. Removing the pencil from your hand when you stop and then spinning you around in your chair so I can kiss your mouth. Lifting you in my arms, intending to carry you down the hall to our bedroom, but having to stop because I can't wait one second longer to take you. So instead, I strip you of your clothing, take you first against the wall next to the easel where a canvas stands drying. I don't know what is painted on it, but whatever it is, I know I will hang it in our home so I can appreciate how talented you are. Your cries, mixed with my groans, echo off the walls, and I have never been more grateful that you soundproofed the library so we don't wake the entire house. So, now tell me, when did you add all that to the third floor?"

"I um... okay... well... it sort of came to me..." A stuttering Larkin is a wonderful sight.

"Tell me," I whisper in her ear. "Tell me, *mi lunita*."

"Two days ago. I needed to clear my mind after a long meeting with Chandler. I sat down and began working on this again. It just sort of spilled out of me, and at first, I didn't even stop to think about it. When I was done, I realized my mistake and almost threw it away."

She takes a deep breath. "Soundproof? Probably not a terrible suggestion, since I imagine the acoustics in that space would most certainly travel down the long corridors. I think I can figure out a way to add that to the design. Of course, until I see the space with my own eyes, measure it, evaluate the structure, only then will I be able to determine if this is actually doable. We may have to tweak a few specifics in the final draft. You should understand."

A low rumble builds in my chest as I listen to her do her best to avoid thinking about what I dared to reveal. I'm not one to usually discuss such matters so brazenly like that. It's never happened to me before, honestly. I'm not sure why I went there this time, but now that I have, it's all I can picture when I look at her sketch. Probably the reason I spin her around and kiss the ever-living daylights out of her until I hear someone clear his throat.

"Sorry to interrupt, Your Majesty." Isaac is standing right outside the kitchen in the foyer. "I believe you said we needed to leave by one. It's ten till now, sir. We are ready whenever you are."

"Thank you, Isaac." I guess all good things eventually have to end. "Shall we, Miss Cross? I believe you have a meeting to get to."

Larkin twirls around quickly and gathers her things. "One, I am so not prepared for thanks to you."

"You are well prepared for it, I'm sure. Come on. Stressing about it will do you no good. What could possibly go wrong? It's not like they will fire you."

Larkin glares at me. "They could if they wanted to."

"Firing the one person in their company who has worked her tail off for them these last several weeks would be bad business. Firing my girlfriend would be reckless and could make their jobs even harder."

She pauses just before we get to the front door where Isaac and his team are waiting. "Your girlfriend?"

"My girlfriend," I say with confidence.

A sly, little smirk appears. "Very sure of yourself, aren't you, Antonio? Think you can say all that stuff you did earlier and suddenly, I will decide to be your girlfriend. Don't I get a say about if I want to be your girlfriend?"

"No," I boldly convey and then shove her toward the door. "You Larkin Moon Cross are officially my girlfriend. We both know it's what you want."

Right before she gets in the car, she spins. "One condition."

"You and your conditions." I roll my eyes. "Please enlighten me, Miss Cross. What is your condition?"

She gets up on her tiptoes and motions for me to lean closer. "That you promise to do all that, exactly the way you described it earlier, once I construct your library."

I growl and look around to see if someone has noticed us yet. "Done. Although I have a condition of my own now as well."

"Okay, I'll bite." She giggles. "Please enlighten me, sir. What is your condition?"

"That when I ask you to marry me, you say yes."

She lowers herself, stunned, and shakes her head slowly. "What?"

"You heard me. I'm not asking yet, Larkin. I said when I do that must be your response. Otherwise, I can't promise to fulfill your request." I grab her chin. "Breathe, love. We have time still before I go about doing such a thing. I have to plan it out, of course, which means I will need to get to know you well enough to understand what you'd like. So, are we in agreement?"

"Yes," she whispers. "To being your girlfriend."

I kiss her lips softly as I mutter, "Glad you made that clear."

CHAPTER 18
Antonio

The Royals

I t's nearly seven in the evening and I am about to call it a day. Not because I don't have a ton of work left in my inbox begging for my attention. There is always something in that box marked urgent. I decided if it were actually urgent Alejandro would have brought it to my attention.

I grab my mail, leather bag, and phone. Like every other working man or woman out there does when they leave the office, I'm no different, really.

Alejandro and Triana are discussing something at her desk. I can't distinguish if it is personal or business. What I can identify is that they are in disagreement and neither aware I am even there.

"Lover's quarrel?" I joke as I step up to her desk.

Alejandro is sitting on the opposite edge facing his wife. "Tell him or I will."

"Tell me what?"

If a look could dismember a man, the one Triana shoots her husband's direction would have done just that. "Ale is only being his typical domineering self and thinks he knows better than I do. I'm fine, just a little tired, that's all."

"Then go home and get some rest. I'm finished for the day."

A shake of his head expresses he either doesn't agree with his wife or he's irritated with me. "She's pregnant. Fourteen weeks. She's not just tired. She's exhausted. I barely get her home and fed before she's off to bed. My suggestion, which I have been told is ludicrous, is to hire her an assistant who can stay late or come in early when needed. I told my dear wife that it would be pertinent to train this person properly beforehand since she will accept the entire twenty-four weeks offered her."

"Twelve. I only get a full salary if I take twelve. So, it will be only twelve, my love. I've told you this, multiple times. You will only take the mandatory fourteen days because we both know how much the king counts on both of us. I told you I'd train someone, I talked to HR today, and they assured me they have it taken care of. My replacement will be here next week. As far as the rest of what you have suggested, it is over the top and unnecessary, every pregnant woman out there gets tired."

"And most of them don't put in twelve to fourteen hour days," he retorts. "Ten at the most is all I am asking for Triana."

"I agree with Alejandro."

"Of course you do, because you have a penis," she barks and then quickly apologizes. "Oh, Your Majesty, please forgive me. I tend to blurt things out like that lately. My usual filter seems to have dissolved with all the pregnancy hormones. I told Governor Colon off this morning when he demanded to know where you were and wanted me to tell him why he was being rescheduled last minute."

"Penis or not, I still agree with him," I inform her through a laugh. "And Aaron can piss off. Just last week he took a personal day, which is the reason he was on my docket today."

"That's what I reminded him of, although he didn't take my reminder so well. I see he joined Governors Hanson and Lyles this afternoon. Bet that was an interesting meeting." My usual non-opinionated secretary gives me hers. "Those men all need to grow up and do the jobs the people have elected them to do. Stop worrying about your private life. They just don't like the fact you may find something they never will.

"All this marrying for something other than love is downright stupid. Why would anyone choose to get married to someone they don't love? I've always thought it quite depressing. No wonder they all wear a sour face and walk around like they have a stick up their backside. Marriage is hard enough as it is. You are allowing someone into your personal life to see all those faults you keep hidden from the rest of the world. I can't imagine allowing someone in like that, let alone sleeping next to someone who I didn't love and trust. When I go home, I want to relax and not have to worry about saying or doing something that will be used against me later.

"So, I commend you for telling them to shove it and rocking the boat a bit. Show them all that even a king can discover love and happiness if he is just willing to wait for it."

My eyes catch Alejandro's, and I notice something in his that makes me truly admire him. He doesn't at all seem bothered by her little rant. Instead, he shrugs in a way that tells me he agrees. Then he turns to face his wife and smiles, truly smiles.

I've seen other men smile like that when they look at their wives or girlfriends. Of course, none of them are a part of my world, men in my world never truly smile.

I want that.

"Thank you, Triana. So, now about this other matter." I make my voice stern but not too stern. "No more early mornings. You are not to get here before eight, no exceptions. Your day ends promptly at six. If by chance you can get out of here before, great. But if I see you here after six, I won't be happy about it. You will also take the full twenty-four weeks offered you at full pay. And your husband will take those fourteen days like you so pointed out, and when he returns, he will shorten his hours. Kids are only little once, so it is important you are both around to enjoy them. I realize it will take us all time getting used to this, but there is no reason we cannot get out of here most days before the sun goes down."

My text tone sounds on my personal phone. Only a few people have that number, which means whoever it is has to be someone important to me. So, I pull it from my pocket and smile.

LARKIN: So how do we do this exactly?

"I need to take this," I tell them as I stand. "See you all in the morning."

> ME: Do what exactly?

LARKIN: This. You. Me. Us.

> ME: What are you really asking me?

LARKIN: I'm heading home. Is it home when it's a hotel room?

LARKIN: I bought a car today. So, I was thinking of driving over, but then there is the fact that you live in the palace thing. I mean, can I do that? Is that okay? Can I, as your girlfriend, just stop by?

LARKIN: Never mind. Forget it.

> ME: Larkin. Yes.

LARKIN: Yes?

> ME: Yes, to all three questions.

LARKIN: So, I give my name to the guards and they will just let me in?

> ME: Yes.

LARKIN: Okay then. So, have you eaten?

> ME: No. Helena, I'm sure, has dinner waiting. There will be plenty.

LARKIN: Oh. Yes, Helena. I forgot about her. Is it okay I come over? I mean, I don't want to intrude or break up your routine with Isabel.

> ME: I want you here. I'll be waiting.

LARKIN: Okay. So, I'll be there in twenty, then.

That gives me more than enough time to change into something more comfortable and drop my stuff off. While I'm there, I inform Helena that we will have company for dinner. The question in her eyes doesn't go unnoticed, even though she tries very hard to conceal it. I get why she is concerned with my decision to invite a woman to my personal quarters.

"Don't look so concerned, Helena. This one is different," I assure her. "Maybe even the one."

"And what do they all have to say about that?" She reaches up and pats my face. "I just worry, that's all. I've known you since the day your mother informed us about fulfilling her duty. I've had the pleasure of watching you grow from a young prince into a powerful king. If she is the one, then fight for her, just make sure she is worth the fight you are about to embark upon."

Her wisdom in all matters is one reason I brought her into my personal residence. She is like a second mother to me and never afraid to voice her opinion. I don't worry about her reporting back to those who feel it is their entitlement to know my whereabouts at all times and want to know how I spend my free time.

I call down to the gate and instruct them to let Larkin through security. Then I order them to add her to the permanent list of those who are allowed access, even access through my private entrance. Make sure that once she enters the main gates, they direct her toward that entrance. Again, I hear a question there, although they don't dare ask it.

As soon as I change into jeans and a t-shirt, I head for my private foyer. There is no way to avoid the palace staff running around at all hours. Most of the cleaning happens when there are fewer people around for them to disturb. The floors, chandeliers, priceless art, and décor are cleaned daily to ensure pristine conditions at all times. Nights are the best time to accomplish most of it.

"Do you need something, Your Majesty? Going out?" A housekeeper approaches me on my way to the door. "They did not inform me you were leaving. I'm sorry for not being prepared, sir."

"I'm not leaving. I have a guest coming," I enlighten her as I continue walking. "Go back to whatever it is you were doing, I've got this."

"As you wish." She nods and hurries off.

I am a nervous ball of energy. Why am I so nervous? I've dated lots of women over the years. Not once have I gotten nervous, not once. But tonight, my hands are sweaty, my pulse is elevated, and I can't stop pacing the stone path down to the driveway.

A light blue Volkswagen slowly makes its way in my direction. It comes to a stop, so I reach out and open the driver's side door. A smiling face peers up at me, and I can tell she is just as nervous about this as me.

"Hi." Her voice is soft. "I think your guards at both gates were unsure about letting me through. They seemed hesitant and checked my ID twice at each gate."

"They'll get accustomed to it. Get to know you quite well and eventually wave you through. I will have Triana print you a badge that gives you full access. That should make it easier." I take her hand to help her climb out.

"A badge? What will it say exactly? King's girlfriend with my picture proudly displayed above it?" she asks as she climbs out.

I tug her away from the door as soon as she is clear so I can shut it. "Do you need anything inside?"

"My bag, maybe. It has my phone and some personal stuff inside. Not sure I want to leave that all here for just anyone to rummage through. It looks like a rather tough neighborhood."

"The toughest," I alert her as I gather her in my arms. "I've missed you."

"I've missed you as well," she tells me as I lean down and kiss her.

When I have properly said hello, I grab her leather satchel and toss it over my shoulder. Then I seize her hand in mine and escort her past all the curious eyes and whispers. Squeeze it slightly, even when I feel her tense up.

"You'll have to forgive them. They aren't used to me escorting such a beautiful woman to my quarters. Again, they will get accustomed to this and you," I express as I open the door to my private residence.

"So, this is where you live?" Larkin glances around.

"This is my humble abode. It's not much, but it's a dry place to lay my head at night." I lead her through the large entry and into the living area.

"Perhaps we should put a rush on Maximiliano Chateau since it is obvious these are such seedy living conditions." Larkin circles as she takes it all in. "Seriously, how do you stand it?"

"Don't encourage him." Helena's voice comes from behind us. "He really does not need any. I'm Helena, and you must be Miss Cross."

"I am. I hope I didn't put any added stress on you by just inviting myself over."

Helena's eyes find mine and I can see right away she likes Larkin. "Not at all, miss. Can I offer you a drink?"

"Larkin doesn't drink." I put a hand on her back. "So tonight, let's all have milk and water with our meal. Is that okay with you, Larkin?"

"Yes, that's fine."

"Larkin!" A loud shriek comes from the front entry as Isabel runs toward us. She is dressed in her *fútbol* practice uniform, and Beatriz is right behind her.

"Cleats, Isabel," I remind her before she steps onto the carpeted area.

"Sorry." She drops to the floor and yanks them off without untying them. "I didn't know you were coming for *cena*. Tonight, we are having Catalan Chicken. Do you like Catalan Chicken, Larkin? Helena's is the best."

"I've never had it before, but I'm sure I'll like it," Larkin informs her.

"Go wash up so we can eat," I instruct my sister. "I'm sure you are hungry after running all around on the field. I know I am hungry."

Isabel runs off to the small bathroom just off the kitchen. "Do you like *fútbol*, Larkin? I have a game tomorrow night. Will you come and watch me? I am very good."

"Isabel. *Apresse se para que possamos comer.*" I holler after her to hurry up as I lead Larkin to the dining area.

"What does that mean?" She asks me as we walk that way.

"*Pare de ser tão mandona. Larkin é a sua namorada? Você a beija? Você a ama? Quer se casar com ela?*" The brat shows off her fluency in Portuguese. Calling me a bossy brother. Asking me if Larkin is my girlfriend. Teasing me about wanting to kiss her, falling in love, and then marring her. I know I am probably blushing.

"Elle l'est. Je pense que c'est le peux. C'est le plan." (*She is. I think I may. That is the plan.*) I reply in French just to determine how well my sister is doing with those lessons.

"*Mon frère, le roi, a finalement perdu son coeur au profit d'une femme. Ne le gâchez pas parce que je l'aime.*" Isabel sticks out her tongue and then giggles as she joins us. Again, teasing me about losing my heart and warning me to not screw it all up.

"Enough you two," Helena scolds us. "Larkin, please excuse them. They are very much brother and sister and often act out."

I take my seat next to hers and grab her hand. "Shall we give God grace?"

I do the honors and make sure to keep it in English. When I am done, Helena serves us. Once we all have our food, she grabs her empty plate and stands.

"Where are you going?" I ask her. "Sit."

"I'm sure you all would be more comfortable talking without me. I will eat with Beatriz tonight in her quarters. Leave it all and I'll be back to put Isabel to bed and clean up. Enjoy." Helena is gone quickly.

"Sorry about all that earlier. We aren't used to having someone around who doesn't speak both Spanish and Portuguese. They were both taught to us not long after we began speaking. English is the primary language spoken in Hermosa Islas, the others are very common and often mixed in regularly during conversations," I explain.

"Why English? Wasn't it a Spanish noble who settled in Hermosa Islas first?"

Her knowledge about that surprises me, and I guess it shows.

"What? I've done my research. Partly for my work. I need to understand the culture so I can do a better job with my designs."

"And the other reason?" I encourage her to share.

She glances over at Isabel, who is studying us very carefully. "At the time, that was my only reason. So, tell me why English."

Isabel answers for me. "King Francisco Eduardo Aragon fell in love with a young English noblewoman after her family abandoned her when she refused to get back on the boat heading to America. The story says that he found her crying in the streets, begging for food and shelter. Her long red hair and pale skin stood out, and he instantly was attracted to her. Ordered her to be brought to the palace where she would remain. He learned English, even forced his staff to learn English. And when the queen died after giving birth to his second child, he married her. He is the first king believed to have ever married for love. His gift to her as his new queen was to make English the official language and require everyone to learn and speak it fluently. The king only spoke English from that point on."

Larkin raises her eyebrows. "He moved her into the palace? So that means she was his..." She leaves it as an open-ended question.

Isabel whispers. "Mistress? Yes. Whatever that means."

I'm relieved to learn she is still innocent in matters concerning subjects like that. Although, I don't believe she would be if my father were still alive. She'd know exactly what a mistress was. I know I did by her age.

"I think it means he loved her but wasn't supposed to love her since he already had a wife." She continues to share her philosophy. "Which is why I believe no one should be forced to marry someone they don't love. Do you agree, Larkin? When you finally marry, will it be for love?"

"It will," Larkin answers quickly. "So now everyone learns English, Spanish, and Portuguese? Don't you find that confusing?"

We both shrug.

"I never really thought much about it. My mother would speak all three to us. She'd say something in English, then repeat it in Spanish or Portuguese. In school, most of us also learn French, since a large number of our citizens have a lineage that can be traced back to them. Two of our kings married French noblewomen who brought several servants with them. They often married locals and eventually became citizens. I think once you learn one language, it's easier to pick up another. I am fluent in all three as well as Italian and Latin.

"*Tu, mi lunita sei la luce che riempie le mie tenebre.* You, *mi lunita* are the light that fills my darkness. *La luce che non conoscevo era là fuori finché non l'ho vista.* The light I never knew was out there until I caught sight of it. *La mia luce che rimarrà con me sempre e per sempre.* My light that will remain with me always and forever."

"Who knew my brother, who is often called the Blind King, could be so romantic. May I please be dismissed? I need to shower before bed and finish my homework." Isabel sighs. "Can you come to my game, Larkin?"

"I wish I could Isabel, but my parents are coming to visit. I haven't seen them for several months because I was living in Mexico City for a year before I moved here." She lets my sister down lightly. "Maybe next time."

"I understand." Isabel stands. "Goodnight."

"Excuse me." I stand as well. "I need to see her to her room and let Helena know she is ready for her."

"I'm not a baby, Antonio. I'm capable of turning on the shower and getting myself ready for bed." She rolls her eyes and then giggles when I grab her and toss her over my shoulder.

"And we have a routine that will not be broken, Princess Isabel. Make yourself at home I'll be back soon." And off we go with a giggling princess bouncing all the way.

"You love her," Isabel whispers in my ear as she tries to pull herself up. "She's very pretty."

"I think so," I tell her. "For now, though, she is my girlfriend. So no more teasing about love and all that stuff, okay. I don't want to scare her off. I want her to choose to stay. This life we live, Isabel, is not for everyone, so we have to show Larkin she can fit in. That our family accepts her for who she is and that we will teach her everything she needs to know. She gets nervous about certain things, like being in the public eye and on display for all to see. Do you think you can help me think of ways to help with that?"

"She loves you too." Isabel giggles when I roll my eyes. "She does. I can see it when she looks at you. Love, Antonio, will be all it takes to help her see this is where she belongs. Just love her. Show her you love her. Tell her you love her. If you do that, then it will be enough and all will work out as it should."

My sister's faith in love and happily ever after is nice. I hope she is right since I plan on doing exactly that.

CHAPTER 19
Larkin

The Royals

I pick up our plates to take them into the kitchen. I've always cleaned up after myself, so doing it now makes this seem normal.

Normal is a word that held a double meaning to me. I've never really felt normal, like I fit in with those around me. I could pretend to fit in when I had to. At work, I could do my job and do it really well. Sometimes being eccentric can be a good thing when you do what I do for a living. It takes a special type of person to see structures differently than others do. Appreciate the lines, angles, and curves that make up a building. Not everyone can fix someone else's work without altering it completely. I happen to be skilled in that I can look at an old building and become entranced by it. Start to sense the mindset of the person who originally designed it. I can then restore it, while improving it, making it possible for others to appreciate it for decades.

My normal was to get through each day without letting anyone ever really see me. To hide behind the veneer that presented me as a functional person who didn't constantly worry she was going to mess something up. In small groups, I was at my best. I could easily talk about my work, or even defend it when needed. This last week defending it was getting rather old and tiresome, though.

When the day ended, my normal was going home to the only place I felt safe, where no one else was and I could sit back and sketch. I wasn't a social person. I socialized at work when I had to. Work gave me more than enough interaction each day. My solitary life had always been what relaxed me these last five years after Randal's departure. I counted on my time alone, where I let the silence lull me in and set my creative mind flowing. During *me time*, I would either work on a current project or permit myself to create. Both were easy for me to get lost in, and before I knew it, hours would pass and I'd have stayed up way later than intended.

So, saying I feel normal taking my plate to the sink sounds strange to me. Everything about this is strange, but not so strange I want to run. I should want to run. Because everything about my life, all the stuff that once gave me the impression I was safe, will no longer be something I can count on. Antonio's life is the complete opposite of mine, yet I find that it—this—for now, feels normal.

I hear the front door open and close again quickly, followed by footsteps. I am almost done putting everything in the drying rack. After doing a quick search, I was able to locate a container to place the leftovers inside. I'm not sure they eat leftovers. Do other people eat the same meal for days like I've done most of my adult life? Freeze extra food, so when one doesn't want to cook, you can just pull out an already homemade meal instead of having to order out?

"Miss Cross, you shouldn't have done that." Helena chastises me from the kitchen door. "I said I'd take care of it when I returned."

"I'm sorry. It's just that when Antonio said make yourself at home, I guess I took him literally. I meant no disrespect, ma'am." I wipe my hands off on a dishtowel.

The woman covers her mouth with her hand. I think to conceal her grin. "It's plainly Helena, miss, and if King Antonio told you to make yourself at home, then that is exactly what you should have done. Never apologize, Miss Cross, for doing something that makes you happy."

"Okay." I breathe a sigh of relief. "Can I ask you something?"

"You can ask me anything, miss." Helena steps closer and grabs a dishtowel then dries the dishes I washed.

"Do you have a night off? A night when Antonio and Isabel are on their own, responsible for feeding themselves. If not, that's fine. I thought maybe if you did, that if you didn't mind me using your kitchen, I could possibly cook for them. If that is not too much trouble. I don't wish to mess things up. I'm sure you have a schedule you like to stick with, so I understand how important that is. So, if it's not, then just say so, and I'll understand." Wow, I sound like a babbling idiot.

"Breathe, honey. If you want to cook dinner, all you have to do is let me know. I can even make sure to have all the ingredients available for you if you provide me with a list." Helena tells me as she puts items away. "I don't really have a night off. Sometimes the two of them like to fend for themselves, so I let them. I am an employee, so I do as my employer instructs me to do."

I take a seat at the counter. "You'll have to forgive me. I'm not familiar with how all this works. I hope I'm cut out for this. I'm not sure I am. Afraid I might be getting in over my head. Terrified, I'll let Antonio down. I only hope to make him happy, want to be happy myself. I haven't been truly happy for a little over five years now. Not since a very dear friend of mine..." The tears roll down my cheek. "I'm sorry. Please excuse me."

What am I doing opening up like this to a perfect stranger? I've never just went off like that to someone I just met only hours ago. This poor woman does not need to see me acting a fool.

Large arms capture me from behind and everything inside me breaks. I shudder like I never have before. My entire body gives out on me as a loud wail escapes from deep down inside. I've been holding myself together for five years, not once really able to let go the way I feel my body doing now.

Why now?

I've cried so many tears for my friend. Gotten angry over it. Threw things when I was alone and yelled at him for not opening up to me sooner. Cursed him for making me feel unworthy and not being enough for him to at least fight. For not giving me the chance to understand his true feelings and leaving me. What he did, how he did it, broke me in ways he will never understand or can fix.

So why am I now melting down and letting it all out in front of a man I don't want to disappoint? A man who makes me experience things I never realized possible. My sentiments for this man scare me, because I know for certain if he ever walked away, left me willingly, I'd never fully recover.

"Shhh," Antonio murmurs in my ear as he allows his body to crumble with mine. "Helena, could you go see that Isabel gets to bed and stays there?"

Oh crap, I totally forgot about Helena. What she must think of this broken woman her powerful king has taken a liking to.

"As you wish, Your Majesty. Take care of that one, sir. She is a treasure and a gift. Well worth fighting for, in my professional opinion. Goodnight, Miss Cross." I hear her feet shuffle down the hall as she does what he asked her to do.

"Shhh." Antonio's body shifts until I end up between his legs, nuzzled against his chest. "Tell me about him."

I shake my head no. I don't dare talk about him.

"Tell me, Larkin. What has dimmed the light of *mi lunita*? Why do you cry for him?" The sincerity of his words, his concern, touches me deeply.

"He was my best friend, my only friend, really. The only person who made me feel like I wasn't an odd ball." I start with that.

"Others made you feel like that. Why? You are the most incredible woman I have ever met." He kisses the top of my head. "I came alive the day I saw you."

"The day he died," I close my eyes, "he came by to celebrate me getting into grad school. Randal was also an architect, very talented. But he told me my talents made him look like the amateur, the apprentice, he would always joke. Encouraged me to never let someone change me and to always create the ideas that were deep inside of me. Urged me to continue painting to get my creative juices flowing, use that as my outlet when I had trouble focusing. He loved my paintings. Said that if I weren't such a talented architect, one who could see into the past, that my art could have paid the light bill easily."

"I'd like to see some of your work." Those words hit me hard.

"I stopped painting five years ago. Haven't picked up a brush since that awful night. The last canvas I painted was for him. One I planned on giving to him for his birthday. It was a surprise. I finished it an hour before he called me and jumped in front of an L-train." The tears soak my cheeks as I vividly recall that moment.

"I'm sorry." He whispers, and there is emotion behind his words.

"He was acting so strange that night. Kissed me in my kitchen for the very first time. It was unlike any kiss I ever experienced before. He told me he should have done it sooner. Said it ruined him. Confessed, he loved me, really loved me. Wanted me to promise him a few things that at the time made no sense to me. Wanted me to finish my schooling and continue doing what I loved. Not a very hard promise to keep for me. It kept my mind from constantly thinking about what I lost that day. He also wanted me to never lose who I was. That one was harder because I couldn't be me without him around to support me." I lose it again. My tears and the pain of it all spill out of me and there is no way to stop them.

"Aww, he did not make you, Larkin. Perhaps he encouraged you, but we all are who we are all on our own. That fiery woman who has put me in my place more than once, that woman, is the one who caught my eye. She takes no bull from any man, and her bark is way bigger than her bite." He tilts my head up. "Were you that way with him?"

"Yes. He always understood when I was holding back and would goad me until I came out firing. Make me get it out and laugh at me most of the time while I was doing it. Don't get any ideas," I warn him, poking him in the chest with my finger.

The corners of his lips curl upwards. "Wouldn't dream of it. I believe I have a completely different reaction when you go off on some tirade."

Dumb and clueless, I had to ask. "What kind of reaction do you have?"

The fire in his eyes heats my core and makes my belly get that funny sensation deep down inside of it. "The tiger inside me comes alive."

I roll my eyes. "The paper tiger. Yes, I remember now."

He chuckles behind me as he tightens his hold. "Be careful, Larkin. The last time you called him that, he pounced."

"I remember," I whisper, as a shiver travels through me.

"What else did he want you to promise him?" Soft lips brush my ear as he whispers those words. "Did it have to do with love?"

"Yes," I admit softly.

He nudges me to stand up. "My butt is numb. Let's go sit in the living area and gaze out over my kingdom while you share that with me."

I allow him to guide me to a sofa. He takes a seat and tugs me down next to him. Once we are seated and comfortable, he uses a remote and turns off all the lights. The view of the city's glow is inspiring. I decide then I want to tell him everything.

"He wanted me to find love. Told me that when I found it, to grab on and never let go. He wrote me a letter. I learned Randal had secretly been in love with me almost the entire time he knew me.

"In the beginning, he felt our age difference was too large. I was a nineteen-year-old college student procuring my bachelor's degree. He was a twenty-five-year-old grad student working hard to achieve his dream and change his stars. So that first year, friendship was all he felt was appropriate. Then he claimed the timing never seemed right. His work, my school, one of us always seemed to be in a relationship or just getting over one. Ultimately, it was a brain tumor that allegedly kept him from making his move. Except, in the end, he did, and then he killed himself." I pause because I need a minute to figure out what to share next.

Antonio, being exactly who he is, seems to understand my tactic and doesn't want me overthinking it. So, he turns his head to stare at me. I can sense his eyes burning a hole in the side of my head. "Look at me."

"No," I tell him, defiance in my voice. "You are just going to make me say what I'm not sure I'm ready to say yet."

"Look. At. Me." How does he do that? Say his words in a manner that doesn't sound harsh, but also leaves no room for question.

No. The word is on the tip of my tongue but won't come out. So instead, I turn my head to glare at him, hoping to let him appreciate how angry I am with him for making me do this.

As soon as my head turns, all my anger dies and is replaced by an entirely different emotion. "Why are you making me do this?"

A hand touches my face and caresses it softly. "Because you need to say whatever you need to say. Until you do, we cannot move forward. I want us to move forward, Larkin. It is significant, and there is only one way to get what we both have been searching for. Tell me."

It takes me several minutes to do as he requests. I stare into those brown eyes until I find my courage. The words pour out of me and I couldn't stop them even though I'd like to.

"He died and I hate him for never telling me how he felt. It was selfish of him to tell me when he knew he was going to die. When he had it all planned out like he did. I hate him for making me question my worth, always wondering why. Never able to ask him all of those questions, because he was a coward and left me. Said all those things in a stupid letter where I couldn't argue with him about it. All those times he encouraged me to rant, and the one time I needed to, I couldn't, because he freaking left me to deal with it on my own. I can't even live in the city I grew up in because it is too painful to walk around and remember. To think about what could have been if he had just been honest with me from the beginning. Every corner, building, and smell, everything holds a memory that sucks the life right out of me. So, I hide in other cities around the world, hoping to forget him one day.

"Most of all, I hate he tarnished every relationship I have ever tried to have since him. He claimed he loved me, but that isn't love. What he did to me isn't love at all, not the kind of love he claims it was. And him telling me he wanted me to find love and hold on to it was a lie. What he preferred was for me to suffer as he suffered, to punish me for something I couldn't fix. I hate him, because he knew me better than anyone and had to have known what it would do to me. What he did shattered me into a million pieces and putting myself back together hasn't been easy."

I can't believe I said all that. I've thought about it many times, but never really said it. Never admitted how much I hated Randal for the pain he brought on after stirring up something unexpected inside of me. Giving me hope for something he knew we could never have.

"You loved him." Antonio's voice breaks through my wandering thoughts.

"I believe I thought I loved him. We were close. He made me feel safe, and I was able to let myself go around him. There was no judgment between us. We were able to just share our deepest thoughts, no matter how weird or wrong they might have been, and the other person listened without passing judgment.

"Until that night, my feelings for him were what they were. He was my best friend, the brother I never had, and the only person I ever felt safe around. Then it all changed after that. I realized he'd been keeping secrets from me all along. That he didn't trust me like I thought he did. That I wasn't as safe as I always believed when I was with him."

I can't believe I am sharing all this with him.

"There is a fine line between love and hate. His confession did wonders for my self-esteem where love was concerned. I began to perceive myself as unlovable, questioned if me opening up completely to him was the real reason he decided not to pursue his feelings for me. Maybe witnessing me at my worst scared him off. Deep down, I started wondering if all those times he laughed at me were more of an expression of his relief, realizing he was dodging a bullet. His secrets put a wedge between us that made it impossible for me to get to know him."

I inhale deeply so I can get this last part out. "And after his death, I felt like I never knew him at all, that our relationship had been one big fat lie. One-sided. I gave of myself completely, invested everything I had, believed him when he told me he cared and loved me. All that was destroyed. The love I thought I had for him quickly turned to hate. And that hate for him has left me suspended in a place no one could ever reach. Kept me from ever letting anyone else in. Left me floating just out of reach, preventing me from ever having to feel anything like that ever again."

By the time I finish, I am once again staring out the large window, gazing out at the city. Sitting here, so high above it all, looking down from above, is a huge metaphor in my mind. My whole life I have always felt like I was looking down at others while they went about life so easily. I was consistently just out of reach to make any real connections with those living happy lives below me.

"Larkin." Antonio's deep, pleasant-sounding voice next to me has a smile forming on my face.

I rotate my head and look at him again. "Maybe all this time I was just waiting for the right person to come along. The only man capable of enticing me to linger just a little closer to the ground so he could reach up and snatch me out of the sky. I didn't love him, Antonio, not really."

His thumb skates across my bottom lip. "How do you know for sure?"

"I just do," I tell him as I run my thumb over his lips. "I just do."

A low growl rumbles from deep inside of him. I know what is coming and I am ready for it this time. So, ending up on my back, with such a powerful man above me, doesn't at all surprise me. His attack on my mouth doesn't shock me or make me gasp.

His babbling in the numerous languages he speaks makes me giggle. I'm not sure he knows he is even doing it. I, without a doubt, am going to have to figure out how to learn to speak these languages so I can understand him when he gets like this. I get the impression he is saying some very beautiful words that would most likely send me into a panic.

When I catch one word repeated over and over again, I begin to recognize it. My brain kicks in again, so I place my hands on his chest and give him a hard push to make him stop kissing me.

"What did you say?" I ask as I run my fingers through the hair hanging over his forehead.

In his perfectly accented voice, he repeats the last words that came out of it. I recognize it as French only because of the way he enunciates the words. *"Je pense que j'ai juste pourrais tomber follement et profondenment en amour avec vous."*

"Amour? I know that word. Why do I know that word? What does that mean? What are you saying, Antonio? Tell me." I try my best to make those last words sound like him when he gives me that same order. I fail miserably.

"In time, *mi lunita*." He leans down and kisses my nose. "I will tell you when I know for sure you are ready to hear the words."

I start to protest, but his lips attacking mine halt me from doing so. I know I know that word. So later tonight, when I am back in my hotel room and trying to get some sleep, I'll google it.

"Excuse me, Your Majesty." A male voice echoes off the walls.

Antonio rises off of me and uses the remote to slowly bring up the lights. "Yes, Gino?"

I also sit up and don't miss the surprised expression on the other man's face when he realizes what he might have interrupted. "My apologies, miss. I didn't mean to interrupt."

"Gino. What is so important that it couldn't have waited until morning?" He asks his guard.

I try not to laugh at the sight of Antonio. He looks a little out of sorts. Not at all like the king he is.

He has red lipstick once again on his mouth. His hair is out of place in several areas, his clothing is ruffled a bit. When he stands, I catch him shift things around down there and realize just how disheveled he really is. Then, when I glance down at myself, I notice I'm not much better.

"There was an accident, sir. Justice Batista, along with his wife and one of his daughters, they have all been taken to the hospital. Initial reports claim it was a shooting. Someone opened fire on the vehicle they were in, killing the driver and wounding one bodyguard. The vehicle flipped several times, and all three had to be cut from it and taken by helicopter to St. Augustine's Medical Center. I thought you might want to know."

"Thank you." Antonio dismisses him and I can tell this means our night is coming to an abrupt end.

"It's fine. I understand." I assure him. "I need to go, anyway."

"We made progress tonight, Larkin." Antonio cups my face. "I will do my best to always be honest with you. Thank you for sharing tonight."

His phone starts going off like crazy.

"You need to take care of this. I can see myself out." I say as I pick up my bag. "Go. Do what a king does and know I understand."

He grabs my face with both his hands. "*Amour* is used in many languages, meaning the same thing... love. I told you I think I might be falling madly and deeply in love with you. I don't want to be like him, Larkin. I don't want you to ever wonder what I am thinking or how I feel. I will do my best to always tell you, because you, *mi lunita,* are worthy and most definitely lovable."

I knew I knew that word. Amour. Love.

He thinks he might be falling deeply and madly in love with me. Well, that makes two of us, then, because I'm pretty sure I have fallen head over heels for this man. There is no doubt about it.

CHAPTER 20
Antonio

The Royals

The last two days have been very busy. I have spent most of my time dealing with what happened to the Batistas. Visiting the hospital, offering my condolences, and doing my best to figure out exactly what went down.

The best anyone has come up with is that someone targeted Justice Ivan Batista. There was a major case recently presented to the five Justices. Two voted for, two against, while Justice Batista was on the fence for several days. A few days ago, he finally presented his and ruled against the verdict. There were a lot of very unhappy people about that decision; especially since it contradicted everything he claimed he stood for.

It was public knowledge he would be at an event the night it all came to a head, making it very easy for any person wanting to achieve their idea of justice to get to him.

This was a hired hit, that much we knew. The family was heading back to their home on one of the major highways after leaving the event. Using a familiar route when a car pulled up next to them and opened fire. Several rounds were sprayed down the vehicle, killing the driver first. Causing the vehicle to veer into traffic, triggering it to flip several times. Two other vehicles were involved in the accident, and luckily no one inside of those were seriously injured.

The Batista's were not so fortunate, though. Not only was the driver killed, so was Lady Eva Batista. Her injuries were so critical that she died en route. Ivan was not fairing so well, either. He is still alive, but no one is giving him much of a chance for survival. And his daughter, Lady Dalia, had a rough go at it for a while but is now expected to make a full recovery. They say she took the news of her father's injuries worse than her mother's death. Having known the family, I'm not sure that surprises me. I was told Eva was very unhappy with her daughter for not securing the crown as planned and that those two have been at it ever since.

I just left the hospital after spending a few moments with her. I'd like to report she was not her typical viper self, except that would be a lie. It didn't take me long to realize she was hoping to use this as her way back into the fold.

Some people never learn, do they?

It took everything inside of me not to call her out on it the first time. The moment I walked into her room, I wanted to turn right back around and walk out.

A nurse was tending to her. In true Dalia fashion, she was giving the poor woman a piece of her mind. Being the rude Lady I have seen now several times over since our breakup.

How she kept that hidden from me I will never understand, because it is very much a part of her true character. She is the rare chameleon viper who nearly slithered her way inside the palace.

"King Antonio, I knew you would come when you heard," Dalia said in that voice that made my blood boil.

"You know, the king and I were practically engaged once. A misunderstanding is all it was. I knew he cared more for me than he has been proclaiming." She was spilling all this, of course, to the nurse, hoping to trap me into doing as she bid.

"Please, come sit, Your Majesty. I have so missed you." Dalia flashes me that vile smile I once so easily fell for, and my stomach churns.

I remained standing firmly at the foot of her bed. "I came to offer my condolences, Lady Dalia. I am very sorry for your loss. Please know the Reyes family is praying for your father. My mother sends her love."

"I always liked your mother. Lovely woman." She patted the bed. "Sit with me for a while. We have so much to discuss. Clear the air between us, so we can move forward."

"I can't stay, Lady Dalia. I have other obligations this evening. I am here only as a courtesy, and you should not read more into it than that. We will do all we can for you and your father. I will punish those responsible to the full extent of the law." I turned to leave, needing to get out of there before she made me say or do something very un-king-like.

"That's it?" Dalia barked out, showing her true colors once again. "I nearly die, and all you can say is all of that nonsense? My mother's death means no more to you than your cold condolence? My father is fighting for his life and you simply promise to punish those responsible?

"To think the people actually believe you have a heart inside that stiff body of yours. That woman you are messing around with, the American, she will never be enough for you. She will never understand what a king's needs are. Never be able to..."

"Enough!" One loud word is all I ever have to say to quiet a room. "I am sorry for your loss. I hope your father recovers. I even hope you recover. What happened to your family is a tragedy, and because your father is one of my justices, I stopped by to see if you were okay. I can see you are just fine and exactly the way I remember you to be.

"And for the record, practically engaged means nothing more than I was smart enough to realize you were a snake in the grass waiting to strike. And if you ever disrespect my girlfriend again, you might want to remember who I am exactly. Bitterness does not suit you well, Lady Dalia. Good day."

I stormed out of there so fast I'm certain my men had to jog to keep up with me. That woman's ability to get under my skin and make me wish we still lived in a time where I could string her up has me fuming. I can't believe I once thought she was the one.

Her insults about Larkin made me want to remind her exactly who I am. And I guess in a way I did, but not in the way I wanted to. Larkin's words in the garden came back to mind about how Dalia knew which buttons to push to get me to react. That she knew how to make me see read and get me to easily take the bait. So, I'd done my best not to give her what she wanted, a reaction that proved she got under my skin. Instead I'd done my best to walk away before I blew up and took her down.

I'd watched the nurse's face twist into a grin when I refused to be swayed and sit with her. Caught her nod when I told Dalia to never insult my girlfriend again. Noticed her lips moving as she muttered the words, *well done, sir*. I left shortly after with Dalia still ranting like she is famous for.

We pull up to the hotel Larkin has been staying in. She is the last one keeping a room here, probably because in another week she will head to Homero to begin work on Maximiliano Chateau. Everyone else has now secured housing in the city.

I still haven't told her that Isabel and I will join her. The summer holiday is starting in a few weeks and I plan on spending it in Homero. Had planned on doing that long before I met Larkin. It was the reason the cottage, where those hired to take care of the chateau lived, had been cleared out and made ready for a king.

It wasn't nearly as big as the twelve-bedroom chateau a few miles down the road, but it would suffice. Six bedrooms, if you must know, four upstairs, all with en suite bathrooms, along with two off the main floor. I wanted to offer Larkin the bigger one downstairs, but was told absolutely not by the Captain of the King's Guard. The room had already been equipped for my needs as king, with all the security measures in place, so that was that. She would have to sleep in the last available room upstairs.

And don't look at me like that. There will be plenty of people living with us to keep things from getting out of hand. Security will be in house, as will Helena and Beatriz, and let us not forget Isabel. During our eight-week holiday, it will be a challenge for us to find space and time to spend alone. But do not think I won't do my best to ensure we at least try.

I wanted to go with Larkin to the airport to retrieve her parents, but was told no by her and Sir Edward. So, I selected option number two and am joining them for dinner at the hotel restaurant. I can't remember the last time I went out and ate at a restaurant. As you can imagine, it is not a simple task setting something up like that. To make things easier on my men, we secured a private dining room so they could give us privacy while guaranteeing all our safety. And of course, we had to enter through a side door so we didn't draw a crowd.

I am running a little bit later than I planned. After I left the hospital, I'd taken a call from Governor Ruth Niles. Seems she heard about my visit with Dalia and wanted to let me know not everyone agreed with several of the senior elected officials. There are those who feel I should have the right to be in charge of my love life. Letting me know I had support from a few to separate my political and personal lives. That conversation lasted fifteen minutes and was refreshing.

The next call that came in was not so refreshing, though, and lasted ten minutes too long. It was from Governor Aaron Colon, and he had way too much to say on the my life choices. Had the nerve to suggest I was disrespecting the crown for even entertaining the idea of going against tradition. Clarified that he would make certain to put the pressure on me by riling up the people. Maybe not using those exact words, yet I understood what he was revealing behind his all too practiced speech. So, by the time I hung up on him, I was not only late but also now determined to make a point and set things straight.

"Isaac, change of plans. Let's pull around the front and enter through the main doors." I then send a text to Larkin.

> ME: Are you already seated in the dining hall?

> LARKIN: No. Sorry. I hope we aren't keeping you waiting. Mother is running late. She is a little nervous about meeting you. You do realize who you are, right?

"Sir Edward says that is a no go, Your Majesty." Isaac is only relaying a message; except I am in no mood to be told what I can and cannot do.

"As your King, I order you to take me to the main entrance. Am I clear?"

"Yes, Your Majesty." He groans afterward, letting me know he's frustrated.

> LARKIN: We are heading that way now.

> ME: Take the elevator to the lobby. I will meet you there.

> LARKIN: Everything OK? Thought we were told to meet you in the dining room?

> ME: Yes. Just do as I ask, please.

> LARKIN: As you wish.

Her sarcasm doesn't go unnoticed.

"Give us..." Isaac starts, however, I open my door and step out before he can finish. "Sometimes, I hate my job."

I hear him cursing behind me, barking orders to the men inside. No doubt I will hear about this, yet right now I have a plan, a need to do what I am about to do.

Like I suspected, the lobby is full of people. Most of them upper-class citizens since this particular hotel doesn't come cheap. The restaurant here is also one of the best and often booked. These patrons are waiting for their tables to open up. It is common to gather in the lobby like this so that those coming and going can identify them. I know, ridiculous, but that is the practice of that particular group, therefore I plan on using it to my advantage.

I shove through the main door and am immediately recognized. The room goes silent in only seconds, and out of respect many of them start to bow. Which of course grabs everyone else's attention who may not have noticed me, and so it begins.

Gino and Franco suddenly appear, flanking both sides.

"Do we have a plan, sir?" Gino's voice sounds amused at the moment.

"I do."

"Are you going to share it with us, or is this another rogue operation?" Again, with the tone, so I glance his way.

"Rogue operation?" I raise my eyebrows as we head for the elevators. There are three.

"I believe Miss Cross and her guests are in elevator number one, sir. I'm also not complaining. The job was getting rather boring, and I am a big fan of mixing things up a bit." Gino is most definitely earning brownie points tonight with me.

"Glad I could spice things up a bit, then. That being said, I should probably warn you it might get even spicier very soon." The elevator dings right after I warn him.

I wait and am very pleased to spot Larkin inside. She is dressed in a lovely deep lavender dress that leaves one shoulder exposed. Her waist is accented with stones, which match the stilettos she decided on. I notice this because I take a few seconds to appreciate the stunning sight of her. I don't even bother trying to conceal the fact I am checking her out.

"Get ready, Gino," I warn as I step forward and offer her my hand. "Miss Cross, looking as lovely as always."

I realize she is expecting me to kiss her hand when I take it to help her off the elevator. That is not at all my plan, and she soon realizes that the instant she clears the doors.

Right there in front of her parents and all those present, I yank her to me and kiss her hard and thoroughly. I don't stop until I hear her whimper against my lips.

When I pull back slowly, I am privileged to witness the slow smile that lights up her face. "So, it's like that?"

"It's like that. I'm done letting others dictate my moves where you are concerned. After all the crap I have had to suffer through these last few hours, I needed a reminder from the one person who always makes me feel alive." I kiss her one more time quickly. "Now, shall we introduce me to your parents, before they wonder if this is how all Hermosa Islaians greet one another, please."

Larkin reaches up and attempts to wipe her lipstick from my lips. "It's not as noticeable as the bright red, but Summer Breeze isn't your color."

"Here, dear." The woman behind her passes over a white handkerchief. "Perhaps you should start carrying one of those with you."

The tinge of red that appears on Larkin's cheeks as she accepts the white cloth doesn't get overlooked. "Thank you, mother."

After I am all cleaned up and now presentable, I tuck Larkin under my arm and extend a hand to her father first. "Senator Cross, it is a pleasure to meet the man who raised such a lovely daughter."

"Charming fellow, aren't you King Antonio?" He takes my hand and gives it a solid shake. "Breaking protocol tonight, I see."

I can see this man understands me, so I just nod once as I turn to the woman next to him. Turning my hand to accept hers, I am pleased when she offers it. I bring it slowly to my lips and then greet her as well. "Dr. Cross, you are equally stunning as your daughter. I see where she gets it from."

And that isn't just a line. I know they adopted Larkin and she looks nothing like her mother. However, this woman is exquisite, with her light caramel skin and black hair that gives away her heritage. An East India beauty that I am certain has turned many heads over the years. Senator Cross is a very lucky man indeed.

"I believe I like this one, Larkin." She glances over at her daughter. "I also believe we are drawing a crowd, Your Majesty. Maybe we should move this to a more private setting now that you have staked your claim."

Larkin gasps at her mother's bold statement as she agitates her head. "Mother, please. Antonio, I do believe she is right about the crowd though. Isaac appears to be getting rather anxious over there."

I turn to discover Isaac doing his best to keep everyone back. His eyes meet mine and I realize he is also getting an ear full from Sir Edward.

"Shall we?" I shift her arm into the crook of mine and begin walking toward the restaurant.

"Sir, it has been requested that we take a less crowded route if you don't mind." Gino is doing his best to follow orders and keep me happy.

"You lead the way, Gino. I will make sure the king follows," Larkin answers for me. "I believe he has caused enough of a scene tonight to make his point. No reason to give Sir Edward any more reason to hate me."

"He does not hate you," I correct her sternly.

"Maybe not, but I know he does not like me very much. I blame you for that, by the way." Larkin tells me as we walk toward a door marked private.

A few minutes later we are seated in the private dining room and all is back to how it was first planned. Things are going rather well in my mind.

I make it very clear that her parents should call me Antonio tonight. I want this to be a relaxed dinner where we can get to know each other better. Both Sam and Eleanor agree, making this feel more like the family dinner Larkin wanted.

The relaxed state she is in right now is refreshing. She laughs openly at her father's jokes and the stories he shares with us. Listens to her mother talk about a few of her more interesting cases and sympathizes with her when she admits she sometimes wishes she could do more. It is clear they are close. They even ask her about her work here and Larkin freely shares. Discusses her upcoming project concerning my home in Homero. Talks about how excited she is to get started, even promising to take her parents to the site, so they can appreciate the place first hand.

I grant her permission to show them any of my homes while here, palace included. They will be here for a week and plan on sightseeing while Larkin is working. Having never been to Hermosa Islas, they are excited to discover something new.

But when the conversation turns to her future plans, all that tension seems to return rather quickly.

"I wish you would have stayed longer in Chicago, dear." Her mother reaches over and pats her hand. "I miss you when you are gone."

"I know," Larkin responds quickly, obviously uncomfortable with this topic.

"Your condo sold rather quickly," Eleanor tries again.

"Yes, I was glad to see that. No need to keep a place I rarely live in. Figured if I ended up back in Chicago, I could stay with you or rent temporarily. Thank you for taking care of that for me." Larkin this time at least says something more than a few short words, although she still seems tense.

"Where should I send your belongings? Here? Are you staying here? Or are you going to Tokyo like planned in a few months?" An innocent question from her mother, but not one Larkin seems all that delighted she asked.

"Tokyo?" This is the first I've heard anything about that.

Her father smiles proudly. "My daughter has been invited to join a team of talented architects who will evaluate several historical buildings and structures. Establish what can be done to save them from becoming ruins. It is a unique opportunity; one she was very much looking forward to. They are only seeking the best of the best, and our Larkin is obtaining quite the reputation."

"I thought this was a five-year assignment?" I realize my tone has changed and taken on a more aggressive one. "You are scheduled to start work on the Maximiliano Chateau in a few weeks. That project alone is projected to take at least a year to complete."

"Six months." She corrects without looking at me. "I should be able to get it done in six months if I buckle down and keep things progressing."

"That seems rather fast with all the changes we have planned for it. Are you sure it will be done correctly in such a short time frame?" I don't enjoy thinking that in six months she could possibly just be gone. Not to mention it does not at all line up with my plan where she is concerned.

"What is it you're asking me, Antonio?" Larkin sets her glass down rather harshly. "And be careful with your words. I've shared our relationship but haven't gone into great details."

"With my words? What are you afraid I might reveal, Larkin?" I wipe my mouth off and stare at her. "Have I not been clear enough with you about all of this. Are you afraid that your parents will not approve?"

"Am I expected to put my life and plans on hold for the unforeseeable future? Decline a job I have been looking forward to since it was first offered to me. It's not every day a person gets the chance to do something like this. And for the record, the Tokyo project got pushed back a year, so I have plenty of time to finish Maximiliano Chateau. Don't you think I would have told you if I planned on leaving as soon as I was finished?"

Her hands are waving around as she goes on. "It's not like I expected any of this when I agreed to come here after Janice quit. Everyone at the firm knows my plans where Tokyo is concerned. Knew that if I decided to go once it was approved, then they'd have to replace me here. My guess is that is why they brought Chandler over once the projects got underway. He would have probably been their first choice had I not approached Zach that morning. He is more experienced than me and has done projects like this in the past."

Her voice fluctuates a bit, but she keeps going. "I don't know what I will do yet, because that is months down the road still. But let me make a few things clear. If I decide to go, I'll go. I like my job, Antonio. I need my work to keep me sane. So, if your plans where I am concerned interfere with anything pertaining to my work, then perhaps, we should reevaluate all of this again. I'm not going to quit my career just because I fell in love with a king and suddenly find myself as his queen. This queen will work if she wants to work, just try to stop me." She shoves her chair back and stands. "I need to use the restroom. Please excuse me."

Her mother stands and follows my fuming beauty, who just revealed a few details I'm not sure she is aware of. I have no intention of pointing them out to her. I only plan on taking pride in the fact that she admitted those things out of anger during a babbling rampage.

"You'll have to forgive her. She tends to dump it all when she gets frustrated." Her father chuckles as he leans back in his chair. "I'm not sure she even realizes she says some of the things she says when she becomes like that."

"I find it rather attractive and have experienced it a few times already." I reach for my water. "I won't say anything if you won't. Will Eleanor?"

"No." He laughs. "So, is any of that going to be a problem, Antonio?"

"Not for me," I honestly admit. "I would never ask her to not work. If that also means traveling, then I will figure out how to deal with it. I may not like it, but the reality of it all is, how can I forbid her from traveling when I do it way more often than I like? Where there is a will, there is away, right?"

Senator Cross rubs a hand over his gray beard. If people didn't realize this man hadn't fathered Larkin, they never would. Unlike her mother, his skin is light and I imagine his hair was once as blonde as hers. Now, it is almost white. He is a tall, thin man with eyes that speak long before his mouth ever does. I appreciate that fact, because I am currently staring into those gray eyes where I discover his approval of me in them before he voices it.

"When Larkin first came to live with my wife and me, we realized we had our work cut out for us. For years we tried to have children, but God had other plans. We were both in our early forties when we accepted the baby no one else wanted. She was just a little over five pounds, looking more like a child's porcelain doll rather than a baby, a fussy little doll that needed us. We fell in love with her right then and there. I think we knew she would eventually be ours.

"We had a very rough go at it. She was a sensitive child all the way around. Small for her age most of her life, didn't start catching up with her peers until around age ten. A fighter. She had to be in order to survive those first couple of years when she was shuffled between her birth mother and us. Those days were hard on Ellie and me. But it was Larkin who truly suffered. Eventually, we were granted her permanently and able to give her all the support she required."

He picks up his drink and takes a sip before going on. "Larkin was our little bird that soared into our lives and has been flapping her wings wildly ever since. We clipped her wings when she was little, kept her grounded for as long as we could. But like every parent eventually discovers, one day you have to let them fly again.

"She flew and landed for a few years in a place we had reservations about, but we knew we needed to let her make her own decisions. One of the hardest things for a parent is not being able to help your child when she finds herself caught in the wind. After her friend's death, she pulled away from everyone, including us. Drifted aimlessly on her own, while suffering in silence. Her work helped distract her when she needed it to. Took her away from it all and allowed her to focus on other matters besides the one that haunted her. Slowly she came back to us, although she was still lost, drifting, and incomplete."

A smile grows on his face. "I knew the second I saw her in the airport that my Larkin had landed again. This time I'm trusting it will work out better for her. You, Antonio, are good for her. Just be careful with her, because she's still sensitive in many ways. Larkin is stronger than she believes, but she worries, over worries sometimes, and panics. The key is to notice the signs and figure out a way to get her to stop thinking. I used to tell her jokes. The stupidest one I could think of at the most inappropriate time. Got her giggling so she'd forget about whatever it was she was stressing over. And when that didn't work, I learned it was time for us to take a break and get some fresh air. Just some words of advice from the first man who fell for the pale, blue-eyed, blonde princess of Chicago."

"Thank you, Sam, that means a lot to me. I promise to take care of her always. Protect her the best I can. Give her everything she deserves. I'll even learn some stupid jokes and see if I can't get her giggling when she shouldn't be." I tell him with sincerity.

Sam nods and smiles. "But will you love her?"

I look him in the eye and don't even blink when I declare the truth. "Until the day I die."

CHAPTER 21
Larkin

The Royals

I splash water on my face to help me calm down. My hands are still shaking from the little rant I had a few minutes ago. I can't believe I blurted that out in front of my parents.

When they called a few days ago to confirm everything with me, my mother questioned me right away about why I sounded different. I hadn't realized I sounded different. However, according to her, my voice had joy back in it.

My parents have been worried about me for awhile now. Always said my light didn't shine as brightly as it once had. They supported me when I left Chicago and worked anywhere my company wanted to send me. Visited me when they could, which wasn't all that often. Called me weekly to check in, making sure I always understood they were there for me if I needed them. So, I knew they paid attention to how I sounded on the phone, even if I didn't.

Without hesitation, I told my mother about the new man in my life. Shared with her how we met and listened to her laughter.

My father and she had a similar encounter. He'd been the one stumbling around, knocking things over when she showed up for a consultation in his ER. A new pediatric surgeon, who until my father's clumsy introduction, ignored all the other male doctors who hit on her.

The gangly blonde handsome doctor, who was normally very suave and charming, known to make old ladies swoon, made her laugh harder than she had in a long time and later secured a date. She always said it was hard to resist a man who literally tripped over his own feet whenever he looked at you.

I then told her he was also the King of Hermosa Islas and the story behind how he told me. Went on to share about the celebration and how I freaked out and why. Heard her sighs of concern, then laughter again when I explained he kissed me to shut me up. Gave her all the details that happened later and listened as her tongue clicked in disapproval, but eventually turn back to awws.

Her sympathy over my struggle when he left me hanging reminded me of all those times she comforted me as a kid. I remember us talking once during that time and how she questioned why I sounded sad. I'd blown it off as nothing and quickly changed the subject. As I said, my parents know me very well and nothing gets past them when we talk. She expressed how she wished I had opened up to her then, so she could have offered me a few words of encouragement. Given me some advice, even on what to do when he came back, although she agreed with how I handled that.

I didn't disclose many details after that. Didn't share all the subjects we discussed after Antonio and I talked Wednesday night. There were facts I wasn't ready to share with my mother; I wasn't sure how she would take it all. Parts of that discussion seemed very private, an exclusive conversation between Antonio and myself that I didn't want others to know yet. It was one that didn't involve those who weren't living the lives we lived.

When I picked my parents up at the airport earlier, I'd only mentioned that we would be having dinner with him. They both were fine with that. Eager to meet the man who had me smiling when I talked about him. My father had wrapped me in his arms and held on tight as he whispered how happy he was to have me back. I nearly cried. Maybe I did, because I was happy to be back.

Since then, we have spent the last several hours catching up. Talking about nothing and everything. Although I avoided going into more details about what had occurred these last couple of days between

Antonio and me. Mostly because I didn't prefer to talk about Randal with them. I knew how they felt. I had finally put all that behind me, and I didn't want to think about it now. All they needed to know was that Antonio and I were dating and that it could be serious.

He'd definitely proven that point when he publicly kissed me in the hotel lobby. I knew he was up to something when he sent me that text. When we talked earlier, the stress in his voice came across loud and clear. I hated he was dealing with things on his own. Going and consoling a family who had something horrible happen to them. I hated it more once I learned it was Lady Dalia's family, for reasons I felt guilty about. If my parents hadn't been coming in, I would have asked if it were possible for me to join him. Support him while he did the right thing and let her know that as her king he cared. I had this gut reaction that warned me she hoped for more and would do whatever was required of her to get it. I didn't trust her and later would inquire about that meeting once we were alone.

I felt like dinner went well after that. My parents seemed to like Antonio. Knew how to address him formally—not at all a surprise, since they have been exposed to world leaders before. (Time out for a minute. Wow. World leaders. I am dating a man who is a world leader. Mind-blowing up here.) Respected him when he asked them to call him Antonio, making everything seem so normal. It had all been going so very well until my mother asked me about Tokyo.

Tokyo. Why had I not thought to mention that before? Probably because I knew that for now, it was on the back burner. Hearing Antonio sternly question me about my timeline, like he was suggesting I would rush a job since I obviously had a better one lined up thousands of miles away from him, bugged the heck out of me. It had burned me after our long discussion a few nights ago when he had forced me to open up. That he thought I would keep something like that from him after everything that had been said that night. After he had expressed his feelings, his alleged feelings, in such a beautiful and honest way.

And that had sent me into a mini-rant. I let him have it in a much calmer way than usual. I didn't speak in that fast-uncontrolled way I had done so many times before. This time I spoke at a more normal speed, even though I let my thoughts just spill out.

Which now has me gripping the sink hard again, as those last words replay over and over in my mind. *I'm not going to quit my career just because I fell in love with a king and suddenly find myself as his queen. This queen will work if she wants to work, just try to stop me.*

My mother's soft hand lands on my back as her eyes meet mine in the mirror. She used the restroom first before approaching me, knowing I needed time to catch my breath before I would be ready to listen.

She turns on the faucet and begins washing her hands. "I like him. I know I said that before, but I mean it."

I start to say something, except the words get stuck in my throat. Consequently, I lean over again and splash more cold water on my face. It's a good thing I have makeup in my clutch tonight.

"He likes you too. A good man all the way around. It's in the eyes. Your father had the same kind eyes." She leans forward as she reapplies her lipstick. "Besides the clumsy man, who couldn't seem to move inside that small room without knocking something else over, capturing my attention. It was the second thing I noticed when he peeked up at me; kind gray eyes that said I could trust him. That's an important thing, you know. To be ready to trust the person long before you ever really get to see them. I have always found the eyes are the windows to the soul. They reveal so much if you take the time to study them."

Making sure to catch my eye in the mirror my mother continues. "Your eyes have constantly given me a proper read on your moods. The first time I saw those soft blue eyes, I knew you were a lost soul searching for your place in this world. You found it with us for a very long time. We were your safe place. But every soul eventually needs to be set free to wander again. You started feeling lost again long before we set you free, though. Found a safe place for a while where you learned some very valuable lessons we couldn't teach you.

"Every person has a path they must travel to discover where they belong. Some find it quickly and easily. Others never find it. They settle for less, sometimes more than once. Some just wander aimlessly, not wanting to settle at all. It's a journey, and one never knows where it will take them, but we all must take it. If a person is smart, she places that journey in God's hands and asks him to help lead her to where he wants her to end up."

She pauses. "I believe, my sweet Larkin, that your path ends here. If you want it to, that is. Of course, there are other paths out there. If you don't trust this is the life God has chosen for you. Although after that little speech, I think deep down you already know your place in this life is with him. You feel it here in your heart. Picture it here in your mind. Know it when you gaze into his eyes and find him looking as intensely back at you."

My mother has always been able to calmly tell me what she believes I need to hear. Reading my mind with just one glance and then saying exactly the right words to pull me back.

I take a few deep breaths and fix my makeup. As I am reapplying my lipstick, I glance fondly at my mother. I have always thought her to be beautiful, and even at sixty-seven I still see it. Very few wrinkles or blemishes, even her dark hair doesn't give her age away. Dye I guess will help with that. My mother claims it's the gift God gave women so they can age gracefully. And my mother has aged as gracefully as possible.

"So, what do you suppose Daddy is telling my King?" I have never called Antonio that before, but I like how it sounds. My King, and I don't necessarily mean a leader with power, but the man who rules my heart. I know, cheesy right?

"Probably one of those stupid jokes he has floating around in his head." My mother laughs. "I hope he doesn't pull out any king or noble ones."

We are laughing when we walk back to the table.

They are sipping coffee while gabbing like men. Right as we sit, my father asks Antonio if he likes chess.

"Sam, no." My mother warns him. "Please, love. Your daughter is trying to impress this man."

My father leans over and kisses my mother as he stares deeply into her eyes. The love that passes between them after thirty-three years of marriage is refreshing.

I want that. Always have. To love someone so much that even through all the trials life throws at us, we end up stronger in the end.

My parents' demanding jobs never got between them. They always supported the other person while encouraging them to do whatever they felt was the path God was leading them down. Showed me that two people could have a happy marriage, even when there were times they had to live apart. My mother repeatedly said it was her knowing without a doubt that my father loved her completely, making things easier. They talked daily, sometimes multiple times a day, to keep the lines of communication open. When the other person needed them, they found a way to be there. The key, my father insisted, was to never take the other person for granted. Never assume they know what you were thinking. Tell them as many times a day as you can how you feel. Show them as many ways as you can think of how important they are to you. Then let those around you witness it with their own eyes, leaving little doubt where your heart and soul lives. You do that not just for your spouse, but also for yourself. Marriage is a work in progress and requires both parties to stay focused.

"Better?" I hear Antonio's voice ask as he watches me watching them.

I turn my gaze his way and nearly fall out of my chair again. One glimpse into those eyes and I see my future as clear as day reflecting back at me. "Yes."

"So, Antonio, do you like chess?" My father chuckles when my mother sighs loudly.

"I do." He answers as he reaches under the table and takes my hand. "It has always been one of my favorite games to pass the time."

"Perfect. Most men like us enjoy chess. It's a strategy game that requires focus. Lose that focus and you lose the game.

"Life and chess are similar in many ways, I believe. We make our move; one we believe will help us win, and our opponent counters. Each piece on the board has rules it must follow. The rook can move any number of vacant spaces forward, backward, left, or right in a straight line. The bishop can only move diagonally as many vacant spaces as available, staying on the same color throughout the game. The knight can move in a two by three rectangle and is the only piece that can jump over another piece, so to speak. The pawn moves one space at a time, slowly making his way across the board. Those four pieces are critical to the game, and you need them working together so you can protect the king. Although, the queen is probably one of the most useful pieces because she can move all over the board, much like the rook. Does what she has to do to protect the king."

There is a pause as my father takes a sip of his coffee. His eyes light up with mischief and I glance at my mother in time to catch her roll her eyes again. "You know what I find ironic about the game of chess? It's how these two pieces reflect the relationship between a husband and a wife. The poor king can only move in a specific order of space, while his counterpart, the mighty queen, can do whatever she likes."

The roar of laughter that comes out of Antonio only encourages my father. He spills out one-liners until both can no longer speak. Some of them I have heard, some are new. My poor mother can only sit back and shake her head while her husband shows his true colors.

"Okay. Sorry. I just couldn't help myself. So, shall we leave these two alone for awhile, Ellie?" My father asks my mother as he kisses her hand.

They stand and say their goodbyes. My father is still chuckling some as he escorts my mother out. She is giving him her little speech about how she can't believe he went there.

"Sorry about that." I take a sip of my water. "He has a very interesting sense of humor."

"Your father is very comical. I enjoyed getting to know him, your mother also, by the way. Miss Cross, is there someplace we can go to talk?" He scans the private dining area. "While this is nice, and seems private, it's not really. Not as private as I'd like, at least."

"We could go to my suite, I suppose. My parents are staying with me, but if I know them, they are heading to bed. It's been a long day for them and it's long past their bedtime."

Antonio stands and offers me his arm. "What will they all say when they see us heading upstairs?"

"Oh. I never thought." I blush. "Maybe we should..."

"Nope. I'm definitely going to your suite. I'm done worrying about what others think. Do you know what bothers me more?" He leads me to the door and then informs his men of our plans.

"No," I answer as we follow them to the elevator.

"None of them would have a problem with me escorting one of the chosen to her hotel suite. They wouldn't find it scandalous. Instead, they'd probably hope that one thing would lead to another, and later it would require a quick marriage." Antonio reveals after stepping onto the elevator. "If not that, then at least they would anticipate a proclamation, stating I am in the process of courting my future queen with an engagement to follow shortly."

"I see." I nervously touch my face. "How long does this courting process usually last?"

"Traditional courting rituals last a few months. It's an allotted time period that gives both parties the chance to get to know the other person." Antonio sounds like he has experienced it before.

"Have you ever courted anyone before?" I don't know why I ask, but the tension that takes over his body tells me it was a good question. "You have."

Sadness covers face as he nods once. "I have."

"Lady Dalia." Her name is the first one that comes to mind. "That's why she is so obsessed with you. Were you two engaged?"

"No!" His voice is loud and unexpected. "No."

My next words come out with little thought. "But that was the plan, wasn't it? It was expected that once you started courting her an engagement would soon follow."

Realization slaps me across the face, as I think about how that woman has looked at him those few times I was around. She knows him better than me probably, how much better I wonder.

Antonio squeezes my hand once. "Yes, Larkin, which is why courting a woman first is always best. When a man courts a woman there is an expectation of an announcement, most of the time there is one. But until an engagement is announced, a man is allowed to simply change his mind, no questions asked. After an announcement, however, it all becomes more complicated. Good solid reasons must be given to break an engagement, at least for a man in my position. Luckily enough for me, it never got that far with Lady Dalia, I was able to just end things."

We reach my suite door and I suddenly have second thoughts about inviting him inside. I spin to face him and am thrilled to see his men have given us some privacy. That makes it easier to ask my next question is hanging on the tip of my tongue. "Did you love her?"

"Can we discuss this inside, please?" There is pain in his eyes. "Please?"

"Did you love her?" I ask again.

Hanging his head, he closes his eyes and shakes his head. "If I did, I no longer do now."

"So, is that a yes, then?" I'm not giving up; I want him to say it if he did.

He yanks the key card from my hand as he mutters several words in either Spanish or Portuguese. I'm not sure which, but the way the words flow from his lips, I know he knows them well. He swipes the card and shoves the door open, nodding for me to enter.

"Is that a yes?" I stand my ground, not budging.

A low growl comes from deep inside of him. Before I realize it, he lifts my feet off the ground and transports me inside. Once we are far enough through the door, he kicks it closed with his foot and sets me down.

I take a step back from him and cross my arms. "Answer me."

Antonio crosses his arms, mimicking my stance. We stare at each other for a very long time. I can see pain so very deep inside of him behind those expressive eyes.

Finally, he throws his hands in the air and roars. "Yes, I loved her! Is that what you wanted to hear, Larkin? That at one time I loved another? That I once thought she was the one? Or that I planned on asking her to marry me? Even secured her a very lovely, expensive ring? I had it all arranged. Knew the perfect location. Practiced the words until I had them memorized. If I hadn't stopped that day to listen to her discussing with her sisters and her mother how her plans were going so well, then I would be married to her right now.

"I loved her once. I don't love her now. There is a fine line, Larkin, between love and hate. She betrayed me. All that love I thought I had for her turned bitter. I thank God every day for showing me who she was before it was too late. Every day, I thank him for allowing me to take a second to just pause and listen. Even on those days when I thought I'd never find what I was searching for and debated calling her. I allowed him to bring to mind how I felt when I heard her bragging about how she fooled me. How she would soon marry me and become the princess she was born to be, the future queen she would learn to be. I thanked him even then. Do you know why?"

I shake my head. "No," I whisper.

"Because I had faith that God would one day lead me to the one woman out there who I could love, who could love me. Me. Antonio. Not the King of Hermosa Islas." He swallows hard. "Now I thank God for another reason altogether."

"What other reasons?" I drop my arms and can sense my breathing quickening.

"One reason Larkin, not other reasons. I thank him for one thing and one thing only. You. I thank him each morning I wake up for leading me to you." He steps forward quickly and gathers me in his arms.

Our lips collide hard, and I wrap my arms around his neck to hold him there. I can understand that because I too have given God thanks for him.

Neither of us says the words, not yet. I'm not sure why, really. Maybe we know it's not the right time yet. But I know we feel them, and that gives me hope that one day soon one of us will admit it. I guess the question is who will do it first?

CHAPTER 22
Antonio

The Royals

The summer holiday is only a few days away. Last week, Larkin moved to Homero so she could get started on Maximiliano Chateau. That was nine days ago, and today is the first time I will see her since her departure.

She visited the palace the night before she was scheduled to leave. It had become a regular event, her stopping by after work. Sam and Eleanor even joined her a couple of times for dinner while they were here. I gladly gave them a private tour, with Isabel leading the way. My little sister entertained the older couple with her knowledge and interesting stories about the legends of Hermosa Islas.

Most of the time, Larkin's visits occurred later, after her parents had settled in for the night. Once Isabel and I finished our nightly routine and she was getting ready to turn in. My woman would drive over, much like I guess others who were dating did, so we could have some private time together.

And no, we didn't just make out like teenagers during those hours. I probably would have been happy doing that, but not Larkin. She always had a plan when she showed up. Some way to force us to be open about topics that displayed who we were. There was so much we didn't know about each other, and she was determined we were going to learn it all.

One night, she made me sit down with her on the living area floor while we listened to music. We talked about who her favorite artists were and why she liked them. She even had a playlist of her favorite songs, and I wasn't surprised to hear the variety mixed together. Her favorite band is Imagine Dragons and the first time she heard their song, "Smoke and Mirrors", was during one of her sad times where she could relate to it completely. She also likes James Bay, said his music always seems so deep and from the heart. Admitted to being a closet Justin Bieber fan, even, but swore if I told anyone she would deny it.

I can honestly say I'd done nothing like that before. Relaxed on the floor with a bunch of pillows surrounding me and just listened to music. It took me a while to get comfortable. It wasn't until I peeked over at her, decked out in her black stretchy pants and sweatshirt, bobbing her head to the music, did I realize how important it was. She looked immersed in the music, and young, she looked so very young. Gone was the professional woman who dressed in her pantsuits with her business style pulled back hair, the one who took charge of the room as soon as she walked inside of it. Larkin had shed her the moment she stepped into my quarters. The person I was observing was the woman Larkin was beneath all that. And I found I liked that woman even more than I admired the other one.

Each night, I had learned a little more about the other side of Larkin Cross. I also discovered something else about her I adored during the hours we spent together.

One night, it was the fact she could catch popcorn with her mouth when she tossed it up in the air. I adored the way she laughed when she threw it at me and I missed almost every single time. Popcorn wasn't something we typically ate. I've probably had it five times my entire life. I now keep a box of it in the pantry, just in case Larkin decides she wants some.

Another night, it was how serious she looked when she sketches. When she'd shown up one evening, I, unfortunately, needed to step away for a few minutes to take a call. Once I returned, she was sitting on my couch madly dragging her pencil across a sketchpad. Totally oblivious to anything around her, focused solely on what was in front of her. I later discovered it was an image of me standing in front of my large window, gazing down at Aragon, dressed in only a pair of lounging pants. My hands were pressed against the glass. My legs, shoulder length apart with my head down, and the muscles on my back taut. It was a fairly accurate portrayal of my physique, and since Larkin has never once seen me shirtless, it surprised me. It was how she envisions me. As soon as she realized I was there, she quickly shut the book and blushed.

Of course, there were also those times when we would kiss and talk and kiss. I enjoyed the kissing sometimes more than the talking. Although the talking gave me insight into where her mind was. Plus, I enjoy sharing my thoughts with her, then listening to hers as well.

She'd ask questions like what was it like growing up as a prince. What could I say about that, really? I didn't know there was any other way to grow up. I suppose it is way different from most, but not for us, not for those born into this life. I started nursery school when I was four, where I learned how to read and write in both English and Spanish.

At six, they enrolled me in primary school, where I was educated, much like everyone else who lived in Aragon. I played sports: *fútbol*, lacrosse, and handball, just like most boys did. I also had lessons with my private tutor. I studied proper protocol on how to act like a prince, how to address others below me, how others should always address me, and everything that went along with being a member of the royal family.

At twelve, they shipped me off to boarding school in Spain, where I hung out with others like me. Being a prince was nothing special there. We were a dime a dozen. Maybe not exactly, but every person there, in one form or another, was raised in prestigious homes with privileges.

I met one of my closest friends, Fernando Martin, whose family was in the banking business for generations, during that time. When we graduated, the two of us went off to university together in England. Which is where he met his wife Sonia, a truly lovely woman who made my friend work for her affection. The other young ladies didn't care for her, always claimed she was too plain for a man like Fernando and didn't fit into his world. That, I believe, is what drew his attention to her in the first place, so not long after we graduated, he married her. They now have three children and live in France. He owns a very flourishing business and raises his children differently, breaking the cycle, he claims.

Which is when Larkin seriously looked at me and point-blank asked me, "Will our... I mean... will any child of yours be expected to live the same life you did? Go off to boarding school at twelve? Of course, they will, never mind."

I liked it when she just said what she was thinking. Our child is what she meant, and I got the impression she wasn't sure how she felt about that.

My father didn't give my mother a choice with my education. She was told how it would be, and there was no room for argument. My brother, Esteban, followed in my footsteps almost exactly. Being second in line for the throne—the backup, as he liked to joke, although I don't believe he finds it so funny anymore—he needed to be equally primed.

When it came to Lorenzo and Gabriela, mother was given a few options. Neither of them was shipped off to boarding school but instead enrolled in one of Hermosa Islas' best, which was in Prieto, very close to the home she kept there. Gabriela switched schools after the kitchen fire in Prieto, to one equally as respectable here in Aragon. Lorenzo went off to university when he was older, although I hear my sister hasn't decided what she wants to do yet. We have ample universities here where she can obtain her bachelor's degree.

Isabel's education so far mirrors my younger siblings. I see no need to ship her off when she gets older. I rather like having her around.

So, I answered Larkin's question as honestly as I could. "I don't know. A private tutor will be a must for learning certain duties that are expected of them. I cannot teach everything to them, but I will take a hands-on approach, prepare them differently. As far as the rest, it all depends on what the mother wants. If I am going to be known as the king who breaks tradition, I might as well do it all the way around."

Larkin rolled her eyes. "Whatever. I guess if you say so."

"So, you don't care if I send our firstborn off to boarding school at twelve?" I knew she would react, which is why I said it.

Again, with the eye roll before she responded. "We don't have a child, so there is no need for me to worry about that."

"But one day, Larkin, one day we will," I boldly declared.

"Please don't." This time those eyes seal tight, as if by closing them, she wouldn't have to deal with my declarations.

After everything that had transpired between us that last week, I needed her to understand my affirmations. "Don't what? Express that we are no longer just dating? That I have decided to court you?"

Those eyes of hers flew open rather quickly. "What? What do you mean? I never agreed to more than just dating."

Wrapping her in my arms, I lowered her onto the couch, generating a lovely squeal that always snuck out when I caught her off guard. I could think of a handful of times from my past when I trapped a woman below me like that. Where I pressed our bodies together to establish how well we might one day fit. Something I have decided I really, really like about Larkin is how perfectly she seemed to fit. It's as if our frames were designed to accommodate the other.

"Then perhaps you should." I leaned forward and kissed her lips briefly. "I'm not interested in just dating you, Larkin. I want us to talk about important subjects, like where we will send our son when he is old enough for secondary school."

"We don't have a son." Her stubbornness had my fingers digging into her side, which caused her to giggle. "Stop! Plus, who's to say I will give you a boy."

"Sex education 101, if I recall correctly, Miss Cross, declares you don't get a say in whether I implant a boy or girl inside of you one day. I believe I determine that." I continued to tickle her because I was pleased to hear her at least playing along.

"What if you don't have any boys inside of you, then?" Her giggle developed quickly into a full belly laugh.

"I have at least one. Are you suggesting that we could possibly create the third true queen to ever rule in Hermosa Islas? Scandalous declaration you are making, *mi lunita*, very scandalous. They will not be happy should that happen; it could cause an uproar." I stared into those pale blue eyes of hers. "Agree."

Playfully, she shook her head while doing her best not to laugh.

"Agree, or I'll be forced to do something drastic." I could only think of one thing that would hopefully get her to conform. I wasn't sure she was ready to hear it; however, I would do what needed to be done to get her to agree.

"One condition." That lovely smile told me I was going to concede to her condition.

"Let me hear it."

"That we take this one day at a time. No more baby talk. I know there will be topics we need to discuss. How many children you expect me to have for you. What will be expected of me. What rules I need to be aware of. I'm sure you'll need to hire me a tutor of my own to ensure I learn all they will require me to know."

"I'll teach you, Larkin. Everything. All of it, I'll explain it to you. I won't be hiring a tutor who will try to push his/her agenda down your throat. Make you like all the others. I'll be the one who will decide what you are required to know, help you understand the laws, guide you on how to address others, and how to have them address you. I'll do it because I don't want an institutional queen by my side. I want you. I only ever want that person to be you."

Larkin closed her eyes and softly agreed. "Okay, then. I hope I don't screw this all up."

I only laughed at her before I kissed her senselessly. No way would I allow her to screw it all up. She couldn't, as far as I was concerned. As long as she stayed true to herself and didn't try to become what others were going to expect her to grow into, that wasn't possible.

I meant what I said. I don't want an institutional queen by my side who knows all the proper ways to act and speak, who can pretend with the best of them. I want Larkin just the way she is. I want her standing there in true Larkin form. So nervous she cannot speak at first, then can't shut up because of the nerves. Relying on me to help her get through it all. Doing all of it not because she has to, but because she wants to. Doing it all because she loves me enough to choose this life, one that downright terrifies her.

As my driver pulls into the long drive of Maximiliano Chateau, I think about all of that. I haven't seen her since that conversation. Never informed her that once Isabel's summer holiday began, we would spend it with her here. Thought I'd surprise her.

Isabel will join us in a few days. She is visiting her other grandparents, Sofia's parents. I don't keep her from them. I feel it is important she knows her mother's side of the family as well.

Which means I am arriving with only my team for now. Isaac and Gino came up early to get matters sorted. They are waiting for us when we pull up to the house.

"Pleasant drive, Your Majesty?" Isaac asks as he opens my door.

"Not bad, Isaac. How are matters here?" I'd asked them to be discreet when they showed up.

"Miss Cross was a little surprised to see us. We told her we were here to check on things, that's all. Make sure security was tight around the property and that she wasn't having any trouble."

I stretch my body out after being confined to a vehicle for the last couple of hours. "Good. Where is she now?"

Gino is smiling way too big for such a question. "I believe she just finished for the day. Invited us to join her for dinner in about an hour. Said she'd like the company, claimed she was lonely. We told her we'd think about it. A man has to eat, right? She informed us she'd call after she cleaned up so she knew how much to make."

"I'll make sure to put aside something for you, Gino." I notify him as I tread past. "Please do not disturb us unless it's a life-or-death emergency."

"As you wish." Isaac and Gino reply at the same time and then head for the back entrance that leads to the security office.

I, however, head for the front. I am pleased to find the door secured and use my key to open it. There is loud music playing over the speakers. I'm pretty sure she told me the artist's name was Rihanna, and right now she is singing about being lost in paradise. I can hear Larkin singing along with her very loudly and very off-key. She has no idea I am here. Probably didn't even hear the front door open over the music. From the sound of things, I imagine she is completely engrossed in her music. The song switches to a different one, and now she is directing me to sell her candy. I chuckle as I listen.

I slip off my shoes and place them next to the door. Then start to advance toward the kitchen where I can hear her moving around. I stop just outside the door so I can listen to her doing her best impression of the woman singing. And before I can get moving again, she comes darting out of the kitchen and runs smack into me.

Larkin screams and then knees me right in the jewels.

I drop to my knees and stare up at her as I grab my crotch, unable to take my eyes off the image before me.

Isaac and Gino come running from the back to establish what the problem is like they are trained to do. They both stop dead in their tracks and gawk as well.

I'd move if I could. I'd jump up and cover her body, so they would not be able to observe her partially naked form if I could. Except right now I'm pretty sure my royal jewels are in my throat, preventing my words from escaping. Finally, I am ready to force my voice to follow my command. Although, by then, they were both spinning on their heels and heading out, anyway.

"Leave us," I choke. "Now."

"As you wish." They are doing their best to cover up a laugh.

Larkin's eyes are wide. "Oh... I'm sorry. Are you okay? I just reacted."

"I'll live, I believe." I blink a few times. "You should probably grab some clothes."

Realization crosses Larkin's face as she glances down, remembering she is only wearing a sports bra and boy-cut style knickers. I only know the style because Isabel wears them. I've had the privilege of shopping with her and Helena while I had to listen to them discuss all the different styles knickers came in. Apparently, this style is best when doing active type work or sports. Doesn't ride up on a woman. Whatever the case may be, I can assure you I am a huge fan of them right now.

"Snap. Crackle. Pop," Larkin blurts out and darts for the stairs.

The back view is even better than the front. Her round cheeks are peeking out from the bottom. That, I can promise, is not helping with the pain between my legs. It is only causing more because my male appendage has decided he needs to make himself known right about now.

I fall back and lie on the ground, staring up at the ceiling. It's probably a good thing she unmanned me, otherwise, I might have done something really, really stupid.

CHAPTER 23

Larkin

The Royals

How had I forgotten that I stripped out of my clothing after I walked in earlier? For the record, I rarely run around the house in my underwear. Today was the exception, and I have a good reason for it.

Construction work can be rather filthy. I am not always given the opportunity to get my hands dirty. Most of the time, I am only present for a portion of the work. This job, however, is different for many reasons. Some that I don't enjoy thinking about, even though in the back of my mind they are all floating around. So that means I am getting a firsthand experience of what a job is like from start to finish.

Today I had the privilege of crawling around the walls—secret passages are often built in these old structures—making sure they were all stable. I even found a few passages not mapped out in the original plans. Some were extremely tight spaces that the larger man accompanying me couldn't possibly fit into. I barely fit, almost got stuck a few times, and had to use my climbing skills to get out.

While I found it fun and exciting, there was no way I could leave those spaces untouched. A child could get hurt playing around inside those areas, so they would have to be widened, reinforced, or demolished completely. I hated the thought of demolishing them, but there is no way I can leave them if they aren't safe. Not only because I didn't want Isabel finding them and then getting seriously hurt. I didn't want any child who might one day live in this home with Antonio finding them and getting hurt. (And that is all I am going to say about that, so stop trying to goad me into saying more.)

Meaning, I had to go back to the drawing board and study the original blueprints. Map them all out again to make certain they accurately reflect the structure so I can decide what the best way to tackle them.

When the day was over, my jeans and long sleeve t-shirt were coated in grime. Mud, dirt, and cobwebs that had to be decades old, if not older, completely covered me. So instead of tracking all that through the cottage, I stripped them off in the backroom.

I knew the guys, Isaac and Gino, were out doing a security check around the grounds and wouldn't be back for a while. I tossed them in the laundry basket I brought down earlier without ever once thinking anyone would see me. Headed to the kitchen and washed my face and hands off so I could grab the meat out of the freezer.

I elected to make lasagna after talking to Antonio's men. It was something that would keep, even if they decided not to join me for dinner. I could freeze it for later in the week when I was too beat to cook.

I had also turned on the stereo right after I washed my hands, needing some upbeat tunes. The house was too quiet, and I was getting lonely. So, I chose an artist that would bring my spirits up, turned it up loud because I could. Then I began pulling out everything I needed just to establish I didn't have to make a run into town.

Once I was done, I headed for the stairs so I could wash this grime off me before cooking. Imagine my surprise when I ran into a brick wall. Without taking the time to let my mind recognize who it was, I just reacted. Did what I was instinctively trained to do and brought my knee up hard, making a very solid connection with someone's groin.

It wasn't until I watched the man crumble to the ground, saw those brown gorgeous eyes staring up at me, that my brain registered it was Antonio. The grimace on his face did not match the sparkle in his eyes.

The way his body was protecting those royal jewels I just crushed did not at all seem to make that heat inside of them fade.

His words, "Leave us," came out sounding choked and forced.

I felt so bad. Knew I had caused some damage and prayed it wasn't serious. Hoped I didn't break him down there, although at the time that had been my intention.

I had completely forgotten I was standing there in a pair of black boy-cut panties. They were the seamless kind that absorbed sweat and set low on my hips, ending straight across the tops of my thighs. At least I had a sports bra on instead of a regular one. Both were my standard undergarments when I was working on site. I dressed for comfort all the way around when I knew there was a chance I might need to do some climbing, crawling, and lots of bending.

So, when he told me he was fine and that I should probably grab some clothes, I thought I was going to die.

"Snap. Crackle. Pop," I uttered, embarrassed, as I darted for the stairs, taking them two at a time.

Now I was about to head back down to face the man I not only gave a good kneeing to but also a PG-style peep show. I'm not sure a man has ever seen me in my underwear before. I mean because there are plenty of perverts out there who may have used their skills to peep at me through a window a time or two during my days in Chicago. I'm pretty sure the guy across the way had his telescope aimed at my bedroom window. But I have never intentionally shown a man mine before. Antonio has now seen them twice. Both times were unplanned and equally embarrassing.

Dressed in a pair of loose gray cotton shorts and a pink t-shirt, I make my way back down. I left my hair loose, still wet. I didn't want to waste more time than necessary for two reasons. The first being I wanted to check on him and make sure he didn't need me to do something, not sure what exactly. And the other being that it has been way too long since I've seen his face, kissed his lips, wrapped my arms around him, and took a really good whiff.

I find him seated in the living room area with a bag of ice pressed to his groin area. He has his legs spread wide, and by the grimace still pasted on his lips, I know it really hurts.

"Hi." I bite my lip as I step into the room.

Gino steps out from the kitchen, carrying a glass of water and a couple of pills. "Remind me never to sneak up on you, miss. I'm rather fond of my manhood."

"Well, at least we know that is one less thing we are going to need to teach her. She will unman a potential threat before he even sees it coming." Isaac is leaning up against the doorframe leading to the security office. "Well done, miss. The worst pair of blue balls I've seen in a while."

"I didn't... I mean, how was I to know... were they really blue?" I take the water and pills from Gino.

Gino is chuckling. "We don't know for certain. Not like we actually took a peek. I'm sure when he takes a piss, there will be a little blood. Blue balls are more a reference to the condition we found him in after you left. Nice set of knickers, by the way."

"Gino," Antonio growls.

"I believe you were in agreement, sir. Thus, the reason for those blue balls." Again, he chuckles and I begin to understand the meaning of his words.

"Stop saying blue balls," Antonio grunts out slowly. "And you will forget ever seeing Larkin like that. You are dismissed, gentlemen."

Isaac nods and leaves, but Gino turns toward me wearing a smile. "I meant no disrespect, miss. Honestly, I was a little surprised to see such a work of art. How long have you had it?"

I instinctively reach around and touch the place on my side where the work of art he is talking about rests.

"Gino. Do you want me to jab your eyes out before I fire you?" Antonio shifts. "Please refrain from discussing it again."

"You didn't like it?" He sounds shocked. "Or is it you're afraid I'll tell someone about it? Not my place, sir. I believe Miss Cross put it where she did so she could appreciate it while keeping it well hidden when needed. I'm sorry if I said something I shouldn't have, although in my opinion there is no reason to keep it a secret. Something like that, miss, should be proudly displayed."

"Thank you, Gino. I got it right before I left Mexico City. I did it on a whim. I saw it in the window when I was passing by and just had to have it. An inspiration, I guess you could say. It was sort of freeing to me." I hand Antonio the glass of water and pills. "Plus, the colors kind of spoke to me."

"What is he talking about? What colors? I only remember black." He growls again as he swallows the pills.

Gino gestures with his head as if saying he believes I should share. My guess is that Antonio's mind was focused on two things earlier. His very sore man parts and the fact I had very little clothing on. There is also the fact that it was on the side that was facing away from him, so when I turned and ran up the stairs, I was probably too fast for him to notice.

I make a quick discission and lift my shirt on the left side as I spin around. Gino has seen it, after all, so it only seems fitting to let Antonio as well. "This."

It's not really all that large, probably the size of my hand. Like I told Gino, I got it on a whim. It was the design, along with the beautiful colors, that drew me into the tattoo parlor in the first place. Then it was the artist, a woman named Raven, who finally talked me into getting it. She took one look at me and claimed my body as the perfect canvas for that particular piece. When she was finished, I had to agree. I loved it.

Antonio shifts again and groans. I suspect for other reasons than the pain in his groin. His large finger traces the center spine of the colorful feather. The contrast of color against my pale skin makes it look painted on almost, and I can sense him studying it closely.

My legs buckle when his lips brush against my exposed skin. And I yelp when he yanks me off my feet and drops me into his lap. With one hand firmly on my tattoo, the other wraps around my neck, he draws me to his lips. The kiss we share makes up for all those nights we spent apart and has me wondering how I have survived this long without them.

"Hello, *mi lunita*," he whispers against my lips. "I've missed you."

"Hi." I kiss him again softly. "I've missed you as well. What a lovely surprise."

My stomach growls, and he laughs. "Hungry? Perhaps we should put this on hold for the time being and feed you."

I pull back so I can look at his face. "Do you like lasagna?"

He nods as his hand continues caressing my side. "I also like this. It makes me hungry for other things, Larkin."

His hand on my skin makes me greedy for other things as well, but I know that can't happen. I stand and start walking toward the kitchen, pulling my shirt back over my side. Out of sight, out of mind, right?

"Are you going to be okay?" I ask over my shoulder.

A loud grunt comes from behind me as he stands. "Yes. So, what do you need me to do?"

I laugh as I grab a pan and hand it to him. "Put water in this. Fill it three-fourths of the way and then put it on the stove. Turn the burner on high."

Antonio takes it and walks over to the sink. He does exactly as I instructed him and then turns around to face me. "Done. Now what?"

I add a little water to a skillet so I can brown the hamburger and then place it on the burner. "Do you know how to brown hamburger, Your Majesty?"

Large hands encircle my waist as he yanks me back. Dropping his lips to my ear, he mumbles, "Antonio. I am always only Antonio to you." Then he nips it slightly. "Yes, I believe I can do that."

I bump him back and hear him grunt in pain. "Sorry. Are you sure you shouldn't take a look at it?"

"I did. It's fine. Trust me, everything is working just fine." He reaches down and shifts things around. "You have quick reflexes."

I get everything else ready while he browns the meat. Cook the noodles. Make the sauce and pour it over the meat when it is done. I have him grab me a casserole dish and then spray it. Then I assemble the lasagna while he watches me closely. I lick my fingers a few times, not thinking much about it. I typically only cook for myself, so I guess it's become a habit of mine.

As I am adding the finishing touches and start to do it again, he reaches over and captures my hand. I am about to apologize until he brings my messy finger to his mouth and sucks off the content instead. "Hum. Good."

I shiver and he grins like he always does when I do that.

Yanking my hand back, I walk over to the sink and rinse them off before shoving the pan in the oven. Setting the timer, I gather up all the dirty pans as I fill up the sink. I'm a clean as I go kind of cook.

Antonio grabs a dishtowel and starts drying the items I have washed. "That was fun."

I grab what I need from the fridge for the salad. "More fun when you have someone to cook for. Will the guys be joining us?"

His answer is quick. "No."

"Oh." I pause and look up at him. "Why? There will be more than enough."

"Because, Larkin, I didn't come up here to eat dinner with them. I came so I could have dinner with you." He puts the last of the pans away. "They can eat later after we are done if they want."

"Okay." I take the salad bowls over to the table and set them down. "So, this is like a date, then."

I feel him behind me before I hear him there. The heat of his body so close to mine that he has mine warming up. "Yes. We are going to do this a lot, these next eight weeks."

I swirl around. "Eight weeks?"

"Isabel is on summer holiday. You are stuck with me for eight weeks." He leans down and kisses my forehead. "Can you handle that?"

"You are staying here? In this house? With me?" I know I sound skeptical about that.

"Yes." He says it so nonchalantly. "The girls will be here on Monday. Helena, Beatriz, and Isabel. Meaning, we won't be completely alone, but we will do our best to find ways to spend time alone. The private sitting room next to the office may work best."

I take a step back. "I have to work, Antonio."

He smiles at me. "Yes, I know. You are working on our home and I thought..."

"Your home," I correct him. "I am working on your home, Antonio."

Sometimes it's better not to say anything at all, in case you were wondering. This seems to have been one of those times. Correcting him seems to have put him in a state that is reflected not only in his posture but also in his voice.

He crosses his arms and slowly breathes in through his nose and out through his mouth. When he finally looks at me again, I realize I am about to get an earful. Fortunately, the timer goes off, giving me the perfect reason to escape.

I pull out two extra plates, placing larger portions on them than I do my own. Adding a little salad to the side and then setting them on a tray so I can carry them to the office area.

I excuse myself as I carry them down the hall to the open office door. "Knock, knock."

Both men look up from the television they were watching and quickly stand.

"Dinner." I walk inside and don't miss the shocked expressions on their faces. "What?"

"You shouldn't have served us, miss." Isaac takes the tray from me. "We could have come and gotten it ourselves after you both ate."

I wave my hand at him, dismissing his suggestion. "Whatever."

"He's right." Gino takes one plate and sits back down. "You are not supposed to wait on us. We are here to serve you, miss."

I cross my arms, letting them know I don't agree. "Why? Because I am dating your King?"

They both nod their heads several times as they take a bite and make very satisfied faces.

Isaac swallows and mumbles. "This is delicious."

"Thank you." I stare at them for a moment. "I'm no one special guys. I'm just a woman like most others out there in this big world. I work for a living, thus the reason I am here right now. You've both seen me in my underwear for Pete's sake."

They both blush and Gino smiles as he speaks. "Yes, but we've seen lots of women in their knickers, miss."

My face must reveal my thoughts about that statement.

"That came out wrong. I mean over the years." He grunts. "I don't mean any of King Antonio's women, there have been none besides you, miss, not since I've worked for him. I meant in general. Isaac, I'm sure was privileged to..."

"Shut it, Gino." Isaac cuts him off. "Antonio doesn't make it a habit of getting his women in their knickers. His father, however, I believe was going for a record of some sort. I had to interrupt him a time or two.

"Now this business about you not being special, not true. I've been around awhile, miss. Seen my share of things over the years. What you have with the king, it's a rare thing indeed. Not very many people find what you have, less so in this tight community. While I understand this is all new to you, you also need to start understanding the role you will one day take part in. I do believe that you, miss, will make a very fine queen and I will gladly serve you when the time comes."

"Please don't." I close my eyes and rub my forehead. "One day at a time. That's how I make it through all this without getting sent off to the nuthouse. One day at a time."

They respond in unison, I know they weren't being ostentatious to make a point, but their words hit me hard, no matter. "As you wish."

The same stupid response they give Antonio. I spin angrily and stomp down the hall back to the kitchen. When I get there, I find him in the same stance he was when I left, and right now, I am in no mood to deal. I ignore him as I grab our plates and then carry them over to the table and place them firmly down. As I'm taking my seat, I give a few orders of my own. "Sit down and shut up."

Antonio's expression fades slightly as he takes his seat. "Grace?" He cautiously asks me.

I take his hand and bow my head while he gives thanks, but as soon as he is finished, I tug my hand free and start eating. It is quiet. The only noise is the clinking of our forks as they bang against our plates. I stare at my food and try to keep it together. But the longer we sit there, the harder it becomes. Soon the tears spill from my eyes and there is nothing I can do to stop them.

CHAPTER 24
Antonio

The Royals

"**S**it down and shut up." Those are Larkin's last words before we sat down to eat.

I didn't argue with her. The tone of her voice was enough to get me to bring down my anger so we could discuss this the right way, although the tension between us remains.

The silence as we eat only seems to make it worse.

I could really use a glass of wine. A nice zinfandel would bring out the flavors in the food and also help take the edge off. So, I stand and make my way to the wine cooler. Grab the bottle of wine I am looking for, two wine glasses, and a corkscrew. After I open it and let it breathe for a few minutes. I pour and then carry them back to the table, setting one in front of Larkin as I take my seat.

I am aware she doesn't normally drink, but I hate drinking alone. It's a glass of wine, one glass. Wine is good for the heart, mind, and soul. One glass a day with dinner should be acceptable. And I bet if she tried it, she'd like it. I won't force her to drink, but I will at least offer it to her when I pour myself a glass from now on. If she doesn't consume it, then she doesn't and I'll pour it out, then do the same the next night. My mind is made up, and I am prepared to defend my actions if she should question me about them now.

Larkin is staring at her food as she slowly shovels it in her mouth and chews. It's all very meticulous and done in a way that suggests she is doing it all out of rote, not enjoying the food she is eating. Such a shame really, because the food is amazing. One more thing I have decided I like about her.

Watching her earlier, as she prepared this meal, was one of the loveliest experiences I have ever been a part of. Her teasing me while she moved around like she owned the kitchen, almost had me forgetting who I was. At that moment in time, we were just Larkin and Antonio, a woman, and a man, doing what half the other couples like us do every day. Or at least that's how I imagined it, I'm not sure that's how it works. Nonetheless, I decided that is how I wanted it to work from now on between us. I want to prepare dinner with her every night for the rest of my life. Want to watch her taste the food as she prepares it. Licking her fingers off without giving it a second thought, all while I listen to her chatter to herself as she does.

I reach for my wine glass and swirl it around slowly before taking a sip. When I set it down, I glance her way again and notice she has stopped eating and has dropped her head. Her hair has fallen over her shoulder, concealing her face from view.

When her left hand lifts and wipes something off her cheek, I watch her more carefully. When she does it again, I reach out and brush her hair back over her shoulder so I can determine the problem. As soon as I spot the tears, I don't care about anything else.

"What is the matter?" I caress her shoulder, showing my concern.

"I'm never going to be able to do it." The sadness in her eyes guts me when she raises her gaze to meet mine.

Sliding my chair back, I snag her arm and tug. I am pleased when she doesn't fight me, but instead stands and takes a seat in my lap without further prompting. Wrapping my arms around her, I wait for her to settle before resting my head against hers. I can feel her body trembling slightly in my arms, and I don't like it.

"Do what, my love? What are you afraid you will not be able to do?" I run my hand along her arm. "Tell me please."

Her fingers play with the buttons of my shirt. "I've never seen you dressed like this before."

"Avoiding the question, Larkin, will not make it go away," I tell her.

And I don't dress like this all that often, really. Today, before I left the palace, I changed into a pair of tan shorts and a short-sleeve button-down shirt. It's the start of the summer holiday, so I figured I should dress the part.

"You look like every other man out there, dressed like this." She lets out a labored laugh. "But you're not just a man, are you, Antonio? No matter what, you are always more than that, and you can't turn that off just because the day is over. You can dress as they do, but you can never truly be like them."

Her statement speaks volumes. I have never been like everyone else. Dressed in the same uniform, looking like the other boys on my *fútbol* team didn't make me one of them, I was still Prince Antonio. There was no escaping the life I was born into. No matter how hard I tried to pretend I could just turn it off, I couldn't, ever.

"You get used to it. Forget."

"Do you?" she asks, not believing me.

I can't lie to her. "No. You just learn to accept it eventually, I guess."

There are times accepting it is even grueling. Days I wish I had been born just a boy from Aragon instead of the prince. Other days, I freely accept my role and do my best to lead the people the way they count on me to. It isn't as difficult as it once was, I suppose. When everything rested on the sovereign's shoulders and only his/her shoulders. I am at least able to distribute the responsibilities to others, those who were elected by the people.

In reality, most of the daily tasks now rest on the elected officials' shoulders. While I am the head of the constitutional monarchy, the six members of the King's Council can outvote me. They hold the majority of the power when push comes to shove. Unless I have friends seated on the council who have the same viewpoints as I do, they could do as they please. I am truly only the tie-breaking vote with a title that sounds really, really important. One that usually even intimidates them when I need it to. And yes, as king, I usually like to throw that back in their smug faces. I was born into this position and will remain here until I die or hand it over to my heir. They are only here for a limited amount of time, so it is always wise to remind them of that fact.

"I'll never be able to do that. I wasn't born into this world, Antonio. I don't understand all these stupid rules. I'm going to mess up regularly and someone will always be there waiting to correct me when I do." Her entire body crumbles in my arms.

Does that mean she doesn't want to play by the rules? Or is she trying to tell me something else completely?

My body tenses now. "What did they say to you?" I know my voice is stern and harsh, that is because I don't like knowing my men made her feel like she messed up.

Larkin sits up and stares into my eyes. "Nothing. It's not so much what they said. I mean that. So, don't go all alpha male on them for only doing the jobs they are trained to do. They were only following the rules that have been drilled into them long before I ever showed up and messed it all up."

"Stop saying that! You didn't mess anything up. And I don't go alpha male on people." I lift my chin and clench my back teeth together in denial.

Larkin takes my face in her hands and runs her thumbs over my tense jaw muscles. She leans in and kisses both sides, along with that tight brow of mine. "Yes, my sweet man, you do. It's not your fault. They raised you to be an alpha male at his finest. Taught you that everyone within earshot of this deep, graveling voice is to do as you tell them to do without question. Your people have also been taught to follow, and they do so out of respect for the position you represent. Very few people out there are allowed to defy the king or even tell him no. So, the alpha male inside of you is hard for you to set aside."

"I don't want to be like that with you, Larkin." I close my eyes, afraid that earlier when I reacted to her correcting me, it might have frightened her. "I authorize you to defy me, and even tell me no, whenever the urge arises."

She kisses the dimple on my chin. "I'm not complaining, Antonio. The alpha male inside of you serves you well and gets the job done. As king, you are intended to be the only one standing tall while demanding others listen to you. I imagine one day I might even like that side of you for other reasons altogether."

I gather her hair in my hand and tug it slightly so she has to shifts back some. Hearing those words awakens that tiger inside of me again. Then I go after her mouth as alpha as I can right now. Taking it like a man hungry for so much more, needing more.

"What is it you don't believe you can do, Larkin?" I ask again once I have had my fill for the moment.

"Pretend to be one of them. Follow their stupid rules. Treat others as if I am better than them. Let them treat me like I am better because that is what they have always been told. I understand they believe that... one day this could all be... that I could one day find myself as a permanent part of your world." Her stumbling over her words, searching for the right ones, lights the wick inside of me.

"If I want to take those men dinner, I don't want to think I am lowering myself to do so. I don't want to feel as if I can't clean, do laundry, scrub a toilet or two, or even cook your dinner, all because I now have this title hanging over my head.

"I can't pretend I give one inkling about any of that crap. Treat those around me as simply servants whose only job is to serve me and do as they are told. It's not who I am. I don't believe one person is better than another just because they happen to live in some fancy castle." She blows out a frustrated puff of air. "I just can't do that."

I stare at her in complete awe and fall deeper by the second. "You truly want to be able to clean a few nasty toilets?"

She shrugs. "A few, perhaps. Fifteen, may be a little more than even I'm willing to do, though, so I would appreciate some help."

I slide my hands upward so I can hold her face in them and chuckle. Fifteen toilets I believe is the exact number Maximiliano Chateau has. "You will do just fine, Miss Cross. I shall inform the staff they are to treat you however you wish them to. Which I know still goes against what you are saying. But they will need to be trained in the new way and that means telling them your wishes as often as is needed, since I never plan on letting you go.

"You, Larkin, are a blessing God has given me, and I never, ever want you to doubt that. I also never want you to wonder what I am thinking or how I feel about you. So, I am going to tell you and you are just going to have to figure out how to deal with it."

Tears fill her eyes again as her breathing gets uneven and falters. "If I must, then I guess I must."

Gazing directly into her eyes, I wait a beat. "I love you, *mi lunita*. I love you and only you. I've never once told a woman that before, but I plan on telling you often so you don't forget." I lean forward and kiss her lips, then feel them trembling under mine.

Very slowly she responds with the most beautiful words ever spoken against mine, letting the tears from her eyes wet my cheeks. *"Rey de mi corazón, yo también te amo. Yo también te quier."* (King of my heart, I love you too. I love you too.)

This is not the first time a woman has said those words to me. I have had my title as Prince added to all kinds of mushy objects. Prince of hearts, love prince, my heart's prince, or ruler of my heart, are just a few examples of the ones the ladies have bestowed on me. They were all just words mixed in hopes to make me feel something for them. They never worked, nor did I believe them when they all claimed to love me. I knew they were just saying the words, not once suffering from the emotion that went along with them. Which is always the reason I never repeated them back, well, along with the fact that I didn't love them.

But hearing Larkin do her best to utter those words in one of my native languages, lets me know they aren't just words to her. I know how challenging it must have been for her to learn them well enough to feel like she could speak them to me. Her self-conscious mind would not allow her to butcher something like that, which means she has most likely spent a few weeks repeating them in her head, making sure she got each syllable exact.

I didn't plan any on this. None of it even crossed my mind. So, I am equally surprised to hear the next words slip from my lips. *"Maintenant, je vais parler de l'avenir. Je t'aime et je t'aimerai toujours. Je vais te demander d'être la reine de mon cœur et d'accepter de m'épouser."*

Larkin giggles. "I have no idea what you just said, although it sounded so beautiful. *Hermosa mi amor.* But could you please repeat it in English?"

"You've been practicing your Spanish." I grin fondly at her.

"Si, señor. I listen to it every night before I go to bed. There's an app

for that, you know. It claims I will be fluent in it very soon. I guess only time will tell. But what you spoke was not in Española, that was French. And I'd like to know what you said so I can counter properly."

I think long and hard about it.

"You promised me I would never have to wonder what you are thinking. That you'd always just tell me, so tell me." She uses my own lousy words against me.

She is correct though; I promised her that. I nudge her to stand and take her hand in mine. "Okay, but first I need to make a run to my bedroom. Then we shall take a walk. While we walk, we will talk. While we talk, I promise to tell you what I said."

"Okay." Larkin nods once. "You promise this isn't some trick to get me to forget about it all."

"No trick, I promise." I lean down and kiss her lips. "No trick, but I need you to keep an open mind and listen to my words while I talk. Can you promise to do that?"

She bites her lip and shrugs. "I can try. Why do I get the suspicion you are about to knock my feet out from under me and send my head spinning?"

"I love you, Larkin. Remember that and the rest will be easy." I wink at her as I take off towards my private quarters.

Once I am inside, I close the door and head for the large closet. Inside is a safe where I keep all my personal belongings and family heirlooms. A habit one learns when they have other people cleaning up after them. Leaving anything lying around is sometimes too tempting, even for the most honest of people.

While I was waiting on Larkin to return earlier after she unmanned me. Gino brought in my things from the car and placed them in my room as I instructed. I came to my suite to have a peek at the damage done to my poor jewels, which by the way were absolutely normal looking, not even red. I would have sworn that they'd be red, perhaps a bit bruised. Even though they were still throbbing, there was no visible damage. Nor did I imagine there would be any physical harm since the staff attached to my jewels was functioning just fine. After I assessed the damage, I went to my bag and retrieved a few items I wanted secured inside the safe.

CHAPTER 24

I am here now to retrieve one of those items. I didn't plan this. Okay, I didn't plan on doing this the first night I was here. My plan was to spend all my extra time with Larkin while here. I figured that sometime during this eight-week holiday I would finally move this courtship along. I mean, we only dated for a little over a week when I decided dating her wasn't enough. So logically, I imagined that once I started courting her, it too would eventually not be enough, and I'd want to make it a more permanent relationship. Give her the title I had seen her in almost since the beginning. Not the title, but the one that would let everyone know eventually she would own that title.

I realize this seems quick. But must I remind you that things are often done differently in my world? Engagements are often arranged long before they are announced. Most of it is all for show.

Typically, in my world a man and woman are seen together at a few events, that is the dating phase. Then they begin the courting phase, which lasts a couple of months, depending on how quickly they want to move it along. Engagements can vary. Some are quick, mostly because there is already an heir on the way and one doesn't want to have the public making accusations.

You didn't know that monarchs cook faster than other babies. I was born seven long months after my parents married. Princess Isabel was a record, I'm sure; her birth was a very quick four months. And as we all know, a king only weds a virgin and consummates his marriage for the first time on the wedding night. So, like I said, monarchs cook quicker, or at least those first ones do. Funny how the rest seem to take the full forty weeks.

I may be the first king, in a long line of kings, to have waited until my wedding night, but I will wait. Larkin has enough to deal with; she does not need to hear all the gossip that would accompany her should our first time result in producing an heir. Accordingly, I will not take her in any way until she is my wife.

Reaching inside the safe, I pull out a black velvet box I picked up the other day. The ring I once thought about giving Lady Dalia was a family heirloom, my great-grandmother's ring. One she would have expected to be offered, and I guess it was a good thing I hadn't planned on disappointing her. (Sarcasm at its best there, folks.) This ring was not an heirloom, though, at least not one of mine.

I had my friend Fernando put the word out that he was looking for a very unique and old engagement ring. A gift for his wife and it had to be unique, one of a kind. Something artistic looking, around a carat, and could possibly be made to look like a set. It took three calls and several snapshots from him to uncover the one I thought would be perfect for my special lady. The yellow and white gold band spoke antique, the flowers handcrafted on the side gave it that artistic appearance, the high setting made the diamond appear as if it were placed high on a crown. Plus, the jeweler had already created the perfect ring to accompany it, with a mixture of yellow and white gold, including small diamonds that hugged both sides of the first band. He had it sent to the palace for my approval, and I bought it upon sight.

I shove the box in my pocket after looking at it closely again. It was the ideal, imperfect ring for a woman like Larkin, and I knew she would love it. What I didn't know was if she would accept it.

If you ever thought men like me don't get nervous, you can think again. Most of the time we don't let things bother us, I guess. People do what we want when we want them to do it. We snap our fingers and they come. There are very few things we worry about, because for the most part, I guess we don't have to worry; we let others do it for us.

But nothing about this relationship has ever really been easy. Larkin is the one woman who could truthfully tell me no, have me dropping to my knees as I beg for her to change her mind. So yeah, I'm nervous, because, for the very first time in my life, her answer to this one question is the only one I care about.

CHAPTER 25
Larkin

The Royals

I t doesn't take Antonio long to return with a jacket he has draped over his arm. I'm not buying that he went to his room to retrieve a jacket, but I say nothing.

He reaches out and takes my hand, then leads me toward the security office in the back. We pause at the door where both men stand as soon as they see us.

"Sit." He motions for them to do as he says.

Neither man moves.

"We are going for a walk. Taking the path up to the orchard so I can check to see how the trees are looking." He reaches into his pocket and shows them a device. "I grabbed the tracker, so should you need to know where we are, you will have no problem locating us. However, we are not to be bothered unless it is a family emergency, or the world is about to end. Are we clear?"

"As day, sir." Both men nod as they travel around the room, doing what it is they must do for us to leave.

"All clear, sir. Team one is checking the orchard now. By the time you arrive, they should have moved on. A perimeter check was done ten minutes ago, and we received a thumbs up. What time should we expect you back, sir?" Isaac glances up from the laptop he moved to right after Antonio told him of our plans.

"Two hours at most." He is getting anxious, I can tell.

"We will buzz in one. Remember to respond within five minutes or expect a second buzz. No response and you can be sure that team one will be on you in two." Isaac sets a timer that I see counting down now on all visible screens. "Good to go, sir."

"One more thing." Antonio waits for both men to look up at him. "Kitchen needs to be cleaned. Take care of it. Larkin was kind enough to cook dinner for us, so it's the least we can do so she doesn't need to do it when we get back."

Gino straightens and crosses his arms. "We? No offense, sir, but I believe you are passing the buck."

A wicked smile crosses Antonio's face. "Does it? Well, since I was the only one in the kitchen with her earlier, helping. Seems only fair that you all get this job. Now see that it gets done."

We turn before the guys can respond. I can hear them arguing about who will get the privilege, but don't get to establish which one ends up losing.

As soon as we step outside, a chilly breeze blows, so Antonio lifts his jacket and drapes it over my shoulders. "Early summer evenings can sometimes get a little chilly. Thought this might come in handy."

"Thank you," I tell him as I slide my arms through the sleeves. "I haven't spent many evenings outside since arriving. Where are we going again?"

He points toward the field that dips down and then backs up to a large grove of trees. I've seen them but never ventured off in that direction yet. It's the opposite way of the chateau, which has been my focus since my arrival.

We discover a rocky path that has obviously been maintained. "What kind of trees?"

"Apple and pear. There are Gala, Jazz, and Zari apples; they are just now getting started. The pear trees are Concorde or Gorham. They were already here when we bought the property. There is also a strawberry patch in the east fields, blackberry bushes toward the west, and wild gooseberries all over the estate," he informs me as we walk slowly, surveying the land. The chateau sits on hundreds of acres of rolling hills that are very pleasing to look at.

"You once said you liked this place and thought it would make a great family home. Why?" We are just walking up the hill toward the orchard.

Antonio pauses and scans the field. "It's very peaceful, don't you think? No noisy traffic. No people rushing around in a hurry to get wherever it is they feel they need to go. It's just you and the land out here. If it takes you an extra five minutes to get where you are going, no one cares." He starts walking again, tugging me behind him gently. "Do you like it?"

"Yes, although I've never lived anywhere but the city. The quiet at night can be eerie until you get comfortable with it. Each night has been better and better and now you are here so..." I stop there, not feeling like I need to finish.

"I'm here now, so what, exactly?"

I guess I was wrong about not needing to finish. "Suddenly, I'm kind of partial to the quiet. Feels sort of like a bubble that could be way too easy to get lost in. A good way to forget about the outside world and all the responsibilities that are just beyond the hills waiting for your attention."

"A bubble." He repeats those two words as he helps me up the last part of the rocky path. "I like that."

Antonio continues walking in silence as he strolls down a row of trees. I simply follow because I have no idea where we are going. It also gives me a chance to appreciate the larger-than-life man in front of me. The one I told nearly thirty minutes ago that I loved him.

If anyone walked by us right now, they'd not realize who he was, I'm sure. He seems relaxed in a way I've never gotten to witness until now. Dressed in everyday clothing, wearing a new pair of tennis shoes, or should I say, ones that once looked new before we started this walk, on his feet. A very tall ordinary man who steals my breath almost every time I look at him.

He finally stops and turns with a smile pasted on his face as he motions for me to have a seat. I glance to where he is gesturing and see a rock bench. If I had to guess, I'd say it's quite old, like as old as the home I am currently working on.

I take a seat and nearly forget to breathe when I catch sight of the view. I have never wished I had my art supplies with me more than I do right now. We must be facing west at the moment, or at least in that general direction. The sunset is sending up the most perfect colors of purple, pink, orange, and yellow, all mixed in a way only God can truly mix them. The large chateau sets just to the south at an angle, surrounded by newly green grass and overgrown fields.

Without thinking, I speak the first thought that pops into my head. "I want to paint this. I want to stand here with a canvas and my paints and capture this view. Hang it in the library I am going to build for you. I want this to be the first painting I have done in over five years."

Antonio finally takes his seat next to mine. "I thought it might inspire you once you saw it."

"You were so very right about that. The colors are exquisite. The view is breathtaking." I am staring out over the land, memorizing it so that later I can try to sketch it with my colored pencils.

"I agree one hundred percent," he whispers near my ear. "Breathtakingly beautiful."

I shift my eyes to determine if he is looking at what I am. He's not, of course, he staring directly at me. "Stop ogling and study it before it disappears. God painted this picture for us to enjoy, and you are too busy gawking at me and missing out."

"Guilty as charged." He chuckles but switches his gaze toward the horizon. "Could you live here with me? Away from all the city noises and busyness if you got to sit and look at this every evening?"

"I need to work, Antonio. My work will take me elsewhere sometimes. You do realize that, right? Sometimes months at a time." I breathe in the clean air slowly.

"When you aren't working, could you, though? Would you want to live here? Raise a few little ones with me here?"

"How many little ones?" I twist so I can regard his face when he gives me his answer.

He rubs a hand over his jaw. "Tradition has let that be up to God. As a chosen servant of him, it has always been custom for a man, or woman, in my position to let him decide the number of descendants he allows. My family is rather small compared to some past ones. My father was the eldest of nine, his father had eight siblings."

I know my facial expression has to be priceless. No way am I birthing eight children, no way, Batman. Four seemed like a rather large number to me even, if I'm being honest. Two was the number I always had in my head as an acceptable one. I'd always wished for a sibling. Three might even be something I'd consider, but that would all depend on how brutal labor was. I might have one and declare never again. Pain and I are not the best of friends.

"So, you are telling me they all just took their chances and kept having babies just because? No. No, I don't think I could do that, Antonio. That is why God gave man the knowledge to create all these different forms of birth control." I am having a tough time wrapping my head around this. "Or even let us figure out that if we did a little cut, snip, and tuck on a man, he could no longer father children."

Instinctively, Antonio reaches down and covers his male appendage. "Why must you always want to do him harm? He's done nothing to you."

I giggle. I hate it when I giggle like a schoolgirl. "Yet. Although I do believe for all those before mentioned offspring to be a possibility, he has wicked proposals on what he'd like to do.

"You're serious, though, about this birth control issue? Should I agree to all of this one day being mine, I'd be expected to keep birthing children for you? I guess that explains why they designed king and queen quarters. Eventually, the queen smartens up and sleeps separately from the ever so potent king, which means I should take a good look at that space in the chateau. Make sure it has all the amenities I would want or need."

"You will do no such thing. Your place will always be next to me in our bed. Separate quarters were done for many reasons in the past. I suppose that your suggestion might be one, although the main one I came to learn was so that the king didn't feel guilty when he wandered."

Antonio reaches out and takes my hand in his. "I will never be a wandering spouse, my love. I hated how it affected my mother and grandmother. Embarrassed because neither of their husbands were discreet about it. My father invited his mistresses to stay in the palace, urged them to stick around until he was done with them. He possessed a few at a time and paraded them around to make my mother jealous. After she finally moved out and left him, it got much worse if you can believe that. I'm actually surprised he didn't father more children."

"Did he not practice safe sex? I mean, you know, because you just never know. I mean, I know condoms break and all, but I believe they were invented for more than one reason."

I can't believe we are actually having this conversation. "So, you've never? I mean, because you are thirty and I'm sure lots of women have thrown themselves at you. Offered you to use them however you wanted. Not just because you are king or were the prince, really. Although I'm confident that would be very tempting for many of them, to be able to say they had been with you for that very reason. But also, because you are a very handsome man, a very large man, so I'm certain they've often speculated if you are equally large all the way around. I mean, you know, because there are those women who always seem to be debating about the size of a man's package. Not that I've ever wondered or anything, or thought about it, really. Oh, please do something to stop me from embarrassing myself anymore. Otherwise, I am just going to keep..."

Antonio smiles as he leans forward and kisses me, so I am forced to stop talking. I love it when he kisses me, anytime, really. The man knows how to kiss, or at least he knows how to kiss me.

"I've never been with a woman like that, Larkin. Yes, over the years, I've received several invitations. Women can be very blunt when they want to be. I, however, had no desire to be with any of them.

"Safe sex was preached to me, much like I am sure it is with many other young boys. My father sat me down before I left for boarding school, and we had a very detailed discussion about it. I was twelve, remember, so sex with a young lady was the last thing on my mind. But he made it clear that even at twelve there would be those who would try, and he was right, there definitely were. By fourteen, he sat me down again and handed me a box of condoms. Told me to carry at least one with me always so I would never be caught off guard, or have to rely on the girl to provide one for me. Made it very clear to never let the girl provide, because one can never trust another person completely. So, of course, I did, because at that time I did as my father suggested. Thought maybe a few times I might need it, but didn't in the end for many reasons. By sixteen, however, I stopped carrying them. That was after I walked in on my father giving it to one of the younger servants who was supposed to be working. I decided right then and there I did not want to be like him. Vowed that I would do my best to not be like those who came before me. I would marry for love and only love. Even save myself for that woman, so I would not be able to compare her to another.

"You will be my very first lover. Will I be yours?" he asks as he pushes my hair behind my ears.

"Yes. I've never even come close. I had a boyfriend once try to convince me to, but when I wouldn't, he ended it. I never dated a guy that did it for me, I guess."

Time to be honest, right, so I might as well lay it all out for him. "It actually terrifies me. I have trouble even using tampons when my period is at its heaviest. I still use the smallest size and even then, they are extremely uncomfortable. My doctor assured me it's a common issue for women who have never had sex and still possess that barrier God designed down there. Many of her younger, less experienced, patients suffer, so she presented me with a few options. One was to remove the barrier for me. Another was I could do it myself. Last she said there was a surgery that could be done to open it some. Eventually, my mother and I opted for the surgery. However, my doctor explained that until I became sexually active, stretched it out a little on a more regular basis, I'd continue to have issues. So, there is that, and since pain and I are not the best of friends, I figured I'd just wait it out until the right guy came along."

Wow, that was not as dreadful as I thought it might be. Probably because Antonio didn't seem shocked by my extreme honesty. He only nodded his head slightly as I talked. When I finished, he leaned in and kissed me again, letting me know how he appreciated me not shying away from that subject.

"I promise to make it not so terrifying for you, my love." Antonio cups my face. "I shall be extremely gentle with you in all areas. I never, ever wish to hurt you. And to be clear about the children business, we shall have as many as you, my love, choose to give me. I am fine with us using birth control or even getting cut, snipped, and tucked if it means you will allow me to continue loving you in the most intimate of ways."

"I know," I whisper. "I mean, it could take us a very long time to get me ready for you.

"I'll enjoy every step along the way, I can assure you of that," he whispers back. "Worrying about it will only make matters more difficult, so keeping you relaxed will be my goal when the time comes. Of course, I also want you to enjoy it so we can do it as often as you are comfortable with."

I don't even know how to respond, so I don't. Instead, we sit there in the fading sunlight and stare at each other, letting it sink in for a few minutes.

"I love you, Larkin." Antonio finally breaks the silence. "Earlier you spoke from the heart. They were such lovely words. So now I will speak from mine and hope I do this right.

"Those words I said earlier. The first part was basically that. I also said I love you and will always love you. I mean that deep down inside, I know you are the woman for me. The one who will always be there for me when the road seems long and hard. Loyal to me, to us, and not let others whisper in your ear as they try to remind you how you got to where you are right now. You landed here on your own. No one helped you or organized our chance meeting, except God, perhaps. Meaning you will owe no one any favors, and that, my dear Larkin, makes the reality of this whole affair seem, at times, unreal.

"A man like myself does not, by chance, run into anyone. There is always a person behind the scenes who is playing puppet master. We possess what many others only ever dream of having, a no strings attached kind of love. I know what that typically means, but it means something different this time. It means we are free to make our own choices, without the influences of those who always seem to want to have a say. The only attachment will be the bond we form between us, and it will be so strong no one will be able to pull us apart."

Antonio leans forward and kisses my lips before he stands. He reaches inside his pocket and pulls out a velvet box. His hands are trembling and right about then I hear a buzzing sound.

"Perfect timing, gentlemen." I hear him grumble. "I need to answer this or they will never leave us alone."

"Sure." I swallow hard as I stare at the box he is now squeezing.

"Checking in. All is good. We should be heading back within one." He pauses for a moment while he listens. "Isaac, I swear that's not funny. It will be your head if that happens. Then Gino will become my new head of security. Now if you will let me get back to business?"

"What's not funny?" I ask him when he hangs up his phone. "Are they watching us? Do they know what you are about to do?"

"No one is watching us. I can assure you of that. And it's their job to know these kinds of things, whether or not I tell them. So, my guess is yes, they know and evidently, they are way too familiar with me. Can we please just forget about being interrupted and get on with it?"

"Are you nervous, Antonio? Are you afraid I'll give you a different answer than the one I believe I promised I'd give you? Do you not believe I am a woman of my word?" I can't help but tease him in his moment of uncertainty. He is most definitely a man on the edge right now, so I plan on taking this all in. I don't imagine there will be very many times in this life where I will get to witness him like this.

"Funny, funny, witty little woman, you are, Larkin Moon Cross. I only want you to answer my question with complete honesty. I don't intend, nor did I ever really, on making you keep your word unless it was absolutely what you want. So, if you are not completely sure that this life is one you can deal with, then..."

I rise to my feet and place a finger over his moving lips. "I guess you will never know that answer until you ask the question. Now, as you said earlier, shall we get on with it?"

One nod is all I get.

The man's confidence has long been forgotten. He is not the king right now. Not the ruler who declares something and expects it to be done without question. He is only Antonio, the man I love. And he is standing here before me, ready to do and say anything to get me to agree.

He drops to his knees—yes knees—and grabs my hands. Bringing them to his lips as he kisses them before he lets the right one go. His eyes meet mine and he stares at me like no other man ever has.

"Be the queen of my heart, Larkin, own it like no one else ever will or has. I beg of you, my love, to agree to all of this. Accept me for who I am and say you will marry me."

I hadn't even realized he'd slipped the ring out of the box until he slides it on my finger. The fit is almost perfect. The unique design has me staring at it longer than I intended. It's not a new ring. Instead, I can identify it as an antique, a ring that has a story behind it. My mind wanders off and imagines the first time a man offered it to a woman.

"Larkin, you are killing me here, my love." I catch the panic in his voice.

My eyes search his again, and the emotion I discover has me dropping to my knees. I take his face in both of mine and squeeze it tight. "Sorry about that. Lovely ring, by the way. Ask me again."

He grunts. "Accept me for who I am and say you will marry me."

"There isn't a force in this world that could keep me away from you, my sweet, handsome man. Yes. Yes, I will marry you."

Remember the alpha male I said lives inside of him? That is very true, but there is also a very insecure boy who hides in his shadow. One that as soon as I speak those words, collapses onto his haunches, and wraps his arms around my center. He presses his face against my stomach and begins weeping, letting it all out.

I don't question him about it. This isn't a sad cry. This is a deep down release of something that has had him trussed all his life, making him feel like he may never escape the confinements this kind of life brings. So instead, I lean forward and hold him against me while I caress his hair.

His hold tightens. "I love you, Larkin."

Kissing the top of his head, I smile, even though I know he cannot see me. "I love you two, Antonio. I promise to love you always."

Finally, he pulls back and stands. Even all red-faced with tear-stained cheeks, this man is still absolutely the most stunning man I have ever laid eyes on. He tugs me to his side and together we stand there in silence and watch as the sun disappears behind the horizon.

CHAPTER 26
Larkin

The Royals

Eight weeks, in case you didn't already know this, really isn't very long. It feels even shorter when you appreciate the time you have with someone is limited.

A lot of things can happen, however, in those eight weeks. Some good, some not so good, and then some that are just interesting. But no matter what, one thing remained constant during all those situations. The love Antonio and I had didn't falter once. If anything, it was strengthened.

I'll start with the good, of course.

I've never been in love before. I figured that out rather quickly after spending these last several weeks with Antonio. How I felt in the past did not even compare to what I felt for this man.

It was the simple things I found the most revealing to me. The little gestures meant more than the time we set aside each evening to do what couples in love often do.

Kissing is what I mean, just to be clear. Not once has Antonio tried to take things past that. Well, not really. He'd voiced his thoughts on how he wanted our relationship to progress. Clarifying that he intended on waiting until our wedding night to express his love in that way. Guess he figured he had abstained this long, a few more months shouldn't be that difficult. I agreed.

It was the fact that he woke early enough every morning to get the coffee started for me. Made sure I had a hot cup waiting on the counter as soon as I descended the stairs. Cooked me frozen waffles with sausage for breakfast most mornings. If I wasn't in the mood for waffles, then he'd make toast or a bagel if it sounded better. I didn't have the heart to inform him I wasn't a breakfast eater. The love that seeped out of him by that gesture was enough to get me to learn to become one.

Then there were all those times he showed up with lunch. Nothing special really, just sandwiches. I knew Helena didn't prepare those sandwiches; the man bringing them to me had. And while that may not seem all that big of a deal to most, it was a huge one for me. He could have easily asked either of the other women at the house to prepare us lunch, and they would have done it without question. Instead, he took the time to not only bring me my lunch most days, but fix it for us as well. Love in its truest form.

The last touching gesture was when he took me back up to the orchard at sunset, lugging my art supplies with us. When we got there, he'd toss out a blanket, set up an easel, and would then lie back and let me do my thing. We would stay until the light was no longer suitable enough for me to see what I was doing. Then he'd repack it and carefully transport my canvas back down.

Since I hadn't painted in a very long time, it took me almost two weeks to finally be satisfied with my initial work. Then it took another couple of weeks to finish it exactly how I wanted. And not once had the man complained when I tossed out the unsatisfied creations. He only sat back and relaxed, sometimes sleeping, patiently waiting on me to get it just right. It was the fact he understood my need to paint, sketch, or doodle as my form of therapy. That he made sure when he sensed me stressed, he would drag me up that hill.

Now for the not so good stuff. The keyword here is *not* so good. Nothing about it is horrible, but some of it definitely caused ripples.

After our private outing in the orchard, we knew once we announced our engagement, there could be a slight uproar. So, we wanted to establish a plan before letting the cat out of the bag. Except somehow it got leaked two days later, which had been harder on Antonio than me. The fact someone had betrayed him, us, had sent him into a fury. I don't think I've ever seen a person so infuriated. He'd gathered his guards and ripped them up one side and then down the other. Demanded that they locate the person responsible for sharing something so private and then instructed them to make an example out of that person.

Turns out it wasn't one of the staff after all. It ended up being his sisters' doing. Isabel texted Gabriela as soon as she spotted the ring on my left hand. Gabriela happened to be with several of her friends. One of them had read the text when it came in and blurted it out. It was all a very innocent mistake, and both girls felt terrible about it.

Isabel had been terrified to tell her brother after hearing him yelling. She finally had a meltdown in the kitchen with me when she overheard him going off again after his team hadn't been able to locate the person. I wrapped her in my arms and comforted her the best I could. Then shouted for Antonio to come into the kitchen and shut up. I informed him what happened, and that his reaction to the stupid incident was the reason we were still dealing with it. I'm not sure who was more surprised about my lecture, Isabel, Antonio, or his men.

So, after everyone calmed down, we made an official statement. We called Alejandro and disclosed the details we agreed could be shared. The three of us were able to come up with a suitable press release that gave a brief statement about our relationship.

It stated that we met four months earlier when I joined the architectural team scheduled to come to Hermosa Islas to work on several historical properties. Both of us were attracted to the other person, and at first, Antonio kept the fact of who he was a secret. Reminded his people how, while that seemed impossible, there were many world leaders out there that most of them would not recognize if they walked right up to them. Shared that after the big celebration at the palace, we began dating. Not all that long afterward, Antonio decided he wanted to court me. During that time, it became very evident to us that what we had was unique and quickly turned serious. We had fallen in the best of ways and realized it was love in its truest form. Which is when Antonio decided to ask me to be his wife. There was no mention of what that meant, that by becoming his wife I would also become their queen. He didn't want to mention any of that. He wanted to make a point. He wasn't asking me to serve as queen, but to be a wife first and then accept any responsibilities that came along with that. Sounded reasonable, I guess.

Once the palace released an official statement, it was time to deal with the fallout. The nation seemed to be split on how they felt about the king's choice. Which put some strain on our budding relationship.

I went off one night after reading a reporter's opinion on the matter. He called me a dumb American girl who was living out her childhood fantasy about meeting a prince and falling in love. Claimed I didn't know the first thing about being a real queen and should step aside and let someone more qualified take the job.

The job.

Those had been the words that sent me into a tirade and had the entire house, besides Antonio, running to their safe corners. I paced the floor while giving that jerk a piece of my mind. I went on about how he made it sound like I was an uneducated, babbling, stupid blonde bimbo. All because I didn't recognize Antonio, since I had never once heard of Hermosa Islas until a few months ago. I wondered if he could tell me who all the world leaders were if only given a picture. I wanted to know what any of that had to do with being Antonio's wife. Did it not matter that I was madly in love with their king? That I'd chosen this life, not because of the stupid privileges that would be given to me, but because of the love that filled my heart whenever I saw him?

I ended the tirade by pointing my finger at my beloved fiancé as I made it clear I was going to show them just what kind of queen I could be. That I'd be the one who would change these stupid rules while proving any woman with half a brain could do *the job* as long as she had a man who loved her standing by her side. Declared that we were going to be the best king and queen duo who ever ruled. I might have gone a little overboard toward the end, but dang it, I was really, really pissed.

When I was finished, Antonio rose to his feet and stood there for several long minutes. I started noticing how his breathing was labored and that he was clenching his jaw. He was also far enough away, making all of him visible to me, meaning I didn't need to divert my eyes to catch the reason for all of that. The large, thick, elongated bulge, just slightly to the right, was sort of hard to miss—quite literally. It was even harder —pun intended—to miss when he stalked me and pressed his body firmly against mine as he wrapped me in his arms. Which is about the time I recalled him once telling me he had his own special reaction when I went off and let it all out.

For the first time in my adult life, I actually had a few extremely naughty thoughts and wondered what it would be like to have a man do certain things to me. Guess that is why I may have pressed harder against him and did a little maneuver with my hips. Which explains why I ended up getting shoved up against the wall only a few feet away. We stayed like that, continually repositioning our bodies, practically having sex with our clothes on. His hands never wandered, and neither did mine, but our sexy parts sure seemed to be trying to get very well acquainted. If Isaac hadn't come in when he did, I'm pretty sure I would have learned a few more details about what occurs when a man gets extremely aroused.

And that was the interesting part of our time together. Interesting, because I had a challenging time keeping my hands off Antonio after that. I mean, I didn't do inappropriate things, not really. It was more like I had a really tough time not thinking about what might have happened had we not been interrupted. That seemed to encourage me to touch him a lot more than before. I would purposely bump into him when we were cooking. Reach over to get something and let certain parts of my body brush against his. Let my hands roam a little more when we started getting intimate. Kiss him so passionately at times it activated all kinds of unusual responses I had always thought were exaggerated by those who talked.

Eight weeks of all of that made it go by faster than one might expect. And this week has been the longest one of my life. We've talked daily since they departed Sunday to return to Aragon Palace. But all the elements I had gotten accustomed to were suddenly gone, and I found myself alone again. I learned I didn't like the solitude as much as I once had.

I am heading to Aragon now, after a very long day. After I make a stop by the office, I will proceed to the palace. Tomorrow we are scheduled to throw an official engagement party. I have been told afterward we could start discussing dates and begin planning a wedding.

I had no idea how I was expected to plan a wedding when I was attempting to renovate a chateau. It was taking a little longer than I first predicted. We are a month behind schedule. Those passageways are causing most of my current setbacks and headaches. Closing off the ones I deemed too dangerous wasn't as easy as it should be. Nor was reinforcing the ones I kept. No way was I going to take a risk or leave any chance of them not being stable. So instead of working on those items we had originally scheduled, the structural engineer and I spent our time inspecting those passages. I knew I was going to have some explaining to do.

I enter the office a little after six and head for the main conference room. I knew they were waiting for me because I called before heading this way. So, I'm not surprised to find them discussing one of the other projects while they wait.

I am, however, surprised to see Zach here. He rarely visits overseas offices unless they are having a personnel issue. And that's when it hits me, and I realize I haven't been summoned here to discuss those delays at all.

Bradley dismisses the other team and then asks Chandler to close the door. The only people left are Cameron, Zach, Chandler, and, of course, Bradley. Cameron dials a number and Timothy's face suddenly appears on the video screen hanging on the wall.

Chandler's smug expression alerts me I am not going to enjoy this meeting.

"Larkin, thanks for taking the time to stop by and meet with us today." Zach starts the meeting. "We have a few issues we need to discuss."

"Did I do something wrong?" I ask, already knowing that answer. Don't they say if you have to ask that question, then you already know the answer? Although I don't think I do.

"Technically, no." Cameron answers.

"Is this about my work or my personal life?" I once again ask, but this time I'm not sure what the answer will be.

I know for a fact there is no policy about dating clients. While it is frowned upon, and not encouraged, there is no written rule prohibiting it. Nicolette Manchester is a prime example of why the policy was never composed. She is engaged to one. And that client went after her, making it very clear what his intentions were from the beginning. She tried to blow him off, even pass his business over to another. But he had refused and driven her insane for several long months.

"When did you hear about the Hermosa Islas project?" Bradley asks me as he flips through some papers.

"When I returned from Mexico City. I needed to get out of Chicago. You know why I was looking for a project that would get me out of there as quickly as possible. My original Tokyo trip got pushed back, so I knew I had time to take something else on. Janice happened to be there late one night, and we talked. I came to Zach the next morning." I have no idea where this is going.

"You don't remember Chandler mentioning something about it in Mexico City?" Cameron asks, watching me closely.

"No. We did not discuss other projects while we were there. I remember him saying something about wanting to get assigned to a project when he got back, but I don't recall what project it was. Is he claiming otherwise?" I glare at the man they just mentioned.

"What about reading an email from Janice, asking you a few questions that pertained to it?" Zach has a huge question in that question, and I can see my answer better match up with what he already knows.

"Honestly, no. I read several emails daily. Maybe you can jog my memory since you seem to think I did?" Yes, my patience is wearing thin. "Look, why don't we just cut to the chase here. Stop beating around the bush and just ask me what you want to ask me."

The room goes completely silent.

I cross my arms and wait. Stare at each one of them. Look them directly in the eyes. I even frown at the video screen as I glare at Timothy. I wait to see if any of them have the balls to accuse me of doing something unethical.

Timothy finally breaks into a stupid grin. "Nicolette warned us not to take you on. She said this all had to be a coincidence and that you would never use this company like that."

"I don't understand." I lean back in my chair, making it clear I am still pissed and would like an explanation.

Zach shakes his head in disgust, but not at me. "It was brought to our attention that someone unintentionally sent a few emails out with confidential documents attached. Janice Bcc'd two such documents to you and Chandler. She sent one to him because she wanted him to look it over before inviting him to join her once he returned. The one she sent to you contained client information that should never have been sent out in the first place. Both were supposed to be private correspondence between the client and her. Neither should have been Bcc'd and should have been brought to our attention immediately once they were."

"I don't remember an email like that. I would have reported it had I gotten one." I am still confused. "Wait, what kind of information did this email have in it? Are you suggesting that I knew all along who Antonio was? That I got myself assigned to this project to do what exactly, seduce the man, perhaps. Are you freaking kidding me right now? Tell me one time when I've ever once shown any interest in doing something like that. During the Seattle project, when the client came to me asking about our dating policy where clients were concerned, do you remember my response?"

Zach's amused response doesn't calm me down. "You called Nicolette."

"Actually, I called you, except you were unavailable, so I asked for a senior manager. She was the only one available. I called because I didn't want anything to look as if I was taking advantage of a situation. That client was in the room when I called while on speaker. I asked Nicolette about the policy, then I had him explain why I was asking."

I remember that day very clearly.

The client, Jerrod, was a very well-off man. He ran one of Seattle's top businesses, electronics I believe. He was in his late twenties and not all that bad looking for a self-proclaimed nerd. We were there because he'd bought an older building he needed to renovate. Wanted to turn it into several lofts and then sell them. The building was in the historical district, so he needed us to help him stay within all the regulations and whatnot.

That day we were discussing my plans for the project. When we were done, he asked me if Manchester International had a policy about staff dating clients. Instead of answering him right away, I called the Chicago office. I wanted to make it extremely clear from the get-go that I had not been the one to pursue. I couldn't think of a better way than to let my superiors answer that question for me.

Nicolette answered him and then asked him to give us a few minutes. Took the time to clarify that I was not obligated to accept. If I wasn't interested, then I had the right to turn him down. And if it became an issue, she'd deal with it.

We went on three dates. He never asked for a fourth and once I finished the project, I moved on. Got a great review from him even, and that was that.

"We weren't..." Bradley speaks, but I cut him off.

"Yes, you were. Or maybe you were only doing it because someone tried to suggest my reasons for taking this job so quickly. How many men have I dated?" I know this sounds like a silly question, but it's not really.

"How are we to know that?" Chandler laughs mockingly. "Your personal life isn't this company's business."

"Thank you." I straighten up. "My point exactly. My personal life is nobody's business but my own unless it is affecting my work."

"I believe you just made my point for me." Chandler leans back in his chair, now looking smugger than before.

"Are you freaking kidding me?" I glare at him. "That is a bald-faced lie, and you know it."

"Is it? Tell me, Larkin. Would you have spent all this extra time on the Maximiliano Chateau issues if it weren't intended to be your future home? Those passageways are a nightmare and should all be removed. Instead, we are wasting resources and time just so you can build yourself a much swankier home." He slaps his notepad on the table and points at it. "The cost alone is slaughtering the budget. We are weeks behind. And then there is this proposed library, don't even get me started on that one."

I am about to rip Chandler a new one when there is a knock on the door. Bradley stands and opens it to let whoever it is inside.

Since I am on the edge of my seat—half seated, half standing—as soon as this guest walks into the room, I do what seems to come naturally. I fall out of my chair and land firmly on my rear. Will I ever not react like that when this man strolls into a room? I don't imagine so. And like the first time, I roll over onto my hands and knees so I can stand.

"There is no need to start kneeling in my presence now, my love."

His words remind me of that first time, and I once again slap his offered hand away. "Oh, shut up. I'm just surprised to see you and you caught me off guard, that's all."

Antonio chuckles as he reaches down and cups a hand under my arm. "I have missed being told to shut up this week. No one else has the courage to speak to me the way you do."

As soon as I am back on my feet, he wastes not one second to give me a proper greeting. Not at all concerned we are in a room full of my colleagues, or that it might not be an appropriate time for showing such affection.

"I hope you gentleman will excuse my behavior," Antonio tells them when he breaks the kiss. "But five days is way too long to go without such a kiss. I hope you all understand."

"I uh... sit down and be quiet." I point to the now empty chair next to me. "You should have waited until we were done here."

"Perhaps." Antonio takes his seat and then motions for me to take mine. "But I was invited to join you, so that might have been considered rude."

"Invited by whom?" The voice I am beginning to despise asks.

"By me." A female voice responds from behind us.

Hope is standing there looking rather upset at the moment. "Is that a problem, Mr. Sloan?"

"Baby girl, you are looking rather lovely. How are you, sweetheart?" Timothy asks when he spots his daughter.

"Hi, Daddy. I'm good. Can we move this along?" She takes the now vacant seat on the other side of me and then whispers. "Dang, girl. We have so much to talk about."

"I don't believe you were invited to this meeting." Chandler addresses Hope, not even seeming to care Timothy is on the video call.

"I asked her to look into a few concerns, Chandler." Timothy's voice is stern. "I wanted her opinion about some of those discrepancies you pointed out about the work being done at Maximiliano Chateau. Had her review the entire project and then give me her honest opinion on what she thought should and shouldn't be done on this project. Afterward, I urged her to meet with King Antonio to find out what he wanted done. Get his thoughts about how it was all going. All of it, by the way, not just Larkin's project."

"No offense, Timothy, but Hope doesn't have the experience or knowledge to properly evaluate a job of this magnitude. She is..."

Timothy cuts him off, "My daughter. I said I asked for her opinion. And no one says the words, no offense unless they intend to offend. Go ahead, Hope, tell me what you have learned. Let's see if we agree."

"I did as you asked. Went back to the original proposal that..." She pauses and looks at Antonio. "Can I call you Antonio or do I need to add the title?"

A sincere smile crosses his face. "Antonio is fine, Hope. Thank you for asking."

"No problemo. So, like I was saying. I went back and looked over Antonio's original proposal the two of you discussed when you agreed to these five, I believe it was five, projects. Focusing mainly on Maximiliano Chateau for now.

"It stated that he wanted the integrity of the structure to remain. That he hoped it could be brought back to the original design with some minor changes. One major change is the tower, since he had no use for a tower that was once used to hold prisoners inside. He wasn't sure what he wanted done with that section of the home. He only knew it needed to be completely revamped and made into something useful and pleasing to the eye."

She stops there and looks over at me. "Wow, is all I can say about the design you came up with for that area. I so cannot wait to see it completed."

"Thank you. I just sort of came to me." I sigh, remembering how I couldn't stop the night I came up with it. "I can't wait to build it."

"What else, honey?" Her father obviously wants to keep this discussion moving along.

"Oh. Sorry. Yes. So, I called Antonio in for a meeting and asked him about his thoughts on the project. He said he was aware of what Larkin was currently working on. That the two of them had discussed it thoroughly while they did a walkthrough of the passages, and later together decided which ones would be saved and which would not." She nods once. "Oh, and he also said we should take any future concerns up with his fiancée. That she was a lot more knowledgeable about these sorts of issues and he trusted her completely. Assured me she would come to him if there was a concern and that together they'd tackle it. Just thought you should know his feelings about that one."

"That's convenient," Chandler grumbles.

"Did you say something, Chandler?" Hope scowls at him.

He scowls back and sits up nice and tall. "I said that was convenient. We all know who his fiancée is, and that he is telling us all to go..."

"I'm doing no such thing, Mr. Sloan. I'm simply delegating this over to the person I know will follow my wishes on the matter. Larkin and I have talked about my ideas for Maximiliano Chateau in detail." Antonio's tone discloses his opinions toward this man loud and clear.

"And when did you discuss these ideas?" There is an equally unimpressed tone in Chandler's voice.

"The first time was during a morning meeting I scheduled after a very late one with you." My man squares his shoulders.

"You mean the morning after your date with her. Again, I believe that seems rather convenient." Chandler actually rolls his eyes. "I'm pretty certain post-coitus meetings aren't ethical and probably not the best time to discuss work."

I've never seen a man react so quickly in my life. Before anyone could respond to Chandler's outrageous statement, Antonio has him out of his chair and halfway across the table, clutching the front of his shirt. "Ever disrespect Larkin like that again and I'll end you. Do. I. Make. Myself. Clear." He growls and then shoves him backward, sending Chandler flying back into his chair. "Perhaps if she wasn't required to repeat herself because you can't seem to understand her logic, then she wouldn't have passed out on me in the elevator. We could have gone on that date I had planned, and then met her at the office like I had scheduled that next day here. Since that wasn't the case, I'll admit I took advantage of having her being near, not as near as you are suggesting, and took the meeting. Not that I need to explain any of that to you, Mr. Sloan, because I don't, nor does Miss Cross. You would be wise to drop the matter and move on."

Straightening his shirt, Chandler sits back up, appearing a little shaken. "Are you seriously going to let him get away with that? Isn't it obvious what is going on here?"

Now it is my turn to have a go at him. "You mean because things between us didn't work out the way you expected, so now you are out to sabotage me? Yeah, that is becoming very clear to me."

Chandler rests his arms on the table and blinks a few times. "I don't know what you're talking about, Larkin. I believe you are the one who kissed me that night and then backed out later when things got heated. I've tried to move past it, not making a big deal out of it. You are the one who made things complicated by ignoring emails, calls, and business dinners when I was extending a hand to fix it. And since my arrival here, you've done everything possible to impair my project, by not being available when I requested. I had to start over again because the sketches you gave me were inadequate and garbage."

Hope stands to her feet and leans over the table so she is nearly in Chandler's face. "I call bullshit. Complete bullshit. If Larkin had to suffer your not-so-subtle advancements, along with all those very inappropriate comments while in Mexico City, and did so without punching you, she deserves a medal. I've had to bite my tongue many times for several weeks while reminding myself that one day I will get the pleasure of reminding you of who I am. I guess today is that day. Daddy, please grant me the satisfaction?"

"Yes, my dear, you may." Timothy smiles at his daughter. "Thank you, by the way, for being my eyes and ears over there. I knew I could count on you to come through. You are well on your way, honey. Keep up the excellent work. Gentlemen, if you will excuse me, I have a date with my wife."

Chandler glares at Hope like he would like to take her out. "What is it he is giving you the pleasure of doing exactly?"

Reaching down, Hope pulls out a stack of papers with this wicked smirk on her face. "These are sexual harassment accusations filed by three employees since you have been here. Two women who for now wish to remain anonymous and me. Did you think I would let all that slide? I haven't yet filed them with HR because I am giving you a choice. You can do the right thing and hand in your resignation, go home, and start over somewhere else without the scumbag reputation, or you can fight these. I promise you I will locate every woman inside this company who you have intimidated. Encourage them to come forward. I'm sure there is evidence that can be uncovered if we know where to look. As you know, all emails are monitored and stored. I think I'll start with Larkin and then see if Janice would like a stab at you. What will it be, Mr. Sloan?"

I'm not sure I could contribute, but then again, maybe I just wasn't paying close enough attention. "I'm in."

Chandler abruptly stands. "I'll send it within the hour. Best to get away now before this mess all blows up in your faces, anyway."

"Our apologies, Larkin." Zach leans back in his chair as soon as Chandler storms out. "We just wanted to establish how he would react. We've been watching him for a while now. Heard about what happened between you two in Mexico City. Unfortunately, it wasn't the first time he's behaved badly or had been warned about it, either. Bradley and Cameron thought it would be best to transfer him to determine if he would display his true colors for them.

"You're doing great by the way on all projects. Your work speaks for itself. We have no problem whatsoever with this relationship that is transpiring between the two of you. Timothy sent Hope here for two reasons, actually. One of them was to see if she could tempt Mr. Sloan and get him to approach her as he has done to so many others."

"Wow," is all I can say as I scan around the room. "Remind me to never cross you, Hope Manchester."

"No worries about that, Larkin. I like you. I like your man there as well. How about you help a girl out and let me come visit you at Maximiliano Chateau so you can show me around? While I'm there, we can go over all your Aragon Palace notes since I am taking over that project now. Deal?"

"Deal."

CHAPTER 27
Antonio

The Royals

We just left the most interesting meeting I have ever been a part of. I think I was almost as shocked as Larkin about what transpired during it. Even though I never really thought much of Chandler, I had a hard time believing the nerve he had. I mean seriously, what kind of man is so sure of himself to harasses the founder's youngest daughter and believe he will get away with it? I guess it just goes to show some people believe if they have gotten away with it so far, then it means they will continue to get away with it.

Good for Hope for volunteering to take a man like him down while not giving her cover away. From what I know of the woman, she is quite a force to reckon with. I'm pretty sure she can hold her own and not many people out there get to her. So, for her to play the role of the victim must have been difficult.

I escort Larkin to her car, and once we get there. I hold out my hand for her keys. She just looks at me for a few minutes like she is trying to figure out what I am asking her for. "Keys, love."

"Do you even know how to drive?" Larkin reaches in her bag to retrieve them.

"No." As soon as I see them in her hand, I snag them. "Figured, we'd put our lives in our own hands. Of course, I know how to drive, I just don't get the privilege to do so often anymore."

I walk around to the passenger's side and open the door. "My lady."

The smirk on her face declares she is amused right now. As she slides past me to sit, she utters, "My king."

Hurrying around to the driver's side, I spot my men in the cars that will surround us. That was the deal I had to make with them in order to be allowed to drive Larkin's vehicle. There would be four cars with at least two men in each—the driver and the observer—all of whom are armed. I also had to carry my tracker and then give Larkin the one I had made for her. I'm not sure how she is going to feel about that, or how she will accept a few other details I am about to reveal.

I climb in and wait for the signal. While I wait, I reach in my pocket and find the tracker that is now hers. "Here, you are to carry this with you at all times."

She stares at the device in her hand that looks kind of like a coin. "In a pocket, I take it. What if I don't have a pocket? Is this a GPS tracking device? Does it pick up sound?"

"It needs to be on your person, so I guess you have to figure out a place to put it." I move my eyes toward her chest. "I'm certain you have shoved a few items down your brassiere before. Gabriela keeps her mobile phone in hers when she can't carry a purse. That device is much smaller, so it should be fairly easy to hide inside." Shamefully, I keep my gaze on her chest while I talk. Sadly, I've thought a lot about them lately, especially after witnessing her in a swimsuit.

While I was in Homero, I took Larkin and Isabel to the natural spring we have on the property. It's hidden in the north woods near the bluffs and the entrance of a cave. The spring bubbles up from the twelve-foot-deep pool and is around seventeen degrees Celsius—or sixty-four degrees Fahrenheit for those of you who are like my Larkin. On a hot summer day, the water is rather refreshing, and since summers can reach as high as thirty-three degrees—near ninety—it is a fun activity to do. A natural pool that doesn't need to be maintained like a regular swimming pool does. Plus, it provides water for the house. Several other springs on the estate help water the trees and animals—that is when we add some animals.

One jump into the cold water had forced my focus on the peaks that instantly emerged under her suit. Making my mouth water and my very friendly member wanting to come out to play. So, I calmed him down by jumping in the water myself and staying in it for as long as my body could tolerate.

And because my gaze is still fixed on her nice bosoms, I don't miss it when she drops the coin-shaped device inside. "You do have a point there. I think I should always put it here since I will always wear one."

Blinking away some very debauched thoughts, I peek out the front window and realize my men are waiting on me. "Time to go. That device is tracked by your team and mine."

"I don't have a team." Larkin is shaking her head in confusion. "Please tell me I don't have a team."

I pull out of the underground garage and follow the lead vehicle. "Your team will work with mine. Amanda is your head of security. Dane will be her right-hand man. Emmett and Quinn are the other two members who will be assigned to you full-time. The rest of the team will coincide with mine."

"When do I get to meet these poor people assigned to me?" She crosses her arms. "And why don't I get a say on who is on my team, or if I even want one."

I reach over and take one of her hands in mine. "First of all, *mi lunita*, it is a must, to ensure your safety at all times. If you don't like anyone on your team, then you tell me so I can have that person replaced. I know this is all new, love, but there are those who would do you harm to get to me, an unfortunate reality of your new life."

Larkin goes silent and turns to stare out her window. When she recognizes the vehicle next to us is one of ours, she mumbles. "I guess I shouldn't have wasted my hard-earned money on this lovely form of transportation."

"Larkin," I say her name affectionately, "if you want to drive it, then drive it. I've already made a few specifics very clear to everyone. One of them was that you have never had security before."

"I've had security. When my father first became a U.S. Senator, there was a threat and the Secret Service was assigned to our family. I hated every single second of it and was glad when they backed down a bit.

They are still around, not on me of course, but both of my parents have someone protecting them," she informs me.

"I told them to do their best to offer you the freedom you are accustomed to. Made it very clear I didn't expect you to up and just quit your job, so they were going to have to figure out how to deal with it." I squeeze her hand. "They've been dealing with it all week."

"What?" Larkin appears alarmed and then embarrassed about something. "They've had eyes on me all week? Like, you're saying that I was never alone, even when I thought I was? A heads up about that would have been nice, Antonio. Gaw, hope they enjoyed the show, then."

"What show?" I've asked for a report back from them daily. "Do you mean the fact that you have been climbing rooftops and scaling walls?"

We stop at a light, so when I glance over at her, I notice the tint of red on her cheeks. "That too, I guess. Part of the job."

"Mm, huh? Don't you have men working with you who could have done those tasks?" I want to order her to not do something I know is dangerous, but I don't.

"I suppose I could, but sometimes seeing it with my own eyes is better and I don't have to worry about them missing something. I was careful. Followed the safety procedures this time." She bites her lips together.

"Do you not always follow those procedures, Miss Cross?" I know the answer before she gives it to me.

"I plead the fifth." Her voice has this tinge of a giggle to it.

"The what?"

"The fifth. It means that I am invoking the Fifth Amendment."

I am utterly confused right now. "I believe that deals with the relationship between the sovereign and his council."

"Not your constitution, the U.S. one. To sum it up, it says I don't have to say anything that might incriminate me; I can choose to plead the fifth. I plead the fifth."

"That I suppose would be the tenth here. Although, it states that if a person chooses to not answer those types of questions, then they are revoking their rights to freedom if there is enough evidence to hold them. So, pleading the tenth means, while you admit no guilt, you are also in a roundabout way admitting it, then forcing your government to prove it. You also understand that until then we will incarcerate you." I inform her as we pull into another underground garage. "Do you still want to plead, my love? I have no problem holding you prisoner."

"Did they report about all my adventures or just the ones that put me in danger?" Larkin is obviously avoiding my question.

"I assume all." I pull into the designated spot and turn off the car. "But I'm not certain. Why are you blushing?"

Larkin closes her eyes and begins speaking rapidly. "It was hot, okay. I'd spent hours inside the walls on a very hot, muggy day. I figured a nice swim would feel good. Since I assumed I was alone, and not far from the spring, I just said why not. Had I known I was under surveillance, I'd have gone back and grabbed my suit, or at least kept my bra and panties on. I thought I was..."

Yeah, she doesn't get to finish the rest, because my mouth firmly lands on her. The thought of her naked in the natural pool, after a long hot day of working, has my mind going places it should not. How I so wish I could have been there to witness that.

And no, her team left that little detail out of the report. They said she went for a swim but didn't say it was an X-rated swim. I'm sure once they realized her intent, they left her after securing the area; I hope that is the case.

After I have tasted her sweetness enough to almost do me in, I draw back. "They left out a few details."

"Where are we?" She swallows, aiming to regain some ground.

"Maison de Deveaux," I tell her as I get out and make my way to her side of the car. "Figured, it was time I take you on a proper date."

This genuine smile lights up her face as she takes my hand. "A date?"

"Yes, a date. I've yet to take you out on a customary date, so tonight I plan on rectifying that." I tuck her arm in mine and we follow my team. "Figured we start with dinner, take in a show next, end with me dropping you off at your door. Much like I imagine most of your dates have gone, and I wanted to experience my first one with you."

"You've never been on a date?" Larkin glances up at me, shaking her head. "But you've dated before."

I lean down and kiss her forehead. "And most of those were outings where my date escorted me to an event. Of course, I did a little dating in boarding school and college. But tonight is different, you see. I am taking my lady out and showing her off. Letting it be known I am most definitely spoken for and very proud of that fact. Showing her a good time and hoping to impress her."

"You didn't try to impress all those other young women?" She bumps me slightly. "I don't believe you."

"I did, I guess. Hoping to steal a snog when the evening ended." I lean down so my lips are near hers as we step off the elevator. "I never wanted more from them, though. Never dreamed of them and woke up wishing they were lying next to me. Ached for them. Missed them the second they walked out the door."

"*Bienvenue votre Majesté et vous votre Grâce.* We are honored to serve you both this evening. I believe you requested a table overlooking the lovely view. If you would follow me." The host bows and then leads the way.

My team came earlier and secured the place. The other patrons do not miss the fact they are all about to dine with their King and start to stand. I stop the first gentleman with a raise of my hand and motion for him to remain seated. I cannot escape the reverent bow he bestows me though, so I nod and continue. Luckily, there aren't many tables for us to pass, so we aren't force to endure that the entire way.

"The chef has prepared something special for our King and his guest, if that is suitable for you, sir?"

As I am pulling out Larkin's chair, I ask. "My love, is that okay with you?"

"Sounds lovely." She glances at the wine bottle and makes one request. "Could you please bring me some tea?"

"Hot or cold, Your Grace?" The host asks her.

"Cold. And it's just miss or ma'am. I hold no title and I do not wish for one." She reaches for her water. "Oh, and could you also bring me a small pitcher of water? If it's not too much trouble, that is?"

With a slight nod, the host replies, "No trouble at all, miss. May I speak freely, Your Majesty?"

"You may," I tell him as I take my seat, interested to hear what this gentleman is thinking.

"A treasure as lovely as this one surely is a gift from above. I believe your choice is a much better one than those who were all but forced upon you. Well done, sir, well done.

"And miss, I must correct you, if I may. The title you hold may not be one you have been handed. It is one, however, you were born to be one day, and it fits you better than anyone else. It shall be an honor to one day soon, address you with such deserved regard. Wear it well, miss, and take pride in the fact that you've earned it by simply falling in love with the right man."

Larkin watches the man depart, completely unable to speak after his honesty. She finally directs her attention toward the large window overlooking Aragon. Reaching for her water I catch the glistening sparkle in her misty eyes.

We are seated directly across from each other like everyone else in this restaurant. However, she seems too far away across the table like that.

During our summer holiday, we ate dinner every night together. She always sat in the chair next to mine. My leg often brushed hers during dinner. My foot sometimes slid behind hers, tugging it closer, where I'd find my foot rubbing hers intimately. We'd talk about subjects couples often talked about. Her day at work and some of the bumps she ran into. All the unexpected issues I had to deal with because some didn't respect my holiday. We'd share, listen, and even offer advice if the other person asked for it.

Isabel of course was present during that time and Larkin never left her out. Would ask about her day and listen closely to all the adventures my little sister found while roaming around the grounds.

Therefore, I stand and move my chair to the spot next to her. At first, she is too busy gazing out the window to notice I have moved. It isn't until my knee bumps hers as I sit, that she jerks her head around to find me there. When I slide my leg behind hers and draw it closer, I feel that discernable shiver that always moves through her when we touch.

"What are you doing?" she whispers.

"Getting comfortable." I easily reply and reach for the wine bottle.

It's a chardonnay that has a hint of vanilla in it. I do as I have done so many times before and pour a glass for her and myself. So far, she hasn't once taken a sip of a glass and I haven't once said anything about it.

"Why do you pour me a glass when you know I never touch it?" Her gaze is focused on the white liquid in her flute. "Why do you always have a couple glasses during dinner?"

I grab the stem of my wineglass and swirl it around a bit. "I like the taste of an excellent wine. I pour you a glass in case you'd like to have one with me. This particular wine is a chardonnay. It has a smooth velvety texture with a rich citrus flavor and a hint of vanilla." Putting the glass to my lips, I take a sip and let it moisten my lips and tongue.

She is still staring at it when I get this idea. I take another sip and let the wine invade my mouth completely. After I am satisfied I've gotten it well coated, I lean forward and set my glass down. Reaching across the short distance, I turn her head so she is facing me and kiss her lips softly at first.

I swear I only meant to leave the sweet taste of the wine on her lips so that when she licked them, she'd get a sample. However, it is extremely difficult for me to just kiss Larkin and not want to take things deeper. Very soon our soft kiss spins into a more intimate one. My tongue slips inside her sweet tasting mouth and toys with hers.

It's the awareness of someone standing near that has me drawing back. Our very jovial young server stands only a few feet from us, holding a steaming platter of escargot and two smaller plates. He sets the dish between us and tries hard to hold back his amusement. "Anything else, Your Majesty?"

"We are good, thank you." I sit back in my chair and watch Larkin lick her lips. "Well?"

Larkin reaches up and touches her lips. "Well, what? Are you asking me about that kiss or the wine?"

A deep chuckle sneaks out and I know we are attracting attention. "Well, let's start with the kiss, since you brought it up."

"It's the kind that could get me into trouble, that is for sure." She is still agitating her head.

"And the wine?" I place a few escargots on her small plate. "It will go well with that."

"Are those... are those snails?" Her uncertainty discloses she has never had them before.

"Yes." I show her how to eat one and then watch her struggle a bit with it.

She finally gets one free and deposits it in her mouth. I see her make an unpleasant grimace. Quickly she grabs a napkin and spits it out as discreetly as possible. Then grabs her wine and downs half the glass. She waits for a few and then finishes it off, holding it in her mouth this time for a few seconds before swallowing. When that doesn't seem to quite do the job, she reaches for mine and finishes it as well.

I try not to laugh. I really, really do.

"Is the wine intended to deaden your taste buds so you don't throw up?" Larkin asks me as she sets my glass down and then reaches for the bottle.

I stop her so I can refill both our glasses, afraid she was thinking of tipping the bottle to her mouth. "Not a fan of escargot?"

Grabbing the glass of tea the server brought her, she wobbles her head. "That's just a fancy word for slimy icky snails."

After I finish the bite in my mouth, I reach for her again to draw her near. She fights me, but my words stop her and she gives in to my advances. "I love you so very much. No more slimy icky snails for you, then."

After a much simpler kiss, she whispers against my lips. "I love you too. But if you try to slip that nasty tongue in my mouth, after you ate those disgusting little snails, I just might puke in your mouth."

The rest of the dinner goes off without any more unpleasant food mishaps. We talk about our week apart, share all the ups and downs we faced. There is a lot of touching throughout it. A few more kisses take place during dessert when she gets some of the mocha de crème on her upper lip. I just cannot resist licking the rich creamy mousse off of hers. Any excuse to put my lips on Larkin's is a good enough one for me.

The chef stops by our table to make sure our meal was satisfying enough and then offers his congratulations.

As we are about to leave, the manager makes his appearance, making sure to let us know we are more than welcome to return anytime we desire. Assuring us that there will always be an open table to accommodate the most romantic and passionate couple to ever step foot in this place. He announces it was lovely to watch and admits he wishes all his patrons understood the importance of sharing such fire while enjoying an intimate meal.

I escort my love out the main doors this time. I drank a little more wine than I first intended and am suffering from it slightly. At least I believe I am. I'd probably go so far as to admit it is a big possibility, the reason I am a little light on my feet, has more to do with the woman next to me. We climb in the back of one of the SUVs and settle in nicely, heading for our next destination.

CHAPTER 28
Antonio

The Royals

I'm pleased to see Larkin listened to my request about how she should dress tonight. Our next destination has a more prestigious dress code. Most of the audience will be dressed a little nicer than we currently are, or maybe it's the section we will be seated in that goes all out. Although we will be housed in my private box, so I instructed those joining us to dress a little more casually tonight. So, the dress she chose fits, and I am delighted with how well it fits.

Larkin must be feeling the wine as well. She twists her head and places a kiss on my arm as she nuzzles closer. "Why did you let me drink from your glass? I shouldn't have done that. Drinking more than one glass was a bad idea as well. I'm feeling a little... free."

She discloses this as her hand lands on my thigh and starts tracking the inseam of my dress pants. I watch her hand as it unhurriedly trails up and then stops mid-thigh.

"I've never touched a man here before," she whispers loudly as she draws circles along the spot. "Or here." Her hand trails a little higher. "Or here."

I grab her wrist to halt her progress. "And tonight, my sweet Larkin, that is as far as you will go. One more inch higher and things could turn rather interesting."

I may have blocked her hand, but I can do nothing about where her eyes land. Nor can I hide how her touch was affecting me down there.

"Does it hurt?" she whisper shouts, and I know Gino heard her by the cough he lets out to cover his laugh. "It looks uncomfortable."

"Larkin." I growl her name as I squeeze her hand. "Shut it, please."

"Sorry. I'm just... I think I should... I mean..." She releases a loud, long breath and this time when she speaks, her voice is not hushed at all. "Is it true what they say? I read confident men tend to have a reason to act like that. Plus, you have very big hands, long thick fingers to go with those bigger than life hands. Rather enormous feet to hold up this impressive frame of yours. All that suggests that the size of your penis is rather impressive as well." Another sigh reveals she has no idea what she disclosed. "It's really going to hurt, isn't it?"

The vehicle comes to a stop right outside the theater. There is no way I can jump out just yet. Her questions have put me in quite a predicament.

"Oh geez." Larkin is still staring at my lap. "You are going to ruin my girl parts with that monster you keep hidden in your pants."

Two doors open and close rather rapidly as my men get out to give us some privacy. That catches Larkin's attention, and she giggles uncontrollably. "Did I say all that out loud?"

I reach down and shift things around down there. "I'm afraid so."

Her giggle turns into a full-blown laugh, and that makes me laugh as well. Which surprisingly helps me calm down enough so I can get out without suggesting we were performing iniquitous acts in the back of our vehicle.

We are some of the last patrons to arrive. On our way to my box, I order us a few coffees, knowing we could probably use them. Someone will deliver them as soon as they are ready. We take the last few steps and enter the large box secluded from all the others.

Already seated inside are my brothers and their dates, as well as Gabriela and my cousin, Mercedes. I lead Larkin to the front row and am pleased to find my good friend Fernando and his wife Sonia are also here. They are dressed just like I instruct, thankfully, and wearing the best smiles I've seen in a very long time.

Fernando stands and performs his famous full body bow. "Your Supreme Majesty, grateful you finally graced us with your presence."

"Ferny, you do so know how much I enjoy watching you show me my due respect." I use the familiar name I came up with during those first few weeks of boarding school.

Sonia tries to yank her husband back down. "Stop. Please ignore them, Larkin, these two can be quite the duo. I'm Sonia. The bowing fool is my husband, Fernando."

Fernando straightens his form, then reaches out and snags Larkin's hand in his. "It is an honor, my lady. Ant told me you were the reflection of the moon, although he forgot to mention you are the image of the celestial stars as well. We should not waste such beauty on a simple man like this one. Surely you have better suitors knocking down your door."

Larkin glances my way. "Well, there were a few. However, none of them were able to..." She leans in toward him and I wonder if that is such a good idea. Glancing back over her shoulder, she whispers, "I felt a little sorry for the poor man. Such a sad sight to witness, really. I've read about them before but never actually met one."

Fernando takes the bait with an amused grin. "Met one what?"

"A paper tiger, of course." And just when I'm about to remind her of how much I hate it when she refers to me as one, I find myself guffawing instead when she calls him out. "You, I'm sure, are also familiar with such a creature. I believe it is the same reason Sonia was attracted to you."

"You wound me, my lady." Fernando places a hand over his heart. "But you will do, for sure. You will keep him most definitely on his toes; much like that one does me. A paper tiger, that is a very brave thing to call a man, Larkin. You should be careful referring to a man in such a way. He might pounce on you rather quickly, and then what would an innocent celestial such as yourself do?"

The lights flash to signal we should take our seats right as the attendant brings us our coffees. We sit so we can focus our attention on the stage below.

The music starts, and Larkin sits back in her chair. I watch her the entire time as she takes in her very first opera, *Madame Butterfly*. Each expression she undergoes takes form on her face. The raw honesty that is

Larkin bleeds, and I want nothing more than to experience all of it with her for the rest of my life.

"What did you think?" Sonia asks when it was all over. "I remember the first time I attended the opera; it was an eye-opening experience."

Larkin is still staring at the now empty stage, with its red lights illuminating it. "I loved it. I mean, even though I didn't understand a word that was sung, I could follow the storyline. I never realized how spectacular one could be. I always thought I'd be bored to death and want to leave. I hold little patience for sitting still, a flaw of mine, I guess."

Fernando stands and offers his wife his hand. "Shall we, my love?"

I follow his lead and take Larkin's as we make our way out of the box seats. My brothers, along with their lady friends, are all waiting for us, as are my sister and cousin. I introduce Larkin to everyone. The two women with my brothers are both friends, and from what Esteban told me earlier, he is doing it as a favor for Lorenzo. Apparently, Lorenzo made a promise to the young woman with him a while back, and a man never breaks his promises. A really good man drags his brother into those types of promises so they can suffer together.

My plan is to make a swift getaway. I bear no interest in sticking around. While it is customary to go down to the house lounge and mingle with the socialites, the knowledge that tomorrow night I will see most of them again makes me not want to fake it tonight.

Fernando and Sonia are the lucky ones. After a message comes across her phone, informing them that their youngest little one is having trouble settling, they are able to make their escape.

I try to follow them out the door, but get intercepted by a group of women and their escorts as they approach us. And wouldn't you know it, one of them happens to be Lady Dalia. Tonight, she is with a young solicitor, Lord Declan Olivier. I believe he works for her father—who, by the way, pulled through but still has a long road ahead of him.

"Your Majesty, I think a celebratory drink is in order." Lord Declan declares as he approaches us. "Why don't we let the ladies do what ladies do best, while we men enjoy a smoke and brandy? After all, I do believe that is the traditional custom the night before the big announcement.

246

We should do your very last night of freedom right, don't you agree, gentlemen?" He turns and encourages those with him to nod.

I slip my arm around Larkin. "I'm sorry, Lord Declan, but I don't believe Larkin would be comfortable with a group of women she is unfamiliar with."

"Do you not think we would play nice with her, Your Majesty?" Lady Genovese tries to act offended. "Let Princess Gabriela and Madam Mercedes join her. She knows them, no? 'Tis tradition for the betrothed to enjoy one last little celebration apart. There are so many of us who would love to congratulate her on a job well done, sir."

I glance over at my sister and cousin. Both look as if they just won the lottery. Larkin's gaze must follow mine because she pats my arm to capture my attention.

"I'm sure we will all be fine. A drink and smoke will take what, thirty minutes at most. Surely I can hold my own with them for thirty little minutes." She pastes on a smile; one I know is fake.

"There is really no need..." I start to tell her we can just go; except I don't get the chance because she rises on her tiptoes and kisses my moving lips.

After she has shut me up, she mutters against them. "Promise you will suck out the venom if I get bitten."

I don't care what any of them will say about what I am about to do. This woman has a way of making me not care about anything except her. I yank her hard against my body and kiss her furiously, drawing a whistle from my brothers and a few others who follow their lead.

When Larkin whimpers and her knees buckle slightly, I draw back so I can admire her face. Hooded eyes, flushed cheeks, and swollen lips, all reactions I caused are what I find. "It will be my pleasure, love. I believe I possess the only antidote; all you need to do is ask and I shall give it to you."

"I love you, Antonio," Larkin tells me as she leans back and says my name loud enough for those around us to hear. "Now go enjoy a drink with the guys while us women shoot the breeze."

I yank her against me one last time before I let her go. "I love you, *mi lunita*. I love you more than words will ever be able to express."

Lorenzo grabs me by the back of my neck and chuckles. "Larkin, I do believe my brother, the all-mighty king, is smitten. I promise to return him to you soon."

And like that, we are walking in one direction while the women head in the other. Larkin hooks an arm with Gabriela and Mercedes as she utters something softly to them both. The two young ladies fall into her and they all laugh.

What bothers me is the scowl the other women give them. I don't trust Dalia or Genovese. Those two are the most conniving, dishonest souls I have ever met. When Dalia's sisters join her, I start to think this was a terrible idea.

"Calm down," Esteban says as his eyes follow mine. "Winnie will look after them and try to keep the rest in line."

I raise my eyebrows at him. "Winnie? Since when has she taken on the name Winnie? Winifred is probably the only Batista sister I trust. Karina and Paschal will hold Larkin down while Dalia sinks her fangs in and releases her venom. I should rush back there, toss my woman over my shoulder, and haul her off before they ruin her."

Lorenzo tightens his grip on my neck. "One drink, for heaven's sake, is not long enough for them to corrupt her. Plus, from what I've witnessed so far, Larkin isn't a helpless victim. When the claws come out, if they come out, she will know how to handle it. It will be good practice for her, actually. We all know eventually she is going to get stuck in a room with them and they need to understand they cannot intimidate her. Otherwise, she is going to get chewed up and spit out very quickly."

That doesn't help me feel any better, even though I know my brother is right. The brown liquid Esteban places in my hand, however, seems to help, so I ask for a second one.

Before I know it, an hour has passed and I am feeling a little buzzed. I've smoked a good Cuban, drank about three brandies, and conversed mostly with my brothers. The other men have interrupted us a few times. Offered me congratulations—some were sincere, most were not. I couldn't care less if they approve, honestly.

I am about to stand and excuse myself, feeling like I've wasted enough time with these gentlemen when I notice Gino entering the room. He doesn't look at all pleased as he gestures toward the front. I quickly rise to my feet and excuse myself as I make my way to him.

"Is there a problem?" I ask as I follow his eyes.

Gabriela and Mercedes are stumbling around, chatting with a few gentlemen. They are obviously drunk. The legal drinking age in Hermosa Islas is eighteen, so they are not breaking any laws. However, it is not a good idea for a person in their position to be seen inebriated.

"Where is Larkin? Why is she not looking out for them?" I ask as we walk that way, finding it strange.

"Maybe because she too has had one too many. Seems the ladies separated her from the main flock to conduct a little meeting of the exes." He grunts. "They are in the solarium."

"What do you mean, a meeting of the exes?" I pick up my pace.

I ignore those who try to talk to me as I make my way through the crowd. I come upon my sister and cousin first and pass them off to Gino. "Take them home now."

"You are such a party pooper," Gabriela grumbles.

"And you are drunk. Explain that to mother when you stumble in." I don't have time to argue with her. Later, however, we will, and she better be ready.

"I got them," Lorenzo assures me. "You go grab your woman. I just heard from Lord Declan that the scorned trio is having a heart to heart with her."

My feet move faster now. I don't know what the means exactly, but understand it is nothing good. When I get to the solarium, I slow and pause right outside the entrance.

"Why are you telling me all of this?" Larkin's voice is weak and broken.

"We want to make sure you understand exactly what you are getting yourself into. I believe tonight's opera was a wonderful metaphor for it all, actually. Men always want what they cannot have at first. The idea is rather exciting to them. But eventually, they return to what is best for everyone," Genovese's spiteful voice exclaims.

"You're just his little plaything, honey. A man who respects you doesn't feel the need to kiss you like he did earlier in public. That there was proof to us he only perceives you as his possession and not his equal at all." That voice belongs to Karina, I'm certain.

"And then there is the fact he gave you that." Dalia's tone sounds disgusted. "That means nothing to him at all. If he were going to truly marry you, then he would have given you his great-grandmother's ring. It is tradition to use a family heirloom, not some cheap custom jewelry."

I feel a hand shove me in the back.

"Go, or I will, sir." Gino has never looked more like he wants to kill someone than he does right now. "That, Your Majesty, is the minor details they've been sharing. I came to retrieve you as soon as I realized what they were up to. But I got distracted by Princess Gabriela and Madam Mercedes. So only God knows exactly what lies they have been filling her head with."

"Have the men pull the car around," I instruct him. "And no matter what, those ladies in that room are to be removed from all further royal events. Their names are to be blacklisted, and I don't care who I piss off. Are we clear?"

"As day, sir." He nods once.

I stand tall before walking into the room, and am immediately detected. The four spiteful women stand looking rather guilty.

"You are dismissed." I glance around giving my order.

Two, move.

Two stand their ground.

Lady Dalia Batista and Lady Genovese. The second woman has had it out for me since our days in boarding school. She and Dalia became acquaintances and equally bitter women after I dumped her lying lady butt.

"I said you are dismissed. Leave now or I will ask Gino to remove you. It makes no difference to me as long as I no longer am forced to look at either of you." When they don't seem to believe me, I glance over my shoulder. "Gino."

"We are leaving." Genovese makes the wiser choice.

Lady Dalia, however, decides she wants to get one last jolt in before she departs. "You should always remember that all is fair in love and war, Your Majesty."

I snag her arm and stare directly into her eyes, letting her know she will not win. "Many wars have been fought over a woman, Dalia. I am prepared to win this one. Are you prepared to lose?"

"I will not lose, Your Majesty. One way or another, I will be victorious. It will be my pleasure to watch you fall and drag her down with you. Are you prepared for that?"

Not wavering, I lean forward and growl through clenched teeth. "I will fight for her with every breath in my body. I will not fall. And she will be the one to hold me up, give me the strength needed to do what needs to be done. And when the dust settles, together we will lead this nation into the future and a brand-new world. The question, I guess for you, Lady Dalia, is in that new world will you survive the fallout?"

"And when they strip you of your title, will you even know what to do?" She is a fighter; I will give her that much.

"I will. If the only way to be with Larkin is to denounce the throne, I will do it without a second thought. But it's not the only way, now, is it? You and I both appreciate that." I let go of her arm. "You are dismissed."

Dalia glances over her shoulder and smirks. "It really is a shame that one can be so easily taken down. It was like taking candy from a baby. Good luck fixing the damage, Your Majesty. One should always remember the truth can be a very venomous poison that eats away at a person's once earned trust. I'll be waiting to strike again when the time is right."

I really would love to see that woman put in her place, but right now my concern is the woman in front of me. The defeated expression on Larkin's face guts me to the core. I drop to my knees and study her carefully.

Where shall I begin?

Larkin

The Royals

I tried to play it off that I was comfortable socializing with those women. Pretended I believed them when they claimed to want to congratulate me on winning over Antonio. I knew it was all one big fat lie, but I wanted to prove I could survive it.

I've known a lot of conniving people in my life. Kids in high school used me when it was convenient and then turned around and stabbed me in the back the rest of the time. I even dealt with a few of those types as an adult. Chandler Sloan is the first name to pop into my head.

None of them ever stood a chance with this particular group of women. Conniving doesn't even describe them. They know exactly what they're doing and how to do it. Vipers, that is what Antonio has called them many times, and I am learning how they earned such a label.

Shortly after we left the men, they started in. First, it all seemed so unplanned. I guess that is the word I am searching for.

Karina, Dalia's sister, asked to see the ring Antonio gave me. So, I proudly displayed the treasure I wore and realized quickly none of them were at all impressed.

Well, none except one. "Oh, an antique. I bet it took him several days to track a ring down like that."

"Fred, please." Paschal makes a face. "That is not a ring at all. He presented that thing to you and you still said yes? Oh, honey, we have so much to teach you."

Gabriela grabs my hand and smiles. "I agree with Winifred. I think it's a lovely symbol of the love my brother has for Larkin. His friend Fernando helped him locate it. Sonia said the two of them visited several exclusive jewelers in Geneva, having no luck. A trip to Paris, as a last effort, was when they stumbled upon this priceless gem. These snobs wouldn't recognize a heartfelt gift if it fell into their laps."

I can tell the snobs want to chastise Gabriela and call her a silly girl, but they won't. Her princess status prevents them from belittling her, so they wait it out.

However, that doesn't stop Dalia from chastising Sonia. "Well, we all know Sonia has absolutely no taste whatsoever. Did you see how she was dressed tonight?"

When a few younger women join us, they others encourage Gabriela, Mercedes, and Winifred to join them. Alluding they only want to take me around the room for more introductions. That it would be so much more exciting for these three if they socialized with ladies closer to their own age, rather than hanging with us.

Again, they didn't strike right away. They slowly helped me get comfortable with them and did as they claimed they were going to do. Introduced me to a few women who were at least better at pretending than they were.

Finally, Lady Genovese suggested we go sit in the solarium and enjoy a few drinks. And that is when the real motive for why they dragged me around becomes very clear.

After we've taken our seats and they cleared the room, Genovese begins. "Did you know I once dated... Antonio? It's okay I call him that, isn't it? I mean, you do, so I can as well, can't I?"

"I am fine with it in a setting like this, I suppose, although I don't think you should get accustomed to it. From the beginning, he has insisted I use his first name and only his name. Declared to me, he is, and always will only be, Antonio. I'm not so sure that is how he feels with anyone else, though, so for now I agree it is okay to use only his name." I inform them as if I have the right to make that decision.

"Interesting. I've never known a man to not want to be reminded he is an important man, and no one is more important than our King." Dalia provides her opinion. "Perhaps he just doesn't wish to make you feel lesser, so he tolerates it."

"Perhaps." I glare at her. "Or maybe it's because I allow him to be simply Antonio and wouldn't care if he were nothing more. I'd love him either way, and he knows it."

"That is so very kind of you, Larkin. Letting him feel like a simple man rather than a powerful king." Dalia is not holding back and her tone does not go unnoticed.

"So, I dated him as I was saying. Did you know that?" Genovese blinks a few times. "I was his first."

"His first girlfriend?" I don't appreciate what she is insinuating.

A nefarious grin takes over her face. "That too, I guess. Are you a girlfriend if the only thing you do for a young lad is bring him pleasure? I suppose when you are fourteen and fifteen, that is how young lovers begin. He definitely ruined me for the other boys. None of them compared in size and were all such a disappointment. You appreciate what I mean, right? Not very many men out there can claim to possess such a large package. Dalia, wouldn't you agree with me?"

I down the drink they handed me moments earlier, not wanting to hear any of this. They exchange a look that communicates they are enjoying this way too much, and most likely aware that I am not privileged enough to know what they mean.

"Well, when Antonio and I dated, he was no longer a lad; he was all man by then. A good man, really, one who tried so very hard to stay the course and not waver. But if you offer a good man what he really wants or needs, at just the right time, even he can slip up. I was so very close to sealing that deal. At least I got the benefit of grasping I was going to need to get myself prepared better than I had been. Karina always said I had a big mouth." Dalia glances over at her sister, dragging her into this sick joke.

"That's because you do. Biggest mouth I've ever seen, at least." Karina nods her head once. "Although I believe I recall you enlightening me even your big mouth had trouble taking him."

The glass I was holding in my hand slips and shatters on the floor.

She so did not just say that about the man I love. Disrespecting him like that to get a rise out of me. "Please stop. Have you no respect at all?"

"Oh, I respected him a few times that night, Larkin. And if his twit headed brothers hadn't shown up and disrupted our fun time, this little fling you are having with him now would have never materialized." Dalia points her drink at me. "It's only a matter of time before he realizes an innocent, insecure woman like you will never do. Have you ever even seen a one-eyed snake before, touched one, or licked one until it cried? That's what I thought.

"You are no match for a man like Antonio, nor are you a worthy adversary for any of us. All is fair in love and war, dear sweet Larkin. Are you convinced you are capable of handling all that comes with the job you will be required to do once you marry him? Or will you suffer one of your famous panic attacks and let the entire world understand what a babbling fool you truly are?"

I am not one to curse, but there is always a time and a place for a person to just say it like it is. "You bitch."

"Is that the best you can do?" Dalia sighs, as if she is disappointed.

"Why are you doing this?" I ask, trying to figure out the best way to knock them right off their high stools.

"We only want to make sure you understand exactly what you are getting yourself into. I believe tonight's opera was a wonderful metaphor for it all, actually. Men always want what they cannot have at first. The idea of it all is rather exciting to them. But eventually, they return to what is best for them." Genovese explains, sounding oh so pitiful.

"You're just his little plaything, honey. A man who respects you doesn't feel the need to kiss you like he did earlier in public. That there was proof to us he only perceives you as his possession and not his equal." Karina adds her two cents.

"And then there is the fact he gave you that." Dalia points at my precious ring, looking so disgusted. "That means nothing to him at all. If he were truly planning to marry you, then he would have given you his great-grandmother's ring. It is tradition to use a family heirloom, not some cheap custom jewelry."

I am going to throw up.

Grabbing my stomach, I press slightly against it to remain calm. The anger these women are able to draw out of me has me frozen for now. I know if I start doing my predictable wordy response, it will only fuel the flame. So, I bite down hard on the inside of my cheeks and focus on the one thing right now that brings me joy.

I stare at the oval diamond encased in white and yellow gold prongs. The precious stone catches the light and sparkles just right. I am reminded of how nervous Antonio was right before he gave it to me. How his hands shook and his Adam's apple bobbed with each swallow. Staring at it reminds me of the way the sunlight caught it that first time he slid it on my finger. The way it reflected little rainbow beams in the most vulnerable brown eyes as he gazed up at me. The light in his eyes began to shine the moment I dropped to my knees and told him yes.

I study the design surrounding the ring and remember in that moment, I encountered the man no one else ever has. I held him against my chest and soaked up all the love he has inside of him. I got to experience him letting go for the first time in his life, as he opened up completely to the only person he has ever really let inside. Remembered how on that hill, in that orchard, with both of us on our knees, was the first time either of us completely allowed another person in. That moment bonded us in a way that could not be broken.

When I finally allow my mind to refocus on the room, I realize Antonio has cleared most of it out. Right now, he is holding his own with the woman who is determined to sabotage us by bringing up the past and making me question everything.

Except her plan has backfired on her, because what they did only makes me want to protect Antonio more. It makes me want to wrap him in my arms and bring him back inside the bubble that is us. I am determined to be his safe haven. The place he can be whoever he wants to be, needs to be, where he doesn't need to worry if I will ever betray him. I only plan to love him like no other woman will ever be capable of —especially any of these spiteful women.

I watch her storm out confident she has accomplished what she set out to accomplish. Wearing a smug expression on her face as she glances back the second she reaches the door, letting me know she believes she has won this round.

Gino shoves her in the back to get her moving again and then turns his own on the room. He is prepared to stand guard to ensure we are not interrupted while we deal with this insignificant problem.

Once again on his knees, Antonio is in front of me. Gone is the confident man who has stood his ground so many times. He is replaced by a man who is uncertain of what he should do. I hate seeing him like this, hate that those women planted a seed of doubt in his mind.

"Larkin." His voice whispers my name as if it is the only name he has ever spoken.

I reach up and seize his face with my hands, holding it steady. Not saying a word, I lean forward and begin placing soft, small kisses on his lovely face. I kiss his eyes and feel the wetness leaking from them, so I kiss his cheeks to wipe it all away. When I finally find his soft lips, I press mine firmly against his and hold them there.

I detect the hiccup that shakes his body as he tries hard to hold it together. So, I tilt my head and run my tongue along the seam of those lips, tasting the saltiness that stains them. As soon as he lets me inside, I take it one step farther and do my best to devour him. I suck on his tongue, nip at his lips, letting our teeth click together when it gets a little aggressive.

He breaks the kiss and then jerks my head back quickly so he can look at me. "Larkin."

"I love you, Antonio. I love you and there is nothing those women could say that would taint the love we share." I brush my thumbs across his cheeks. "Nothing, do you hear me?"

He nods once. "What did they say exactly?"

"Things that they thought would get me to question your true feelings for me. They wanted to paint a certain picture of you. One that portrayed you in a not so desirable light. To pressure me into envisioning you as someone I know you are not." I brush a few wild hairs off his brow. "It only made me see them for the vultures they are."

"I never..." He starts to tell me something I already know.

"I know. And even if you had, that is the past. We all have a past Antonio, even I've done things I wish I could take back." I lean forward and kiss his lips again. "Can we please get out of here now?"

Rising to his feet, Antonio takes my hand in his and pulls me up with him. "Never again, Larkin. Those women will never again be allowed anywhere near you. I will not allow it."

"I'm fine. I'll be better prepared next time." I inform him, meaning that next time I will be ready to put them in their places when they start.

"I'm sorry you were forced to deal with them." He places a finger over my lips, revealing he wants to say something and not be interrupted. "I never once slept with them. Things may have gotten carried away. I was young, and I was naïve. Blinded both times by lust and a desire to want more, but not understanding what that truly felt like. There were always those who were willing, and as a young hormonal boy I mistook their affection and willingness for that more."

He pauses, so I insert my thoughts here. "You don't need to explain, Antonio. I know."

Bringing our joined hands to his lips, he kisses mine and smiles. "I know you do. However, I need to say this so there is nothing else that can be said about it. Genovese was the first girl to... show me how good certain acts could feel. We went to boarding school together and as you can imagine, there were places kids snuck off to so they could get away from the eyes of those responsible. During an adventure that involved alcohol and stupid young teenage fascinations, things between us went further than they should have. She was the first of a very short list of girls that happened with, and she was the most daring. Not just with me, either. Ferny and she had a few go-rounds. She had a reputation, and she lived up to it, still does.

"When I was sixteen, I told you about what I witnessed with my father. That was also when I met you the first time. The combination of the sweet bold girl in the garden who stole a piece of my heart, and the realization that if I continued down the path I was heading, I'd be just like him. I decided to not indulge anymore, to be different, and look for a different type of girl who wasn't just interested in what was between my legs."

There is a tinge of how much what he is about to say hurts him in is voice. "Dalia and I met in college. We knew each other before, but never hung out. Different friends, I guess. Or maybe I just avoided hers because I knew her type. She'd done a really good job over the years of learning what I didn't like about most of the women who dared to approach me. The first time I ran into her was after one of those other women had all but thrown herself at me. Asked me if I ever grew tired of all that stupid fakeness and then did her best impression of the young woman. I laughed so hard that I cried.

"For several months we were only friends. She never sought to be more. Waited for me to make my move, so certain I would. And of course, I did, and at the time it felt good to have someone who I felt like I could be me around. Relax and not worry. After a fight with my father about something, I'm not sure over what, she was there and things just sort of happened. I tried to stop her at first, but one touch and a few well-spoken words, I allowed lust to once again take over. I thought I was falling in love with her, hadn't revealed it to her yet, but I was planning on it. Consequently, I allowed my body to lead the way and pushed away those voices that advised me to stop before it was too late. If my brothers hadn't come by to check on me, I would've done something I regretted even more. I never slept with her, but I allowed matters to go farther than I ever allowed them to go before. Guilt ate at me for a long time after that. And that feeling kept me from allowing it to ever happen again, no matter how hard she tried."

He sighs, "That is the extent of it all. There was no one after her. Until I met you, no woman has ever tempted me. No one, Larkin. No other woman has ever stirred up those emotions deep inside of me. None of those previous women made me aware of the aches of longing I suffer from now. You are in a league all your own, and that is why you've done the one thing those women never could."

"And what is that, Antonio?" I ask as I stare into his eyes.

"Brought me to my knees. Knocked the wind out of me more than once. Secured my heart inside your chest so it will always be with you, so I cannot exist without you. Shown me what love is, real genuine love. So, now you are stuck with me." He leans down and kisses me softly. "Shall we make our escape now?"

"I love you," I whisper against his lips. "You've done the same to me, you know. All of it."

Antonio secures my hand in his and lets Gino know we are ready to leave. The whispers, glances, giggles, all of it does not go unnoticed. I realize what they are all thinking. The group of vipers has obviously been making their rounds while we talked. They have been feeding these hunger gossipers with a bunch of lies and loving every second of it.

All that does is set a fire inside of me. Gives me an idea. One I am certain Antonio will be more than willing to go along with. I wait until we get in the car though before I share it with him. I'm done letting them think they can stop us from being happy and living the life we both want. So, I decide to take a very bold step and seize the reigns once and for all.

CHAPTER 30
Antonio

The Royals

I blankly stare at her, positive I misheard. Surely, I rearranged the words that came out of her mouth in my head. I know there is no way I heard her correctly, no way.

"Okay, so maybe I was wrong. Never mind then, I guess we can mark that off as me overreacting to a very unpleasant exchange. I mean, you're right. We should stay the course and do this the right way. I was simply letting all that get to me. Letting my anger feed my desires. I merely thought if we moved this along, then that would shut them up rather quickly. Of course, that isn't the only reason, but it crossed my mind. I mean, I definitely would love to see for myself what all the fuss is about and all. They acted so fascinated with your anatomy that I thought I might appreciate my chance of deciding if they were telling the truth. And well, I won't get that chance until... so I guess since it's what we both want. Of course, that is only the bonus fun stuff that occurs, I guess, or so I've been told. I mean, because all I want to do is claim you as mine and let those women know they better keep their distance. You are indeed mine. No one is ever going to be able to say anything that will hinder the love we have. Thought if we could get this show on the road and be done with it, then we could put all that crap behind us and start moving forward. But if you'd rather wait the proper allotted time, I understand. I'm shutting up now." Larkin pats my cheek as she turns her head and stares forward.

I continue to gawk at her.

The car is silent for several minutes before I break into the biggest stupidest grin ever. "Ask me again."

Larkin jerks her head around quickly with a wounded expression on her face. "What? No."

I lean forward and whisper softly. "Ask me again. Please?"

"No."

Gripping her face, while giving it a gentle squeeze, I pretend to be her, making her mouth move with each word. "Oh, Antonio, my sweet man. I have this wonderful splendid idea, crazy really. How hard would it be for us to get hitched tonight?"

She tries to talk through my manipulations. "That... not what... said."

"Ask me again." I release my grip. "Ask me again so I can give you a proper response."

Rolling her eyes, she swats at my hand and sighs. "Maybe I've had a change of heart now."

"Ask me again, Larkin, or I swear to you I will..."

She growls at me, "Fine. Antonio, I was thinking that maybe I'd like to get married."

I tap her finger like I did the first time she said it and repeat my words. "We are love. Have you come up with a date?"

She nods and turns those pale blue eyes on mine, holding my gaze. "I have. I think I'd like to get married tonight."

"Tonight?" I try not to burst.

"Yes, tonight." She, however, is getting irritated with me now. "But I guess you don't want to, so fine. We..."

"Tonight, it is then," I interrupt her and let all my love for her reflect in my eyes. "But I must insist we do it right."

A lovely giggle emerges from my woman. "Is there a right way to elope?"

"Aww, there is, I assure you." I clear my throat. "Gentlemen, I require some assistance. I need to make a few stops. I also need to place Miss Cross in one of the other vehicles so she can get herself ready. Call

Helena and ask her to have the dresses that were sent to the palace brought to the queen's quarters, all of them. Make sure a seamstress is on hand in case some adjustments need to be made. Tell them to prepare the Throne Room and to call the palace vicar and let him know I've requested his services. Send a car to each of our family members and inform them they have been summoned to the palace and should dress properly. Call Dr. Devon Wilson and instruct her she needs to do the previously discussed examination tonight."

Larkin has been quiet until now. "Is that necessary? I mean seriously are we still living in the Dark Age where that kind of examination has to be done? Do you think those other women would have passed?"

We've been back and forth about this many times over the last several weeks. Had several arguments dealing with this particular topic and none of them ever ended well. However, I am not giving in, especially now. I want no one to question our reasons for marrying so quickly. I don't want them to spread more lies, and so I am going to insist I get my way here.

"Of course, none of those women would pass such an examination because none of them are virgins." I don't keep my voice down, which explains why Gino and the driver nearly choke and start chuckling. "You however, are, and therefore it will be recorded in the matrimony documentation. Much like it was done many, many years before when a doctor would verify what I already know to be true."

Crossing her arms as a sign of her defiance, Larkin lifts her head. "It's ridiculous and degrading. I suppose there will also be onlookers present when you steal my virginity that first time as well, to prove it was you who deflowered me. Gino, would you like the honor? After all, you've already witnessed me in my underwear. Or maybe we should invite one of my security teams members to join us, since they were privy to my little skinny-dipping episode."

The car comes to a stop and Gino twists to face us. "I believe I will pass, miss. And for the record, no one was privy to that little episode. Amanda ordered everyone to head back when she realized where you were heading. Called Quinn to join her so they could secure the area and give you some privacy. And stop reminding him of the knickers incident, it never leaves him in a good mood." He then gets out of the car, leaving us to deal with this.

As soon as the car door closes, I grab her and yank her into my lap, forcing her to straddle me. My hands land on her thighs and shove the skirt of her dress upward so she is able to sit exactly where I want her, need her, to sit. The heat from her center, as it comes into contact with mine, has my hands tightening around the outside of her stocking covered legs.

Larkin's hands are resting on the back of the seat to steady her body and keep it from getting too close. I can see her holding herself up so she doesn't come in direct contact with me. Her hair is unfastened, making it hang freely around her face like a curtain. Those icy blue eyes bounce around as my fingers dig in and slide higher.

I don't warn her because I know if I do, she will try to stop me. Instead, I slide my hands over her rear and yank her center hard against me. It's not the first time I've ground my hard length into her, nor will it be the last. However, it is the first time I have done it while holding onto her like this, where I encourage her to move her hips. I allow one of my hands to shift forward so I can run my thumb over the warm, now damp material.

"This is mine, Larkin. Only my eyes will ever get to appreciate what it looks like when I take you that first time. No one else will ever be allowed to set their eyes on you in the thralls of passion. That will be for my eyes and my eyes only." I run my thumb hard against her and listen to the whimper that slips out.

Removing that hand, I reach up and snag one of her hands and place it between us. Wrapping my hand around hers, forcing her to cup my heavy shaft as I draw it up the length of it. I watch her chest rise and fall as she does.

"I am also yours. This is the effect you have on me and the first time you take it, there will be no one near to hear your cries. No eyes but yours to witness my undoing when I bury myself deep inside of you and get lost there. That will be for your eyes and only yours."

She closes her eyes and licks her lips, unaware of what that does to me. Not understanding it reveals her desires and makes mine grow. I release her hand and plunge my hand in her hair so I can drag her delicious lips toward mine. We kiss, letting the realization of what will transpire later tonight take over.

I pull back and slam my head against the seat. "Did you go on the pill as we discussed?"

Larkin drops her head to one of my shoulders and inhales. "What? No. I was going to wait for us to set a date. I mean, because I assumed, we'd have more time, you know."

I place both of my hands on her back and rub. "That's what I thought. I'll ask Gino to take me by the chemist. I'll also let Dr. Wilson know we are in need of birth control and have her explain your best options."

"Why do you need Gino to stop by the pharmacy?" She asks but then answers her question with a laugh. "Well, that will surely be one for the gossip columns. King Antonio was witnessed purchasing a box of condoms late one night. Can you imagine the stories that will emerge?"

"I could make Gino purchase them." I kiss the top of her head. "He wouldn't mind. I'm sure he has bought them before."

"I bet most of the guys on your security team have. What if you skip the pharmacy altogether?" She draws tiny circles on my chest. "I mean, since I am having the virgin examination to prove I am actually a virgin. Isn't the idea also so that when the queen becomes pregnant, no one questions who the father is. Although the blood-stained sheets the following morning would probably be proof you successfully popped my cherry."

I pinch her side and listen to her yelp. "Sometimes the words that emerge out of your mouth surprise me. And I don't just want her to do the examination to confirm your virginity. Dr. Wilson is one of the best gynecologists we have. I explained your little issue and how you were concerned about it being painful even after surgery. She said she had a few ideas on how to help us achieve a less painful experience that first time. Recommended after her examination to snip the hymen so it would be easier. Told me it would be less painful and she could give you a numbing first. Even leave a little so I would get the pleasure of expunging it if that is what you wanted. She takes patient confidentiality very seriously, and I trust her to not disclose any of this to anyone. I don't wish to hurt you, my love, and if this is the way to make things easiest, then I think it is the way to go."

"How did I get so lucky?" She whispers against my chest.

"I am the lucky one, Larkin. Never, ever doubt that. So, you would be okay if a little heir decided to make an appearance?" I run my fingers up and down her spine.

"I would be okay with it, yes. My cycles are sporadic, so it may take us some time to get it right. We may require some assistance to regulate my cycles. So should a little heir decide to make an appearance in nine months, I'd be okay with that." She lifts her head, so she is looking at me. "I love you, Antonio. I imagine I will love any child you implant inside of me equally so."

"Not afraid of how it will affect your work?" I have to ask.

"No." She laughs. "My mother worked full-time and still managed to raise me. My father held down a job as well most of my life. Plus, we have Helena and Beatriz, even Isabel, who I am sure will be willing to help out. We can hire another nanny if we need to, one who can travel with me so the little one can go with me, or us even. It's a brave new world, right?"

"Yes, it is." I lean down and kiss her nose. "So then, I guess that's settled. Now get out so I can figure out how to make this work."

Larkin gracefully climbs off my lap and fixes her dress. Then she leans over and kisses my lips hard, leaving me breathless. Afterward, she climbs out of the car and is escorted to the SUV parked behind us where Amanda and Dane wait for her.

Gino climbs in the driver's seat this time, joined by Isaac. Both men spin with raised eyebrows and stupid smirks on their faces. They stare at me for a few moments while they wait for me to give them instructions.

"Well?" I ask, wondering how much they got accomplished while I felt up my fiancée.

"Are you kidding me?" Gino throws his hands up. "That's all you have to say?"

Isaac, the more professional of the two, only clears his throat before he lets me know all my orders have been filled. He admits a few of my family members had questioned him intensely about my state of mind. Even let me know Larkin's parents would be picked up at the airport as soon as their plane lands in the next hour and taken directly to the palace. They were coming to celebrate our official engagement announcement with us tomorrow. He was able to speak with the Senator who didn't seem surprised about the change.

When he is done, I stare at them for a few moments, and then just say what I am thinking. "You both have... you both are... I mean... aww screw it. I need some advice, okay. You're both experienced, right?"

Both men nod, and I realize they are enjoying this way too much.

"So, it's no secret I am lacking in that department." I can't believe I am discussing this with my men. "Any advice on the subject would be appreciated."

Gino, ever the smart ass speaks up first. "Peg goes in the hole. The front one, not the back, is best to steer clear of that one. Well, unless you are into that kind of kink, but I don't suppose that would be something you'll gain knowledge of this first time."

I've never wanted to flip someone the bird before, but I'd like to do it now. "I know that much, *gilipollas*. I mean, how do I make it easier for her. Not only is my beautiful woman lily-white, but she also has a few physical issues that could make things more challenging. Then there is the fact that I am not a small man."

Gino starts to speak, but Isaac punches his arm and motions for him to drive. He then turns around and begins messing with his phone, typing rather rapidly. After a few minutes, he spins back around and winks at me. "All is taken care of, Sir. Everything you will need will be made available to you in the left top drawer next to the bed. More is always a good idea the first time. Take your time and explore. The best way to distract a lover is to find her sweet spots and pay them a great deal of attention. And only do what you both are comfortable doing. The rule of thumb is that you will know when you are both ready if you pay attention to her body. Big or not, it will fit if you take the time to prepare her and keep her relaxed. I don't doubt you will have no problem distracting her when the time is right. It may be best to try a position that lets her be in charge of how fast she wants things to progress. I'll send you a link to a site I came across that has helped me and..." He stops and clears his throat. "Helped my partner and me get what we both need. She is a petite little thing and some of my previous favorite positions didn't work for her, us. And when you care about the person you are having sex with, it is always important to make sure she enjoys it as much as you do."

"Care or love, Isaac?" I ask, because I believe I detect a tone in his voice that says he more than just cares for the woman he is talking about.

"I agree with His Majesty. You sound like a lovesick puppy over there. Maybe we can ask the vicar if he can do a two for one tonight and you can stop pretending you leave the palace every night." Gino does a quick glimpse over at Isaac and laughs. "Did you really think you could pull one over on all of us? *Let me escort you to your room because we know how dangerous these palace halls can be late at night. I'd be glad to join you on a run to the store; there are a few items I could also use. One shouldn't walk the grounds after dark alone. Give me a second and I'll walk with you.* And then of course there were those early mornings in Homero when you would have to sneak her out of the guardhouse before the main house woke and missed her. We just figured you two weren't ready to come clean. But dang man, you share some shit like that and I think maybe you just need a little nudge."

"You have a big mouth, you know that, Gino? One of these days I am going to enjoy rubbing it right back at you. Don't think I don't notice either." Isaac mumbles back at Gino, making the other man straighten his frame.

"Notice what?" I ask.

"Nothing." They say in unison.

"Love. It is most definitely love. I just haven't had the valor to share my feelings with her yet, but it most definitely is love, the kind that makes a man do really stupid things." Isaac peeks over my shoulder. "You know what I mean, sir?"

"I do, Isaac. And just whom do I need to congratulate for bringing Isaac Nadeau to his knees? Not, Amanda, she hasn't been with us that long. Nor do I suspect it to be Quinn, she isn't a tiny little petite thing." A light bulb moment goes off and grab his shoulder and give it a solid squeeze. "How long?"

"Excuse me, sir." Isaac realizes when he turns around that I have figured it out. "Six months approximately, sir."

"Right around the time, she broke up with her long-term boyfriend. The one who cheated on her more than once, the one I threatened to have thrown into the tower. Well, that explains a few things, now doesn't it?" I smile fondly at him. "She is a good woman and you are a very lucky man. So, when are you going to make an honest woman out of her? You can't keep this charade going much longer before Helena or Isabel figure it all out.

Isaac closes his eyes slowly. "Isabel knows, sir. I mean we are dating, not the other. She thinks it is cool and promised to keep it on the down-low. Bea is very protective of her and makes sure we keep matters very PG around her."

Well, the things you learn when you open up. Now I guess I just need to figure out who Gino has his eye on. He pretends to be a playboy, but I know it's all an act. I'm not saying he's a saint—he is not a saint— but he is no playboy, either. He most definitely has his eye on someone; otherwise, I imagine he would have more ladies on his radar.

CHAPTER 31
Larkin

The Royals

I t all sounded good in my head. It even sounded perfect when I said it out loud earlier in the car. I'll admit it sounded wonderful after that when we were discussing our plans, and he was touching me in a way he hadn't dared to touch me until then.

But the moment I stepped into the queen's quarters, it hit me. I was able to play it off at first and hide the fact I was freaking out. Not sure Dr. Devon, the gynecologist, bought my story about being okay, though. She kept asking me if I needed something to calm my nerves. Reassuring me the examination was not all that unusual and won't take long, a basic pelvic examination essentially. And she was right about that. It was like every other pelvic exam I'd ever had, and it was very uncomfortable.

"Can I ask you why you have suffered like this for so long?" Dr. Devon inquired while she was down there messing around my vajayjay. "King Antonio said that you had surgery at one time."

"I did. I was eighteen. So, I guess the only thing I was worried about at that time was being able to insert a tiny tampon. The idea of sex was far from my mind." I tried to focus on the ceiling.

"I've been a doctor for many years now, Miss Cross. Seen my share of young, inexperienced women. Yours is no different. The doctor, I would say, did a decent job opening it up so you could insert a tampon. My guess is that you've always had some discomfort during an exam like this, though." I nodded when she glanced over at the sheet covering me. "Most of your hymen is gone. A portion is still intact, and that could be what is causing some of your discomfort when inserting a tampon."

She explained the way a woman's secret region has to be stretched. Described it as one of the most unique organs God designed. A snug, narrow cavity that could do wonderful miraculous phenomena, such as birth a child and return to that firm cavity. Each one is capable of accepting all the different sized male genitalia out there, could be trained to take a larger size completely with very little pain if done correctly. Went into more detail than I was ready to hear, but I tried to listen so I would hopefully one day be able to enjoy sex. She patted my legs closed and smiled when she was finished.

"Larkin, there is no need to be concerned about you experiencing discomfort during intercourse. I don't believe you will. I removed the last bit of your hymen to make things smoother later. It won't go in my report. No woman needs to experience pain, or fear pain, during intercourse. It should be a satisfying, intimate encounter between lovers, a very natural one that leaves no room for unnecessary emotions. So now you can relax and let your new husband show you the joys of that kind of intimacy."

Of course, after she left, I ran to the bathroom with my purse in hand. Found a tampon and inserted it to see if I felt a difference. Surprisingly, I did, which gave me a tinge of hopefulness for later. Well, until I looked at the slender tampon and realized it was the size of one of my fingers. Antonio's fingers were so much larger than mine.

Right as I am finishing up with my hair and makeup, there is a soft knock on the main door. Helena is in the apartment with me—quarters, I guess, is the right word—but this is an apartment. She is getting it ready for her and Isabel. They are going to spend the next few days here to give Antonio and me some time alone. Said it was easier to move them than him since it was only for a few days. I was heading back to Homero on Tuesday so I could get back and complete the work on the home the three of us would share one day.

I nearly cry when my mother's face appears in the mirror I am gazing into. Spinning in my chair so I can look at her. I knock over my glass of water and spill it down the front of me. Good thing I am still dressed in my robe.

"Oh, Larkin, you will forever be the clumsy girl who worries when there is nothing to worry about," she tells me as she grabs a towel and begins cleaning up the mess. "Breathe, my sweet little bird. Breathe and understand your father and I support you one hundred percent. This is your home now, so there is no reason to put it off any longer. Claim that man as yours and show them that my Larkin Moon was born to free him so he too could fly with you."

"I love you, mother." I throw my arms around her. "You must be exhausted from your trip. I'm sorry."

"Your father and I were able to sleep on the lovely plane your soon to be husband sent us. Now come let us get you dressed. There is a very impatient man out there waiting for you. His mother told me she has never seen him so unnerved before. Both his brothers are having their fun with it, though. If I don't take you out of here soon, I'm certain he will barge in to see what the holdup is." She unzips the garment bag and gasps.

I step in behind her and stare at the lacy white simple gown I selected. It looks like a vintage one, but it isn't. The A-line skirt is beautifully decorated with French tulle—that's what the seamstress told me, at least. Lace overlays the deep sweetheart neckline, held up by a star-shaped pattern with narrow straps in the open back. It even has a tulle train that can be detached, although it is not very long, so I don't understand the reasoning on that. The gown could not be more perfect, and I know my mother is thinking the same thing I am.

"Larkin." She covers her mouth. "It is exactly like I imagined."

"It's not my design mother, but I thought the same when I saw it. It's almost exactly like the one I used to sketch as a little girl." I reach out and touch it. "A sign, I believe."

"Most definitely a sign, my sweet girl. God sometimes has a very unique way of letting us know he planned this out long before we were even capable of putting it all together. And just because it is a path that follows his plan, does not mean the course is easy. Often, God's path can be rather rocky, but stay the course and keep your eyes on him and it will be manageable. Trials and tribulations are a part of life that we cannot avoid. Picking the right person to walk through them with you is what is key to surviving them. You, my dear girl, have done a wonderful job doing just that." My mother certainly has a way with words.

That doesn't mean I am still not freaking out right now. It only means that I am freaking out a little less than before. And as soon as we have the dress on and everything seems to be in place, she calls my father to come and escort us to where the others are waiting.

So here I am, standing just outside the main doors, trying to remember to breathe. My father is by my side, doing his best to keep me calm, making all the guards keeping watch snicker at his stupid jokes.

"Do you know why the King of Hearts married the Queen of Hearts? They were perfectly suited for each other." He chuckles. "Okay, let me offer you some words of wisdom. I have, after all, been married to your mother for almost thirty-four years. It wasn't always easy. We had our ups and downs along the way. Got in a good fight or two where she wanted to use her skills as a surgeon and open me up a few times, I'm sure. So let me provide you with a few words of encouragement that will hopefully help you in this journey you are about to embark upon."

Squeezing my arm he shares, "A successful marriage requires falling in love many times and always with the same person. You may not always feel loved or even experience that feeling of being in love, and the best way to rectify that is to do something about it. Don't expect Antonio to be the one to perceive the signs. See them with your own eyes, and then take charge. Be the one who does what needs to be done to rekindle the flame that may have dwindled to a few hot coals. You make the effort, and I guarantee you that man of yours will quickly follow. We cannot expect our spouses to read our minds. Even after thirty-four years, that woman I married is still an intriguing mystery to me."

I can hear the chuckle in his voice. "Share a bowl of popcorn every so often. Lots of things can happen during that time. Conversation typically takes place; even a simple conversation is important. Hands often bump when you reach into the bowl at the same time. Forcing you to touch the other person. And one cannot share a bowl of popcorn unless seated next to the other person. So, it brings you together, close enough to feel that person's physical existence. Not to mention, we all know how popcorn is a very sneaky invention that often falls into places we men find very fascinating."

"Daddy," I squeak out. "I cannot believe you."

"Yes, you can. I believe you used to chastise me when I would throw popcorn at your mother, so she could catch it in her mouth. You always said I was aiming lower just so I could watch her retrieve it. You were not wrong about that, Larkin, and the older I get, my aim has only gotten so much worse."

Gino chuckles as he opens the main door. "A man after my own heart. I do believe I like your father, Larkin."

"Everyone likes my father, Gino. He is a very free-spirited man and often overshares." I roll my eyes.

"But tell me, Larkin. Are you more relaxed now than you were before?" My father adjusts my hand resting on his arm. "Shall we, my beloved daughter, get this show on the road?"

I am so much more relaxed than I was before. My father's playful spirit has once again taken my mind off of the fact I am about to become a married woman. Not just a married woman, but also a queen. I still do not feel like I deserve such a title. I fear it will all return when the doors open completely. The moment I see the long march we have to travel to make it to the front, my breathing falters again.

Until I spot my man, dressed in that same suit he wore the night I was first invited to a palace celebration. He looks as stunning as he did then, with one noticeable exception. The moment our eyes lock, I suddenly become aware that he is as equally nervous about this as I am. Or he was. Now he just seems eager to get this ceremony over with so he can finally put all his past uncertainties behind him and live the life he has always dreamed of.

Don't ask me too much about the ceremony, because it would be a lie if I tried to tell you I knew what was said. Most of it is one big blur that I was trapped inside while staring at the man whose eyes had put me in a trance.

I remember repeating our vows, traditional ones. Exchanging rings. Taking communion as a way of promising to keep God in this marriage. Repeating some words, I didn't quite understand—Antonio translated for me, something about how I would not only be faithful to my husband but also faithful to the throne. Making a sacred vow to reign over Hermosa Islas and obey the king, not only as the ruler of this country but also over the house we would establish together. Promising to forsake all other loyalties that would interfere with my duties as the king's spouse as I take my rightful place by his side.

Afterward, Antonio took a sash from one of his brothers and draped it across my left shoulder as he repeated a verse that I assume makes it official. He repeated it in English so I knew what he was saying. It basically stated that as king he presented me with his colors, proving that I was now queen and together we would rule over his land.

Then he turns to present me to those in attendance. Everyone delivers a respectful bow. At that time Prince Esteban walks over to one throne and picks up a very heavy looking crown resting on a pillow. Antonio takes it carefully off the pillow. He smiles fondly at me as he places the priceless jeweled crown on top of my head, securing it way easier than I imagine I would have. Prince Esteban then places an even larger, more masculine crown atop King Antonio's. Once that is done, Antonio blinks a few times and turns to the vicar and nods. The man emits a bunch of wordy words and then declares us king and queen before he permits Antonio to kiss his queen. Which he does, and I believe I swoon right there in front of our families.

We do a procession of sorts, I guess. Unlike any I have ever seen done before. Antonio takes my hand and walks me up the last few steps of the platform to the two gold-covered thrones designated as the king and queen's. He stands in front of them and waits for me to understand what we are about to do.

"You want me to sit in that?" I glance behind me, feeling unworthy.

"Yes, Queen Larkin Moon Reyes, I want you to take your place by my side and sit on the throne that is rightfully now yours. Shall we, *mi lunita,* affirm our united reign? Tis usually tradition that the king sits first, but I want to make a statement that proclaims you as my equal in all things. Tomorrow evening when we do this again, when I introduce you to my kingdom, it will be a sign that I have publicly declared you as my equal. It will affirm that I do so willingly, expecting all others to treat you as they would me. Let us make a statement and be the best king and queen duo to ever rule Hermosa Islas." He leans over and kisses me and then we sit down together, at the same time, as he holds our joined hands high for all to see.

And the reality of what just happened washes over me. Holy freaking Captain Underpants. I am now a queen, a genuine queen who others will look to for guidance. Suddenly, I burst into a nervous laugh that I am sure has to seem a little crazy.

Antonio

The Royals

I wait for her to stop laughing as I hold our hands high. She means no disrespect; I know this. My family knows this as well. So, we patiently wait for her to calm before continuing.

Through the last bits of laughter, Larkin tries to apologize. "I'm sorry. That was so not appropriate."

My elbow is now resting on the arm of my throne, so I tilt toward her and bring her hand to my lips. "I believe it was the most genuine reaction ever to transpire in this room. Reality can sometimes hit us hard, making laughter the only suitable way to deal with it. Never apologize, my dear wife, for letting your emotions free. A queen never apologizes unless her king orders her to. I will never order you to do anything."

"Are you my king now?" She lets out a very sweet sigh and smiles sincerely.

"I am. I am your king. I am your equal. I am your husband. I am your lover. I am your most trusted confidant. I am whatever you need me to be from this point forward." I kiss her hand again. "And you are my everything."

A throat clears, so I glance up to find my brother, Esteban, standing at the top step. When I nod once, he kneels, letting only his knee graze the step, and then proceeds. "Congratulations, Your Majesty. I vow to be of service to both of you whenever called upon. It is my honor to be the first to welcome our Queen to the fold."

Larkin giggles as she offers her hand to Esteban. "Prince Esteban, thank you. Must we keep this so formal?"

Esteban, being the spokesperson for the family, tells her the truth. "Yes. Here in this sacred room, formality shall always prevail, Your Majesty. However, if it is your wish outside of these four walls, I shall address you in whatever manner you request."

Lorenzo is next. He bows in the same manner as my other brother. "Your Majesty sure knows how to shake things up a bit. Nice to see Larkin... pardon, I misspoke. Nice to see Queen Larkin has successfully removed the stick Father shoved up that royal butt of yours. My Queen, you are looking divine this evening. I believe tomorrow night you will make a few women have to choke on their words. It will be a show I would pay money to attend."

Gabriela and Isabel walk up together. Both speak briefly to me before making a comment about Larkin's dress, expressing how lovely it looks on her. They are equally thrilled to have another woman in the family, one who will hopefully remain on their side.

My mother follows them, so I rise to receive her, and Larkin follows. After she has kissed both our cheeks, she motions for us to sit back down. "Your Majesty, you have done what no other sovereign before you ever has. You have found love in its truest form. I charge you to cherish your chosen queen always. I charge you to be faithful to her in all things. Be the example, my son, to the next heir the two of you will one day create. Never back down when those who wish to witness you fall come for you. They will come; therefore, you must unite and hold strong.

"Queen Larkin, I am beyond overjoyed to welcome you. You have given my son the one thing I never could. You have offered him the power of love. I charge you to love him like no one else ever could. Be the safe refuge he can turn to when he needs to rest and unburden his soul. Provide him with the strength needed to be a good and wise leader. Stand by his side as his equal and never forget that he chose you over all the others."

Larkin stands again and wraps my mother in her arms. "I promise I will, Your Royal Highness. I promise you I will."

Larkin's parents stand and begin to do the same as the others. However, I stop them. "No need to bow before us. I am not your King and she is most definitely not your Queen."

"Probably best because I am certain to mess it up, anyway." Her father extends a hand and then yanks me hard against him. "Fine man you are, Antonio, fine man indeed. Love Larkin with all your heart, mind, and soul. Cherish each day as if it could be your last. And always buy her a dress that has a zipper in the back, because a dress that zips up in the back will bring a husband and wife together. First, it will be to assist her so you can take her out and show her off. Later it will be so you can lend a hand as she does her best to slip her out of it. At that time, you should take full advantage of the situation, maybe even allow her to help you slip out of your clothing as well."

I cannot help but chortle at this man's sense of humor. "I will keep that in mind, Sam. I can tell you are a smart man since you have held on to your beautiful wife for so many years. Eleanor, you are truly a treasure and almost steal the show with your beauty."

Eleanor pats my cheek before she leans in to kiss it. "A charmer to the core, this one. Take care of my darling daughter. Protect her when she needs it. Soar high together, away from all the pressures this life is sure to bring. You do that and you and I will always get along. But hurt her, keep in mind that I am very skilled with a scalpel."

"Point well-made and understood. I promise to never give you a reason to prove that to me." I kiss both her cheeks and watch as she and Larkin have a mother/daughter moment.

As soon as they are done and join the others at the main door, I take Larkin's hand and tuck it in the crook of my arm. Then I lead her down the aisle and out the main doors. We walk through the portrait gallery and down the long corridor. She is very quiet the entire walk, and I have to wonder what she is thinking. As we turn the corner that leads to my quarters, I decide to speak.

"So, it's been a long evening." I start there.

"It has." Her eyes glance up at me. "Dinner at a very fancy French restaurant."

"A lovely evening at the opera." I smile.

"A most interesting introduction into the life of a socialite. I'd say we could eliminate that part, but then I'm sure if we did, we would not have ended it like this." Larkin leans her head against my arm. "So out of curiosity, how many first dates do you imagine end like this?"

I pause outside my door and stand there so I can take her all in. I want to remember this moment for the rest of my life. "I'm guessing, not many. And to be fair, ours wasn't really a first date. It was, however, the first time I had the pleasure of taking you out and showing you off properly. I believe I said I wanted to take you to dinner, and a show, then end it by taking you home and giving you a proper goodbye."

I lean in and kiss her lips softly, knowing that if I am not careful, things could get out of hand quickly. Kissing her is a risk because it always makes me desire more. More before tonight was not a possibility, but now she is my wife, so more is anything she will allow me to have.

Larkin pulls away and backs up against the wall next to the door. "So, now that we've done the proper goodbye kiss. Are you going to show me the not so proper one?"

Sliding the key into the lock, I wait until I hear the click and shove it open. Stalking her like the tiger she has awakened inside of me, I dip down and scoop her into my arms. The yelp that echoes down the dark long corridor hasn't ever sounded so lovely.

"Not exactly," I warn her as I carry her across the threshold and kick the door closed. "I was thinking of showing you the proper way a husband shows his wife how much he loves her." A shiver travels down her body and I catch the heat building in her eyes. "Are you nervous about this?"

She shakes her head as she stares at my lips. "Not really."

"Will you let me love you tonight, Larkin?" I start walking to the master suite. "Mark you as mine?"

"Yes. Please," she whispers and then attacks my lips with a kiss that has me halting my progress so I don't run into a wall or drop her.

I shuffle my feet again, knowing that if I don't get moving soon, I will take her here in the hallway. After the link Isaac provided me, I realize wall sex might be a possibility, keep me from going so deep that first time. Although I'm not sure wall sex is the way I want to take her this first time.

As soon as we are inside the room, I set her feet on the ground, but don't stop kissing her right away. Instead, I wrap my arms around her and tug her snug against my body, and then shuffle her backward until I feel her bump into one of the tall bedposts.

There is a bench at the bottom of the large king-size bed, so I instruct her to take a seat. Once she is seated, I get rid of the sash I placed on her earlier and lay it next to her. Then I remove my medallion, jacket, vest, and cufflinks, shoving them in the pocket of my pants.

After I loosen the top few buttons of my shirt, I kneel and take her foot in my hand so I can gently remove her heels. I bring her dainty feet to my lips and kiss each one of her toes as I allow my hands to massage her calves.

"What are you doing?" Larkin mutters softly while she watches me.

"Loving you." My response is simple. "Shhh... let me have my fun."

Another one of her famous shivers takes over her. I do so love it when I feel her react like that. As if the anticipation of what is coming has her body trembling with excitement.

I tug her to her feet and spin her around so I can assist her out of her dress. The thin straps hook together easy enough. A simple flick of my fingers has them separating. I push them to the side and lean forward so I can place soft, loving kisses on her spine and shoulder blades. The soft velvety skin on her back makes me want to rip this dress right off her in a very primal move.

"Tomorrow, this dress will not survive to be worn again. I am going to rip it from your body just to show you I can." I inform her as I nip the tender skin just above the zipper.

"Only if you promise to let me do the same with your clothing," she whimpers over her shoulder as I draw the zipper down, loosening the gown.

I slide my hands under the material and tug on it so it falls off of her frame.

"Deal," I mumble as I drop to my knees and kiss the small dimple on her back that rests just above the curve of her ass.

My gaze travels up and down the length of her appreciatively. The shimmer that radiates off her porcelain skin is intoxicating. I truly believe I could just stare at her and be a very happy man. Luckily, I don't only get to look, I can touch and kiss and smell her as often as my heart desires.

Larkin spins so she now faces me. The front view of her makes my head spin. The way her hipbones show just enough to make her midsection appear perfectly flat. Even her belly button is the perfect indention, causing my mouth to water. So, I kiss it much like I would her mouth and she burst into laughter.

"Stop." She squirms. "That tickles."

I growl and shake my head as I drag my mouth to her hips and nip the hard bone. "You are the most gorgeous woman I have ever laid eyes on."

Grabbing my head, she lifts it upward. I have to tighten my arms around her so I don't tumble backward. Her perfect breasts tilt up toward the ceiling, making those rose-colored nipples protrude from them, beckoning for attention.

I realize she was about to say something, but the sight of them has me on my feet. In a move I didn't know I possessed, I lift her off the ground by the globes of her rear and bring her breast to my lips. And while I am feasting on her, I fall with her onto the bed so we are now lying side by side.

Her nails dig into my hair, holding my head in place as she squeaks out these soft, high-pitched purrs. All that does is light the wick inside me, igniting the flames of passion that have never taken over before. The fire starts to burn away my resolve.

"Antonio," she cries out. "Oh please... stop."

I jerk back, afraid that maybe I am hurting her. "Okay. What's wrong, my love?"

Larkin is practically hyperventilating. "You have... too many... clothes on."

Sliding her body down the bed, she shoves me onto my back and climbs on. Her fingers fumbled with the buttons of my shirt. When I try to help, she slaps them away. Once she has it undone, she pushes it aside and begins tugging at my undershirt.

I sit up to shake off my shirt. Just about to remove my other one, when she tugs it up and over my head first. Accordingly, I tumble back onto the bed and watch as Larkin takes a slow scan of my physique.

I'm not a hairy man, but I do possess hair on my chest and down my naval. My olive tone, in contrast with her porcelain, is a very impressive sight.

Larkin draws little circles with her nails around my now hard nipples and then leans forward. Her lips touch my burning flesh, and I moan, knowing that she could very well be the death of me. I lie there and try not to move while she worships my body like no other woman ever has. Her soft hand traces the lines of my abdomen, and then she caresses the moles that circle my navel, before dipping her tongue inside. That move nearly has me exploding in my pants, so I reach down and tug her back to my mouth, allowing me to kiss those lips again.

The feel of her fingers fumbling with my pants has me rolling us over onto our sides. I throw my leg over hers and haul her body closer to mine. She finally gets the fastening to cooperate and slides the zipper down. I kick my shoes off and then draw back so I can study her face.

Her eyes divert south as her thumbs slide underneath my waistband to shove it over my hips. I have to lift so she can free it, and then I kick my legs until my pants slide off. Next, she runs her fingers over the Balenciaga label on my black briefs. Yeah, I am a brief guy, never understood why men had so many choices, really. I say plain briefs do the job just fine.

"I've never heard of this brand before." Larkin shifts her gaze to meet my eyes and watches mine as her hand slides just below the band. "Are they expensive?"

My breathing picks up slightly when her hand slides closer and closer to where I want her to touch me. "Don't know. Don't care."

She stops her movement and starts to retreat that hand.

"Larkin, love. Please don't stop." I thrust my hip and watch her swallow.

Even after my protest, she manages to pull her hand all the way free as she sits up. "On your back."

"What?" I shake my head with disapproval.

Rising to her knees again, she shoves against my shoulders. "On. Your. Back."

I oblige and roll onto my back, but not before I put my mouth on her breast again and give it a good hard pull. "Now what?"

Larkin slides off the bed and stands. She wanders over to her dress and picks it up, draping it over the back of a chair. In fact, she picks up all our discarded clothes and makes sure they are off the floor and laid out flat.

"What are you doing?"

"Keeping our clothes from wrinkling while I work up the nerve to tell you what I am going to do next. I just required a little pep talk with myself. I suggest you get used to how I am, since you will have to spend the next forty or so years dealing with me. Sometimes I just need to move. Staying still too long makes me edgy. I mean, not that I was getting edgy, not really, I guess. I just needed to move because I started to overthink things and let a few unpleasant thoughts enter my mind. Meaning, I needed to move around a bit so I could refocus and shake a few voices free." She stops moving, places her hands on her hips, and just stands there.

I rise to my elbows and stare at her gloriously sexy body. Scooting to the edge of the bed, I decide to sit up so I can admire her fully. "Okay. So while you are standing there, giving yourself this pep talk, do me a favor?"

Several brief expressions cross her face as she tries to process my words. "Okay, sure."

Standing to my feet, I point to her white lacy knickers. "Take off your knickers."

Larkin glances down and shrugs. I can see her debating it over in her head.

"Don't think about it. Just do it. On the count of three, okay?"

She nods once and blinks a few times. Once her thumbs are in position, I count down quickly. "One. Two. Three."

Larkin wiggles out of them. She doesn't notice I have removed mine as well until she glimpses back up. Hers are stuck halfway around her knees. So, when she tries to take a step toward me, she gets tripped up and ends up on her knees, and then does a face plant.

CHAPTER 33
Larkin

The Royals

Now that is one sure way to impress your man. Trip over your lacy panties that are still tangled around your knees, and fall smack into his very large, very impressive, very...

"Larkin. Are you okay, my love?" Antonio is not even trying to hold back his chuckle. "You are determined to kneel before me, aren't you, my love? Come on, up you go."

His very impressive appendage is now jutting straight out between his legs, jumping toward his stomach. I can't take my eyes off the massive thingamajig that is...

"Up." He tugs on my arm and tries to help me stand. "No more falling onto your knees before me. If anyone is going to fall to his knees, it shall be me. Here, let me help you out of these tricky little knickers."

Antonio squats again and removes my lacy panties carefully. He drops fully to his knees, while he runs his eyes over the length of my body, making it heat. He bends over, and at first, I am trying to figure out what in the world he is doing until his lips kiss my knee and I feel the sting.

"We need to take care of these abrasions." He says as he kisses the other one. "You should be more careful, honey."

I say the first thing that pops inside my head. "And you should warn a girl before setting that prodigious apparatus free. How do you walk around with something like that between your legs?"

He glances down and shrugs. "One foot at a time. I didn't mean to startle you. I only thought if you were going to be standing in front of me nude, I should be equally vulnerable. Want me to put him away for now?" Not hesitating, Antonio reaches for his briefs and stands so he can slide them back on.

I snatch those expensive briefs from his hand and toss them across the room. "No. I don't want you to put it away. I prefer you to lie back down on the bed so I can get a good look at him."

When my feet suddenly lift off the ground, I shriek and find myself bent in half, now staring at his gloriously tight backside. I reach down and pat it, and swear if I wasn't tossed over his shoulder like this, I'd have swooned. Instead, I shiver. His entire back is just as stunning as his front. His muscles shift when he walks, making me want to lick them all.

"What did you just say?" I hear him ask as he uprights me and sets my bare butt on the cool granite counter.

He opens a cabinet, sprays something on the gauze in his hand, and presses it to my knee. I nearly kick him in the nuts when he does that, but he is fast and moves out of the way just in time. "Please do not break him tonight. The last time you kneed me, it took a few days to heal. I hope to let our sexy parts get acquainted."

"What is the devil's fire are you putting on my knee?" I jerk again when he places a clean piece of gauze on my other knee with that crap on it.

"Just an antiseptic to clean it out. You are worse than Isabel. She gets these kinds of abrasions from *fútbol* and doesn't squirm nearly as much as you do." He grabs two new gauze pieces and does it again, but at the same time.

"Look, Darth Vader, do that again and my sexy parts are going on strike." I grab a handful of his chest hair and tug. "That freaking hurts, and I told you pain and I are not friends."

"Ouch." He gently reaches up and removes my hand. "You are adorable when you get like this." Retrieving another spray bottle from his cabinet, he shakes it before aiming it at my knee.

"No way, Dr. Kevorkian. You are not spraying anything else on my poor battered knees." I cover them with my hands.

Lifting the bottle, Antonio lets me read the label. An antibiotic spray. When I remove my hands, he leans forward and kisses my lips. Then he does something really smart and drops those lips to my bare chest, enclosing that warm mouth around my very sensitive nipple. Once I am distracted, he sprays my knees and I hardly feel it. This is how I am suggesting he takes care of all my future injuries. And since I am accident prone, I foresee a lot of fun times in my near future.

I moan in protest when he stops and reaches into the cabinet again. This time he had two large square bandages in his hand. After he places them on my knees, I take one look at them and frown.

"What?" He touches my chin and lifts it. "Why are you pouting?"

"Because I am the ultimate klutz. Name one other woman who would have fallen on her face as I did. Now I look like some poor oaf who can't do anything right."

Antonio rubs his nose against mine. "My oaf, who makes me laugh. You name one other woman who makes me feel the way you make me feel. Someone who causes me to forget who I am to the rest of the world. There isn't one, Larkin, because God broke the mold when he created you with me in mind. I love that you can look past everything and appreciate the man who hides inside of this shell. Now I believe you had something you wanted me to do, shall we get back to it?"

"Yes." I shove him and jump off the counter. "Go lie on the bed while I pee. I'm in here and now I have the urge, so I'm going to take care of that first."

He motions for me to do what it is I need to do while he walks back into the bedroom. I admire him until he closes the door, and then I grab the sink with both of my hands and stare at my reflection.

"Did you get a good look at that?" I ask her.

She nods back with eyes the size of silver dollars.

"Yeah, that is going to take some time getting used to. My vajayjay is going to revolt when he tries to put that inside of her." I swallow hard. "Maybe if we distract him enough, he will forget about the fact that he didn't actually slide it in. Any suggestions?"

"Larkin?" I hear his voice on the other side of the door. "Are you okay? I thought I heard you say something."

"I'm fine. Just singing to myself," I lie. "I'm washing my hands now."

"Okay." His voice is low. "Larkin?"

"Yeah." I splash water on my face.

"We don't have to have sex tonight, honey. We can just fool around a bit if you want. If you don't, then we can cuddle. I know that you..."

I yank the door open and point to the bed. "Shut up. Why aren't you lying down as I instructed?"

The smirk that takes over his face makes my heart swell. "Yes, my queen. Your wish is my command."

He grabs my waist as he backs up toward the bed. "What does my queen wish for?"

"Please don't call me that." I sense the panic building. "I'm trying to maintain a certain amount of control here."

"Larkin." Antonio sits down on the bed. "Breathe. It's just you and me. This is our bubble and no one else exists right now. What do you want to do?"

The love in his eyes gives me the courage to tell him what I want. "I want to see what those other women were talking about."

"Larkin, do not..." Antonio frowns, but I cover his mouth with my hand to stop him from objecting.

"I need to do this, Antonio. For me, it is important. If they... if they had their lips or mouths on you like that, then I wish to do it as well. Their smug little faces, while they recounted how you allowed them to do that, bothered me. I know I said that your past is not us, and it's not, but they... I want to erase them from your mind."

He mumbles behind my hand. "I don't think about them ever."

I tilt my head to look at the ceiling and roll my eyes. "And I simply forgot about the first guy who felt me up."

"You will forget him." Antonio grabs my breast and squeezes. "I'll make you forget everyone but me. Okay. Okay. I get it."

He slides back on the bed and gets comfortable. Grabs a few pillows and tucks them under his head. Then he pats the bed next to him. "You don't ever have to do anything you are not comfortable with."

I crawl up next to him and stare at his large erection. Antonio reaches over and takes my right hand in his, interweaving our fingers. I take my other hand and bravely wrap it and around him. The soft skin that encases his long rod surprises me, so I run it up to the mushroom-shaped tip and then back down again.

His fingers twitch in mine and a low groan resonates in his throat, so I ask him, "Do you like that?"

"Very much. *Me trae mucho placer mi amor.* Brings me so much pleasure," he whispers as his Adam's apple bobs. "I love it when you touch me. *Tu tacto es como un fuego que ilumina lo más profundo de mí y arde tan bien.*" (Your touch is like a fire that lights the deepest parts of me and burns so good.)"

I get brave and lean forward to graze the tip. His words are so rapid now that I don't understand him at all. I believe he mixes all of his languages. Now feeling a little braver, I let the tip slip between my lips and breathe in the musty scent of him.

I never thought I'd do anything like this. Never imagined I'd put a man's privates between my lips and enjoy it.

But I do.

I shift my body some so I can run my tongue from the tip to the base and then back up the other side. I do that a few times before I slip it back inside my mouth and take a little more of him this time.

"*Mi amor.* My love, stop." Antonio warns me, but I refuse to listen to him. "Larkin, I... I am going to... aww... forgive me, my love."

He no sooner gets the words out when I take him deeper into my mouth, a hot creamy liquid hits the back of my throat and coats my tongue. I'm not sure if I am supposed to spit it out or swallow it, so I just do what comes naturally and swallow. And when I release him, more spills out and lands on his stomach. It continues to run down my hand that is still pumping him. I can feel it pulsing under my fingers as the liquid squirts out a few more times. And then he softens slightly under my grip, so I release him. Not really thinking anything of it, I lick the warm liquid off my hand and then lean forward and clean it off his stomach.

By then Antonio has recovered enough to understand what I am doing, and before I know it, I am flat on my back with him hovering over me. We have been in this position many times before with our clothes on, but this is the first time with them off. The sight of him has me squirming, anticipating what his next move will be.

"You are very good at that, my love. You didn't need to swallow or clean up my mess. Now it is my turn to return the favor. I have never done this before, so bear with me." He kisses my lips and then slowly places soft kisses down my body.

I am trying to figure out what he is talking about when I feel him grab my leg and place it over one of his shoulders. Getting ready to protest, I start to rise but quickly fall back down when his tongue slips between the slit of my sensitive center. I try to speak, except my voice isn't working. The only sounds that come out are squeals and squeaks as he licks me like I have seen others lick an ice cream cone.

"Larkin, you are one delicious delicacy." He grabs my other leg and brings it over his other shoulder. "Yes, that is much better. You smell like..."

"Please don't tell me how I smell down there," I whisper the same time he figures out the scent and reveals it.

"Like rain on a hot summer day."

I really hope that is a compliment.

"I love going outside after the rain and taking a deep breath of the fresh air. Now all I need to do is bury my face between your legs and..." He inhales and I swear I melt into a big puddle of goo.

I'm not sure what I expected really, but it wasn't this. My entire adult life, I assumed I'd forever be agonizing about what is sure to come next. But right now, I cannot think at all, I can only feel. The way his hair brushes against my thighs as his head bobs between my legs. How his tongue glides over my flesh down there, so he can lick every single part of me. The way his hands grip my legs, as he holds me down while he devours me like I am some sort of treat.

Antonio stops and I wiggle, trying to get him to start up again. "You like that?"

"I love that." I open my eyes and stare at his, which are now peering up at me from his position.

"Me too." His eyes don't look away, but his tongue darts out and laps at me down there again. "I am going to enjoy doing this often."

One of his hands shifts to the inside of my thigh and he pushes against my leg until my knee lands on the bed. Then he rests it on the inside of my groin and holds my leg there, doing the same with the other. Afterward, he dives back in for a good tasting, rising to his knees as he breathes.

Without saying a word, he drags his right hand up my thigh and lets his fingers play with me. I whimper and wiggle as his touch has my skin breaking out into goosebumps. Then, without warning, his other hand joins in. One holding my bits open for him, while the other seems to learn how all those parts of me work.

He presses the pad of his thumb against a bundle of nerves, and I swear as I lift one foot off the bed. The wicked gleam in his eyes as he peeks up at me, right before doing it again, sends a shiver through me. That is when I feel his pinky at my entrance, slowly circling it, letting the tip press in slightly before retreating.

I want more, need more. "Antonio."

One more little circle and I feel it slide in easily all the way and moan. He pulls it back out and does it again. I swear my body orders my brain to relax and let him have his fun.

"More," I whisper.

I feel him remove his pinky and slip a slightly larger finger inside. Stretching the entrance even more as it glides in and out easily. The pressure building inside of me is almost too much.

"More," I say a little louder this time. "Two fingers."

Antonio runs both fingers along my now slick center before sliding them in with ease. His expression, as he moves his fingers inside of me, has me wanting even more. So far there has been no pain, just a little pressure as he stretches it out.

"More." I circle my hips. "Three now."

Leaning his body forward, he kisses my lips before he says anything. "Getting greedy."

"Yes," I tell him as I nip at his bottom lip. "Do it."

He crashes his mouth against mine at the same time he adds the third finger. I want to cry out, but his kiss prevents me from doing so. And this time he curls those fingers and begins dragging them against my slick walls. His thumb presses against the nerves again and the combination of the two sends me down a black dark hole as my body quivers from the inside.

Antonio breaks the kiss, and I cry out when all the pressure building inside of me finds its way out. I can identify his hard length as it slaps against my center while his fingers continue to manipulate my body. And right before my body goes limp, he withdraws his thumb and uses his erection to stimulate that nerve. Once again, I detect the hot liquid spilling from it as it coats my core.

I start to protest when he removes his body from mine and slides in behind me. Want to tell him he should probably take advantage of the fact that I have no energy to stop him from robbing me of my virginity. That I want him to do it while I have no coherent thought running through my overactive brain, except the words won't come out.

My love wraps his powerful arms around me, hauling my limp body against his as he places the most loving kisses against my ear. "Enough for now. I'm spent. You're spent. We rest now."

"But." One word is all I can get out.

He's right. My body needs rest and I am fading rather quickly.

"No buts." He kisses my ear again. "That my love was the most satisfying sexual experience of my life. Watching your body soar as I manipulated it with my touch was enough to satisfy my need for now. There is plenty of time for more later after we get some sleep. It's late and tomorrow we have a very busy day to get through."

I yawn. "Okay, but that was your best chance to deflower me."

A low growl and chuckle escape from him at the same time. "I want you coherent, Larkin, when I deflower you. On the verge of what just happened, but of sound mind when I take you that first time. I want to feel all that convulsing around my sensitive flesh, as I drive you wild. Now hush and go to sleep."

Twisting my head, I find his lips and kiss him fervently one last time and then confess to him. "I want that too. I want your prodigious gorgeous sword to ruin me completely."

CHAPTER 34
Larkin

The Royals

The glow from the candles I lit a few hours ago bounces around, illuminating the most pulchritudinous man I have ever laid eyes on. The structure of his frame suggests he was built to be a powerful warrior, one who could easily lead others into battle if we lived in a different era.

His long muscular legs are pieced together with strapping thighs and burly sculpted calves. When he walks, the various muscles that make up his legs contract. It is a sight to take in and one I did my best to memorize.

The curve of his rump has no softness to it at all. It is as firm as it looks. I have stroked my hands over it a few times now. I needed to touch it. What can I say? You'd touch it too if it were so close. I wanted to lick it, but I didn't want to wake him just yet. Later, I crave to hold it in my hands while he drives his king-size male appendage deep inside of me.

Right now, he is lying on his stomach with his arms tucked under his pillow. Making his biceps bulge and flex. Forcing the muscles in his back to appear tight in the shoulder region. It all disappears around the curvature of his perfect spine. Coming together again impeccably where the valley meets his rump.

I am sitting in a chair adjacent to the bed with my sketchpad and pencil. I have been sketching him since I located my bag and lit the candles I found hidden in the library. Unable to go back to sleep after waking, I did what I have always done. Except this time, my subject has an astonishing effect on me.

A low moan catches my attention, so I glimpse up from my sketch and realize he has flipped over. I watch as he reaches down and scratches his bare, lifeless, yet still rather impressive member. Giving it enough attention to bring some spunk back into it.

Flipping the page in my book, I start all over again. Outlining his form as I watch in awe as every part of him seems to slowly wake and come back from dreamland.

I don't find any of this vulgar or inappropriate. I'm sorry if you do. If I were merely some anonymous woman sitting here, perhaps I would. However, I am not. I am this man's wife and so I undergo no shame at all admiring his body with lustful desire.

Brown, hooded eyes search for me, and when they find me, a mischievous grin appears on his face. He tucks the arm closest to me under his head, while he keeps the other right where it is. Wrapping his fist around his now almost fully erect organ, he strokes it slowly.

I continue to doodle, now a little more frantically as I watch his hand do what I have been dying to do for a while now. He has worked it until it is standing tall and proud and even weeping just a little. Then he pats the bed as he rolls over onto his side.

Sliding my pencil into the spiral spine of my sketchpad, I set both on the table next to me and stand. I don't miss the way his eyes scan my body, now covered in a white lace robe with only a few flimsy ties to hold it in place. As I walk toward the bed, he throws his legs over the side and sits up.

When I stop a few feet from him, he motions for me to step closer with a wiggle of his finger. And once I am close enough, he simply reaches up and tugs the ties as he watches the robe drop open, only stopping because my breasts have caught the fabric. Antonio slips his hands around my waist, heating my cool skin, hauling me closer until he can capture the tip of my right breast in his mouth through the lace.

I throw my head back and whimper at the way his manipulations make me feel alive all over. He does the same with the other, and I swear I could lose it right here and now. When he is finished, he shoves the material off my shoulders and drags me down with him as he tumbles back onto the bed.

For a very long time, he only kisses my lips, tunneling his tongue in my mouth slowly. A sweet kiss that expresses he plans on taking his time with me. Warming my body until it is on fire and ready to take what he has to offer me. Then his hands roam and caress my body. Paying homage to my breasts and nipples. Working them to hard points, making them ache for more, which is when he drops his mouth to them and sucks.

While Antonio manipulates my breasts, his hand travels south and cups my center. After his spell down there last night, he is more familiar with where everything is. Teasing the bundle of nerves first, before retreating and sliding those long greedy fingers back to my entrance, where he dips only the tips in before going back to the other. He plays this game for a while until I want to beg him to do more.

Instead, I decide to have a little fun of my own. My hands have been caressing his back up to this point. The next time he teases my entrance, I dig my nails in and drag them down his spine, getting the reaction I wanted from him.

One long finger dips inside of me, and I moan. When he retreats, I let one of my hands land on his hard globe and squeeze it the best I can. The tight muscles don't give like the soft tissue I possess in mine does. And then I locate the crevice between them and trace until my fingers contact the valley between his heavy sacks and back hole. I have no desire to play with that, by the way, not something I imagine he would even enjoy.

Two fingers enter me now, so I allow my nails to gently draw a line to his family jewels and then palm them. Massaging them very gently, not sure how sensitive they may be; and I have no wish to hurt him. Plus, our future children live somewhere inside his testicles, so taking care of them seems prudent.

As soon as I feel his mouth leave my breast and start kissing his way up to my neck, I rearrange my hand again. This time its destination is the long hot rod that keeps bumping my leg. Wrapping my fingers around him, I then drag them up and then back down, much like I watched him do earlier.

Antonio nips my chin and then pulls his head back so he can look at me. Our eyes lock right before he dips the tips of three fingers inside of me, with a fourth nudging just outside the moist cave that is I.

I shake my head no, yet he nods his yes before he slowly pushes all four of them inside. I can feel the burn and gasp at the intrusion, not sure I can take much more. That's when I feel one of his fingers curve and nudge against a sensitive knot deep inside of me. He drags them in reverse just as slowly, before urging them back inside, a little deeper this time.

It burns and I feel my eyes beginning to water. I know I am about to cry. I understand what he is trying to do, but I become less confident the longer he keeps it up and it doesn't seem to get any better.

A few seconds before I am about to ask him to stop, he pulls them out completely and sighs. That is when he reaches over me and opens the drawer next to the bed and begins digging around. Once he locates what he wants, he lays it next to my head and fiddles with it a little. His hand then returns to my lady parts. I realize then he has added some lube to his digits and is about to try again.

Again, I shake my head and must make a face that warns him I'm unsure about all of this. His lips land on mine, where he bites my bottom lip hard enough to cause me to forget his intent. When he retreats, I grab his with my teeth and bite down the instant his four fingers are thrust inside of me. The taste of metal fills my mouth, so I release his lip as I cry out, more out of surprise than pain. This time his fingers are not slow, they move fast and with purpose. So, I grip his member a little harder and try to keep my pace even with his. The fire inside me is building and I know I am about to go up in flames again soon.

Suddenly I am being twisted away from him, facing the window that right now is acting more like a mirror. I watch as he maneuvers our bodies, bringing my top leg to lie over his as he yanks my butt to rest against his stomach. I can feel his hard, hot sword brushing against me down there. He slides an arm under my head, tilting my head so I am now looking directly into his eyes.

A beat or two passes as we gaze passionately at the other person. Then he slowly lowers his head and gently kisses me at first, but the kiss quickly turns into more. His tongue begins taking my mouth, much like I imagine he is going to take me elsewhere very soon.

I feel his other hand spread more lubrication just outside my entrance, and then he dips a few fingers in to coat it all very well. When his fingers retreat, I expect my mind to start working overtime as it anticipates his next action, except it doesn't. Instead, I suddenly feel more relaxed than ever and end the kiss so I can look at him.

The tip of his erection is placed just outside the point of no return, so I reach up and run my thumb across his cheek. Slowly, he guides himself in and I feel my eyes rolling into the back of my head.

I'm not going to lie to you. Antonio is a large, well-endowed man, so there is real pain as my body stretches to accommodate him. I can sense my eyes watering and burning with each slow half inch that is forced inside of me. I realize he is only barely inside when pulls back to the tip and then pushes the before mentioned appendage a few inches back inside.

I once read that a man whose penis reached six inches was considered large. The average circumference is typically less than five inches, which is about the gap between a woman's middle finger and thumb when touching. I measured my hand once from my palm to the tip of my middle finger, and it was close to six inches. Meaning that the hard silk rod, now barely inside of me, is bigger than that by no less than an inch, maybe two. And the girth of it was vast enough my fingers couldn't touch the closer they got to the base, barely able to at the tip.

Did I mention he was only a few inches inside of me? Meaning he has a great deal left before he is all the way in.

My senses seem to return so I can now open my eyes again. When I do, I am able to identify the very focused grimace on Antonio's face as he holds back. I appreciate he is doing his best to do this slowly and trying to make it feel good. But at the same time, this slow progression is only dragging out the discomfort.

Remember how when I said earlier, I'm not a very patient person.

Try to keep that in mind as I finally have had enough of this drawing out and let my thoughts be known.

"Either do it or don't. Stop with the freaking torture. Pop my flipping cherry already." I grunt through clenched teeth.

Antonio halts all movement as he tries really hard to speak. Sweat beads form on his forehead as he nips his bottom lip. "I don't want to hurt you."

"News flash, stud. When you have a freaking zucchini between your legs, rather than the typical cucumber, there is bound to be pain involved when inserting it into my virgin sheath the first time. So, either be a man about it or hand in your man card. Otherwise, I'm going to think the paper tiger has..."

Oh, I really should learn to keep my mouth shut. His lips clash with mine as soon as I mention the paper tiger. In one swift thrust, he is so deep inside of me I swear my body split in two.

The only good thing about that is at least now I know I will die a very satisfied woman. Because that move not only split me wide-open but also sent my body into orbit. I am flying high above the earth as flashes of colorful light explode all around me. When I come back down, Antonio's body is thrusting feverishly inside of me, causing it all to build back up again.

Oh yes, I am going to die in this bed while this glorious man teaches my body all about the joys it will miss once I'm gone. Subsequently, I decide if I am going to expire anyway, I might as well go out with a real bang.

I elbow him and force him to refocus for a second. Long enough for me to lift off of him—which you should know wasn't an easy task—and shove him to his back. The confused expression on his face has me sniggering a bit. Remember how I seem to laugh at the most inappropriate times, like in the Throne Room earlier when the reality of it all became clear to me?

"Why are you laughing?" He snickers too, I think, because I am.

"Shut up. Stay on your back. Best enjoy this, while you can, because I'm pretty sure you just killed me with that little maneuver. So, since I'm going to expire any second now, I might as well do it taking you for a ride one last glorious time." I climb on top of him, positioning my knees just outside his hips. I pause above his still erect member and notice it twitch slightly as I wiggle to make sure I'm right where I need to be. "You ready for this wild ride I'm about to take us both on?"

Antonio sits up quickly and slides us toward the headboard with his back firmly rested against it. He bends his knees and positions his hands on my hips to hold me motionless while he explains. "Not as deep like this."

I lean back so my rear rests against his legs. "How do you know this?"

Rubbing his thumbs along my hipbones, he confesses something that has me in stitches. "I asked the guys for advice, so Isaac sent me a link to a webpage that explained the positions that would be best these first few times."

I fall forward and drop my head to his notable chest and start to chuckle again. "Isaac and Gino?"

He grunts. "I was trying to..."

Raising my head, I kiss his lips, still laughing. "Shhh. So that painfully slow torture earlier was from this site?"

"You didn't like it." He drops his head back and gazes up at the ceiling.

"I didn't hate it. Not after you grew a pair and started moving." I kiss his jaw. "My sweet, sweet man. Thank you."

Then I rise to my knees again and grab his lethal weapon, placing it between my legs and lower just enough to let the tip slip in. Positioning my arms on his shoulders, I brace myself, take one breath before I slam home.

There isn't any pain this time, but I do suspect I could not possibly take him if he were wider. Which is when my eyes grow, as I begin to realize he is expanding rapidly inside of me. Before I talk myself out of this, I decide to move. I lift my body up and then slam back down, up, and then slam back down. Building up a rhythm that feels just about perfect.

I glance down between us, thinking that I am doing well, taking so much of him, until I notice there is still more. How in the ever-living realm am I supposed to fit all that inside of my body?

Where there is a will, there is a way, right?

"Move so I can take it all," I order him.

"Larkin." His grip on my hips tightens. "This is good."

"But not great, so move your royal tushy, or lower your legs, or whatever you have to do so I can take all of you now." I pinch his neck.

He mutters a slur of words and we are repositioning again. Once again, I find myself on my back with him hovering over me, somehow still inside of me. Griping my wrists, he pins them to the bed. Before I am able to complain, he hammers the rest of the way inside and doesn't let up. He pounds forcefully; propelling my body up each time our bodies collide.

I want to touch him, need to touch him. "Let me go."

He does, so I bring my arms around his back and down to his muscular globes. My eyes flutter as my focus fades again. This time, though, I can detect my inner muscles trying to hold him where he is deep inside of me, getting greedy about it when he retreats. So, I raise my legs to wrap them around his rear, and I swear somehow, he seems to go just a tad deeper. He must hit the button that was designed to send my entire body into one giant spasm. My legs lock around him, my toes curl, my hands clench, and the rest of my muscles contract and hold.

The most primal roar I have ever heard spills out of Antonio, echoing off the walls. One last thrust and his body trembles and jerks as he empties hot liquid inside of me.

Once we calm down, and he has rolled us onto our sides, I nuzzle in and ask what is on the tip of my tongue. "Am I dead yet? Or do you suppose we might be able to do that again before I expire?"

Antonio's chest is now vibrating and drenched in sweat. He smells better than he ever has, so I hope and pray God spares my life. What a shame it would be to go my entire life without knowing how wonderful sex can be. It would be even worse, I imagine, to figure it out and then have it taken away.

"You're not dead or dying." He kisses the top of my head, still laughing. "Give me some time to recover and take a breather, then I promise to do it again. So, tell me, *mi lunita*, what were you over there sketching when I woke up."

"I was..." I yawn and feel my eyes becoming heavy. "I was capturing the most captivating thing ever. A sleeping paper tiger in all his glory."

I yelp loudly, and once again find my body trapped under his. So much for that nap, he said he needed. Looks like round three is about to begin right about now.

CHAPTER 35
Antonio

The Royals

I t is always hard to determine how others will react. You often predict one reaction and then get a completely different one all the way around. Therefore, I've learned to never assume anything until after everyone has all the facts.

Tonight is the night we were scheduled to announce our engagement. People from all over this country have been invited. Most of them are powerful members of the community, those who are considered upper-class citizens.

Several invitations have also been sent to those who have in some way caught the attention of the royal family. A person suffering from a life-threatening illness, a member of the armed forces or law enforcement who was injured while serving, or perhaps someone who has done a spectacular job reaching out and making their community a better place to live. That number is not as big as the first, but in my opinion, they are more important than the others.

Therefore, when the seating chart was constructed, I opted to have them seated closer to the front rather than being placed in the back. I know I will hear about it later from those who believe they have earned the better seats. But this is a brave new world and things are about to change.

Right now, I am standing in my designated spot, greeting everyone as they arrive. I hate this part. To me, it only stretches these events out even more and is a waste of time. Typically, I have passed this task off to my mother, who seems to enjoy it much more than I do. Which is why I have her here, standing next to me.

A few of my guests seem confused and have questioned why Larkin isn't here. I simply explained she was running a little late, needed more time to get all beautified for her big debut. And everyone has seemed to accept that explanation, until a malicious group of women and their escorts arrive, making me wish I had enforced my ban. But Larkin and I agreed to allow them to attend tonight's celebration. It was sort of an extension of kindness, a second chance, so to speak, to determine if the other night might have just been a fluke.

"Your Majesty." Lady Karina takes the lead tonight. "I hope we didn't frighten your fiancée off."

"I can assure you that you did not. I should probably thank your little cluster of ladies; seems you sparked a little fire inside of her." I pass her off to my mother so I can greet the next viper.

Lady Paschal's sinister grin explodes on her face. "Your Majesty. No harm, no foul, then. Perhaps she'd be interested in attending one of our charity fundraisers soon."

"Perhaps. Although right now I'm afraid she is quite busy with her work. Her current project is very dear to both of us, so until she finishes, I just don't see her being available to do so." I pass her off and paste on a very fake smile as I greet my next guest.

"Well, I guess she will have to choose what is more important to her once she becomes queen." Lady Dalia starts her incline forward, intending to press an inappropriate kiss on my cheek.

Thankfully, my mother intervenes.

"Lady Dalia." She reaches over and tows her toward her. "Looking as lovely as always."

"Thank you, Your Royal Highness. I was just going to say that King Antonio looks rather ravishing this evening as well. Too bad Miss Larkin is missing out. She needs to learn the importance of punctuality, I do believe. One can never be too careful about leaving such a fine-looking man all alone." She air kisses my mother's cheeks.

"She will be here..." I start to tell her *soon* when a small hand lands on my back.

"Who will be here?" Larkin's voice asks as she steps between my mother and me.

We had agreed she would not be a part of this. That way, no one would question her attire. However, I get the impression she got a whiff of the stench when they walked in, or someone alerted her of it. Either way, I am happy she is here now. She looks as stunning as she did last night, and this time I get to truly appreciate how this dress fits her. My mind is no longer occupied with other scenarios; worried she'll change her mind or come to her senses. She is forever mine and I am hers. Together, we will stand.

"That's a very lovely white gown you have on. A little bold, don't you think for a modest event like this one. One typically saves a dress like that for a much more formal occasion." Lady Genovese is the next person in line.

"I don't know, Gen." Dalia slowly drags her eyes over the gown. "I think she looks like the perfect little lamb. I'm sure that was the look she was going for."

I am about to put an end to this and have them escorted from the premises, but my lovely wife squeezes my hand and plays innocent. "Something like that, yes. I'm certain the more events I attend, the better I'll get at choosing my attire."

"I'm sure." They sarcastically agree as they exchange a look.

"My love." Larkin spins to face me. "I could use your assistance if it isn't too much trouble. Seems I am not as well equipped as you at getting it to stay put without falling right off."

I can hear the women all mumble to themselves as they listen to our private conversation. "Not at all, *mi lunita*. Lead the way."

"Esteban said he would be glad to take your place here while we finish getting ready for introductions. Are you okay with that, Angela?" Her use of my mother's given name so freely is not done out of disrespect. It is done to display her familiarity and prove to the others she is allowed to do so.

"Yes, I believe that is a wonderful idea." My mother's tickled expression about my wife's sneakiness cannot be hidden. Neither can her words or actions, when she leans forward and kisses both of Larkin's cheeks very respectfully, an action typically only done with a family member. "You will do just fine, dear. Glad to see you took my advice to heart."

Larkin glances over my mother's shoulder at the women now gaping in her direction. "I have been dealing with difficult situations most of my life. So, I guess you could say I have been well trained for this."

I tuck her hand in my arm and lead her out the back way. As soon as we round the corner, I whirl her around and trap her body against the wall so I can kiss her. Her small hands start to push me away, but when I press my full body against her, she grips my shirt instead.

"Get a room." Lorenzo's voice chuckles from behind us.

"I swear if the only reason you asked me to take his place, Larkin, was so you two could go at it again, I'll buy you prunes for Christmas." Esteban leans up against the wall next to us. "Aren't you two adorable?"

I pull back and glare over at my brother. "Don't you have someplace to be?"

"I do. But I'm waiting for a few because right now Lady Maribel is greeting mother. She is doing her best to delay so she can..." Esteban's voice breaks off and he gets this fierce expression on his face. "Why is Winnie here with Hector Colon?"

Lorenzo and I both step in behind him. Sure enough, Winifred Batista is standing next to a very handsy older Hector. She doesn't seem as motivated about it as he does. And it is not for the first time I notice my brother looks like he could hurt someone.

"Excuse me." He marches through the door as he steps in next to my mother.

We all watch as he greets them, taking a little longer with Winifred. He even leans forward and seems to whisper something in her ear, and I watch as she blushes.

I also notice Hector does not find his action amusing at all, so he steps up behind her to move her along. He too leans in to say something, and her body straightens. It expresses more about what I am witnessing.

"Who is that?" Larkin asks, watching as well.

"Hector Colon. His father is governor of the southern district.

Rumor has it that Aaron is training Hector to take over his job after his term ends. And by the looks of that, I'm guessing he is negotiating a marriage for his son, with a woman whose family has been trying to shun her for a very long time." I lean down and kiss Larkin's cheek.

"I don't understand all of that. Doesn't she get a say?" Larkin glances up at me with a huge question in her voice.

"She probably has a trust or dowry that is large enough to get her to agree to just about anything. Stating that unless she marries a man of her father's choosing, those funds will never be made available to her. The fact that she is still very young means she hasn't quite gotten the courage to tell him no yet. I don't get it, either, love, but the fact is it happens still." I take her hand in mine. "Perhaps she will get the nerve to do so after she sees how happy we are. Perhaps we will start a revolution of sorts and end all these silly arrangements once and for all. Or maybe Esteban will finally do what he has been eager to do since that girl turned eighteen."

We make our way to the dressing area. I quickly change into my more formal official attire. I greeted everyone in a dark suit and tie that displayed my colors, with my sovereign crested pin attached to my jacket. I didn't want to give anything away by dressing too formally. Like the other women so non-discreetly pointed out, this was one of the less formal events that took place here at the palace. It was simply a dinner party, so most of our guests were not displaying their most elegant wardrobes. Dressing much like they would if they were going out for a fancy dinner at one of the nicer restaurants in Aragon.

So now I slip into my tailored tux, gold vest, and replace my tie with the king's medallion. I rarely wear a sash, mainly because I hate them, but tonight I place mine between my jacket and vest, so Larkin and I match. She will not have to wear one after tonight if she does not wish to. I believe the new crown I had forged for her will be the perfect statement for later events. Its jewels of rubies and sapphires, encased in the purest gold, resemble the colors chosen to represent my reign, and it should do just fine.

Tonight, however, she will wear the customary Queen's crown that has been passed down since the Reyes family claimed the throne. Redesigned slightly a few times while maintaining the original jewels and gold. It is a little heavier and can become uncomfortable, I imagine, but if secured correctly, it will stay in place and not move. Luckily, my mother has taught us all how to properly secure a crown. And since only a royal's hands are allowed to touch this crown, I am here to assist my lovely wife while I teach her at the same time.

There is a knock on the door before it opens slightly. "It is time, Your Majesties," Isaac's voice announces through the cracked opening.

"We are fully dressed." My Queen announces. "What do you think, Isaac? Am I going to make a statement or just get the gossipers whispering?"

He takes his time to look her over and then smiles. "Most definitely a statement, my queen. The gossipers will whisper no matter what, but this time, the whispers will be about the statement you are sure to make. You look divine, and King Antonio is most definitely setting the bar high. Shall we make our way to the Throne Room and let the festivities begin?"

Typically, our guests would be instructed to take their places in the dining hall. However, tonight is not at all typical. We have asked that they be left in the Throne Room, where we will greet them as a family united. A formal introduction of a new family member has always been done in this manner. This introduction will be no different, except for the fact that my guests are unaware that a member has been added to our fold.

The back doors are opened and the introductions begin. I can verify the confusion on many of their faces as each member of my family is introduced before they enter. It is not how things are normally done when attending a dinner party, and so the whispers begin.

I am excellent at reading lips, a critical gift I picked up on as a lad. A few are asking why do you suppose we are being introduced to the royal family. Others are suggesting that we have gotten a little pretentious and making them all suffer through such an unnecessary event. And then there are those who are making remarks about the fact that my fiancée must feel the need to feel important. Therefore, I am appeasing her and making a big production of this whole debacle.

As soon as Princess Isabel makes her proud long walk down to the royal family platform, where she joins my mother and sister, the trumpet signals my royal entrance. I am standing alone at the back, for now, awaiting the presenter to speak his designated words.

"Your Majesties." He bows and motions toward the door. "King Antonio Ramon Reyes and Queen Larkin Moon Reyes."

I reach out and bring my lovely Larkin into view. The entire room seems to gasp at the sight of her beauty. I must agree with them, she is one exquisite queen indeed.

Tucking her arm in mine, I turn to her. "My Queen."

Blinking slowly, she glances up at me and smiles. "My King."

And together we begin the long stroll that leads to the thrones. We hear several congratulations during our unified march, along with the murmurs that ascend after we pass by. Larkin holds her head high and offers each person a genuine smile and a respectful nod.

I am proud of her for not letting them get to her. I know deep down she is most likely freaking out and will need me to calm her later. Let me assure you, I have no problem reminding her of the reason she agreed to marry me. It will be my pleasure, and hers, to wash away all the stress that sometimes shadows an event like this. I believe all this will be much easier now that I have my Larkin to help me shake it all off.

When we approach the steps, I put her hand in mine, motioning for her to continue ahead of me while I offer her assistance. This is a most taboo gesture, so when I hear the audible objections, I twist my head and let them know I will not tolerate it. Once we are standing in front of our designated thrones, I bring her hand to my lips and kiss it.

The Throne Room falls silent. This room was designed so that all in attendance could hear a simple whisper if spoken from where I am standing. So, I don't need a microphone to give my prepared speech.

"We would like to thank all of you for joining us this evening. I can identify several reactions and expressions on the faces staring back at us. Many of you are probably shocked, maybe even disappointed, that you were not informed this venue has been changed from a simple engagement party to a celebration of our recent nuptials. I... pardon me, I misspoke. I mean, we meant no disrespect by keeping you all in the dark."

A female voice echoes off the walls. "Yes, you did."

I know the voice, so I direct my attention to where she is standing with the other women in her group. "I can assure you we did not, and to question me about it is calling me a liar. I will not stand here and defend my actions or my decision to marry the woman of my choosing. I will, however, enlighten you that it was executed properly last night in this very room. The vicar conducted the traditional ceremony that not only united us as husband and wife but also unified us as your king and queen. My family and Queen Larkin's were present to share in the sacred ceremony with us. A choice we made as a couple.

"And for those who have assumed a union like this goes against the conventional protocols that have been laid out and always followed. Let me remind you that, as King, I say what is and what is not acceptable. And it is always acceptable to marry for love over conventions that are outdated and should have been abandoned long ago. There will be no more arranged marriages or marriages of convenience performed from this point forward. We will allow our children to freely choose their spouses. My brothers and sisters are also free to marry for love. The royal family will no longer entertain negotiations.

"This is a brave new world and there will be many modifications to how the royal family conducts its personal affairs moving forward. We no longer live in the Dark Ages, so it is time we bring this family, along with this country, into the twenty-first century. Accordingly, tonight Queen Larkin and I, King Antonio, for the first time in the history of Hermosa Islas, formally announce that we will rule as one. I, King Antonio, grant my Queen equality in all things."

Larkin squeezes my hand as she prepares to speak. "And I, Queen Larkin Moon Reyes, accept the equality my King wishes to grant me, with one exception."

We argued about this early this morning when I told her of my plans. She has no desire to have any say in the way the kingdom operates, the political aspects of it. I however strongly disagreed with her and warned her that if she tried to pass on it, I'd simply not accept it.

"I will gladly voice my opinion on all matters when asked, support my husband in all things, and stand by his side, united as his equal. But should we disagree, or should I feel the need to not provide an opinion, then the King's decision will be mine. After all, I believe the Lord made the husband the head of the house, because there cannot be two heads, otherwise things would never get done. As a loyal servant of God, I chose to follow his law in this matter and submit to my husband when I must."

Well, I believe I said earlier that one never knows how others will react in certain situations. Case in point. Apparently, my wife has been busy endeavoring to figure out the best way to pass on those political responsibilities, and I must say I am very impressed.

"I accept my wife's amended proposal." For good measure, and because right now I just really want to, I lean down and kiss her. "Shall we make this official?"

My loyal family starts and my faithful audience follows. "All hail to the King and Queen. May your reign be long and prosperous, a strength that will lead us and make us a stronger nation."

The crowd shouts and bows. "All hail to the King and Queen."

I take my Queen's hand and raise it high, and much like we did last night, we take our seats together. I glance over at her and notice she is doing her best not to burst into laughter as she did then. So, I lean over and whisper in her ear to hopefully make it look like I said something funny if she does.

"Welcome my love. I must declare that you are absolutely the most gorgeous queen to date. I propose we fix the portrait currently hanging, replace it with a more fitting one. Perhaps you would be willing to paint it."

Larkin giggles and rotates her head so she can study me when she declines. "I don't paint portraits, or at least not the kind that would be appropriate to hang for all to see. The one I plan on painting of you will be for my own private viewing. No other eyes but mine will be allowed to look upon it."

Forget about her bursting into hysterics. I beat her. The sound of my laughter bounces off the walls as I throw my head back, knowing she unknowingly just announced to the entire room about her plans of painting a nude portrait of me.

CHAPTER 36
Antonio

The Royals

If you assume our announcement went over without a hitch, then you haven't been paying very close attention. There will always be those who believe they know better. Those who think they can get away with almost anything and never have to pay for it.

Once everyone was escorted into the dining hall, and we took our seats, the gossipers started. Larkin and I did our best to ignore the whispers and focus on ourselves. After all, this was our wedding reception, therefore we planned on having a good time and incorporated a few traditions from both of our countries.

Wedding cake traditions, in case you didn't know, vary around the world. Here in Hermosa Islas, each table is presented with a segment of the cake after the bride and groom serve the family. However, in America, the bride and groom cut the cake and then share a piece before the rest is offered to their guests. We opted to combine the two.

The large cake was rolled out, and I heard Larkin giggle nervously when she spotted it. The white and gold cake was eight tiers and taller than me, which is saying something. I guided my wife to the obnoxious ensemble, and together we cut it. She broke off a portion and fed it to me, and I did the same for her. I heard the way several didn't find it appropriate, but I didn't care. And I proved that when I took the remainder to the cut cake and shoved a large portion of it in my mouth before I grabbed my wife and kissed her. Making sure to smear some icing on her lips so I could lick it off, which I did, as she shamelessly did the same. We washed it down with a bubbly glass of champagne that she insisted we try to do while interlocking our arms. I believe I may have spilled a little and laughed a lot. Then when we were done, we served our family while the servers distributed cake to the rest of our guests.

When that was over, it was time to dance, which, as you might have guessed, was not a top priority on my lovely bride's list. She wanted to skip dancing altogether, except dancing at a wedding was what made the reception tolerable. Not to mention I have been eager to get her back on the dance floor and display some of my best moves.

That's right, this king knows how to dance. My brothers and I have perfected our skills over the years. It was how we got through all of those required events we were ordered to attend as young princes. At least when we were dancing, we weren't obliged to hold meaningful conversations and could switch partners frequently. After all, it was our job to make all the young ladies in the room feel special, and thus, we did our best to do so.

Tonight, however, I plan on dancing with one woman and one woman only. And while I am dancing with her, we will not only communicate with our mouths but our bodies. I've never danced like that before, never wanted to. However, tonight I want to seduce her right there on the dance floor and then later finish that seduction in our private quarters.

As you might imagine, I am a fan of several Latino artists, so I chose our first song accordingly. 'Bailando' is the very first song Larkin and I will dance to.

I had my sister, Gabriela, do her best to teach Larkin some moves this morning. You know, what most people consider salsa dancing. A little swinging of the hips, handclaps, how to move her arms while doing so. We all got a good laugh watching her uncoordinated form attempting to learn while being unsuccessful.

Lorenzo stepped in eventually, sliding his body behind hers while I dance flawlessly in front of her. He placed his hands on her hips to help her locate the beat, swaying his with hers. I'll never forget when she told him to just give up because she obviously didn't possess the dancing gene. Except my little brother was not giving up on her, said every person had the dancing gene; they just needed to figure out how to activate it. He then found a song he believed would activate hers, 'Bailamos'. He instructed her to listen to the words while he moved behind her. Instructed her that dancing is an expression of our emotions. Sometimes it's all about having a good time, letting off some steam, whereas other times it's about connecting with the person you are dancing with. A seduction to attract the person, keeping his or her attention the entire time. I'll never forget the blush that took over her face as Lorenzo whispered something in her ear.

"What did you say to her?" I growled at my brother as he chuckled behind her.

"Chillax, Antonio. I only instructed her that dancing was a lot like making love. *Hacer el amor es un baile entre amantes, donde sus cuerpos encuentran ese ritmo perfecto para expresar el amor.* (Making love is a dance between lovers, where their bodies find that perfect rhythm to express love.) Do you disagree?" Lorenzo encourages Larkin to step closer. "Now, Larkin, dance like you have found your perfect rhythm."

That worked almost flawlessly, and I hated that my little brother had figured out the key before me. Not really, but you understand what I mean. Because if you knew Lorenzo as I know him, you'd know he just has a way of figuring stuff like that out. And while I worry about my little brother in the way he can charm the women so easily, I know one day there will be a woman who will be immune to his charm. That will be the woman he falls for, and once he wins her over, because I have no doubt he will, she will have a man who will love her as only Lorenzo can.

So here we are, just the two of us, dancing to one of my favorite songs. Larkin is swaying her hips perfectly to the rhythm on the opposite side of the dance floor. We are mimicking each other, doing a line dance of sorts while we work our way to the other. Once we meet in the middle, she sways seductively in the center while I move perfectly around her for a few beats. I eventually slide in behind her when I'm ready and we salsa together effortlessly. Her arms ultimately find their way around the back of my neck as my hands caress her body. One of mine travels up her arm, where I release her hold so I can spin her perfectly like we practiced. Out once and then right back in, bringing her flush against my body right where I want her. Which is how we remain for the rest of the song. Her arms around my neck, mine secured firmly against her back as we dance the way lovers do.

The cat whistles, that my brothers and Fernando start, begin as soon as the song ends. They produce the loveliest blush on my beautiful wife's cheeks and get her to relax. She throws her head back and laughs like she does when it's just the two of us, which means I do the same.

The next song is the one she chose, and I have to say I agree it is absolutely perfect. 'I Choose You', seems to sum up our relationship almost perfectly. I adjust her in my arms, taking one of her hands in mine so I can lead her easily around the dance floor. We have all but forgotten about the rest of the room as we focus on only us. But this bubble cannot last in a room of a few hundred. As soon as the song ends, the crowded hall reminds us of their presence when they applaud.

The deejay then invites everyone who wishes to join us and of course, they do. Not everyone may agree with this union, but I've never known anyone to turn down free food and a good dance party.

My love and I dance a few more songs before we make the rounds around the room. Our first stop is to welcome our honored guests. They don't normally get invited to such an event and are speechless when we sit down with them.

My wife was the one who took her seat next to the female constable who was shot in the line of duty. She still wears a sling to keep her shoulder from moving more than necessary. Larkin asks her if there was anything we could do for her or her family. When my wife learns they are foster parents, she shares her own story with them. Thanks, them for stepping up and looking out for children who are unable to look out for themselves. When she stands to leave, she motions for her parents to come meet them, and as we walk away, they were swapping stories.

Our next table is of a single mother who brought her son who has been diagnosed with Tourette's. This time Larkin asks the young man if it would be okay if she sat next to him. Of course, the smart boy has no problem with a beautiful woman sitting beside him. Once again Larkin opens up to this thirteen-year-old boy and his mother. Talks about how she was diagnosed with ADHD when she was a young girl and how it affected her. Shares how tough school was because she couldn't focus on subjects that didn't interest her.

When she notices the young boy has a backpack with him, she requests to see what he has inside and is pleased to learn he often draws when he gets overwhelmed. So, of course, Larkin asks if she can have a piece of sketch paper and a pencil. Explains how as she got older things seemed to get a little easier for her. Then finally discovered that even a girl like her could secure a job she was good at. While they talked, she sketches half of the young boy's face perfectly; it looks exactly like him. When she is finished, she thanks him for allowing her to work off some of her nervous energy as she signs and dates her work.

Right as we are about to move on, a Black Eyed Peas song starts and her whole face lights up. It was a song she claimed had to be played when we handed the deejay the list of suggested tunes. Turning toward the young man—who I bet never gets asked to dance—my wife does just that. When he seems to hesitate, Larkin waves her hand at him as she informs him there is no wrong or right way to dance to this song. And then she starts jumping around to 'Let's Get it Started' as she drags us out to where my brothers are doing the exact same thing. She waves her hands around as she spins that sweet little body of hers while encouraging the young man to do the same. No one seems to notice when he yelps loudly because he gets excited.

Gabriela even joins us and bumps hips with Larkin. Then she shows them a few of the new moves the young kids are doing these days while we dance for three songs. As soon as Larkin catches the young man is getting overstimulated, she hooks her arm with his and fakes exhaustion.

I escort them back to the table and then offer an excuse so I can have a few minutes alone with my new wife. Except on our way to the dressing room, a very drunk Lady Dalia and her equally drunk coconspirators block us.

"Well, look what we have here, ladies. King Antonio and his pregnant queen. Bet you didn't think we'd figure that one out, did you? Only one way a woman like that one snags a man like you." She slurs as she downs her flute of champagne.

"Not pregnant." Larkin counters at the same time I also speak.

"You should watch how you speak of the queen," I warn as I attempt to step around the group.

"Or what? We are moving away from the Dark Ages, are we not? So, I figure that means we can just call it like it is. Did she spread her legs for you right away? Or did she play hard to get?" Dalia snags the flute from her sister Paschal. "Now see that may have been where I played my cards wrong. Perhaps I should have feigned the, *I didn't give a shit about any of this*, instead of the *don't you hate all these fake bitches* one."

The lot of them giggle, and that only encourages her. Dalia walks right past me and gets right in Larkin's face, staring at her with scorned eyes. "And here I thought we had said all the right things to get you tucking tail before heading back to the land of the free. You are better than we gave you credit for. We won't be making that mistake again, Your Majesty, I can assure you of that. Welcome to the club of ladies who have had the privilege of appreciating what a real man carries between his legs. When you tire of it, just let one of us know and we will be more than happy to help you take care of him."

"Enough," I say it like I have so many times before, and the smarter ones seem to disperse.

"Oh. Yes, I agree, Your Majesty. You definitely have enough to go around." Dalia blinks slowly and dares to scan my body. "Don't you agree, Queen Larkin? I hear it's better to know who your husband is sleeping with than to..."

A loud slapping sound echoes off the walls as I watch Lady Dalia stumble backward.

"The bitch just slapped me." She glares behind her, only to notice her friends have all abandoned her. "You little slut whore. How dare you slap me like that, do you know who I am?"

My wife advances quickly, making Dalia backpedal until she finally bumps the table behind her. "I do. You are Lady Dalia Batista. Do you know who I am? You don't, do you? You thought you did when you cornered me last night in that room and tried to share all your dirty little stories about the man I love. But what you didn't realize is that I have been dealing with little insecure worms like you my entire life. I was able to decipher your little game long before it even started. What you failed to understand was that I don't play by your rules, never have, and never will. It doesn't matter to me if you like me or hate me. I couldn't care less if your little posse of worms over there likes me or hates me. I care about one person in this crowd and one person only. I don't just care about him, I love him."

Dalia glares at my wife as if she just slapped her again with those words.

"You love no one but yourself. I actually feel sorry for you. What a lonely life you are doomed to suffer through because of that. You are right about me wanting all this but wrong about why you think I want it. I have no desire for power or all the amenities that will be tossed at me because of who I am now. The reason I want all this is because the man who holds my heart is a part of all of this. I didn't want to fall in love with him. Mainly because I knew that this crème de la crème would be a hard one to infiltrate and make me susceptible to people who are too nosey for their own good. Making my private life hard to keep private. I understood I was going to have to step out of my comfort zone and deal with crazy nutcases like you; ones who believe their shit doesn't stink. When in reality it probably stinks worse than most, and so you feel the need to throw it around, causing it to land on the rest of us.

"So, I'm sorry to disappoint you that I don't portray the white lamb you thought you were going to lead to the slaughter. I'm more like a feral cat that looks cute and weak and easy to manipulate. But corner me and I come out with my claws extended, ready to do what has to be done to protect those I love.

"Now if you'll excuse us, we need to get some fresh air. Seems the air in this corner has gone a little stale and is making me sick to my stomach." Larkin spins on her heels and makes a beeline for the side door.

I am about to follow when I see my siblings gather a few of their friends and mine. They spread out and cover the exits. I quickly realize what is about to happen, so I jog after my wife and get to her right before she gives up our location.

CHAPTER 37
Larkin

The Royals

I am fuming mad.

I mean like the kind of mad that has a person seeing red. If I stand here one second longer, that feral cat I referenced myself as will scratch Dalia's eyes out. Now wouldn't that get all those skeptics talking? Imagine what they'd say if I got into a catfight with one of their preferred ladies. My guess would be that most would side with Lady Dalia and use my outburst as a reason I was a poor decision of Antonio's, and the reason one should stick with tradition.

Almost having reached my destination, I pick up my speed when Antonio catches me by the waist and steers me in a different direction. "What are you doing?"

"Shhh." His hand covers my mouth as he explains, or at least tries. "They are searching for us right now. Stay low and keep your voice down."

I notice he is doing his best to keep his large frame below the rest of the crowd, which, if you remember, is tricky when you are six and a half feet tall. The sight of him attempting to be inconspicuous lightens my earlier mood.

"Who is searching for us? And why don't we want them to find us?" I quietly ask him.

We make our way to the back hall where the bathrooms are located. He does a quick glance one way and then the other before shuffling me down the corridor.

"Quick, in here," he orders as he pushes open a door and shoves me inside.

I take a step forward and try to figure out where he has steered me, but it is dark and tiny. "Where are we?"

"Linen closet. Shhh. Fernando and Sonia were right on our tails." Antonio slowly closes the door until we hear it click.

"*Êtes-vous sûr de les avoir vus de cette façon?*" A male voice asks clearly in French.

"*Je suis. Vérifiez la salle de bain des hommes. Je vais vérifier les dames,*" a female voice responds.

"*Vide. Vérifiez cette porte, Fernando.*" The voice I now suspect is Sonia's orders.

"*C'est vide aussi. C'est bloqué et je ne pense pas qu'ils aient eu le temps de s'y faufiler avant que nous soyons sur eux,*" Fernando tells her as he wiggles the door handle.

My stomach is currently in my throat and I am doing my best not to giggle. Antonio's ear is pressed against the door. Why I don't know, although it is quite adorable.

A male voice echoes down the corridor. "Any luck?"

"*Nada.* Sonia thought she saw them head this way. But unless they are hiding in the ceiling, I don't see how." Fernando tries the door again before we hear footsteps click away.

"Are they..." I start to whisper, but Antonio's hand covers my mouth.

"Ant." Fernando taps on the door like he knows we are inside. "We are now even brother. I will hold them off the best I can. However, if your brothers get wind we saw you, they will sniff you out. Good luck, my friend."

We don't move right away.

Antonio gives it a few beats before he opens the door and dares to stick his head out. Then he motions for me to follow him again. We slip into the main room and slither our way along the wall until we reach the preparation area. Once we are deep inside the large kitchen, I ask why we are hiding.

"It's a traditional cat-and-mouse game. We are the mice and if they catch us, we will be escorted back into the reception. At that point, it is the others' responsibility to keep us there for as long as possible. The objective is to make it to our quarters without being seen." Antonio explains.

"Fernando, let us go. Why?" I ask as he pushes open an outside door and peeks out.

"I helped Sonia and Fern make a clean getaway at their reception. They had been caught twice by that point, so I felt sorry for him. Fern respected his lovely bride and had kept personal affairs between them biblical. Sonia was wisely sheltered growing up. Until college, she hadn't lived away from home, and in our world, that is a rarity, which is why Sonia didn't fit in with the other socialites. As you can imagine, when Fern started giving her his attention, they began making her life miserable." He jerks the door closed quickly, urges me around a corner as he puts a finger to his mouth.

The door flies open seconds later and several feet trample inside.

"Spread out and check every cranny," Lorenzo instructs everyone. "They have to be in here somewhere."

Antonio leans close and whispers in my ear. "Take off your shoes."

I slip off my heels and hand them to him. He places them next to his on a shelf and then peers around the corner. Without saying a word, he grabs my hand and we tiptoe back toward the door, slipping out without being detected.

Then he starts running and I know I cannot keep up. "Slow down. I'm not going to make it."

"Yes, you are." Antonio stops, spins around, and yanks me down at the same time. "Shhh."

"Brother." Esteban's voice calls out through the darkness. "Isabel and Triana are guarding the garden passages. You will not make it out that way."

"Where to now?" I ask quietly.

"We aren't going to the garden passages." Antonio keeps an eye on his brother and waits. He points to the left, where there is a balcony one story above us. "That is our destination."

"And how are we going to get to that exactly?"

He points to the tree just in front of it.

"You... you want me to climb a tree in this? I could probably climb that tree if I was dressed in jeans, but no way will I be able to do it in this dress," I enlighten him.

"You can and you will." He walks, dragging me along behind him.

I shake my head, disagreeing. "I can't."

The door opens again and the rest of the gang spills out. Suddenly, I realize if we are going to escape, our time is limited. So, I do what any person trapped in an inescapable situation would do.

"What are you doing?" Antonio watches wide-eyed with a surprised tone in his voice.

"Doing what needs to be done. Take off your shirt and give it to me." I instruct him as I sashay out of my dress. "What? Do you want me to climb that tree or do you wish us to get caught and dragged back inside?"

As soon as he gets a glimpse of my naked breasts, he is shrugging it all off, tossing the leftovers at the base of the tree. Once his shirt is free, he drapes it over my shoulder and drags my mouth to his, mumbling softly against my lips. "*Te amo mucho, mi hermosa y luchadora reina.* I love you so very much, my beautiful, feisty queen."

While I would love to stay here and kiss him right now, we don't have time. I can hear the voices getting closer by the second.

I slide my arms through his shirt and then shove him back so I can button it around me. It hangs mid-thigh and I am very grateful for that, especially since I will be exposed here very soon when I begin my climb. I have experience climbing difficult slopes and buildings, so this should be a piece of cake, right?

"Okay, give me a boost." I rise to my feet and look up to see how high the first branch is. "Have you ever done this before?"

"Yep. I used to sneak in through that window when I missed curfew. We all did. My brothers and I would even sneak out of it so we could play in the garden at night." He locks his fingers and waits for me to step in. "Okay, up you go."

I yelp as he practically tosses me up toward the branch so I can grab it. I have no idea how I manage to get up there, but somehow I do, and now I have a dilemma. I can't see where I am going, and since I've never climbed this tree, I want to make sure I don't fall. "Now what?"

Antonio grins and grabs the branch with both hands, easily wrenching his body up. Then he grabs the next adjacent branch and is up it before I even have time to think about how hot he looked doing that. He offers me his hand to help me climb. Together, we scurry up the tree and I have to admit I don't think I have had this much fun in years. The tricky part will be getting from the tree to the balcony, or so I thought. Antonio, however, makes it appear so simple, he climbs out onto the thick branch hanging over the edge and drops without giving it a second thought. As soon as I see him do his leap of faith, I yelp because I am certain he is going to miss it altogether.

Gabriela must have heard me because she points us out. "They are climbing the large oak."

"Bugger," Lorenzo shouts out.

"Is this her dress?" Sonia picks up our discarded clothing and glances up. "Nice play."

"This will be one to send the guards over the edge for sure. When Isaac or Sir Edward hears you climbed that tree, they'll chop it down." Esteban is laughing when he spots us. "Didn't know the queen had it in her, or I'd have posted someone here too. I am glad to see she at least covered herself."

"Never underestimate me, Esteban. I am extremely competitive, so when presented with a challenge I tend to do what needs to be done," I inform him as I accept Antonio's hand so he can guide me onto the balcony.

Fernando joins his wife, wrapping his arms around her as he gazes up at us. "A good woman, Ant, is difficult to stumble upon. A good woman who strips out of her clothing, so she can climb a tree in an attempt to escape with the love of her life, is nearly impossible to meet by chance. I believe the rules of the game state that if we see you, you must rejoin us. However, such a brazen move requires we extend you a pass. Take your bride and claim the prize she has handed you."

"I believe I will do just that," Antonio informs his friend as he grabs me by my waist and tosses me over his shoulder before he walks through the balcony doors.

"Don't you keep these doors locked?" I ask, giggling from my tossed position.

"Yes. I had Gino unlock it when he noticed my siblings acting like a bunch of children." He struts through a room that looks a lot like the library in his quarters.

"Are you going to carry me all the way to our bedroom like this?" Reaching down, I pinch his butt because it is, after all, right there.

"Yes. If I stop, we won't make it to the bedroom." He growls.

Liking how that sounds, I untuck his undershirt until I expose his skin. I have thought about licking him often. I know that's weird, but there is just something about this man that has always made my mind think of him as some delicious treat. A treat that should most definitely be licked and savored slowly. So that is what I do.

My tongue darts out as I lower my head so I can lick his back before I take a healthy bite. I wasn't sure what his reaction would be, although I didn't expect it would be to turn his head and do the same to my thigh that is so easily accessible. Which only causes me to have a reaction of my own I'm not sure he expected, either. I slide my hand down his back and under his trousers so I can fondle his firm butt. I love his butt, in case you forgot. I could spend hours touching it like this and never get bored.

"Larkin," Antonio warns, as the hand not holding my legs finds its way under the shirttails of his shirt and grabs my butt in much the same way. "You are playing with fire, *mi lunita*."

I bite his back again slowly, applying more pressure, all while I dig my nails into his butt cheek. "I enjoy playing with fire."

What I didn't realize was I wasn't playing with a small fire that I often have seen burning in a fireplace. I was dealing with a bonfire that was raging and ready to consume anything it touched. Although I figured it out rather quickly when I was yanked off his shoulder and flattened against the wall between the tall bookcases. The only thing holding me up is his solid body, which is now pressed firmly against mine; while he consumes me with a scorching kiss that instantly lights a fire inside me as well.

I wrap my legs around his waist as my hands try to haul his undershirt off him. He reaches behind with one hand and does it for me, breaking the kiss just long enough to discard it.

Now it's his turn to remove something, and he does so in the rawest way ever. His hands grip the button placket of his shirt, and in one swift jerk, rips it wide-open, sending buttons flying wildly.

It's the hottest freaking seductive act I have ever been a part of. I drop my arms so he can shove it off me and then fling my head against the wall. His mouth captures one of my nipples, and I whimper. I never realized how having a man pay them attention would be so mind-blowing that it'd stop all rational thought altogether.

The next thing I am aware of is the sound of his zipper being lowered, as I hear this whirring noise next to my ear. I have no idea what that noise could be or why it is going off now, nor do I care. And I completely forget about it when I come into contact with the tip of his large erection pressing against my very pulsing center.

"Yes, please." I mewl as my fingers dig into his damp hair. "Do it."

Antonio draws his head back so he can look me in the eye. His brown eyes are dilated and there is this passionate glow to them. One slow, determined blink occurs before he thrusts the length of him inside of me. I see stars as my eyes roll back into my head.

Will I ever get used to that move? I really hope the answer is no, because this is the most transfixing sensation that melts me from the inside out.

And once he starts driving home, something inside of me breaks free. I scream out his name so loud it makes my throat throb. It's like I can't turn it off, and can't believe the loud moans and shrills are echoing off the walls in here. The acoustics of this space surprises me.

The noises aren't just coming from me either; they are also originating from the man pounding into my slightly sore bits, making them burn in a marvelous way.

"Mine." He repeats several times. "You. Are. Mine."

I am about to have the biggest orgasm I have had to date when the door flies open and five men enter with their guns drawn. Light immediately floods the dark room, making sure there is no way we stay hidden. My husband's body jerks as he achieves climax and explodes violently inside of me, setting my own off while I stare directly at them.

Franco retreats first as he talks into his wrist, alerting the others of a false alarm. I wonder how often he has caught a king in this position. He worked for Antonio's father, so I'm sure it's not a first for him.

Dane and Emmett swiftly follow, doing their best to look anywhere but at the two of us. Guess I don't have to worry anymore about if they saw me skinny-dipping. This has to be worse, right?

Isaac utters a few muffled words about not needing to be witness to the two of us going at it like bunnies. Throwing his head up as he verbalizes more in Spanish—I believe it is Spanish—but he is speaking so rapidly I am unable to follow.

Gino, however, stands there the longest as he closes his eyes and shakes his head. He backs up slowly and flips the light off, while he speaks in an audible voice, a hint of a chuckle hidden in it. "You know this is only going to make him grouchy for weeks. You two triggered the silent alarm in the wall safe. Had I known your intentions were to christen his office, I would have warned the cavalry before bursting in like we did."

I glance around the room and realize then we are not in the king's quarters, but inside his office where he conducts all official business. As soon as my husband disengages his body from mine, I reach down and grab the shirt he ripped off of me first before tossing it aside. I pat the ground until I find his discarded t-shirt, which is when I realized I am missing my underwear.

I watch Antonio tuck himself back inside his pants as I ask, "Panties?" I don't remember him removing them earlier.

"Shredded somewhere down there." He blinks a few times.

And then, at the same time, we burst into uncontrollable laughter. Hey, if you can't laugh about getting caught by the men sworn to protect you, then you have a stick too far up your butt. After all, laughter is the best medicine and I am pretty sure this will not be the last time something like this happens.

CHAPTER 38
Antonio

The Royals

I t's been three months since the wedding that not only united me with the love of my life but also gave my realm a queen. If I told you our lives have been smooth sailing since that day, you'd never believe me, and for good reason. Nothing about these last months has been smooth, really.

Let's start with the day after the party where I introduced her to those who I knew would give us the most grief. Luckily, my staff was way ahead of my adversaries and sent the press release shortly after I presented Larkin as my wife. We even agreed to an interview with one of the major networks that always strived to report the facts over rumors.

That interview went something like this.

The male broadcaster announces he is sitting down with us and then explains how tonight is going to go. Shortly after his explanation, he turns to Larkin and asks her flat out. "So, there is one question every woman in Hermosa Islas wants to know before we get down to business. King Antonio has been called the most eligible bachelor and sort of gained a reputation."

Larkin's eyes slide my way. "Is that so? What sort of reputation? I wasn't aware he had one."

"Oh, all the Reyes brothers have this particular reputation. The problem is the press has never been allowed in the palace during the after-hour parties. A few social media snapshots have been posted and left up for a few hours before being removed permanently. The family has always been very protective of social events and most guests have respected that; I'm guessing mainly because they don't want to miss out on the next one. So, tell us, Queen Larkin, is it true that King Antonio can bust a move on the dance floor?"

All the nervous energy that was building up inside of my wife fades quickly as she lets out an authentic laugh and tumbles into me. That move right there was so genuine, I believe that is when my people fell in love with her. "Most definitely. Antonio, Fernando, and his brothers could give Justin Timberlake a run for his money in a dance-off."

"Fernando Martin, the French capitalist, whose company was named one of the top five companies in Europe. I'm not sure everyone is aware of your friendship with Mr. Martin," he interrupts her.

I give a quick response to that before my wife continues.

"Perhaps if you are lucky, I will see if I can convince my husband to allow me to post a video of the dance he performed at our reception. My mother recorded it upon my request, so I could watch it later. Of course, we were also warned not to release it. But maybe it's time for the rest of the world to get to know this family like I have gotten to know them.

"Sometimes, I think we want to believe the life a family like this one lives differs from the one the rest of us live. It does in a way, of course; privileges are granted to them that no one else is privy to. But they also are people with feelings, emotions, and wonderful senses of humor, who often feel isolated from the rest of the world.

"Imagine living life in a glasshouse where there are always those watching your every move. Wouldn't we all aspire to keep a certain part of that life private and out of the public eye? Although I believe a brief glimpse might do the people some good and help them understand why I fell in love with this man."

I have to admit I am impressed with her answer and will seriously consider what she suggests.

The host then moves the questions back to why we are here. "Did you always dream about one day growing up and marrying a man like King Antonio?"

"No." Larkin gives her one word response.

"How do you mean, no?"

"I mean, I had other things I dreamed about. As a young girl, I wanted to be an artist. As a teenager, I realized I had a hard time relating to the opposite sex, so I stopped trying and focused on my art. In college, I met someone who helped me see things differently. Encouraged me to branch out a bit, which is when I started imagining one day finding a man to settle down with. I think I pictured someone less complicated." Larkin glances my way and pauses momentarily. "I never dreamed that a man as incredible as this one would even notice me. I don't know if you've noticed, but this man is in a league of his own, handsome beyond words. The first time I met him, I skidded out of my chair and end up on my hands and knees before introductions could ever be made."

The two of them talked back and forth like that for nearly twenty minutes. I am so enthralled watching her share all of it so freely, I almost miss it when a question is thrown my way.

"What was the first thing about Queen Larkin that attracted you to her?"

I couldn't very well say her ass that was protruding out of the back of a chair, so I went with the second thing I recalled. "Her eyes. There was a purity reflected in them that drew me in. Then shortly after that, it was that mouth of hers."

"Her mouth? Are you saying you wanted to kiss her right from the beginning, Your Majesty?" I can tell this man is hoping my answer is yes.

"No. I mean... that's not what I meant about her mouth. It was the words that so freely tumbled out of them when I offered her a hand to assist her. I may have said something about her not needing to kneel before me. Remember, Larkin had no idea who I was, so she didn't get my humor about the situation. Told me as she batted my hand away, she wouldn't kneel before me if I were King of England."

The entire production crew burst into laughter; at the same

moment, my wife blushes. As soon as things calm down, I explain why I liked it so much.

"People are always going out of their way to make an impression when they meet me. Granted, they are clued in most of the time on who I am. So, the fact this woman treated me like she would any other arrogant male was refreshing."

"Did she continue treating you like an arrogant male after she learned who you were?"

"Yes." I reach over and entangle our fingers. "*Mi lunita* has always dealt with me like a simple man, never discriminated against me just because I held some outrageous title that I had no part in obtaining. I did nothing special to achieve my role as King, and she has looked upon me no differently because of it. I never wonder what she is thinking or question where we stand, because she openly shares it all with me."

"Tell us about how King Antonio proposed."

My wife's eyes meet mine. I know the answer she is going to give them before she even says it. "I'd rather keep that between us, if you don't mind. I will, however, reveal that it was a very touching moment, one I will forever hold dear to my heart. He is quite the romantic and pays attention to details. Knows me well and made sure to knock it out of the park and seal the deal."

"Knock it out of the park?" he asks, and I laugh because Larkin definitely says things I don't get at times, either.

"Yeah. A homerun." She laughs. "Baseball analogy."

He shakes his head and moves on quickly to the question I know everyone really wants to learn. "Why did you all decide to marry so quickly?"

"Why do others elope?" Larkin throws a question right back at him. "There are many reasons. We love each other, most importantly. Our lives are very busy and the thought of planning a wedding was overwhelming for me. I'm not one who enjoys being put on the spot."

"But you are now queen. You will be in the public eye forever."

Larkin blinks slowly and takes a controlled breath. "I know. A reality that became clear to me moments after the I dos were exchanged. Anxiety is something I struggle with, therefore a private ceremony with the ones most important to us allowed me to not fret as much about what was going on around me.

"Let's face it; there are those who don't agree with this marriage at all. They claim I am not worthy. Believe that a woman who was raised to take on such a role is more suited for this job and would have voiced those opinions over and over again, hoping to dissuade me from spending my life with the man I love. Sometimes love is enough to get you to do the unthinkable and take a leap of faith. In this case, it was. I know Antonio will have my back on all matters. Help me understand this new role I am now expected to portray. Not fault me when I say or do something that may seem uncouth of a queen.

"I guess what I'm saying is, why should we expect these elite few to settle for less? Shouldn't every man or woman out there be given the right to choose the person they want to spend the rest of their lives with? Why do you suppose men and women in these positions, where we have limited their choices, have affairs or divorce? The pressure of this life is great enough as it is. So, if you don't love the person you are married to, the one you are expected to have children with, what kind of sad, lonely life would that be? We figured it was about time to break the cycle and mix things up a bit, follow our hearts first and let the rest eventually work itself out."

The host turns to me as the biggest sincere smile takes over his face. "A rare jewel, this one is, Your Majesty. I can see why she captivated you. Just sitting here, I can assure our audience that the love you two share is real and very powerful. Would you like to add anything? Explain maybe why you elected to have her undergo a tradition many would consider an invasion of privacy."

"The Maiden Exam is what you are referring to?"

He nods, so I continue. "I wanted to douse any rumors that would surely follow after a rushed marriage. Larkin has no reason to be ashamed of why I requested it done. Nor did I have a reason to doubt her. Plus, I would not have put her through it if I wasn't already certain what the results would prove. I did it to keep those who wish to discredit us at bay. No other reason. I requested Dr. Devon Wilson to perform it because she is highly respected in our circle, and no one would ever accuse her of fudging the results.

"Now understand this as well. I myself would have subjected my body to the same type of exam if one were possible for a man. Proven that I had practiced abstinence as well. But there is no such exam, so I guess you will all have to take me at my word as King."

He ends the interview by discussing our decision to rule as one. Asks what it means exactly, wondering if that is constitutional. I assure him it is and that while most kings and queens don't come out and proclaim a united reign, they often go to the other person for advice. We are just being open about the fact that I plan on allowing my wife to be my biggest adviser.

The feedback we received was about what I expected. Those who have consistently supported me continued to. Those who enjoy being a thorn in my side let it be known when this goes south that I had no one to blame but myself. And the people who I reigned over were all over the board about how they felt. Some found it refreshing and thought it would do some good getting fresh blood in the king's office. Others were waiting to see how it was all going to play out, not wanting to give an opinion, but made it clear they liked my wife and wished her luck. And then there were those who assumed I should have followed the advice of those who had repeatedly lent an ear to the king. Followed traditional ways and abandoned love. Pointed out how badly that had seemed to work for Princess Diana and Princess Fergie.

So that all happened within the first week. After that, it was just a matter of letting things settle as we got on with our lives.

Larkin went back to Homero the following Tuesday. My wife was a working woman who took her responsibilities that surrounded her job seriously. She was on a schedule, and if she slacked, she had no doubt those who worked for her would slack as well. They were already behind, and that probably bothered her more than anything else. She prided herself on the fact that when she gave a deadline, she met that deadline. This was one she just wasn't certain she could make.

I went to visit her the next weekend alone. My brothers stepped up and took Isabel for me. Knowing that my wife and I would most definitely need to spend time alone, where we could connect as husband and wife. We both hated that our weeks were going to be spent apart, only giving us the weekends to have that physical contact.

Then, of course, after several weeks of marriage, I had a three-week European tour, where I was meeting with other government officials to discuss issues leaders discussed. Something that had to be done, but most certainly was not my favorite type of trip to take. Perhaps if my wife could have traveled with me, it would have been tolerable. I always felt like my time could be better utilized during those trips. While I accept foreign policy is important, and maintaining positive relationships is beneficial, there are times it feels like I am going through the motions.

During that time, Larkin and I were restricted to phone calls, texting, and FaceTime. If you've ever tried to do the long-distance thing, you understand how complicated it can be. There is nothing like it and a reason so many don't work out. A person must really love the other person—trust the other person—enough to get them through the extended time apart. And since this woman is the air I breathe, we have managed to make it through these last three weeks and even figured out ways to draw us closer.

The first week I was gone was probably the easiest. We'd send private brief texts throughout the day to let the other person know we were thinking of them. Made a point to FaceTime each evening, around seven, her time, so we could eat together and discuss our day. Seeing her face helped, but it also made me miss her that much more. I also made the point to call her each morning before she left for the day because I wanted to be the first person she talked to.

The second week got a little harder. My schedule seemed to be packed full of dinners or early morning meetings. Esteban also joined me during that portion of my trip. Part of his duty was to make his face just as well-known as mine to these leaders, and honestly, it made things a little less mundane. However, it also made it difficult for me to clear as much time for Larkin, forcing most of our contact to be strictly through texting or short late-night calls that often got interrupted.

Week three hadn't been much better, except it wasn't my schedule that was interfering this time. Larkin had finally gotten her team close to finishing phase one. She was putting in long hours to get everything ready for phase two while making sure nothing got overlooked. The one time I was privileged to FaceTime her, was a few nights ago, and I noticed how tired she looked. It reminded me of the time she fell asleep on me in the elevator. I didn't enjoy knowing she was doing more physical work this time around, instead of the desk work she had been performing then. Even though Larkin ensured me she was fine and not overdoing things, I instructed her security team to keep a very close eye on her.

My plane landed back in Hermosa Islas forty-five minutes ago, and we are now heading for Homero. Since I was two days early, I knew I had time to make an unscheduled stop there. Honestly, it wouldn't have mattered if I did or not. Three weeks away from my wife of only three months meant the only incident that could have kept me away would have to have been catastrophic in measure. My team hadn't even questioned me when I gave them instructions to take me to Maximiliano Chateau. I am certain they anticipated the change.

I am lost in thought when I hear Isaac answer his cellphone. At first, I think little about it until he seems to straighten and quickly becomes extremely professional. He is doing his best to keep his voice low while making it clear he understands. I don't miss the fact he has retrieved his tablet, and now frantically works on it while talking at the same time. Five minutes pass before he hangs up the phone and turns to give the driver instructions.

"We need to turn around. Destination Aragon Palace. T-minus twenty would be ideal." Isaac's voice is level.

"Isaac." I only need to say his name to get him to understand. I expect to know why we are making this modification without consulting me.

"Your Majesty, trust me when I tell you that Aragon Palace is where you want to be." He doesn't elaborate, but his tone has me searching for my phone.

When I pull it out, there aren't any messages or missed calls. I decide to send one to Larkin to establish if I get a response from her.

> ME: Where are you?

Her text doesn't come back immediately; in fact, it takes ten minutes for her to respond. When she does, things spiral out of control quickly.

> LARKIN: Why?
>
> LARKIN: I'm fine. Everything is fine.
>
> LARKIN: What did they tell you?
>
> LARKIN: I told them to shut it and I'd handle this when you got back.
>
> LARKIN: It's just a minor setback, really. No need to rush home, because there is nothing you can do, anyway. So, do what a king must do and when you get home, we can discuss it.

"What happened?" I leave little room for Isaac to lie to me, and he is a smart man to realize that.

"Apparently, there was an incident." His straight-lipped expression reports he knew nothing about it until the phone call.

"What kind of incident?" My blood is heating.

"I don't know exactly, sir. Her team is following the queen's orders and keeping the details under wrap. All I know is that when they heard we were heading to Maximiliano Chateau, they felt they should let us know she wasn't there." Isaac sounds almost as irritated as I feel.

"That is complete bullshit. They were to report in each day, and I read each report thoroughly. There was nothing in them about an incident and since when do my instructions not get followed?" I am fuming right now, and as soon as I figure out what is going on, heads will most certainly roll.

"Permission to speak freely, sir." Isaac obviously has something he wants to share that he knows will piss me off.

"Spit it out," I growl.

"I believe you gave Queen Larkin equal authority over all matters. Perhaps she reminded them of that when she gave her own orders on the subject. I'm certain her team feels like in order to do the job they are assigned to do, they also need her to trust them.

"Tell me this, if something were to happen that you felt would be blown out of proportion, if you felt by her knowing she'd overreact, would you not give us the same order? I'm not condoning this, sir, I assure you of that. However, I believe until we can properly assess the situation, we should do our best to remain calm."

I hate it when someone uses my own words against me, my actions as well. Equality in all things does not mean I will be kept in the dark when something happens. Perhaps Isaac is right, though, and I should just keep my cool until I know for sure what we are dealing with.

CHAPTER 39
Larkin

The Royals

I've been back in the palace for two days now. Not by choice, I can assure you of that. Had I had my way, I'd have gone back to Maximiliano Chateau immediately after my doctor's appointment and distracted myself with work. I wasn't given a choice though. Dr. Wilson insisted I take it easy for a few days while I let my body recover.

So that is what I did, even though it is the last thing I wanted to do. I am not great with downtime. I am much better when I keep myself busy and don't have time to think about subjects that will only make me sad. And yes, I had a very good reason to feel sad.

After a trying week at work, an exhausting one, I came to realize I wasn't feeling quite myself. Once I did a few quick calculations, I realized I wasn't just worn out from all the hours I'd been putting in since Antonio left for his diplomatic tour. It wasn't until I sent one of my security team members into town to retrieve what I needed did I conclude I should call Dr. Wilson. I tried not to get my hopes up, not let my mind go there until I confirmed it with her. Except if you've ever been in my position, you'd understand how hard that is.

My team did a great job of not asking me a ton of questions after my appointment. I think the fact I looked worse than I did when I went in, communicated I hadn't received the news I was hoping for. Although it wasn't a complete surprise to me since that morning, my body had begun cramping severely.

I'd witnessed my mother experience three miscarriages. I was four, six, and seven when my parents thought they might be adding to our family of three. After the last one, my father decided it was time for them to stop putting us through the pain we suffered when each one ended prematurely.

For the record, I never felt like my parents didn't consider I wasn't enough for them. It was quite the opposite, actually. I felt like I was exactly where I was meant to be and that God had planned to give me to them all along.

But we all have dreams of having children who are a piece of us. My parents were no different, so I never faulted them for trying to experience what so many others got the privilege of experiencing so easily. It just wasn't in their cards, and once they both came to that same conclusion, it was as if our family became that much closer. We learned to appreciate that we were a family, and would always be a family, even though none of us shared DNA.

I only had to ask my team to take me back to Aragon Palace. They'd driven me there without saying a word.

I was lucky enough to get my emotions in check before Isabel got home that evening. She had been so ecstatic to see me she didn't once ask me why I was there. Instead, the two of us had some much-needed girl time and did stuff we wouldn't be able to do when Antonio was around. Isabel has quickly become the little sister I never had growing up. I love spending time with her because she is a pure soul who brings a special kind of joy with her always.

It wasn't until later that night when I was alone in our large suite that I finally grieved our loss. I ran a hot bath, then dumped lavender and mint salts into it. Once I sank into the tub, and there was nothing left to do but let my mind go there, it was as if I couldn't stop.

My head of security finally came to check on me when she was doing her rounds. Amanda is a single mother of two very sweet girls who currently resided in Aragon with their father. She sees them as often as she can. When we are in town, she makes a point to have dinner with them. It is something her ex also believes is important. While he is no longer in love with Amanda, he loves his girls enough to realize they need their mother as much as they need him. Therefore, they co-parent the best they can, and it seems to work for them.

She had just returned from visiting them and was worried about me. It wasn't normal for a member of the security team to enter our private bedroom. That was typically considered taboo. Unless it was life or death, it was a big fat no-no. But Amanda realized I was in a bad way and had a pretty good idea why. So, she did what a person who cares about you does and broke protocol.

It should completely mortify me. After all, she found me a blubbering mess, soaking in a lukewarm bathtub. I most likely would have stayed there until the water became cold and given myself pneumonia. I'd done that once before, after my friend's death. Let myself get so down that I'd done more harm than good. My mother that time had discovered me and then taken me home with her until I could take care of myself again.

Amanda encouraged me into a warm shower and then helped me get dressed. She'd escorted me down the hall to the kitchen where she made me some tea to help me calm down.

We talked.

She shared with me about her loss in between the two angels she mother's now. Tried to reassure me it wasn't an uncommon tragedy and it didn't mean that I'd never get to become a mother. Her words I knew were meant to soothe, and they did, but that didn't mean it lessened the pain any less. Which is something she also said she understood, and the reason she had encouraged me to call Antonio.

I had refused. He would be home from his trip soon enough, plus it wasn't as if there was anything he could do about it. Combined all that with me not feeling like I could say those words over the phone. When I told him, I wanted to be in his arms so we could both grieve together.

Currently, I am resting in our bedroom.

A few hours ago, I finally completed miscarrying the life we created. Dr. Wilson informed me I had options when I was in her office. One of those was to let nature take its course. She explained a few details to me about what would happen or could happen. If in a few days nothing seemed to be progressing, she wanted me to come back to the office so she could determine if anything needed to be done on her end. The cramping, the heavier flow of blood, and the larger clot that passed notified me I had successfully completed it. I think having to place that all in a sterile container—luckily it wasn't a clear one—so Dr. Wilson could have it tested, was one of the hardest things I have ever done. It was all so final, sad, and depressing.

I'd cried myself to sleep. Woke when I heard my phone ping, indicating a text from Antonio. I have been avoiding talking to him because I knew he'd know something was wrong if he heard my voice. So, we had been texting these last few days, it was easier to hide my mood in a text.

ANTONIO: Where are you?

I think I read those three words a hundred times before I responded.

ME: Why?

Does he realize I left Maximiliano Chateau? How would he know unless someone told him? Amanda promised me she wouldn't, and I had to believe her.

ME: I'm fine. Everything is fine.

Crap. Why did I say that? Now he will know that is a lie.

ME: What did they tell you?

Please for the love of all that is sacred, if I find out someone went behind my back, I'll fire them or at least threaten to.

ME: I told them to shut it and I'd handle this when you got back.

What must he be thinking? Handle this when you got back, really Larkin that doesn't sound fishy. Gaw, you are so bad at this.

> ME: It's just a minor setback, really. No need to rush home, because there is nothing you can do, anyway. So, do what a king must do and when you get home, we can discuss it.

There is no reply to any of my texts; therefore, I know something is amiss. He wasn't due back for a few days still. Now that it was done, my plan was to go back to Maximiliano Chateau. I needed to check on the progress being made, and the best way for me to stay up on it was to get back to work.

I roll out of bed as I send a text to Amanda, asking her to meet me in our quarters in ten minutes. That gives me enough time to comb my hair, wash my face, and add a minimal amount of makeup. I don't change my clothes because the sweatpants and t-shirt I have on right now fit my mood. I do however pull my hair up into a high ponytail to get it out of my way. I plan on going into the library after I speak with Amanda to go over some emails and see if I can get my foreman on the phone.

So as soon as I am ready, I head to the kitchen and brew a cup of coffee while I wait. I go over everything I have neglected these past couple of days while I let myself get a little lost. The list is long, but it will feel good to finally get my mind back on the issues I can control, rather than the ones I can't.

By the time I hear the door open, I am ready to tell Amanda the plan. I'm seated at the table, luckily, when I come to realize the person who walked in isn't Amanda, not by a long shot.

"*Mi lunita.*" His rich voice washes over me, and I crumble exactly like I knew I would.

Antonio has me secured in his arms within seconds and I am being carried into the living room. Together we drop onto the couch.

I nuzzle my face into his chest and let the scent that is my husband comfort me. This is what I have been missing, what I required to keep me grounded. He is my compass that guides me and without him I wander aimlessly, searching for the right path but never able to find it.

"What has dimmed your light, *mi lunita*? Why do you look so sad?" His words break through my solitary moment and bring me back to reality way too quickly.

I know I cannot keep this to myself, that I have no other choice but to tell him. I also know when I do, my man will suffer along with me. "I'm so sorry."

"You have no reason to be sorry, Larkin. You only need to say what it is that you need to say." I can tell he is holding back, trying to decide if he needs to fire a few of my security team.

"They were only following my orders, Antonio. I needed to be the one to break this to you. And because I knew you would be home shortly, I saw no reason to do it over the phone." I hate this, but if I don't just tell him, it will only drag this matter out more. "I went to see Dr. Wilson a few days ago. At first, I thought I'd have something positive to share, but that morning I knew what I'd be sharing was going to break us both."

His arms tighten around me, and I can feel his body tense. "We will try again, my love. When you are ready, we will try again."

My tears soak his shirt. "I know."

And I do.

Dr. Wilson tried to advise me it was just one of those things that happened. In a few months, we could try again, and most likely the results would be different.

I go on to share with him what took place earlier. Tell him the whole gruesomeness of it as I bawl. My husband does not hold back his emotions, either. He freely lets it all go, and together we fall apart, much like I am sure other couples do when they suffer this kind of loss. Being with him right now, while it is sad and emotional, it is also the best I've felt since receiving the devastating news.

The smell of something cooking wakes me. I'm still on the couch, but I am alone with a throw secured around me. The next thing I am aware of are the voices that echo from the kitchen area.

"Do you know if it was a boy or a girl?" Isabel softly asks her brother.

"No. It was too soon. Thank you for being here for her when I

341

couldn't." Antonio sincerely tells his little sister. "I'm sure your sunshine helped ease her pain some."

"I don't know. I could tell something was bothering her, but I figured it was work or the fact that Lady Dalia..." Isabel stops when she catches me walking in slightly shaking my head. "I'm sorry for your loss."

I walk up to her and wrap her in my arms. "Thank you. What are you two cooking?"

"Grilled cheese sandwiches and minestrone. Helena started the soup before Antonio woke from his nap with you." Isabel glances up at me. "She left for the evening to give us some private family time."

Antonio spins around. "What did Lady Dalia do now?"

I gently pat Isabel's shoulder to reassure her I'm not upset she brought it up. "It was nothing. Do you need help?"

Antonio plates a sandwich and hands it to his sister. "Let's eat in here tonight. Get us all some water and start dishing up the minestrone."

Then he directs his attention at me as he assembles another sandwich. "No. Tell me, Larkin."

I hate how he can do that; make the words flow out even when I don't want them to. Grabbing a bowl from Isabel, I ladle in a few while I share.

"As I said, it is no big deal. Last weekend, when I came home for Izzy's game, she and one of her sisters happened to be there. The one that is dating her coach."

Antonio glances at his sister for that answer.

"Lady Karina, although dating is a very loose description, I think. Georgette said her dad dates lots of women and she is just the latest flavor." She makes an adorable disgusting face, one that causes us to chuckle.

"Anyway, so because I was there, seated in the stands like everyone else..."

Antonio glares at me, we've gone rounds about this. He typically sits in the press box or stands off to the side surrounded by his men. Keeping the crowd at bay and offering him the chance to focus on Isabel without being distracted. I however enjoy sitting in the bleachers with the rest of the families. It gives me a chance to practice my socializing skills, as well as lets me get to know the other parents. You can learn a lot about a person if you sit amongst them during a youth soccer game.

Rolling my eyes, I refuse to feel guilty about doing this my way. "Dane and Emmett were both with me. Geez, those men alone are enough to discourage anyone from trying something. Plus, Quinn's niece is also on the team, so she joined us, even though it was her day off.

"Now back to what happened. At halftime, as you know, is when most of the parents finally get the nerve to talk to me. That day was no different. Two moms sitting a few rows ahead of us turned around to be friendly. Said it was nice that I showed my support for the team and Isabel. We talked for several minutes, but interrupted when those two strolled in. Dane and Emmett reacted quickly, as soon as they spotted Dalia, thought it best to ask her to leave. I, however, stopped them."

We are all seated around the table now, and I pause so Antonio can say the blessing. I continue after a few bites because I haven't eaten much these last few days, and this taste wonderful.

"What happened, Larkin?" Antonio is getting impatient.

I make eye contact with Isabel, who is trying hard to not smile. She and I had a very good laugh about it later on the way home, although not all of what went on was necessarily funny.

"Third quarter, Isabel stole the ball from the other team, and I may have gotten a little excited. I jumped up and my popcorn and drink may have gone airborne and landed on both of them. What? I was just having fun." Yeah, it was rather funny. My drink landed in Dalia's lap, while my popcorn covered them both.

An evil smirk takes over Antonio's face. "Please tell me they were dressed more for a night out and not so much for a sporting event."

"Most definitely. Dalia nearly came unglued and said a few things that were very inappropriate when around a younger crowd. Asked me what kind of simpleton I was, acting so ridiculous over something that meant nothing. I told her I disagreed; that it meant everything to Isabel, so it was worth acting foolish. She just kept up the shenanigans, going on and on about how embarrassing it was to have someone like me representing them. Thought there should be some law about not allowing foreigners who have no clue how to act in public when playing such an important role. Finally, after about ten minutes of her word vomit, I'd had enough." I take the last few bites of my sandwich and try to end it there, but my husband wants to hear the entire story.

"Tell me your team finally stepped in and took care of her." He sounds so sure that is the only way to handle her, except it was not.

"No. I took care of her myself." I shove my plate aside and take a few sips of my soup.

"What did you do?" Amusement bounces around in his brown eyes.

Pointing my spoon at him, I call him out. "Do you not think I can handle her? Did you think I would allow her to get away with trying to belittle me in public?"

When he shakes his head and reaches for my hand, I continue. "Good, because I didn't. I very calmly said a few truths to her."

Isabel finishes up and asks to be excused. I am grateful because some of the truths I told Dalia are not kid-friendly and I know Antonio is going to want to hear them all. Once she leaves the kitchen and heads for her room to start her nightly routine, I decide to finish my story.

"I told her that first of all I wasn't playing any role, that this wasn't some Broadway performance. Might have pointed out that if it weren't for foreigners stepping up throughout history, to leave their homes and serve this country, several of your great rulers would not exist, you included."

That's right, Angela is not a Hermosa Islas natural-born citizen. Her family moved here when she was a teenager from Spain after they promised her to Prince Ramon so she could get to know her future husband better.

"I said that I took my duty as queen seriously. And that while I may still need to learn a few things, it didn't mean I was so far removed from matters I had no clue on the power I held in my hands. That with a simple nod or eye contact with the right person, I could have her forcefully removed simply because I did not like her. Although, I promised her I would not do that, because I learned long ago that an act like that only adds fuel to the fire. Instead, I cautioned her to tread lightly, because she was causing a scene and would most likely be asked to leave by someone other than me if she wasn't careful. Then I continued to watch the rest of the game."

344

"Why do I get the suspicion that isn't all you said?" Antonio brings my hand to his lips. This man knows me so well.

"As we were leaving, I may have paused next to her and her sister. Extended my hand, making it appear like I was making peace with them. Then I might have gone on to say a few other truths. I may have mentioned that it was a good thing she never got the opportunity to experience you fully because if she had, and then you dumped her manipulative little ass, she'd be ruined for any other man. I may have even declared there was no way I'd ever tire of you, either, that you most definitely knew how to use what the good Lord had blessed you with. Then I offered to pay for her dry cleaning and had Quinn give her the number of the one we use and instructed her to put it on our tab."

I know none of that was appropriate, but it sure felt good watching her shrink within herself. She most definitely understood what I was telling her and perhaps realized she was never going to be able to slither her way into the life I unintentionally took away from her. It was time for her to move on and stop with all these stupid games.

CHAPTER 40
Antonio

The Royals

Another few months have passed. It is also a brand-new year. One I have high hopes for.

The last year seemed to be full of so many unexpected events. Some good, like Larkin, some not so good. In the end, though, it turned out to be the most important year of my life.

I am hoping this next year is even better.

We are starting it off exactly how I want. It took some hard work all the way around, but we managed. I have finally moved my main office to Maximiliano Chateau, and I couldn't be more thrilled.

For now, we are going to live in the cottage. Living apart wasn't working for me, or Larkin, either, really. We did so much better when we spent the majority of our week together. There was no reason I couldn't do my job here as well as I did it in Aragon. One week a month I will have to return so I can meet with the King's Council, while I also handle any other business that might come up. Otherwise, everything could be done via satellite, or if it was urgent, then I could either return to the palace or they could come to me. I can promise you I will make them come to me as often as I can get away with it.

I enrolled Isabel in the local school. She is very excited about getting to know all her new schoolmates when it starts up again in a few weeks.

While I realize she will miss living in the palace, I also know she will love living in Maximiliano Chateau.

Alejandro and Triana are proud parents of a little girl, Doreen. She is a little over three months now. Triana has three more to go before I will allow her to officially report to work, although I get this nagging suspicion she is unofficially doing some work from home. Her replacement, Violet Blanc, has been working out just fine, keeping my schedule how I like it and getting everything done that needs to be done. Which is why Violet will remain at the office in Aragon Palace and run things there, assisting me during those times when I return.

Alejandro and Triana are also making the move with us to Homero, renting a house in town for now. Eventually, they will take up residence in the guesthouse. That way, they can be close when I need them and will also use our au pair for little Doreen.

Maximiliano Chateau's final date suggests we will be able to move in come early spring. Larkin, as you can imagine, is not at all happy about the fact she is three months behind her original schedule. There were several snags along the way that seemed to put each and every deadline behind, postponing phase three until after the first of the year. Which is the phase where she will get to build that library she designed.

They waited to start this portion of the project for several reasons. Other areas of the chateau required some critical work. Structural work was required so they could complete all the final stages at once. Phase three was not just about the library—which would be Larkin's main focus—but also about the finishing touches that needed to be completed in the rest of the home; minor details that could now be finished.

So when Isabel and I arrive one day behind her, I'm not at all surprised to not find my wife where she was supposed to be. She has been so eager to get her hands on the tower. I knew as soon as she received the green light, she'd be in there preparing it.

I am, however, surprised when I hear her voice echoing loudly as she argues with Gino and Dane. It makes me wonder what she is up to that has them both ready to wring her neck.

"Your Majesty, I must insist you come down." Gino is typically laid back, but right now, he does not at all sound relaxed.

"Insist all you want, Gino. I am not coming down until I am good and ready to do so." I also recognize the stubbornness in that voice. "Hope, pull that rope so the pulley will shift just enough for me to reach this. Perfect."

"Miss Hope," a very stern Dean grumbles. "It would be very wise of you not to listen when she instructs you to do something like that. It will be your head if the queen falls and gets hurt. You two should not be doing these dangerous…"

"Shut up." Both women shout at him at the same time.

"We are not amateurs, Sir Dane." Hope's sarcasm does not go unnoticed.

"It is just Dane." I hear him curse loudly. "Woman, you are going to kill her if you keep messing with those ropes like that."

Hope and Larkin are now laughing.

I walk through the door right as Larkin gives Hope another order. My eyes travel up the ropes in the other woman's hands, to where my wife dangles three stories up—actually, I believe it is more like four. Larkin is in a harness that is strapped to both her legs and torso. Currently, she is leaning as far back as she possibly can with a tiny wire brush in her hand, wearing eye protectors and some kind of hardhat secured on her head. Like that dang hat would do a darn bit of good if she plummeted headfirst into the concrete slab below our feet.

"What the hell?" I bark out as I glare at both men just standing there.

"Don't look at us like that." Gino points his finger at me. "She was already up there before we realized what these two were up to. They told us they wanted to check a few things out. They didn't tell us they were going to risk life and limb just so she could clean and repair the ceiling."

A loud yelp has all three of them looking up.

"Heads up," Larkin shouts as something falls to the left of me. "Oops, that was close. Good thing I have a backup brush with me. Hope, to the right a bit."

I have no words to describe all the crazy reactions traveling through my body and mind right now. Hope seems to know what she is doing and even has the nerve to see if she can rile us up a bit more.

"You know, if you guys were any good, I'd let you take over here so I could join her. But one wrong move and poor Queen Larkin could end up being another victim of this tower." Just her saying that makes me want to order Larkin to get her butt down here where she is completely safe.

"Don't egg him on, Hope. I completely trust you; you know what you are doing. Besides you and I both know how dangerous this looks. How very dangerous it is, which is why we take all the extra safety measures to make sure accidents don't occur. Plus, the way you are holding onto those ropes, as if my very life dangles in your hands, makes you look like a real badass. Now stop messing around and get your ass up here to help me." Larkin is looking at us all from her upside-down position, laughing. "I can't believe they actually fell for that."

Hope drops the ropes in her hands and I swear we all flinch, expecting Larkin to plummet to her death, except she doesn't budge. Then we watch in awe as Hope straps into a harness of her own, clips herself to one of those ropes, and, like magic, gets hoisted to the ceiling. Once she is up there, she secures her body to a whole other system of ropes and begins acting like Spiderwoman, moving across the ceiling with ease.

"But it's so much fun messing with them. I told you it would be. I bet they've never seen anything like this before. This really is beautiful, such a shame it was hidden all those years." Hope begins doing what Larkin is doing.

We stand there and watch them for an hour. I cannot take my eyes off of her hanging up there without a care in the world. Both drop several more tools, hollering out each time to warn us. By the time they start their descent, I am about to lose it.

"We will leave you to deal with them, sir." Gino obviously understands my dilemma.

I nod and as soon as Hope's feet touch the ground, I encourage Dane to help her. "Perhaps you could escort Miss Manchester back to her car."

Dane snickers, a little insulted that I ordered him to take on the firecracker, Hope Manchester. "Did I do something to deserve such a task, sir?"

"Larkin, are you coming down soon?" Hope hollers back up at my wife, who is clearly absorbed in a dream up there.

"Yeah. Just making sure we got it all. Looks good." She makes her way toward the ropes and starts doing whatever it is she needs to do to descend.

"All right, well I'll see you in the morning then." Hope rolls her neck a few times. "King Antonio, you look as dashing as ever. Lovely home you have here, by the way."

"Thank you, Hope. So, you are on her team now?" I take my eyes off my wife for a second.

"I am." She glances over her shoulder. "You two be careful now."

While I wait for Larkin to slip out of all her safety gear, I pick up all the brushes they dropped. As soon as I see her walking over to the corner to put her things away, I slide in behind her.

"That was a cruel joke," I inform her.

The low rumble of her laugh goes straight to my groin.

Things between us have slowed down a bit. First, it was because I knew sex was the last thing on her mind, so we dialed it down and reverted to the days before we married. Her body and mind needed time to heal. I also needed time to connect with my wife on a more intimate level. And if you think the most intimate level possible deals with sex, then you couldn't be more wrong. Discussing all the dreams we have for our future family can be very intimate. It was also a subject we had put off until then because Larkin hated getting ahead of herself.

We discussed names we might like to name our children. She was very aware that the firstborn often bore the name of his/her father in one form or another, and that the second-born usually did as well. So she thought it would be fitting if we named our firstborn according to tradition and after another king who took a chance. If we had a son, she liked Nicolas Antonio. Should we be blessed with a girl she suggested Nicolette Antonia. I was in awe of the fact she had taken this to heart, and I agreed with both of her choices. It was some of the other unusual names that she threw out there that had us both laughing and disagreeing. It's probably a good thing we don't have to name all our children before we have them.

It also encouraged us to seriously talk about how many children we would like to have. After losing a child, I can imagine it often changes a person's perspective on what they thought they wanted. It had, for both of us, at least. Larkin admitted it scared the daylights out of her to think she could possibly give me a basketball team—that would be five, by the way—or worse yet, a baseball team—nine in case you are having trouble figuring that one out. But she had decided that if God wanted to bless her with children, even an unmanageable amount, she would consider herself blessed and accept them as miracles gifted to her from above. Even though she quietly revealed that if I felt the need to get a little snip, clip, and tuck, she'd be all for that too, of course only after we had at least one of each.

"Hope's idea." I hear her whimper when I press my front into her backside. "Wow. That's quite an impressive predicament you seem to be in, King Antonio. Perhaps I should check to see if I have something handy that could assist you." The frisky side of her has returned, so I decide to take advantage.

"Are we alone?" I rub my hand over her jean-covered backside. "Please tell me we are alone."

"If you are asking me if there are other people here working, the answer is no. They won't be back on the job until tomorrow. Hope arrived early and stopped by, talked me into getting started." She straightens and I allow my hands to slither forward and form a triangle around her front. "Are your guys around?"

My guys are probably in the vicinity, but no one should be inside the house. "Outside, yes. Inside, I do not believe so."

"Dr. Wilson called me today." Larkin's voice is almost a moan as she reacts to my fingers toying with her center. "Said my blood work was good. Told me that the results were what she expected. Informed me that if we wanted to try again, we could."

Thank God, is what I am thinking. "I'm game if you are," is what I say.

When you haven't made love to your wife in almost three months, mainly because you both had decided to not take that chance, you start thinking about certain fantasies. Trust me, we've done lots of other stuff. Both of us have done our best to drive the other person absolutely insane, trying to one-up the other at times. So as soon as you get the green light, there is very little that will stop you from pressing the pedal to the floor. If Larkin claimed she wasn't ready yet, I'd slam on the breaks.

Except she doesn't. "How fast do you think you can get inside of me?"

Fast, baby.

My fingers flip the button to her jeans free and I have the zipper down within seconds. Her jeans are around her ankles now, making it so I get to appreciate the way those boy-cut knickers hug her. I don't take long to admire them though, because I need this woman.

As I drag them down her legs, I warn her. "This will not be gentle, *mi lunita*. If you need me to be gentle, please tell me now so I can modify my approach."

"Just. Need. You." Her broken speech hints she is aching for this as much as I am.

I love this woman. I never expected to find a woman I could truly love. I have, though. I have found a woman to love in a way very few people I imagine get to experience.

My pants are now around my ankles, along with my underwear. There aren't many hidden spots in this room. Windows surround us, so anyone watching will be able to see exactly what we are about to do, what we will do. I, however, can only focus on one thing right now, and I am holding on to that person's hips at the moment.

I run my length between her legs as I tilt her forward. She can only spread her legs so far, so I hope I don't hurt her.

"Grab your ankles, baby, and hold on," I instruct her.

She does exactly what I direct her to do with this glorious grin on her face. I place my tip at her entrance, and without giving her time to think about it, I slam home. Knocking that grin right off her face and replacing it with a blissful expression.

"Oh, wow." Larkin whimpers. "Geez. That. Is."

I don't let her finish before I am pumping my hips and I am not doing it in slow, easy drives, either. I am taking her hard and fast and can feel her insides responding to each harsh thrust. It takes us no time at all to get to where we both want to be. As soon as I hear her voice shriek out, letting me know she is where I want her to be, I fall right there with her.

Literally.

We climax and then end up tumbling forward until we hit the concrete slab. Thankfully, I am able to slide out and roll to my side before I crush her beneath me.

"Are you okay?" I ask when I catch my breath.

Larkin says nothing, so I grab her shoulder to roll her onto her back, where I can see her face. She isn't talking because she is laughing so hard no noise can escape from her. Her hands motion between us like she is trying to explain with that motion alone.

One look at us and I get it. We most definitely look ridiculous, with our pants around our ankles, while lying on the concrete floor after one hell of a sexual performance.

I join her laughing and I know this woman was created for me and only me. No one else could make me forget I am king the way she does. No one would be able to make me laugh with my pants down around my ankles. No one could get me to not care about the fact that my men could walk in and see us looking so disarrayed.

I'm certain that when God made this woman, he made her with me in mind. Therefore, I will thank him every day for leading me to her when we both needed it. No one will convince me that God didn't orchestrate all this, because only God could bring us together the way he did.

So, there you have it, the story of how a man of my status found love, real genuine love. I wasn't supposed to find it. It wasn't part of the plan so many had for me. It took me having faith in what I believed in and not letting those around me steer me away from those strong beliefs.

I am King Antonio Ramon Reyes, of Hermosa Islas, and I am the first king in its history to marry for love and only love.

Epilogue

LARKIN

Three Years Later

You didn't think we would leave you hanging, did you? Make you wonder if or when our firstborn made an appearance? Speculate if it was a boy or a girl? That would not be very nice of us now, would it?

So, let me give you a quick little rundown of the last couple of years. Well, I can't tell you everything, because there are parts of this family's story that aren't mine to share. If you are really lucky, perhaps they will share it with you when they are ready to do so.

I didn't believe Antonio when he told me that monarch's firstborns didn't take as long to cook as the rest of the world. But after doing my research, I learned that appeared to be the case. There were only two other firstborn births in the history of Hermosa Islas' monarch families that were past the nine-month time frame. A few were hard to say one way or the other, but close enough you definitely started trying to do the math.

Our baby, however, took a record of fourteen months to cook.

Princess Nicolette Antonia Moon Reyes came to us two months after our one-year anniversary. She possesses her father's black hair but has inherited my blue eyes. The contrast of her darker tinted skin, and those eyes, makes them almost glow. I know for sure one day they are going to drive the boys crazy, which means her poor daddy is going to have his hands full.

I also know you are curious about how I handled childbirth. I'm not going to lie to you; I opted for an epidural and thought, now this is how all women should labor. Until the medication wore off three hours before Nicolette was born, which is when I thought my insides were going to fall out. I almost gave up, except my husband wouldn't let me. He asked all unnecessary personnel to clear the room, leaving only Dr. Wilson, Antonio, one nurse—and, of course, me. Then, in true form, he gave me an order like only he can do. Fifteen minutes later, I was holding the product of my hard labor and bawling because she was so very beautiful. I just might agree to do it for him a few more times now that I understand the pain is worth the results.

Right now, I am on the third floor of my studio, painting a portrait of my two favorite people. My mother took this photograph with her camera when she was here for a visit last.

Oh, that reminds me.

My mother and father will move here in a few more months. My father's seat in the Senate ended a few months ago. My mother handed in her resignation around that same time. I am even building them a house on the east side of our property so they will be close to us. It was a no-brainer for them, they said. There was no way they wanted to live an entire ocean away from their grandchild—or me, so they claimed, although I think Nicolette was the main reason, and I don't blame them. Either way, I am thrilled they will be around, and so is Antonio.

It's a little past midnight. A full moon is shining in the window next to me. I am studying the image of Antonio holding our baby girl above his head, making her giggle.

He is the perfect father. I knew he would be. The way he was with Isabel was a sure sign of that. Every night before she goes to bed is their designated time. He holds her while he reads her a story. He is also teaching her both Spanish and Portuguese in much the same way his mother taught him. I am better at understanding it now. Hopefully, by the time our children are fluent, I will be as well.

I take a step back to let the paint dry before I attempt to add to it again. I'm definitely not a portrait painter and wouldn't be hired to do this for a living. However, I am not painting this for anyone but me. It will hang in my studio along with the few others I have dared to render.

My absolute favorite hangs above one of my desks, so I can look up at it for a distraction when I need to. It's not one I'd let anyone but me or those I consider close stare at. My mother has a difficult time looking at it, says it is a little too much for her. But I often find Hope staring at it when she comes by to work on a project with me. I think she does it more when she knows Dane is sure to interrupt us. He is a very jealous man, but if he doesn't man up soon, I am not confident he will get his chance.

You want to know about the painting. I'll give you a hint. I used one of my sketches from my wedding night as my inspiration.

Get your head out of the gutter. I said I allowed those close to me to admire it. Do you really think I would let them appreciate a portrait of my husband if he were completely nude? No, I would not.

That portrait hangs in my bedroom closet behind another less obvious painting of our home. I only look at it when I'm alone, and no one but Antonio and I have laid eyes on it. He claims I have a wild imagination. I, however, believe I didn't even come close to doing him any justice.

The painting above my desk has a sheet draped over his most private areas. And since he is lying on his stomach facing me, it only covers a portion of him. His eyes are most definitely staring at me, giving me those bedroom eyes that melt me from the inside out.

I sense him before I hear him moving in behind me. Lately, I have been having trouble sleeping, a sure sign my body is preparing for what is coming in a few short months.

His large, warm hand brushes my hair to one side so that his lips can have free rein of my neck. He is very good at letting those lips warm me up before he even touches me anywhere else.

"What are you doing?" He whispers.

"Looking over the blueprints for Fort Serna. We start on that project in a few weeks and I want to make sure I know it inside and out before then." I glance over my shoulder. "What are you doing?"

"Looking for my bed partner." Antonio lets his hands run down the front of my robe until he finds the knotted sash. "I thought we agreed you'd stop working late at night. You need sleep. My son needs to get his rest as well."

My head falls back when the sides of my robe fall open and his hands land on my slightly rounded belly. "Son, huh? Are you sure you gave me a boy this time around? Maybe we are growing a second princess in there."

One hand travels up to my breast, while the other treks south. I am at his mercy right now and he knows it.

Hormones are real tricky things during pregnancy. One minute they have you feeling like you could toss your cookies, and the next they have you wanting to eat everything you see or smell. They also make you moody and extremely horny.

It's not like I left my husband unsatisfied a few hours ago when I slipped out of our bedroom. I had ridden him hard and put him into a very blissful coma before I wandered off to do my own thing.

"Antonio," I whisper his name as he pinches my nipple while toying with my center.

I am weeping for him easily, and he can surely detect it. Probably explains why he spins me around on my stool and scoops me into his arms. I nuzzle right in and inhale the cinnamon and mint scent that is purely my man.

He doesn't take me against the wall inside the library. Right now, my belly is just big enough to get in the way, so instead he carries me down the corridor to our suite.

Don't worry; we have had a lot of wall sex in that special space. He did exactly what he promised he would do so very long ago, not all that long after we moved in, actually. He's done it so many times that I am very glad we soundproofed it so no one could hear our cries when we made love in that room.

Once he carries me across the large space to our bed, he removes my robe before removing his own. Then he slides in behind me, and much like he did that first time, he makes very slow, punishing love to me.

Drives me completely over the edge, knowing that the only way to get me to sleep is to force my endorphins to kick in after multiple orgasms. When he knows I am on the verge of breaking, he pounds into me until I cry out and see stars.

No matter how many times he does that, I have learned it will always feel the same and a surefire way to make certain I not awake this time after I pass out. And just like every other time I make certain to tell him how much I love him in case I don't make it, positive this time may just do me in.

As my mind drifts off, I recall the first time I saw this man walk through the door of my boss' office. I remember thinking then that whoever gets the pleasure of loving this man one day had better appreciate it. Well, I can assure you, ladies, I appreciate it several times a week and twice, sometimes on Sundays.

If you enjoyed the story of King Antonio and Queen Larkin, please consider leaving a review. I'm also on Goodreads and BookBub. If you use those, I'd appreciate it if you'd do the same there. Reviews are how authors gains more readers when recommended to others.

Here is the link to Unexpected Princess, book 2 in The Royals, the story of Esteban and Winifred.

I have several other books available. There is a list of those available either in the front or back of this book.

Thank you and Happy Reading!!!!

The Duke

FALCON GLOBAL NOVELLA

One kiss was all it took...

All I want is my freedom. All my father wants is to chain me to the highest bidder. I have one last opportunity to live on my terms before my choice is taken from me.

Darius Falcon, also known as The Duke, enters my world. He's an arrogant prick who won't take no for an answer. Refusing to change course once he sets his sights on me. Too bad he won't get to keep me for more than a week.

Then one day he materializes from the shadows to save me from a monster. It's then I wonder if now is my chance to take control of over my future. Maybe when you wish upon a hunk, dreams really do come true.

Only Available to Newsletter Subscribers.
https://dl.bookfunnel.com/xn53pw0g4o

Acknowledgments

I want to give a few shout out to those who have made this book even better.

Thanks Ashley for helping me edit this book after joining my team. I can always count on you to make sure I don't screw it all up royally. You're an amazing editor and you make my life so much easier.

To my readers who have loved this book from the beginning. Your encouragement to keep writing and to give you more of this family has been amazing. I continue to write because of you.

Thanks to my family. Your willingness to let me do what I love, no matter how crazy it gets, means the world to me. I love you guys, always.

* Updated 4/20/24

Also by C. R. Riley

Unexpected Princess
My Noble Fight
Her Royal Highness
Fearless Warrior

About the Author

Contemporary romance author C. R. Riley is celebrated for creating worlds and characters that don't always follow the rules, including those she futilely tries to set herself. But the best characters always find a way around them, often surprising her with their willingness to make each and every journey unique, if not emotionally satisfying.

Her Kohl Family series has been called the perfect epitome of contemporary romance with a twist of the unexpected. The characters tackle tough topics while making you fall in love with them, and despising those baddies who deserve it. Each story is a unique standalone. That cares over in her Modern-Day Royals series, which features characters who are unlike any royal put to the page before. And of course, combining her love of football and baseball she adds a steamy sports romance, Love of the Game which follows a family of athletes on their separate journeys to find true love.

You can find all her romantic and out-of-the-ordinary series on Amazon and free in Kindle Unlimited. Never miss a new project update or book release by signing up for her newsletter or follow her on social media, accounts listed below.

I'd love to hear from you and do my best to personally answer emails.
crriley@crrileyauthor.com

Newsletter Signup:
https://www.subscribepage.com/o5t3m0

Website:
https://www.crrileyauthor.com
LinkTree:
https://linktr.ee/c.r.rileyauthor